PRAISE FOR KOURTNEY HEINTZ'S
THE SIX TRAIN TO WISCONSIN

"*THE SIX TRAIN TO WISCONSIN* is an engaging story that deftly explores the mysteries and secrets of the heart and mind. Kourtney Heintz has crafted a story that is hypnotic and uplifting—you won't want to put it down."
—**Paige Shelton**, *New York Times* bestselling author of *Farm Fresh Murder*

"*THE SIX TRAIN TO WISCONSIN* is like a breathless thrill ride on an out-of-control freight train rushing through the darkness, at a pace that never slows down, never lets up, and never compromises. There are enough twists and turns and near misses to make you hang onto your seat by your fingernails, and at the end, respite and a satisfying conclusion that makes the crazy ride worth it."
—**Jenna Bennett/Jennie Bentley**, *USA Today* & *New York Times* bestselling author of the *Do-It-Yourself Home Renovation* mysteries & the *Cutthroat Business* mysteries

"A richly layered novel, *THE SIX TRAIN TO WISCONSIN* gently pushes at the reader's expectations, then exceeds them, turning what could almost become kitschy in more inexperienced hands to something with an almost literary bent (if the literary genre ever decided to dabble in the paranormal)."
—**Readers' Favorite** reviewed by Kayti Nika Raet

"Heintz's debut weaves psychological insight into a suspenseful, sci-fi-tinged thriller and produces a welcome variation on the classic marriage drama."
—**Kirkus Reviews**

"Readers will be hooked by Kai's special powers and the ways in which they make her life difficult."
—**Publishers Weekly**

"*THE SIX TRAIN TO WISCONSIN* combines a brilliantly conceived plot with deep psychological insight and compelling writing to produce a wonderful reading experience."
—**BookPleasures.com**, Sandra Schwayder Sanchez, Book Reviewer

2014 National Indie Excellence Awards Winner
2014 Readers' Favorite International Book Awards Winner
2014 International Book Awards Finalist
2014 EPIC Ebook Awards Finalist
2013 USA Best Book Awards Finalist
2012 Amazon Breakthrough Novel Awards Semifinalist

Highway Thirteen to Manhattan

To Friends of Betsi,

Enjoy!

Highway Thirteen to Manhattan

The Six Train to Wisconsin Series

KOURTNEY HEINTZ

Kourtney Heintz

Aurea Blue Press

HIGHWAY THIRTEEN TO MANHATTAN
THE SIX TRAIN TO WISCONSIN SERIES — BOOK 2

Trade Paperback Edition / November 2016
Aurea Blue Press

By Kourtney Heintz

Edited by Jessica Jernigan
Cover Art by Creative Paramita
Internal Design by Nick DeSimone
Internal Photography by Kourtney Heintz
Author Photograph by Brett D. Helgren

Printed in the United States of America

Dedication

To Maxine Kilger for opening your heart and your home to me and letting me see all that Butternut was and is.

CHAPTER 1

Kai

Like most daughters, I loved my parents, but right now, I wanted them anywhere but here. Hospitals are always hard, but my parents managed to make it harder. My head was already pounding from all the thoughts and emotions coming at me. Not just from the patients and their families and the doctors and the nurses, but also from my mother and father. Instead of shielding their thoughts and trying to make it better for me, they let their emotions crash into me.

My mind wasn't strong enough for all this. Neither was my body. Tubes eviscerated my right hand. A giant bruise blossomed beside the newest IV line. A cast wrapped around my left wrist. My broken pinky finger had been set and taped to my ring finger. The back of my head was held together with stitches. Beneath the blanket, my body was covered in bruises.

I didn't feel any physical pain because of the medications the doctors pumped into me. They said I needed it to recover, but it made my body feel like it wasn't mine. And the steady drip of opiates didn't just steal my physical pain; it left me unable to form the psychic shield I needed to protect myself from the misery swirling around me.

Mom sat in the chair closest to my bed. She wore one of her flowing peasant blouses and faded jeans. Her hair was pulled back in a messy bun, and light brown strands slipped loose to hang around her face. The corners of her hazel eyes were pinched with worry.

Her hand hovered over my arm, unsure where to touch me—if she should touch me. Finally, she laid her hand gently on my thigh. "You just need to rest here for a few more days."

She was wrong. I needed to get out of here. Away from all these thoughts as soon as possible. "I want to go home."

Mom shook her head. "You need to let the doctors help you." *Like they did last time.*

Her thoughts slammed into my brain. She thought hospitalization was the solution to everything.

"Please. Look at what's happened to you. You can't go home until you're better," she said. *I can't lose you. I won't let that happen.*

I didn't know how to reassure her. Yes, I'd almost died, but being here was hurting me more than it was healing me. I swallowed all the words I wanted to say and hoped for Caleb to come back soon. My brother would know how to talk to Mom, how to make her understand.

The doctor came in to check on me and Mom's agonizing fear rose up. *Don't let her have brain damage.*

Dad patted Mom's shoulder. He looked like an older, surfer version of Caleb. Both were tall and muscular with curly blond hair. Dad's hair was a darker blond streaked with platinum from decades in the sun and salt water. His eyes were greener than Caleb's, but like Caleb's, they were rimmed with purple bruises. When Dad smiled, sun lines radiated from his eyes and cut across his cheeks. But I hadn't seen those lines since he'd arrived at my bedside. Instead, waves of exhaustion rolled off him and rippled over me, right before I heard his thoughts. *I can't go through this again, watching you slip away.*

My younger sister Naomi lounged in the chair in the corner as far from me as she could get. She had Mom's light brown hair and thin frame and Dad's green eyes and height. She looked nothing like me and only distantly related to Caleb. Her long legs looped over the armrest as she flipped through a magazine. *Thanks for ruining Christmas break. I'd rather be anywhere but here.*

I felt the same way.

At least my husband Oliver was gone for the moment. Mom had convinced him to go home, take a shower, maybe even sleep. I couldn't bear his guilt; it was so thick it choked me.

I'd never loved and hated someone so much at the same time. I still couldn't believe he'd called my parents. He knew how bad they were at handling me. How could he have thought that having my family here would be good for me?

Bitterness frosted my thoughts. I was in a hospital, bruised and battered. I'd almost died. That's what Caleb had said. He was the only one willing to tell me the truth. Oliver had said it was bad, but he wouldn't say *how* bad. He couldn't bear to admit what happened to me.

"Who's hungry?" Caleb pulled me out of my thoughts with his question.

He came into my room with a tray of coffee and bagels from a nearby coffee shop. His hair had curled into ringlets. He looked like an angel. Seeing him made everything more bearable. He perched on the side of my bed. As always, he was shielding his thoughts to make sure there was one less mind invading mine.

I looked up into his eyes. He dropped his shield for a moment, so that his thoughts were clear. *Give them another half hour; then I'll get them to leave.*

He reached over and tucked a lock of red hair behind my ear. I felt a trickle of relief.

I was finally alone and waiting for my brother to return when Oliver appeared in the doorway. His tall frame filled the space. His expression was uncertain, like he was afraid I'd send him away. I hadn't done it yet. I couldn't.

He looked around. "Where's Caleb?"

"He went to get me some ice cream." It was the one thing that tasted right with all the pain medications in my system.

Oliver hesitated. It reminded me of how a vampire waits for an invitation to enter. I would have laughed if it weren't so sad.

"You can come in."

He came over to the bed and sat gingerly beside me. "Kai..." He rubbed his hand over his mouth. "How can I help?"

"I want to go home."

"The doctors want to keep you here a few more days. Just to make sure there are no complications. "

"They don't know what's best for me." How could he agree with the doctors? He knew what hospitals did to me, especially in a city like Wausau. He was supposed to be on my side.

"As soon as it's safe, I'll bring you home, I promise."

I didn't believe him. He'd keep me here and my parents would encourage it. I'd be stuck inside this hospital room for as long as they could convince the doctors to keep me. My chest tightened. A rush of anger drove away my exhaustion.

"Why did you call my parents? Why did you bring them here?" I demanded.

"They were planning to come for the holidays already. You know that. I had to let them know what happened to you."

"But you could have just told them to reschedule their trip. You could have made up something that would have kept them away. You should have known that they couldn't handle this. They're just making everything worse!"

"I had to tell them. What if…"

You died were the words he couldn't bring himself to say. Saying them would be the same as admitting how close he had brought me to death.

I sighed and let my head rest against the stiff hospital pillow. All my rage dissipated, leaving me exhausted again.

"They don't know what I need, Oliver."

He reached for my hand, touched an IV tube, and dropped his hand back to the bed. "I thought that, after everything you'd been through, you'd want to see them."

"I never want my family to see me like this." It conjured up too many memories of the last time I was broken. They couldn't separate then from now. And I didn't want them having a say in what happened to me because they would try to keep me hospitalized again. Oliver should have known this.

Guilt swarmed me—his guilt. It filled my throat and cut off most of my air. I couldn't escape it. I could barely breathe around it.

His voice was a strained whisper. "I only wanted to make it better."

"I know." And I did. I knew how much he wanted to fix everything he'd broken. I knew he was trying. And it was tearing me apart. Because I wanted him to fix it and I wasn't sure he could.

It was almost 1 a.m. when Caleb fell asleep in the chair by my bed. I couldn't wake him. Not again. He's stayed up with me for too many nights.

I was so tired. I wanted to join him, but I didn't dare. I couldn't take another nightmare. They were twisted versions of what had happened. And they always ended in my death.

Not that staying awake was much easier. Emotions cluttered my room. Fear, pain, anger, hopelessness. These feelings weren't mine. They belonged to other patients. They were overwhelming, but they were just an inkling of what I would face when my own emotions started coming for me. And they always came for me.

The clock on the wall blurred. I was falling asleep. I tried to fight it, but my eyes felt so heavy. I couldn't keep them open.

I slipped into a dream.

I was right back there in that cave again. The smell of pennies and damp earth assaulted my nose. The clammy coldness of being underground clung to my skin. Lukas wasn't there this time. I was all alone. Somehow, that made it worse.

But I wasn't just in the cave. This time, I was locked inside a gilded cage. I could only take six steps in any direction. I was at Nathan's mercy. Again.

My arms were wings, covered in a songbird's feathers.

A shadowy figure circled my cage. I couldn't make out who it was, but I knew. His name filled my mouth. "Nathan."

He reached through the bars and touched my wing. I felt a spark. I jerked away. But it was too late. He'd done something to me. Twisted something inside me. His powers intertwined with mine.

Shadows filled the cave, and I wasn't sure if it was his darkness or mine. The shadows separated and took form. Hundreds of shadow people converged on me, slipping through the bars of my cage and reaching for me. I couldn't escape them. Everything went black.

Then I was on a bicycle, pedaling into the moonless night. Cold air stung my cheeks and pushed against my legs. But I had to get away. I had to escape Oliver's betrayal. Images played inside my mind of my husband kissing Mickey.

Headlights blinded me. A car smashed into my bike. I flew through the air and slammed into the ground. Each breath I took felt like it was pulled through a broken straw. I wheezed and gasped. Suddenly, I was choking on something hot and liquid. Metallic. I tried to cough it up, but I couldn't. My own blood filled my throat. I knew that my broken bones would never mend because I was dying.

Then I heard Caleb's voice calling to me, "Kai, you're okay. It's just a dream."

The night sky dissolved into daylight. Silver and gold flecks glinted on the tan and black sand. Sun warmed my skin. A gentle breeze tickled my neck. I was at Torrey Pines Beach in San Diego, one of the places where Caleb and I liked to meet in our dreams.

I glanced around, looking for him. Then I saw him moving toward me from the water's horizon. His feet glided over the water.

He was here. I was safe. My heart slowed in my chest. I could breathe again.

As he hugged me, he said, "I'm not sure how long I can keep you here. You need to wake up now."

Caleb's words reverberated in my head and in my hospital room.

My eyes blinked open. I was back in my hospital bed. Caleb was there. Just like when I had awoken from a coma days earlier.

I gasped for air. "Was I screaming?"

He nodded.

"I tried to stay awake."

He brushed the hair off my forehead. "It's okay. I'll do everything I can to get you out of the nightmares when they come for you."

"But you need to rest sometimes."

He gave me a tired smile. "I can survive on a few hours of sleep. You're the one I'm worried about."

"I'm here. I'm okay." Even as I said it, I knew that it wasn't completely true.

CHAPTER 2

Oliver

I leaned forward in my chair and spoke quietly so that no other families in the waiting room could overhear our conversation. "A hospital is the worst place for someone like Kai."

I expected her parents to agree with me, but her mother was firm. "She needs to be here."

She'd said the exact same thing when she locked Kai away in the mental institution. Back then, I didn't have the power to stop her. Now, I did.

"There are too many thoughts and emotions here." Thousands of people came in and out of that hospital every day. And then there were all the people within a half-mile radius—Kai heard their thoughts, too.

I looked to her father, hoping he'd agree with me. Kai had inherited her abilities from him. Surely, he would get how hard this was on her.

Her dad's jaw muscle pulsated before he spoke. "The doctor said he needs to keep her under observation, in case..."

He couldn't say the words: Something went wrong with her brain.

I had the same fear. It's why I wanted them on my side. Because

Kai's life might be at stake.

Caleb leaned against the wall with his arms crossed. "She can't stay here any longer. You see how thin she's getting."

She'd lost ten pounds in the hospital.

"What if something happens?" his mother asked.

"We can bring her back here if we need to," Caleb said.

She wrung her hands. "It's too risky. We can't lose Kai."

Caleb rubbed the back of his neck. "You don't see what's right in front of you. She's getting worse, not better. If you keep her here, she'll lose her mind."

"Don't talk to your mother like that," his father said.

His mother put a hand on his father's arm. "It's all right. We're all worried."

Caleb gave his father a death stare. His father stared right back at him. This could go on for eternity if I didn't do something.

"Her blood pressure is 190/90. We have to do something. This isn't working," I said.

"Let the doctors try another medication," his father said.

It didn't matter what medication they gave her. None of them would ease the emotional strain.

"The mental stress of being in the hospital is taking too much out of her," Caleb said.

He looked like he hadn't slept in days. The rest of her family offered to stay at night, but Kai sent them home. Every other night, she let me stay. I think it was to let Caleb get some rest. Caleb was the only one she wanted with her.

"She's alive," his dad said. Like that was all we could hope for.

"Being here might hurt her more than the physical injuries," I said.

"Hospitals are the best place for people with head injuries," his mom insisted.

She refused to see how dangerous hospitals were to Kai's mental well-being.

"Not for Kai," Caleb said.

His father frowned. "You don't understand. You weren't here last time."

Caleb's entire face shifted. He pulled away from the wall and took two steps toward his father. The fury in his eyes cemented in his voice. "Because you didn't let me help until it was almost too late. That won't happen again."

He turned and stalked away from his parents. I stayed there and listened to their litany of reasons why Kai should remain in the hospital. I didn't want to put Kai at risk, but I couldn't keep her here in agony.

I excused myself and went into Kai's room. Her face was drawn. Even paler than it had been yesterday. Her body was trembling.

I rushed to her side and touched her cheek. "What is it?"

She looked up at me, but she wasn't seeing me. Her eyes were unfocused. She was slipping further into her own mind. "He's dying. She's sick. The little girl...oh God...she's losing her mother.... I can't.... It's too much."

Caleb stood in the doorway. "We've got to get her out of here. Today."

"I know. But we can't just take her out without the doctor releasing her." I didn't want to risk her getting worse. I'd made the wrong decision so many times with Kai. I couldn't make another mistake with her. "I'm working to get you released as soon as possible."

I saw it in her eyes. She didn't believe me. Not after everything we'd been through in the cave.

Kai's eyes shifted to Caleb. "I need to get out. Now."

He nodded. "I'll make it happen."

"Promise?" she breathed.

"Promise," he said.

Some of the tension in her eased. She believed him. "Today?"

"Today."

I raised an eyebrow at Caleb. That was a ridiculous promise to make. He jerked his head toward the hallway.

Kai stared out the window, whispering, "Today."

Caleb and I stepped out of the room.

"There's no way you can get her out today," I said. "I've been trying to talk to the doctor all morning about getting her released."

"That's your problem. You want them to condone what you're doing. Just do it."

"You shouldn't make a promise you can't keep."

"I haven't."

"How are you going to get her released today?" It was already 3 p.m.

He gave me a slow, superior smile. The one he used way too often with me. "While you've been trying to talk to a doctor all day, I've called in a private doctor to expedite the paperwork. Kai's checking herself out."

As usual, Caleb was throwing money at a problem until it went away. "What if she has a relapse?" I couldn't help echoing her parents' fears because they were my fears, too.

"Do you think this emotional and mental stress isn't putting her at risk?"

I knew that, but somehow when it came from his lips, I felt like I had to fight him. "But if she gets sick again?"

"I'll have a helicopter standing by to airlift her back here."

He had an answer for everything.

I was about to respond when Kai's doctor marched up to me and said, "Your wife is my patient. I strongly discourage you from letting her check herself out."

Clearly, Caleb's plan was already in motion. I hated working with him, but if it meant I could get my wife safely out of there, I would. "She's under too much stress here. She needs to go home."

"This is the best place for her to be treated," the doctor insisted.

"What about the comfort of home with a private doctor caring for her?" Caleb asked.

The doctor considered it. "I'd feel better if she stayed here. If anything goes wrong, we can take care of it immediately."

"I can get her back here in an hour," Caleb said.

"I want her blood pressure monitored closely," the doctor said.

"Of course. I'll have my doctor check in on her hourly and send you her vitals. If they haven't improved in a day, I'll bring her back here," Caleb said.

He'd never do that. It was just a lie to get what he wanted, but it happened to be what Kai needed, so I didn't say a word.

The doctor shook his head. "For your sister's sake, I hope you know what you're doing."

Caleb smiled that smug smile of his. "I always know what I'm doing."

The doctor signed the release papers.

Highway Thirteen to Manhattan

CHAPTER 3

Kai

It was so quiet at the Richter farmhouse. I'd almost forgotten how peaceful it was when there were fewer than a dozen minds in my telepathic range. Out in the country, it didn't matter that I was still too weak to build a mental shield. Caleb had even gotten my family to make an effort to shield their thoughts from me.

I stopped taking the pain pills and welcomed the agony of my injuries. I needed it. I wrapped every physical sensation around me like a security blanket. I relished my throbbing wrist, aching pinky, pulsing headache. The knitting of a broken wrist bone. The tightness of the stitches on my mending scalp. The tender bruises all over my body. Every single injury was mine, and I wanted them all. I wanted the pain. I needed it to remind me I was still here. That I survived everything.

Within a few hours of being home, my blood pressure dropped back to normal. My anxiety levels decreased. My pupils relaxed. The doctor that Caleb had hired checked me every hour to make sure it wasn't just a temporary thing. As the day progressed, it became clear that all my vitals were improving.

I felt so much better than I had in the hospital. But I still dreaded what was coming next. The nightmares.

My doctors said they were a common side effect from emotional trauma. Back when I was working at Child Protective Services, I used to see it all the time. The telltale dark smudges beneath children's eyes. The slight tremor when they talked about their dreams. Because they weren't just nightmares. They were their minds reliving some awful moment from their lives that they couldn't get over.

Mine were a little bit worse. My abilities heightened my emotions. My nightmares felt more real to me than my waking hours, and I would do anything to escape what came for me in the darkness.

The day passed too quickly. Night came faster than I expected.

I wanted to enjoy the soft sheets and the warm down comforter. I wanted to sink into the mattress and let everything go. But I couldn't. Because I knew what came next.

I sat up in bed and studied my reflection in the vanity mirror. My dark blue eyes were the only things I recognized. My features looked different. Sharper. Maybe it was caused by the weight loss. Maybe it was what had happened to me. I touched my cheekbone. It felt more pronounced than it used to be.

Oliver was there with me. I turned to him and asked, "Does my face look different?"

"You've been through a lot. You just need to rest."

I choked on a laugh. Rest. Right. In every nightmare I'd had since we'd escaped from the cave, I was being trapped or controlled or hunted. And then I would die. Over and over again. There was no rest to be had. I might sleep, but I couldn't rest.

He left the lamp on beside my side of the bed. "Is that enough light?"

It would make it harder for him to sleep, but it wasn't nearly enough. "Could you put on the bathroom and the closet light?"

When I woke up, I needed to be able to see exactly where I was, even if it was still dark out. I could break free from the nightmares a little faster that way.

"Of course." After he turned on the other lights, he asked, "Do you need more pillows for your wrist?"

I shook my head and he slid back into bed beside me, careful not to jostle my broken bone. "Can I hold you?"

I wanted him to and I didn't want to want him to. When he held me, I felt like I would break into a million pieces, and I couldn't let myself break, so I hid behind my injury. "It's too hard with my wrist."

"I could just lay close you."

He'd done that in the hospital. It had been nice. "Okay."

He curled around me in a careful "C."

"Is this alright?"

I could feel the warmth of his body. His breath on my neck. If I let myself, I could slip back into a memory of what we had been. It was more than alright. Or at least it used to be.

"Yeah," I whispered.

"Go to sleep. I'll be here."

"I know." Hot tears pooled in my eyes. I turned my face away from his. "Thanks."

He must have heard it in my voice. "Are you crying?"

"A little."

"Why?"

"This was what I wanted when I was in the cave. To be back here with you. And now..."

"It's all messed up." He brushed a piece of hair off my forehead.

I didn't trust myself to speak so I nodded.

"Don't think about it tonight."

I couldn't help it. When I was scared, I hid inside us. I went back to one of our memories. To a happy moment of Kai and Oliver: *Koliver*. Our love had been everything to me. But now, every moment of us hurt. To remember what we had had and feel the loss of it. I had nowhere to hide. My sanctuary was gone.

17

"Just not today."

"Not today." He gave me a tentative smile.

After I finished breakfast, he took my tray downstairs. I watched Netflix. Read *Wuthering Heights*. Anything to stay awake. I even doodled a little—at least, that's how it started out, like one of those silly designs you draw in the margin of your notebook to pass time in class. But then, suddenly, I saw an image inside my mind. A lake I'd never been to. But I didn't just see it. I felt the sunlight on my skin. I heard the birds chirping. I was there, and I was trying to capture it all in my drawing. My hand glided over the paper, and there it was: a perfect depiction of a place I'd never seen.

Caleb came in as I stared down at the sketch.

"What's that?" he asked.

"I drew it," my voice came out wobbly. This couldn't be my drawing. I was the goth girl in high school, not the artsy goth girl. I had no talent for drawing. My brother knew it, too.

"You drew it?"

I nodded.

He sat beside me on the bed and examined it. "It's good. When did you learn to draw like this?"

I swallowed, but it didn't move the ball of weirdness trapped in my throat. I looked at the clock. "About twenty minutes ago."

His eyebrows pulled together and creases appeared between them. "That's weird."

"Yeah." It freaked me out, and I didn't want to admit how much, so I shrugged and tried to act like it wasn't a big deal. "Maybe my head injury—"

Concern filled his voice. "The doctor said your vitals have been good. Have you noticed any other changes? Mood swings? Blurred vision? Dizziness?"

"No. I mean I get a little dizzy if I get up fast."

"I'd better let him know about your drawing."

"Can we wait?" Fear coiled in my belly. If there was something wrong, they'd drag me back to the hospital. This time, I feared I wouldn't have any control. I wouldn't have any say over what happened to me. I couldn't take that. Not again.

"This is your health, Kai."

"I can't go back to the hospital," I whispered. "And Mom and Dad can't find out about this." That morning, I'd heard them arguing with Oliver in hushed tones about how risky it was to bring me home. They'd wear away at him if they knew about this.

"Let's see what the doctor thinks."

Before I could stop him, he was on the phone. I listened while Caleb told him about my drawing. They talked for a few minutes. I chewed the inside of my cheek. Caleb kept saying "I understand" and "Of course."

When he hung up, he gave me one of his *you're going to be okay* looks. Slight head tilt, brief smile, warm eyes.

"What did he say?" I asked.

"It might just be an aftereffect of the head trauma. Or the emotional trauma. Children often draw after trauma."

"They don't become gifted artists."

He forced a chuckle. "The brain's a funny thing. It's hard to predict what it will do. He says to let him know if anything else changes. He'd also like you to come in in a few days just to rule things out."

"No."

"No?" He raised an eyebrow.

"It's just a telepathy thing. The doctors can't diagnose those things."

"True. But it could also be a head injury thing."

My voice went wobbly again. "Don't send me back to the hospital."

"I won't." He paused. "But we can go in for a couple tests—"

"Mom and Dad will make me stay in the hospital until the doctors find an explanation. And if they can't..." My chest constricted. I had to take quick, shallow breaths. "I can't be locked up again." I whispered,

21

"Not in a hospital, not in a cave, not in a cage."

"They won't lock you up. I won't let them."

The way he said it—I believed him. The heaviness in my chest eased.

"So let's just keep the drawing between us," I said.

"I can, but can you?" He looked pointedly at my hand. I hadn't realized that I had picked up the pen and started drawing while we were talking.

I dropped the pen. "I don't know why, but it helps."

"I'll help everyone see that." He kissed the top of my head. "As long as you let me schedule those tests."

I nodded. It was the best deal I could make.

In the afternoon, I moved downstairs to the living room. The walls were the warm eggshell that Oliver and I had painted them months ago. The crown molding gleamed from all the TLC we'd given it. Our furniture was comfy. The thick toffee-brown rug under the coffee table had been a housewarming gift from Oliver's aunt Ines.

A fire crackled in the fireplace. The bull and bear figurines that I bought for Oliver sat on the mantle. This was the home I'd built with him—back when I still believed in us.

Last night, I'd let myself forget everything that had happened between us. I'd escaped into the comfort that only Oliver could give me. I'd grasped at one more moment of us. In the light of day, it seemed cowardly. And it felt like a lie, a bastardization of what we'd once been.

The memory echoed in my heart. Agony. Unbearable agony. Worse than any physical pain I'd endured. It wasn't that Oliver had hidden Christian's death from me, but that he'd refused to let me help him carry that burden. It wasn't the fact that he had kissed Mickey when my parents had locked me away in a mental ward; it was the fact that he'd kept it to himself for years. He hadn't trusted me. Now, I couldn't trust him.

And I didn't know what that meant for our future.

I clutched at the handmade quilt covering my legs. My pet turkey, Herbie, shifted closer and rested his head on my leg. He tried to comfort me, but it didn't help.

Almost before I knew what I was doing, I grabbed my broken finger and jerked it backwards. The physical pain stole my breath away—and it distracted me from the emotional pain that threatened to overwhelm me. I knew it was wrong, just like I knew the night before was wrong. But, once more, I needed an escape.

After I took the edge off, I needed something that would last longer. My fingers itched to hold the sketchpad and pencils that Caleb had rounded up for me. It was like something compelled me to do it.

I snatched them up.

When I was drawing, I slipped away from the emotional pain inside me. It was an oasis for me. Nothing mattered but staying there. I propped my sketchpad against my knees. Rested my left arm on the back of the couch in its cast. Bones set to right should heal. If only feelings could be that simple.

By the time I finished the picture, I forgot where I was. I looked up and watched the sunlight stream through the big picture window. It danced on the ginormous Christmas tree that we'd decorated a few weeks ago. I stared at the twinkling lights, needing to feel the possibility of a future. I tried to imagine a perfect holiday with family, even just a normal holiday with family. Maybe that was all we needed.

And maybe I could talk myself into believing that.

CHAPTER 4

Oliver

K ai was so lost in her sketchpad and pencils; she didn't even realize that I was watching her. I couldn't help myself. Having her home was all I'd wanted for weeks. And last night, she'd let me be with her. For a few moments, we'd felt like us again.

The doctors said that it was a miracle that she'd woken up after what had happened in the cave, a miracle that she hadn't suffered massive brain damage, a miracle that she was still here. I was so grateful to have Kai alive, I didn't question if we'd used up all our miracles.

Still I couldn't help wanting her to be my Kai again. The doctors cautioned that there would be aftereffects to that much physical and emotional trauma. That's how Caleb explained her sudden interest in drawing. I wanted to believe him. I didn't want her parents to be concerned, so I acted like it was no big deal. But deep down, I worried.

The first time I saw her at the hospital, all I wanted to do was explain everything. To make her understand why I'd kept so many secrets. To apologize for how my secrets had hurt her.

She'd looked so fragile in that bed. I was afraid to touch her.

Then she said, "Come here," and I was afraid not to.

I shuffled toward her and sat down beside her, careful not to hurt her. When she touched my face I felt it: her love, her pain, and how they were all wrapped together now.

"Can you forgive me?" I asked.

She was silent for a long time, and then her hand dropped from my face. "I don't know if it's possible."

"You did a dozen impossible things to save Lukas." I touched her arm. She didn't pull away.

"Maybe I exhausted myself."

She couldn't talk about it. Not then.

Seven days had passed — 168 hours since she'd woken up from the coma and asked me for more time.

I felt like all this time was strangling us.

But then last night when she'd awakened in a panic, screaming, she'd reached for me. She'd begged me to touch her. It had given me hope that we could rekindle what was between us. Today, however, she'd receded into herself again.

So I just watched her for a moment. Her face was scrunched in concentration as she made dark, heavy marks on the paper. The tip of her pencil snapped. She slammed the broken pencil on the table and reached for another, but it was just beyond her grasp. She was having trouble reaching with her good arm without disturbing her broken wrist or putting too much pressure on her bruises.

"Kai, you're going to fall." I rushed into the room. "Let me get that for you."

"I can do it," she insisted.

Herbie clucked a warning to her. Even the turkey knew she was being foolish.

She didn't listen to either of us. Instead, she kept reaching until she lost her balance. I was able to catch her just as she began to fall off the couch.

"All you have to do is yell, Kai. We're all here to help you," I said.

She just gritted her teeth. "I almost had it."

"You almost fell off the couch." I handed her the pencil.

"I've survived worse."

"And you're still recovering." I peered at her sketchpad. It was a landscape. A lake I thought looked familiar, but I couldn't be sure. It was weird. In all the time I'd known her, Kai had never shown an interested in drawing. I hadn't even known she *could* draw.

She caught me looking at her work and flipped to a clean page. She started a new drawing. From her first tentative strokes, this one seemed different. Less assured. But as I watched it take shape, I felt a flicker of hope. She was drawing our Christmas tree. It had to be a good sign that she'd chosen to draw the Christmas tree—the tree we'd picked out and decorated together.

"It's lovely," I murmured.

She laughed. "It's terrible."

"Well, I like it. That was a good day, wasn't it? The day we decorated it?" I wanted to make her remember us before everything happened.

She started sketching in a present beneath the tree. "Aunt Ines made amazing eggnog."

"I loved your slice-and-bake sugar cookies."

"Thank goodness Aunt Ines brought all those lights." The faintest smile touched her lips.

"Remember the pre-lit tree from Duane Reade we had in New York?" I tried to sit beside her on the couch, but Herbie growled at me. Damn turkey had never liked me.

Kai crooned at the bird, "It's okay, baby."

He shuffled closer to her and rubbed his head on her thigh.

Kai put her pencil down and reached out with her good hand to stroke his feathers. He purred at her.

I took the chair near the couch. Close enough to Kai and far enough from Herbie.

Kai went back to drawing. I wished I could understand everything she was going through.

Not that I didn't have some idea. I'd seen the x-rays and waited while the doctors performed multiple surgeries. And every day I prayed with Aunt Ines that Kai would survive.

While she'd been in the coma, I'd sat by Kai's bed, holding her hand and talking to her for hours. I promised, "If you come back, I'll spend every day apologizing. I'll do whatever it takes to fix us. To be the man you deserve. I won't lose you, Kai."

I hadn't been there when she finally woke up. Part of me wondered if it was Caleb's voice that brought her back from the abyss, but I didn't care. She was back.

But she still wasn't the Kai I had known.

My Kai didn't shut down like this. My Kai always reached out, feeling her way through everything. I was the one who withdrew. I was the one who kept secrets.

"Can you talk to me, please?" I asked.

She didn't look up from her sketchpad. "I'm talking to you right now."

I lowered my voice. "About what happened in the cave. What Nathan did to you. What you found out about me. What you're feeling."

When she did look up, her eyes were dead seas of certainty. "I can't. Not yet."

I touched her arm. "Why?"

"There are things that are best left alone for now. Buried in the back of my mind." Her voice quivered.

I flinched at her words. They were eerily similar to the ones I'd spoken when I was hiding my past from her. "Things like that have a way of coming out."

"Eventually." She smudged a line with the side of her hand. She frowned at it. "I almost died. Twice. What do you want me to say about that?"

I didn't know, but she had to start somewhere. "Tell me about the nightmares."

She shuddered. "No."

"Can I tell you something then?"

She nodded.

"There is only one reason I didn't tell you about kissing Mickey when you were in the institution: I was ashamed. It wasn't because I had lingering doubts about my choice or a secret desire to be with Mickey."

"But—"

"Let me finish." I continued, "It was because I didn't want you to know I'd given up on us. For a few moments, I believed you were gone and I used Mickey to kill the pain. I never wanted you to know that I wasn't strong enough to believe in us, that I'd ever doubted us. Even for a second."

She didn't respond, but I could tell that she was listening to me. She was giving me a chance.

"You needed me to get you out of the institution. You needed things to be the way they were. I couldn't hurt you with one stupid moment." I sighed. "I was so afraid you'd have a setback. That all your progress would disappear. And it would be my fault. I couldn't tell you about it when you were putting your life back together in San Diego or when we were starting over in New York. There was never a time that felt right to say 'I lost faith in us.' I could barely even admit it to myself back then. So I buried it like I buried Christian and my father." The words scraped against my throat.

Kai shifted on the couch. She reached a hand toward me. I grabbed it. Then she said, "I understand your fear. But the secrets, Oliver. The lies."

"Tell me."

"I don't know how to do this," she whispered.

"Do what?"

28

"Find my way through the pain."

"Let me help you," I said.

"I don't think you can."

"I love you. I'd do anything for you."

Her eyes brimmed with tears. "I know. And I love you, too."

I squeezed her hand, but she pulled away and wiped her eyes.

Her voice was raw. "Don't you understand? I love you, but I also hate you. I miss you and I want you back and I wish you weren't here and I wish I wasn't here. I wish that none of this had happened to us." Tears rolled down her cheeks.

"I'm sorry. Sorry for everything Nathan did to you. Sorry for every secret I kept from you. Sorry you got hurt because of me."

She gulped back a sob. "You said that Butternut would be better for me than New York when you dragged me out here. But I wasn't any safer, was I? If we'd stayed in New York, none of this would have happened."

"You weren't safe there. All those people, all those minds invading yours. It was tearing you apart."

"No one ever held me hostage in New York."

"I thought you were going to kill yourself!"

"Nathan almost killed me here. And whose fault is that?" she whispered.

I wanted to know exactly what had happened to her, but I wasn't sure I could bear the guilt. "But you didn't die, Kai. You're still alive."

She looked down at her drawing. "I didn't die" was all she said.

Her voice sounded hollow, like she didn't quite believe it.

CHAPTER 5

Kai

Sitting at my vanity to brush my hair, I tried to take pleasure in doing something that would have been impossible a few days ago. It was my third day home and I could feel my body healing. I was making progress. I wanted to be grateful, but something held me back.

My brain hadn't felt right since I woke up from the coma. At first, I blamed it on the pain meds, but they were almost out of my system and something still felt off. Really off—like I wasn't myself. I couldn't explain it any better than that.

The afternoon sunlight streamed through the four big windows in my bedroom. Large bands of brightness cut across the hardwood floor. Tiny bits of dust sparkled in the air. It still wasn't enough light and darkness was coming. I turned on two lamps.

A soft triple knock on the door told me Caleb was here.

He shielded his eyes as he came in. "Wow, it's like living on the sun." He pushed a blond curl off his forehead. It sprung right back into place. "I don't know how Oliver sleeps in here."

No matter how many times I told Oliver that he could leave, he stayed. He said he wanted to be there in case I needed him. I hated how much I still needed him. "About as well as I do, I think."

"After everything that happened, I guess missing out on a little sleep isn't the worst punishment in the world." Caleb's words were light, but their meaning hung heavy in the air. Caleb had never quite trusted Oliver, and now he blamed my husband for everything that had happened to me.

"Sometimes, I can feel him watching me."

"In a creepy way?"

"As if he thinks I'll disappear."

It was more than that. Oliver needed something from me, something I couldn't give him: He wanted absolution for everything that his secrets and lies had cost me. But I couldn't separate him from the pain he'd caused me.

"We were so close to losing you," Caleb murmured.

"I feel like I'm never going to be like I was."

"The bruises are fading," he said. "You're getting better."

"I mean mentally. Emotionally." I fidgeted with the hairpins on my vanity.

"Maybe it's something physical. That should be easy enough to handle."

"And if it's mental?"

"Then we'll handle that, too."

He made it sound so easy.

It wasn't going to be easy. Like this drawing thing. I tried to tell myself that drawing soothed me. It did, but there was more to it than that. When I chose to draw, it was relaxing, but it was nothing like when I *had* to draw—when an image took over my brain and my hand.

I'd already caught my mom giving me strange looks while I sketched. She was eager for a reason—any reason—to put me back in the hospital. Any hint of a mental problem would be more than enough for her. For my dad, too. Maybe even for Oliver.

"Do me a favor. Don't tell our parents and Oliver we're going back for more testing until we get the results. I don't want them to worry over nothing."

"We'll be gone for at least half a day. What do you want to tell them?" he asked.

"I'll think of something."

I could see that he had more to say on this topic, but he decided to let it drop.

"How are the dreams?" he asked softly.

Fear skittered around inside my belly. "Bad."

"What do you see that makes you scream?"

"Don't you see it?" I whispered. Every time was different, but it always ended the same.

"All I see in your nightmares is darkness. Then I shift the dream landscape to something safe and familiar."

Maybe I was protecting him from it. Maybe it was something I had to go through alone. "Sometimes I'm Christian riding his bike. Sometimes I'm me trapped in the cave. Sometimes I'm someone I don't even know. But it always ends in my death."

I flashed back to the moment when Nathan had been shot. I struggled to survive, but I knew I wouldn't. I was trapped with Nathan, inside his mind, and I was going to die with him. My heart raced as the fear came for me all over again. And then I felt something else, the emotion that I was most afraid of—relief that it was all over.

I couldn't talk about this, not even with Caleb. Nobody understood me like Caleb did. Nobody protected me like Caleb did. But what if he thought I wanted to die?

I grabbed the brush on my vanity and pulled it through my hair. Caleb didn't say anything. He was waiting for me. Just like Oliver was waiting for me. Waiting for me to say something I could not say.

Frustration and anger welled up. A rush of emotions that I wasn't ready to feel. I squeezed my splinted left hand. Pain flared in my pinky, coursing through my hand and up my arm. I hissed and panted around the shock of it.

"Don't hurt yourself!" Caleb shouted.

"It's the only way I can keep it all under control." The words came out before I could stop them.

"What do you have to keep under control?"

"Everything inside me," I whispered.

"What do you mean?"

I chewed on my bottom lip, knowing I had to say something, but not sure how much I should say.

"You can tell me anything," Caleb promised.

I had to trust someone. And I trusted him. "It's starting to feel like when I was a teenager."

"You mean when Kadin committed suicide?" he asked.

Just hearing his name brought it all back. Junior year. Caleb was a freshman in college at USC. I was all alone. Until Kadin transferred into my school and made the fatal mistake of befriending me. The bullies taunted him for being the freak girl's friend. I could take it—I was used to it. Kadin couldn't.

Tears burned my throat. If only I had known what it was doing to him. But Kadin had made me promise to never read his thoughts. He told me he could handle it.

The three months that followed were a subject my family never talked about. Mom and Dad thought I was depressed and acting out. If only. It was one of the few times I didn't turn my emotions inward and hurt myself. Instead, I used my abilities to hurt people, the people who'd hurt Kadin.

When my parents finally understood what was happening, they sent me away to Grandma Guhn's. She lived fifty miles from my high school, way beyond my telepathic radius. She was the only one who could bring me back from that place where hurting others made so much sense. I'd promised I would never be that girl again. But, now…

Caleb rested his hand on my shoulder. "You've managed it before."

"I had Grandma Guhn back then." She was dead now. My nightmares stopped me from reaching her in the In Between. But there was more to it than that. "It's different this time. *I'm* different this time."

He took the brush from my hand and gently ran it through my hair.

It felt so good. I started to tell him, "Make sure you cover..." But I hated saying it, so I thought it at him instead. *The bare spot.* The place where they had shaved my scalp and stitched it back together. It was only an inch, but it felt so much larger. Maybe because those blows to the head almost killed me.

"It'll grow back," he said.

"It will take months. And it won't be the same." Nothing would ever be the same.

"You're going to be okay." Caleb's words felt like a wish and a chant rolled together.

CHAPTER 6

Oliver

The grave was blanketed in snow. Iced-over tree branches crackled above me. I stared at the gray granite headstone inscribed with the name *Richter* for a few moments before I knelt to lay a wreath of holly and ivy against my grandparents' final resting place.

Every day, Kai's family hovered over her. The house felt too full of her family. I wished it were just me there nursing her back to health. Caleb could have rented a place for them all to stay, but he endured the small guest room with a shared bathroom so that he could be close to Kai.

I had to leave my own house just to hear myself think. I hadn't even known where I was going when I left, or what had drawn me to the cemetery. Maybe I needed to be with my family instead of my wife's.

Aunt Ines believed that the spirits of my grandparents could hear her when she visited, but the idea of a soul lingering with its decaying body bothered me. I wanted my grandparents somewhere warm and safe, drinking coffee and talking about what a mess I'd made of things down here.

Still, here I was. The silence thickened around me. The burden of my thoughts weighed on my chest. It didn't matter if only the wind heard me. I had to get them out.

"My first Christmas back in Butternut. Kai's entire family is here. I wish you were here, too."

What I would give to hear Grandpa's gruff chuckle when I gave him his gift. No matter what was inside the box, he'd smile at me and act like it was the greatest present he ever got.

I'd spent so many years running from Grandpa and hiding from what my father had done. I was so worried about keeping Dad's secrets. I never worried about keeping Grandpa in my life. I thought that he'd always be here, waiting for me.

And then he was gone.

The cold chilled my nose. I sniffled. One thought consoled me. Grandpa had never known why I left home. He hadn't been burdened with the knowledge of what his son had done. When John Schneider had killed my friend Christian, my father had covered it up. And, when I discovered what he had done, my father's secret became mine.

For twelve years, I'd buried that memory in the back of my mind. It was the only way to live with it—to push it down as deep as I could and ignore it. At least that's what I told myself.

I blamed Schneider. I blamed my dad. But the events leading up to Christian's death had started with me. I was the reason my friend was out on that road late at night, riding his bike. He was trying to get away from me.

I gulped the cold air, wishing that I could go back in time and make everything right again.

I looked over at my parents' gravestone. It lay six feet away. A lifetime of regret lingered between us. I picked up the flowers I brought for my mother and walked over. The snow creak-crunched beneath my boots. This was the first time I'd visited her grave since I left for college. It was also the first time I'd seen my father's name carved into that headstone.

I nestled a bouquet of white roses into the snow. "I'm sorry they aren't blue, Mama."

Blue roses always made her smile. My grandmother used to make them in her little greenhouse, especially for my mother. Something to do with adding blue dye to the root. Every year, Grandma Richter would cut me a bouquet for Mother's Day, and I'd get to see Mama's big ray-of-light grin. After Mama died, I brought them here.

Grandma's rose bushes were all dead now.

I traced my gloved fingers across my mother's name. *Sophie Alina Richter.* Aunt Ines used to tell me *Sophie* was for her wisdom and *Alina* for her beauty.

I closed my eyes. It was getting harder and harder to remember Mama. I could barely conjure the sound of her voice or her laugh. My throat tightened around a ball of longing.

I'd lived almost twenty-two years without her. So many more than I'd had with her.

I hadn't brought anything for my father. There was nothing left for me to say to him.

I wasn't ready to go back to a house filled with Guhns. When I saw Aunt Ines's tomato-red Dodge Durango parked in front of Cruise Inn Spring Creek, I pulled in and parked beside her.

After the brightness of the snow, it was almost impossible to see inside the dim interior of the bar. As my eyes adjusted, I took in the familiar dark paneling and deer head mounted on the wall. There was even a stuffed black bear in a glass cabinet.

Pure Northwoods charm.

I spied Aunt Ines's purple coat at the end of the bar. As I headed toward her, the owner, Pam, greeted me with a huge smile. Several customers seated in back gave me a nod of acknowledgment. After my picture was splashed across the *Park Falls Herald*, everyone in town seemed to know me—even people who'd moved here after I left.

Aunt Ines noticed the commotion and glanced up. When she saw me, her brown eyes warmed and wrinkled up in the corners.

I made my way toward her. A couple guys stuck out their hands to shake mine or slapped me on the back. They were proud of me. Somehow, saving Lukas and my wife had made me more a part of Butternut than all the years I spent growing up here.

I finally made it to Aunt Ines. She wiped her hands on napkins before she hugged me and dropped a quick kiss on my cheek. "Oh, you're freezing. Where have you been?"

"The cemetery."

Her expression shifted. Part sympathetic, part concerned. "Visiting your mom?"

I nodded. Before I could say more, Pam appeared with a menu and asked, "What would you like?"

"Jack and Coke."

"First round's on me." Pam winked at me.

"Thanks."

That was one of the perks of being a local hero. The police and the newspapers ran with the story Mickey and I told them. Nathan had lost his mind and convinced himself that I was Lukas's actual father. His brain tumor only made our story more plausible. "Local Hero Saves Family from Deranged Father" was the headline in the *Park Falls Herald*. Me being the local hero, Nathan the deranged father.

Mickey and I knew we couldn't tell anyone about what Schneider had done to Christian. Not without real proof. For now, it was my word against his. He was still the chief of police, armed with a bogus statement I had signed saying that my father had been behind Christian's death.

I glanced over at Aunt Ines's plate. It had crispy fries and a giant bacon cheeseburger. "Aren't you coming to dinner tonight?"

She nodded.

I checked my watch. It was almost 5:30 p.m. "How are you going to eat again in an hour?"

"I'm not a Guhn. I can't live on that vegetarian stuff."

My lips tugged into a smile. "I can't stand it either."

"Get a burger," she said.

"But dinner..."

"I didn't make any wiener schnitzel for tonight," she confided. "I don't want to make trouble with your mother-in-law."

I thought about what I could expect at the evening meal without Aunt Ines's fried pork cutlet, and I ordered my own cheeseburger and fries when Pam served my drink.

"You went by yourself to the cemetery?" Aunt Ines asked.

I nodded.

"Next time, I'll go with you."

"Thanks."

She offered me a fry and I took it. "It'll get better, Oliver."

"Will it?" I wasn't so sure.

"Kai will get stronger."

But would *we* get stronger?

A few minutes later, Pam arrived with my cheeseburger. After setting my plate in front of me, she leaned on the bar. Her blue-green eyes sparkled with curiosity. "So what's it like to be a town hero?"

"I just did what had to be done."

"You saved Lukas and your wife. You risked your life for theirs."

"That's what you do for family." I sipped my drink.

She reached over and squeezed my hand. "You're a good man, Oliver Richter." She gave Aunt Ines a knowing look. "You must be so proud of him."

Aunt Ines patted my arm. "I've always been proud of Oliver."

39

Before everything happened, I'd been looking forward to celebrating the holidays in my family home. As I stepped into the dining room, though, my heart sunk a little. This wasn't what I'd had in mind.

Kai's father, brother, and sister were already at the table. Caleb and Naomi were texting on their phones and ignoring their father. That wasn't the worst part.

Kai's father sat at the end of the table in the seat that should have been mine. Kai was at the other end, with Caleb to her right. I tried not to feel like I was being shut out of my rightful place by Kai's family, but I failed.

There was a bit of color in my wife's face, and her eyes were bright. She was sitting up straight, not hunched over in pain. When she was around her brother, it was like she was able to borrow some of his strength. I felt that awful twinge in my heart. Jealousy. I hated knowing that he could do something for Kai that I couldn't—that she wouldn't let me do.

When I tore my gaze away from them, it landed on the antique cabinet against the far wall. Aunt Ines had given it to Kai and me for our wedding china, which had a pattern of bright blue peacock feathers laced with gold. Tonight, it felt like those feathers were mocking me, reminding me that I was a husband without a solid place in his wife's life.

I dragged my thoughts back to the table. More specifically, where I would sit. Naomi sat on Caleb's other side, looking like she would rather be anywhere else in the world. I understood how she felt. There were two seats left. The one beside Naomi had a half-drunk glass of white wine there, which meant Mrs. Guhn had already claimed it. I took my place next to my aunt, grateful for her warm presence.

A few moments later, Mrs. Guhn hovered around the table, holding a huge casserole and fretting at Kai. "You've lost too much weight."

Caleb quirked an eyebrow and Kai fought a smile. They had to be sharing thoughts. I was glad that Kai was letting someone in, but I resented that it wasn't me.

"I believe a hospital stay will do that to anyone." Caleb sipped his wine.

"Well, I guess it's my job to see that she gains it all back." She slid a large slice of vegetarian lasagna onto Kai's plate. Kai was an omnivore, but everyone was vegetarian when Mrs. Guhn was in the kitchen.

"That's too much, Mom," Kai said.

Her mother just stared until Kai had taken a couple of bites.

With a pang, I realized that I should have brought home a burger for Kai.

Once everyone had been served, Mrs. Guhn took her seat and made polite conversation with Aunt Ines. Naomi tried to get Caleb's attention, but she only succeeded in extracting a few one word answers before Caleb resumed his private chat with Kai.

Unlike Kai and Caleb, Naomi hadn't inherited any psychic gifts from their father. She wasn't a brilliant success like her brother. She didn't need the same care as her fragile sister, who had ruined whatever plans Naomi might have had for her winter break. I tried to ask her about her college search, but her parents hijacked the conversation and managed to bring it back around to Kai and Caleb. Eventually, Naomi slid her phone out of her back pocket and start texting. Nobody but me seemed to notice.

Caleb took advantage of a quiet moment to say, "Kai and I are going to go to Wausau tomorrow."

I stared down the table at her. "Are you up for that?"

"It'll be good to get out." She gave me a nervous smile.

"It's a two-and-a-half-hour drive." I'd driven it several times when she was in the hospital down there. "Why do you need to go that far?"

Kai studied her lasagna and mumbled, "Art supplies."

Caleb, whose face was always a carefully controlled mask, looked dumbfounded by her explanation.

Mrs. Guhn tried to sound calm and reasonable, but I could hear the underlying panic in her voice. "Oh, I don't think you're up for a trip like that, dear. Maybe next week."

Mr. Guhn nodded. Aunt Ines looked concerned.

Naomi was the only one who sounded excited by this trip. "I could use some art supplies! Why don't we go instead, Mom?"

Mrs. Guhn was about to reply when her husband cleared his throat and said, "I have to say, this drawing thing concerns me."

There was a brief silence. Mr. Guhn usually let his wife take the lead when it came to worrying about Kai. Even Caleb seemed surprised.

"So, just to be clear, Kai is kidnapped, held hostage in a cave by a madman, has her head bashed in twice, and goes into a coma for days. When she wakes up, she takes some comfort in drawing. And this is what concerns you?" Caleb sneered.

Mrs. Guhn rushed to take her husband's side. "It's not the drawing, exactly. It's just that..." She paused like she was searching for the right words. "She's good at it now. And she wasn't before. She has," she hesitated before saying, "new abilities."

Those last two words hung in the air. Kai's old abilities had been more than enough for her and her family to deal with.

Mr. Guhn added, "Maybe the doctors could run some more tests?"

"Sure, Dad. We can stop by the hospital while we're in the city buying art supplies," Caleb said smoothly.

I looked at Kai's face as she looked at Caleb's, and I knew they were lying about something. I just couldn't quite figure out what.

"When were you going to tell me about this?" My voice bounced off the walls of the dining room.

Kai looked startled, but then she shrugged. "It's not a big deal. I feel fine. When I was working with Child Protective Services, I met a lot of kids who processed trauma with art. I'm sure that's all it is. Caleb just thought we should let the doctors rule out brain damage. That's it."

Her parents relaxed. They didn't like talking about Kai's "abilities" and were eager to be reassured.

I was alone in my outrage. "Is that supposed to make me feel better?"

Kai glanced at Caleb like she hoped he'd fix this for her.

"Her vital signs have returned to normal since she left the hospital. You know that. It's probably nothing," he said calmly.

"Since when are you in charge of Kai's medical care?" I asked.

"Since I started paying her medical bills." His voice was quiet, but it had an edge.

Kai and I had both had insurance before I made us leave New York and our jobs there. Once again, Caleb was taking my place.

"What do you suggest we do, Caleb?" Mr. Guhn was deferring to his son. They all were. It was like I wasn't even there.

"We make sure that Kai is physically healthy, we accept that she's got a harmless new talent, and we don't freak out about it."

He made it sound so easy. I knew it wouldn't be, but what could I say? Nobody was listening to me. Not even my wife.

I pushed the cold vegetarian lasagna around my plate.

The rest of the meal would have passed in strained silence if Aunt Ines hadn't started talking about the weather.

As everyone left the table after dinner, I scrambled to get a moment with Kai, but Caleb remained by her side.

"I'll go to the hospital tomorrow," I said softly for her ears only.

"Don't you have to work?" she asked.

"I can call in. I want to be there for you," I said.

"Are you sure they can find someone with your skillset on such short notice?" Caleb had overheard, apparently.

He loved reminding me that I was a lowly bagboy at the local grocery store. It didn't matter that it was a temporary career choice I'd made to keep Kai safe. For Caleb, it was just another sign of my inadequacy.

I waited for Kai to defend me. She didn't. Instead, she said, "I'll be fine with Caleb. Let's not make a big deal out of this."

"You don't want me there?" I couldn't keep the hurt out of my voice.

"It's not necessary," Kai said.

"We can take my Cherokee," I offered.

"I've got my Mercedes SUV," Caleb said. "It's a smoother ride, better for someone recovering from serious injuries."

"You want me to stay here?" I wanted her to say it.

"It's just easier," she replied.

I didn't know what to say. So I didn't say anything.

CHAPTER 7

Kai

After dinner, we split into two groups. Oliver and Aunt Ines cleaned up in the kitchen with Mom's help. That left Dad, Naomi, Caleb, and me in the living room. I couldn't recall the last time we had all been together like this, but it didn't take me long to remember why my family wasn't big on reunions.

I tried to chat with Naomi. Nothing I had to say was more interesting than whatever was happening on her phone, so I gave up.

I thought about saying that I was exhausted and going to bed, but, as I looked at my father and my brother, I desperately wanted my family to work. Oliver and I might be falling apart, but maybe I could bring Caleb and Dad together again. I just needed to get them talking, even if they were talking about nothing.

I turned to Caleb. "Dad was wondering when you're heading back to London."

Caleb didn't bother looking at Dad. "TBD."

"What?" my dad asked.

"To be determined," I replied.

"Doesn't your boss expect you?"

At least Dad was taking an interest.

"I can work from anywhere with my laptop and Wi-Fi."

"You can trade from home?" Dad asked.

"I haven't been a trader for years." Caleb said it like Dad should have known.

To be fair, I barely understood what Caleb did.

Caleb didn't explain. Dad didn't ask. Maybe the distance between them was more than I could bridge.

They hadn't always been like this. But, after Dad let Mom commit me to a mental institution without telling Caleb what they were doing, well, things had changed. Caleb understood Mom's fears. She wasn't special like us. But Dad was. Caleb thought that he should have done a better job helping me. And Caleb was furious that they hadn't let him be there for me when I needed him most.

This was going to be our first Christmas together in years. I needed for us to be a family. So I kept trying. "Honestly, Caleb, I'm not sure I get what you do."

"I work in private equity."

I scowled at Caleb. He wasn't even trying.

"Not like Bernie Madoff?" Dad's voice was a mix of tentative and worried.

I cringed.

Caleb sighed. "I am not running a Ponzi scheme. I work for a huge investment bank. We have auditors and regulators. We have protocols in place to prevent disastrous decisions."

From Caleb's tone, I didn't think he was alluding to bad investments. Nope. That was a barely veiled jab at Mom and Dad's disastrous decision to commit me. I wondered if Dad got it.

"Well, I'm ready for bed," Naomi announced.

Dad murmured, "I could use some fresh air." He went to the closet.

Naomi rose, stretched, and headed for the stairs.

I nudged Caleb. "Go talk to him."

"But I owe Naomi a Wii zombie game," he said.

Naomi turned. Surprise flitted across her face. The surprise gave way to excitement because she worshipped Caleb and loved spending time with him. Clearly, they didn't have plans. He was just using her to get out of talking to Dad.

"I'm going to kick your butt!" Naomi announced.

"You can try little sister." Caleb headed toward the study, where Oliver kept his Wii.

Naomi followed him.

The front door slammed shut behind Dad.

I grabbed my coat, slipped my good arm into a sleeve, and did my best to drape the other side around me. I slid my feet into clogs.

The cold, when I stepped out onto the front porch, was more than I expected. "It's freezing out here."

"Get back inside," Dad said.

"My doctor says I should get fresh air."

Dad smiled and swept snow off a wooden chair. "As long as you sit down." He tried to hide the hand-rolled cigarette behind his back. It smelled of cloves.

"I thought you gave up smoking." I sat down.

He gave up the subterfuge and took a puff. "Everyone needs a vice or two." He looked up at the night sky. "The stars out here are amazing. They remind you how small you are."

A memory from long ago rushed over me. We were camped out in Death Valley. Desert all around us. Parched earth and coarse sand. A smattering of green desert brush here and there. As far from natural light as we could be. Daddy held me up to the sky. Mom lifted Caleb. Grandpa Guhn had his arms wrapped around Grandma. Naomi hadn't even been an inkling then.

"Remember when Grandpa Guhn took us to watch the meteor shower?" I asked.

"You were only six. You remember that?" Dad gave me a sideways glance.

"I remember everything about Grandpa."

"He was a good man." Dad's voice rumbled in his throat.

"He still is," I said softly.

Dad turned to me, searching my face. "He's dead, darling." He was shielding his thoughts, but I knew how hard this was for him to talk about.

"He left this world." I took a breath. "But I've seen him in the next."

"Kai..."

Something inside me needed him to understand what I'd been through in the cave. "When I got hurt, I went," I lowered my voice, "to the In Between."

His face locked in neutral. He hated when I talked about the In Between. So many people in our family had supernatural gifts. My telepathy always made him uneasy, but my ability to travel to limbo and talk to the dead scared my father. I knew it was creepy, but I needed for him to finally accept it—to finally accept *me*—so I kept talking. "I saw Grandma and Grandpa."

Dad gazed up at the stars. Finally, he said, "You've got to let them go, honey. It isn't normal for—"

I interrupted him and my voice broke. "I've never been normal."

He was quiet again. Then he sighed. "Don't tell your mom. She has enough trouble dealing with our woo-woo stuff."

My shoulders slumped. I stared down at the snow-covered porch. "How were they?"

I looked up into his green eyes and saw the love there.

"I do care about them," he said. "I just care about you more. I can't help them, but I can still help you."

"They look happy, but they worry about all of us."

"That's my parents."

"Grandpa said that you and Caleb are too alike."

He squeezed my shoulder. "He's got that right."

"Neither of you can admit that you need people."

"There's some truth there." He stamped his cigarette out in a snowy patch on the banister. He put the butt inside a soda can he'd hidden in a snowdrift on the porch.

I clutched at his coat sleeve. "I'm here, you're here, Caleb's here. Please, Dad, for me. For Grandpa Guhn. You've got to try. We can be like we used to be."

He pulled me up into a hug. "Your brother won't let me in. You saw how he is. Once he shuts a door he bricks over it." Hurt crept into his voice.

"Promise me you'll keep chipping away at it. Don't give up on him."

He whispered in my ear, "I won't give up on any of you kids, ever."

That gave me a little hope.

When he released me, his expression was laced with concern. "But what about you and Oliver?"

"What about us?"

"Have you given up on him?"

"No, I just..." I rubbed my forehead. "Dad, it's complicated. Oliver and I need time."

Dad sighed. "I thought that's what Caleb and I needed. But time just let the hurt grow."

CHAPTER 8

Oliver

When I was with Mrs. Guhn and Aunt Ines, I sometimes felt like the moderator of a debate that would never end. Whatever Mrs. Guhn thought, Aunt Ines was struck with the opposite view. Wrist deep in soapy water, I scrubbed away at the food particles that stuck to our plates. Vegetables are a lot clingier than meat, as it turns out. Must be all the fiber. I needed to get a dishwasher if we were going to embrace all this "healthy" eating.

After I washed each dish, I handed it to Mrs. Guhn to dry. Aunt Ines wrapped up the leftovers, muttering about how many there were. Not even Mrs. Guhn's own family savored her cooking.

Mrs. Guhn ignored her and leaned closer to me. "Don't let Caleb get to you. We can't all be investment bankers."

I wondered if she had overheard the conversation Caleb, Kai, and I had had after dinner.

"I think it's wonderful that you gave up your career to come here and take care of Kai," she said.

She'd overheard it.

But I hadn't given up my career—not permanently, anyway. When we got here, I had to find work fast, something to cement our stay in town. I took the first thing that came my way and when that didn't work out, I grabbed onto the second. And the third. A job was an anchor in Butternut. I figured when Kai was better, then I could consider something more long term like telecommuting as an auditor. But I didn't feel like discussing this with my mother-in-law. "I needed to put Kai first for a while."

Mrs. Guhn confided, "It's hard to be the normal ones in this family. Just you, me, and Naomi."

I cleared my throat. "And Aunt Ines."

"Yes, of course," she said dismissively. "I'm sorry you have it so rough with Kai. Dylan's powers were always under control. If only Kai could be more like her father."

I'd never seen his telekinesis manifest in the nine years I'd known him. I figured he required focus to move objects with his mind. Kai's telepathy required focus to tune out all the thoughts and emotions around her. If she didn't focus, they overwhelmed her.

"Her power is harder to deal with," I said.

Mrs. Guhn looked doubtful. "I'm not sure she tries hard enough to deal with it."

I did my best to keep the anger out of my voice. "She tries." Mrs. Guhn had no appreciation for how much Kai wanted to help others, even if it meant putting herself at risk. Kai had worked so hard to keep it all together in New York, she had almost driven herself crazy pretending to be okay when, really, she was falling apart.

She wiped the inside of a glass. "Look at Caleb. He's managed to build a great life for himself."

"Caleb's powers only work when he's asleep!"

Mrs. Guhn jerked and bumped the glass on the counter. Aunt Ines gave me a concerned look.

I lowered my voice. "Kai's been through a lot, Mrs. Guhn."

"And so have you." Mrs. Guhn patted my hand. I didn't find it reassuring.

"Kai's not herself right now."

Mrs. Guhn started to say something in response, and then stopped, turning her full attention to drying and polishing the salad tongs.

I went back to the dirty dishes and my own thoughts.

Kai hated secrets, and I'd kept such big ones from her. She'd taught me how to build a psychic shield when we first started dating. She'd accepted that my past was mine and mine alone. She never tried to force her way into my head. But I'd used that shield to hide too much from her, and, when it all came out, she was the one who got hurt.

I was surprised to hear Aunt Ines speak up. "I don't know how she survived in a cave with that madman. Protecting little Lukas and risking her life. I can't imagine how hard it is to come back from that." She was sticking up for me by sticking up for Kai, and I loved her for it.

Mrs. Guhn used that tone of voice that acknowledges and dismisses simultaneously. "Of course it was terrible, but there's no use dwelling on it. It only makes things worse. It always makes thing worse."

Aunt Ines wasn't about to back down. "She's only been out of the hospital a few days. She'll get there."

I saw improvements in Kai. She was moving around with more ease. She was talking to people. "Maybe we're expecting too much, too fast."

Mrs. Guhn didn't reply, and we all went back to cleaning up. The only sounds in the room were the slosh of water, the crinkle of aluminum foil, and the soft clink of clean dishes being settled in their cabinets.

A few minutes later, Mrs. Guhn broke the silence. "Maybe we are expecting a lot. But maybe Kai needs help that we can't give her—help that she won't get for herself."

The *again* went unsaid. But I heard it.

"Don't you remember what happened last time we gave Kai 'help' she didn't want?" I asked.

When Kai's grandmother died, Kai had been right there inside her grandmother's mind. It annihilated Kai. She was catatonic for weeks. And, when she woke up, she wasn't right. She tried to kill herself. Mrs. Guhn had her committed, and Kai receded to a place inside her own head where no one could reach her.

And I tried. For months. I lost all hope. Then Kai spoke to me and reached out to Caleb in her dreams. She welcomed our help. Caleb and I joined forces to get her released. I'd never worked so hard for anything in my life. It took weeks to get her out. And, once she was free, I married her so that her parents could never commit her against her will again.

"She got better," Mrs. Guhn insisted.

"We nearly lost her."

"But we *didn't*."

Legally, her mother couldn't make any decisions for Kai now. I'd never say that, though. Because she held a more subtle power over us. Guilt. She knew I would never do anything to hurt Kai and she had a way of making me feel like the choices I made for Kai were the wrong ones.

"Caleb is here this time. He won't let Kai fall too far. And he'll do what needs to be done if she's past the point where we can't help her on our own." It killed me to admit this, but it was true. I didn't like Caleb, and he didn't trust me, but he was my best ally against Kai's parents.

"Can Caleb stop her from killing herself?" Frustration raised Mrs. Guhn's voice; fear broke it.

"Can Caleb stop her from hurting others?"

I froze. The silverware slipped through my fingers and back into the soapy water. As long as I'd known Kai, she'd only caused herself harm, turning her powers inward. "What do you mean hurting others?"

Mrs. Guhn seemed shocked by my question, as if she hadn't even heard her own words. She focused all her attention on drying the glass in her hand.

I persisted. "What do you mean?"

"Perhaps you should ask Kai, Oliver."

CHAPTER 9

Kai

I hadn't expected to spend the entire day in Wausau with Caleb. In the morning, I'd done the MRI and CAT scan, but we wouldn't have the results until the afternoon. So, Caleb and I had time to go shopping for art supplies after all.

As we walked around the downtown area, Caleb carried the bag with all the sketchpads and pencils and charcoal he'd bought me. There were lots of little shops along the brick sidewalks. We meandered into a bookstore and a soap shop. Then we stumbled across a retro diner.

We took a table in back. We both got burgers and fries with milkshakes. Nothing Mom would let us eat at home.

"Why did you tell everyone that we were going to an art store today?" Caleb asked.

"I panicked. I didn't want them to know about the tests."

Caleb shook his head. "Can I give you a bit of advice? Next time you want to improvise, don't."

I snorted. "Duly noted."

I was nervous about the test results. Something told me they would all be fine, which meant I didn't have a physical problem. And then I'd have to figure out what was really going on with me. I tore pieces from my napkin until I had a pile of shredded paper next to me. Caleb slid the sketchpad across the table and handed me a pencil. Somehow he knew what I needed before I did. A place I'd never seen came to life on the page. Grass I'd never touched, I could smell. The sunlight made me squint. It was like a memory. A memory I'd never made.

While the pencil scratched across the page, everything went quiet inside of me.

"You look so calm when you're drawing."

"I feel like I'm in control. Like I can handle things." I continued to draw as we talked.

"What about when you aren't drawing?"

"Like something is wrong with me. Like I came back wrong."

"Do you think something happened during the coma?"

I wasn't sure. I had no memory of that time. I tapped the pencil on the pad. "Maybe."

Caleb reached across the table and touched my cheek. "It'll be okay."

"How can you be so sure?" I needed to know what had happened to me during the coma. "Something changed. I changed."

His voice was soft. "Yes, you're different. That's okay. Everything must evolve or die."

I appreciated his recognition that I'd changed, but he didn't get it—not really. There were things I could feel and sense that no one else did. Things that were starting to scare me. I glanced around to make sure no one was nearby. Then I whispered, "I need to show you something. Can you come inside my shield?"

He nodded.

To anyone at the diner, it would look like we were both just sitting still and looking down. They'd think our conversation had taken a very awkward turn. If someone actually talked to us, we'd be able to hear them and respond. But, for a few moments, I needed for Caleb to be inside my head.

I closed my eyes and envisioned my psychic shield. Steel beams reinforced it. I'd replaced the crystal walls with huge bulletproof frosted glass windows. I couldn't see out. No one could see in. It was the one place I was completely safe.

I cut a door in the glass and opened it. Outside was a barren terrain. A desert of rocks and shrubs and sand. I saw Caleb standing on the balcony of his titanium tower. He'd picked the strongest metal for his own fortress. He floated over to me.

He took in the interior of my shield. I'd done a little redecorating. Bright chandeliers blazed, illuminating every inch. A soft white leather couch filled an entire corner. The space was as open and bright as I could make it.

Then his gaze dropped to the floor. It seethed beneath his feet. Pulsating reds and purples. "What's that?" he asked.

"My emotions from the cave."

"You've formed an internal barrier around them?" He quirked an eyebrow.

"It was the only way." If I hadn't locked them away, I wouldn't have been able to get through everything that happened.

"I prefer my pain shaken not stirred," he murmured.

I pulled him back toward the doorway he'd come through and pointed outside. The entire landscape had shifted after he arrived. It was composed solely of shadows. They gathered around my psychic shield. Watching. Waiting for me.

"What are those?" he asked.

"I don't know. They've been there for a day now."

"Do they hurt you?"

I shook my head.

"Have you seen them before?" he asked.

"Twice. When Kadin died and when Grandma Guhn died." Both

times, I lost control. The first time, everyone who hurt Kadin paid the price. The second time, I hurt myself.

His forehead wrinkled with concern.

The shadows climbed on top of each other, reaching toward the window that I'd carved in my shield. I rushed to seal it shut.

"They seem to be coming for me," I said.

"We need to figure this out."

Caleb sat down on the L-shaped couch and patted the spot beside him.

I hesitated. Caleb never took what you gave him. He always demanded more. He rested his foot on his opposite knee and leaned back into the cushions. The picture of patience.

I shuffled over and sat down beside him.

"What do you feel in there?" He pointed at the floor.

"There's a darkness in me. I can feel it taking root."

"When did you first sense it?" he asked.

"In the cave with Nathan," I whispered. "There was so much darkness in him. The way our powers interacted, I think his darkness summoned mine."

Caleb was silent, concentrating. "I think you need to go see him."

"But he's still comatose. He won't be able to talk to me."

"You can use your abilities to reach into his mind."

I shuddered. "I don't want to."

"It may be the only way to get answers."

I wrapped my arms around myself. "I don't even know if I can reach him in his coma."

My brother just nodded, but I knew that this conversation wasn't over.

"Are you sure?" Caleb asked the doctor.

I shifted on the exam table. The paper crinkled beneath me. I hated the smell of doctors' offices. Like they'd bottled "clinical" and made it into an air freshener.

The doctor looked over the papers in my file again. "The MRI and CAT scans came back normal. Her reflexes are normal. There's no indication that her drawing is anything but a response to the trauma."

I didn't realize how tense Caleb had been until that moment. I could see the relief trickle into his eyes, but I knew that he was thinking the same thing I was, and that thing scared me more than brain damage. The drawing had to be some new manifestation of my powers. Something Nathan had done to me, or was doing to me.

Caleb insisted that I use a wheelchair. It had been a long day, and the hours of protecting myself from the emotional onslaught of the hospital had been draining. Blue and dark purple fog surrounded me. So much pain and guilt and sorrow. It took all my focus to keep my shield in place.

Caleb's footsteps echoed down the hallway as he pushed me through the hospital.

"So, that was good news." His voice rang with a false cheerfulness.

It made me nervous about what was coming next.

"I know that you don't want to see Nathan, but we're here now. He's here. And we've just ruled out the possibility that there's anything physically wrong with you, so…" He let the words hang in the air.

I was so tired. But it was tinged with terror and fear. The terror of thinking I might be sharing my mind with the man who'd tried to kill me. The fear of what would happen if the shadows came for me and I couldn't contain the darkness.

No matter what, I had to know what was happening to me.

"Take me to Nathan."

We paused in the hallway near Nathan's door. A local police officer was stationed there, waiting until Nathan woke up from his coma.

Caleb squeezed my hand. "I'll be right out here, waiting for you."

I held on tight. "Okay." I took a deep breath and let go of his hand. Caleb helped me out of the wheelchair and I walked toward the officer.

"No visitors," the officer said.

"I just need a moment."

"Are you family?" He peered at me.

I shook my head. "I'm the woman he kidnapped."

He gave me a look of appreciation. "You helped take him down."

Everyone involved in the case knew the story. Bruised and beaten, I'd gotten Lukas out of harm's way. Then Oliver had shot Nathan to save me. Oliver and I became heroes.

"I did what I had to do to protect Lukas."

"You were very brave." He glanced around. "His only visitors are supposed to be family, but I'll give you ten minutes. I'm going to be right outside this door if you need me."

"Thank you."

I wasn't sure what I expected when I went in Nathan's room. Something was different. His face. Then I saw it. They'd shaved off his beard.

He lay so still. Only the beep of the machines told me that he was still alive. In that hospital bed, he looked so much smaller than the man who reigned over my nightmares and held the power of life and death over me and Lukas.

I should have hated him for everything he'd done to me, but I didn't. I didn't feel anything. I was numb.

I'd been so afraid of him, but now that I was in his presence…

My pulse didn't speed up. My breathing didn't grow shallow. I didn't feel anxiety. I didn't feel fear. In fact, I was slowly overcome by the sense that this was exactly where I needed to be.

The silence was deafening. I filled the room with my words. "Do you know what happened to you?"

I hadn't expected a response, and I didn't get one. There was only one way to reach him.

If I opened my shield and reached out, our abilities would interact and he'd pull me into his mind. I'd been inside his mind before, and it wasn't a place I wanted to revisit. But I had no choice.

I dropped my shield.

Suddenly, I was overwhelmed. So many thoughts. They flew at me with such fury. Their voices and emotions echoed inside my mind. I sifted through all the pain and despair and worry that washed over me, trying to find my way to Nathan. But none of them was his.

It was the coma. I still had no idea where I'd gone during mine. Maybe Nathan was lost, too. Desperate now, I did the only thing I could think to do: I laid my right hand on his arm.

As soon as I touched him, the room melted away and I was inside his mind. I sat on a lotus-leaf swing, wearing a baby-blue taffeta dress. The breeze ruffled the stiff fabric and the sun warmed my skin. I held onto the two ropes of twined ivy that supported my swing. When I looked up, the ivy disappeared into the sky.

Nathan sat on the swing beside me. He wore a blue and white seersucker suit, just like he had the last time I'd gone inside his mind. That time, his desires had become mine. I wanted to die because it was the only thing that would help him. I wondered if that was when the darkest part of me awakened.

He looked younger without his beard. His black hair was combed back from his forehead. His husky blue eyes were different. Clearer. Warmer. Not a hint of the insanity that had once filled them. His darkness wasn't as strong as it had been.

"You can swing as high as you want," he promised.

"I can't." My feet refused to leave the ground. "It scares me. So much scares me now."

"I went too far in the cave." He paused. "I had to make Oliver and Mickey pay, but I shouldn't have hurt you and Lukas like that."

"None of us deserved what happened in the cave." Even as I said those words, though, I felt something stir inside me. *Mickey deserved to pay. So did Oliver.* I recoiled from those dark thoughts. I didn't want to have them. But I did.

"It all made sense back then. But now..." He looked confused. "It was wrong."

I felt a bizarre urge to explain his actions. "You had a brain tumor. Lukas saw purple in your head. He told anyone who would listen. The doctors operated and removed it."

"My son saved me?" Nathan puzzled over it. "I can't believe he did that for me."

"He helps anyone who's ill. It's who he is." I stared down at my white patent leather shoes. Despite my digging them into the dirt, they remained pristine. "You've still got a very long road ahead after you wake up from this coma."

"If." His deep voice rumbled.

"What do you mean?" Now that I was here with him, the thought of his death felt wrong. I didn't understand why, but it was true. I wanted to save him.

He stared off at the horizon. "Maybe this is where I belong."

"Where are we?" I asked.

"I don't know. I call it the Neitherlands."

"Is it part of the In Between?"

He gave me a questioning look.

"It's like limbo. Between our world and the afterlife."

He shook his head. "This is somewhere else. Somewhere you shouldn't be."

"What do you mean?"

He just shook his head. "You can't stay here too long. Say what you need to say and then leave."

"Or what?"

"Trust me, you don't want to know."

I swallowed. "You have to wake up then. Not just for you, but for Lukas."

"He must be terrified of me." He looked down at the grass. His brown wingtips gleamed. "It's probably better for him if I don't."

"He needs to understand what happened. Why you did what you did."

"He's such a strong kid." Nathan almost smiled.

"Stronger than me," I whispered.

Nathan tilted his head and looked at me. He had such long, thick lashes. "Sometimes when something breaks, it allows something new to emerge from the cracks."

"I've been drawing in my spare time," I blurted out. "It helps me feel more in control."

"I have to draw this place or it starts to disappear."

"Why?"

He shrugged. "I don't know. It's like I'm all that's holding it together."

I didn't know what to say about that, so I focused on the drawing connection. "When we almost died, I got entangled in your mind. After I woke up from the coma, I discovered I could draw way better than I ever did before. Do you think I got this ability from you?"

"Maybe. I don't know. I don't really understand how any of this works."

I looked up at the blue sky. I stared at the cloud above me until I saw a winged dragon. "But there's more."

"What?"

"I feel darkness inside me." I hated to ask the next question, but I had to know. "Is it yours?"

"Are you on a murderous rampage?" he asked. "Kidnapping innocent kids?"

I shook my head.

"Then it's not my darkness. Because that's where mine took me. This darkness, it's yours."

I swallowed. "How do I stop it?"

His gaze pinned me in place. "I couldn't stop mine."

"But you had a tumor... I'm not..." I couldn't finish the sentence.

"Insane?" He gave me a sympathetic smile. "There's a bit of insanity in all of us." He leaned back and looked up at the sky. "I'm glad you made it out of my mind."

"You pushed me away."

"I wasn't going to take you with me."

"But it would have been the best way to punish Oliver."

He rubbed his forehead. "You were more important."

"Saving me?"

"Letting you live," he said.

I didn't understand the difference, but before I could ask, gray clouds swept over the sky. A cold drizzle began to fall on us.

"You should go." He looked around. "It's not safe here any longer."

"Why? What's going to happen?" I asked.

Everything around us faded away. I felt myself falling. Someone shoved me. I blinked and was back beside Nathan's hospital bed. I snatched my hand away from his arm and whispered, "It's not safe anywhere."

CHAPTER 10

Oliver

A fter Caleb made a crack about my current job, he offered to get me some contract work at his friend's bank, a telecommuting gig writing policies and procedures. A few months ago, I'd have jumped on the opportunity to do what was in my wheelhouse and still be able to stay close to Kai. But, I turned it down. I couldn't stand the thought of owing Caleb for one more thing. And, given that I had no idea when Kai's family was going to leave, I needed a reason to get out of the house. Bagging groceries seemed like paradise compared to another day trapped with the Guhns.

I didn't blame Naomi; she was just being a teenager. But Kai's parents and Caleb—I felt like I had to constantly battle them to keep my place in my wife's life. And I was clearly losing to Caleb. He was the one she'd wanted with her when she had to undergo tests. She didn't just love him, she trusted him. I'd lost her trust, and I didn't know how to get it back.

At least she texted me, "Test went okay. All normal." I wanted to believe that this was good news, just like I wanted to believe everything we were going through was a natural part of the healing process. I tried to tell myself that she needed some space, but she kept reaching out to her family while she was pushing me further and further away.

This morning after Kai had left, I asked her mom again to explain her remark about Kai hurting others. Mrs. Guhn sidestepped my question, like she regretted that she let those words ever slip out. It just gave me something else to worry about. I was almost grateful that the Guhns were still around. Whatever had happened in the past, they'd be better equipped to spot it if it was happening again.

That didn't mean I wanted to spend another day surrounded by my in-laws.

Finally, my manager was willing to give me a shot at the register. It was only because a cashier had called out sick, but I was almost excited about this opportunity for career advancement. I appreciated the meditative monotony of scanning groceries.

I smiled at Mrs. Wiesner when she came through my checkout lane. She was one of the town's old guard and a notorious gossip, but she and her husband had been kind to me when I'd first come back to Butternut. They gave me my second job here—mucking out their barn.

"Good morning, Mrs. Wiesner."

"Lovely to see you, Oliver."

With the pleasantries done, she started pumping me for information. "How's your poor wife doing?"

"Recovering."

"Thank goodness she was there to protect Lukas."

"He's a great kid," I said.

"The Hoffmanns must be so grateful he's safe. I still can't believe that Nathan was behind Lukas's kidnapping. His own father." She waited for my reaction.

"Horrible." I focused on scanning her canned goods, but she was undeterred.

"The Hoffmanns never got over losing Christian the way they did. And now this." She tsked. "It's more than any family should have to bear."

I'd let them live thousands of days thinking that Christian's recklessness cost him his life. The guilt they must have felt, wondering what they could have done differently.

I scanned her items faster, eager to get her out of my line.

"Have you seen Lukas?" she asked.

"Not since he came to see Kai at the hospital." I didn't tell Mrs. Wiesner that Kai talked to Lukas on the phone sometimes. She'd been close to the little boy before they were trapped in the cave together. The bond between them seemed even stronger now. And I didn't tell Mrs. Wiesner that it was my fault that Kai couldn't go see Lukas. With him being Mickey's son, it got awkward.

"What a strong little boy." She heaved a sigh. "Poor Mickey. To realize she married a monster. She must feel like such a fool."

I knew that I should just let Mrs. Wiesner prattle on, but I couldn't help defending Mickey. "No one could have predicted what Nathan would become."

She pursed her lips. "I never liked the way that boy picked on you." Mrs. Wiesner clearly thought she'd foreseen his badness.

"Losing his brother was hard on him." I wanted for this conversation to be over.

"That's kind to say. You're a good man, Oliver."

She believed it. The entire town said it. That I was a hero.

I bagged Mrs. Wiesner's groceries and loaded them into the cart for her.

"Goodness, Oliver, you go above and beyond."

"Just doing my job."

"Please tell your wife I'm praying for her speedy recovery."

"Thanks, I will." I waved goodbye.

As I watched her walk away, her words continued to roll around in my head. I couldn't help thinking about how many times I'd gone above and beyond for Kai. No matter how many mistakes I'd made, I'd come through when she needed me. I'd saved her life. That had to count for something. It should have made me a hero in her eyes, too.

CHAPTER 11

Kai

"So, what happened in there?" Caleb asked.

He had waited until I was safely settled in the privacy of his SUV before he asked me about my visit with Nathan.

I did my best to describe everything that had happened and finished with "He thinks this darkness is mine."

"What do you think?"

"I'm scared he's right." I was also scared that he wasn't telling me the complete truth. I sensed that we were more linked than he let on. Maybe more linked than he even knew.

"Trauma brought it out last time," Caleb murmured.

In high school, I didn't have friends. I just had a spectrum of people who feared and hated me because they knew I was weird.

They had been there when my powers first manifested. They were creeped out when I accidentally blurted out their thoughts or responded out loud to things they were thinking or feeling. Eventually, I learned to shield myself, but it was too late. I was branded a freak.

I tried to embrace it. I dressed goth. Most of the time, the other kids would just shun me. But, occasionally, they turned on me. They'd put my clothes in the toilet during gym. Write awful things about me in the boys' bathroom. Steal my books. Invent awful nicknames and get everyone to call me them. They never tired of letting me know that I didn't belong. Caleb tried to help, but he was two years ahead of me. After he graduated, it got worse.

Then, one day, the new kid sat down next to me at lunch. Kadin. Once the other kids started tormenting him, too, I tried to discourage his friendship, but he told me he could handle it.

I didn't realize until it was too late that I had ways of coping that he didn't. I could go visit Grandma Guhn. I was safe at home. Kadin had a mom who worked all the time and a stepdad who beat him. The torture at school was too much.

He put his stepdad's gun in his mouth and fired it. Kadin was gone.

After he killed himself, I lost control. I didn't hold any of my emotions in. Instead, I lashed out with my powers. I learned how to use them to hurt, and I hurt everyone who'd hurt Kadin.

Chaos reigned over my high school for weeks. No one understood what was making students unravel. No one but me. Finally, my family figured it out. Caleb begged me to stop. But the darkness had taken over.

In desperation, my parents sent me to live with Grandma Guhn. Not only was her house miles and miles away from my school—well outside my telepathic range—but she was also a healer. That was her special ability. She taught me how to push back the darkness and to embrace and control my own gifts.

Caleb pulled me out of the memory by asking, "When you went to stay with Grandma Guhn, what pulled you back?"

"She did. But she didn't just heal me. She helped me face my feelings and learn to control them again."

Caleb glanced at me. "I can help you do that."

If anyone could, it would be Caleb.

Still, as we headed back to Butternut, toward all the mess and emotional pain that waited for me there, I couldn't help wondering if it might be better to just let go and let it all out.

That thought scared me. And it excited me.

I sat at the kitchen table with Mom and Dad flanking me. Mom had toasted some whole-wheat bread for me. I loved the soft, buttered middle, but I hated the crust. Just like I always had. Mom said it was good for me and refused to let me cut it off. Just like she always had. But she couldn't make me eat it. I tore at the crust with my teeth and spat it at Herbie. He caught each bite in his beak and gobbled it down.

"Kai, please, that's just gross," Mom said.

"Do you see how he catches it? He's getting better every day," I said.

Dad smirked and kept reading the paper. "Maybe you can take this show on the road someday?"

"You think? Me and Herbie? Maybe Oprah will come back to do a special?"

Dad chuckled.

"Can't you just give him scraps by hand?" Mom asked.

"Where's the fun in that?"

Dad put the paper down. "She has a point, Mags."

"Dylan Giles, don't encourage her." Mom used Dad's middle name when she was particularly adamant about something.

I hid a smile when I heard it because Grandma Guhn had told me the backstory to Dad's name. Dylan because of the way he swam around in her belly. She knew he'd love the sea. Giles because the first time she saw him, she thought he looked like a goat.

Naomi wandered into the kitchen. Her hair hung around her shoulders in unbrushed waves. It was the same shade as Mom's. I saw so much of Mom in her. Too much sometimes. Probably part of the reason Naomi and I weren't close.

"When are we going into town again? I want to pick up a black bear figurine." Naomi rifled through a box of Nutter Butters.

Mom didn't seem to hear her. "But why do you have to *spit* the toast at him?" she asked me.

"Because he likes it."

Mom groaned.

Dark red thoughts slammed against my shield. Angry thoughts. I drew a window in my shield and opened it a crack. I choked on cinnamon. The taste. The scent. So much cinnamon came with those thoughts.

I hate it. Everything you do is cute. Nothing I do is ever cute enough to get their attention.

Emotions coming to me as colors was normal, but tasting and smelling them was different. It scared me. That hadn't happened since the last time my telepathy spiraled out of control because of all the people nearby. At the farmhouse, though, there were so few people around. This shouldn't be happening.

Then I remembered something. Nathan was an empath who tasted and smelled emotions. I'd experienced his abilities when I was in his head. But I wasn't in his head now. So why was it happening?

My only answer was that my connection to Nathan was more than I realized. My head ached at the possibility. I rubbed my temple.

Do I have to nearly die to get their attention? Or develop a superpower? Mom doesn't even know I'm here when I'm talking to her. I bet Dad doesn't either. God, I wish I were an only child.

Naomi's last thought hurt. "Do you really wish I wasn't here, Nomes?" I hadn't used her nickname since she was little.

"What?" Naomi asked.

Mom rushed to ease the tension. "Kai, you promised no eavesdropping on our thoughts."

"I can't help it if someone is hurling her thoughts at me," I said.

Naomi's cheeks flushed. "I can't stand how everything always revolves around you. It's always about Kai. Always."

Mom looked shocked by her outburst. "Sweetie, that's not true."

"Really? What did I just ask you?" Naomi asked.

Mom's forehead crinkled up. "You wanted a new top?"

"Not even close." Naomi slammed the Nutter Butter box on the counter. "It's like I'm not even here."

"Of course you're here," Dad said.

"Then what did I ask?"

My parents looked at each other. Clearly neither knew the answer.

"She wants to know when you're going into town again, so she can buy a black bear figurine," I said.

Naomi threw her hands up in the air. "Of course, you heard me."

"Don't take that tone with your sister," Mom said.

"Tell her to stop listening to my thoughts!" Naomi shouted.

"My shield is up. Yours isn't, Nomes." I did my best to keep everyone out of my head. But I was also working hard to keep my own emotions inside my head.

"Girls." Dad's voice rumbled. "Do we need to practice building shields again?"

"If that's the only way I'll get your attention," Naomi muttered.

"Shield your thoughts better while your sister is recovering." Mom gently swept the hair back from my face.

Naomi's voice skyrocketed. "I'm sick of dealing with freaks!"

Freaks. The word triggered an avalanche of anger inside me. "What's the hardest part of being the normal one? Is it how comfy Mom and Dad are around you?"

Dad touched my arm. "Kai."

I pulled away. Anger pushed against my shield — my anger. I couldn't contain it all. I didn't even want to anymore. I was tired of worrying about everyone else's feelings. What about my feelings? "Or maybe it was being the kid they could take out in public without any fears? Tell me more about the agony of your normal childhood."

72

Naomi turned chili pepper red. Her emotions filled my nose. Butter cookies of embarrassment and cinnamon rolls of anger. Good. About time she realized how ridiculous she was.

"I HATE YOU!" She stormed off.

"You should have let that go," Dad said.

"You don't know how many times I have let that go," I said. "She's been thinking these things for years."

"So you should be used to it," Dad said evenly.

"She's a teenager. You remember how emotional you were back then," Mom said.

I remembered feeling like a freak and realizing I would never be normal again. Hearing everyone's thoughts and emotions showed me the worst of people. It brought such darkness to my life. It overshadowed everything I did.

My shield stretched under the pressure of containing so much hurt.

"You've never reacted like this to your sister before. She hasn't changed. Clearly, you have. And not for the better," Mom said.

"I do what I have to do to survive. Would you rather I be dead?" I asked.

Mom's eyes widened and she jerked away like I'd slapped her. "How can you ask me that? After everything we've been through with you. Everything we've done for you."

I didn't mean to lash out, but I couldn't stop myself. "I can't be what you want me to be. I never could."

"We just want you to be happy," Dad said.

"Bad stuff happens. And I get to be sad and angry." What I didn't say was that it felt like it wasn't just my pain making me rage at them. These feelings were bigger than mine. They pushed me places I wouldn't have gone on my own. It was scary and it was exhilarating and I didn't want it to stop.

"Sometimes you need help. Your father and I always want what's best for you," Mom said. Her thoughts wrapped around my shield and whispered through the open window in it. *That's why we had to put you in that institution.*

"That wasn't best for me," I said. "I couldn't protect myself in that place."

"You got better," Mom insisted.

How could she rationalize what she did to me? I opened the window in my shield wider and looked out. Shadows danced around me, obscuring most of my view. Down below, in the barren wasteland, I saw her shield. She kept her thoughts protected in an armored tank, but something escaped through the hatch. It darted through the window in my shield. One thought. *Just like my mother.*

Normally, I don't pry, but I needed to know what she meant. I focused on the hatch and nudged it open a little. Something seeped out. Memories from Mom's life flickered in front of me. Her dad in his army uniform. So many medals. The family had been stationed all over the world. Boxes, always boxes of stuff everywhere. Either settling in or packing up. That's how life was.

After her dad died, she was the one who packed up her two younger brothers and herself and moved them all in with her grandparents. Her mother was institutionalized. I couldn't see why. Mom had hidden that well. But I did see Mom was the only one who visited her. She saw her own mother become a shell of a woman, incapable of caring for herself or her children. By the time she was released, Mom was married with her own kids. She didn't need a mother anymore.

I tasted orange candy on my tongue. Tart and sweet. Mom's worst fear came through my shield—that I'd inherited something from her mother. I'd broken because of something she passed on to me. Dad had given me abilities, and she gave me instability.

I hadn't meant to go so deep into her mind. I'd never known that my mother's mother had been institutionalized. I'd only met her a few times before she moved to Europe. It wasn't the ocean that had kept us apart. Mom hadn't wanted her kids around someone so fragile. And she didn't trust her mother to be with us.

All these years, I'd thought my mom had just packed me up and sent me off because she didn't want to deal with me anymore. But now I understood what my breakdown had forced her to relive.

"Mom, I'm sorry."

"It's all right." Her voice was soft now. "You and Naomi will make up."

I bit my lip. She hated it when I poked around in her mind, but I wanted her to know what I knew. "I mean, I'm sorry about your mom."

Something flickered in her eyes. "You aren't supposed to listen to my thoughts."

"They were so powerful."

She got up and moved toward the sink. She stood with her back to me, staring out at the yard.

The kitchen was quieter than a graveyard in a ghost town. Herbie shuffled closer to me, begging for more toast.

Dad's voice startled me when he said, "Therapy is worth considering. Having someone else to talk to can help put things in perspective."

"So, I need to talk to a stranger about what happened in the cave, but Mom never has to talk to me about her mother?"

Mom's hands curled around the lip of the counter. "My mother was sick. She went away. She got better. Same as you."

I felt the rage building up again. "Mom, it's not the same. Not at all." I tried to recapture the compassion I'd just been feeling. "You were just a kid. How did you manage?"

"I did what had to be done." Her voice was like rusted iron—strong and damaged. "There is no need to dredge up my past. You're the one who has to deal with what happened to you."

"We just want what's best for you, Kai," my father added.

I was trying so hard to connect with my parents, but they weren't listening to me. They just kept pushing me to do what they wanted. Everyone else was allowed to have their secrets and their unhappiness.

Everyone except me. I snapped.

"You know what would be best for me? It would be best for me if my family actually believed that I might know what's best for me."

"It's not just about you, Kai. It's never been just about you. And if we had to do it all over again, we'd do the same thing."

"It was our only option," Mom said.

I felt like I had been sucker punched. Knowing what it did to me, they would still lock me up like an animal? I could feel the darkness bubbling inside me. I wanted to lose control. I wanted to make *them* lose control.

"You locked me up in a place where I was surrounded by insanity and misery. You took Caleb away from me when I needed him most, and you didn't even let him try to help me. And you'd do it all over again," I said.

"We would. To protect him." Dad's voice was colder than a winter night in Yosemite.

I looked from him to Mom, trying to comprehend what he was saying. She refused to meet my gaze. "Protect him? From what?"

"From you," Dad said quietly.

They'd locked me away to protect Caleb. Acid burned my stomach. Each word fell from my lips slowly. "You thought I'd hurt him?"

"Not on purpose. But we never thought you'd harm yourself until you took all those pills," Dad said.

Mom added, "And we never imagined that you would lash out like you did after Kadin died."

"We had no idea how your powers would interact with your brother's when you were in that state." Dad reached for my good hand.

I pulled away.

Mom softened her voice, trying to cushion the blow. "We couldn't risk losing both of you."

"So you locked me away?" I'd always known they were afraid of me. But how could they have thought I would hurt Caleb? I was still reeling from that revelation when another one hit me: They'd chosen him over me.

That's when I stopped trying. That's when I gave in.

Darkness poured through me. I hated them.

My mouth went dry. "Does Caleb know?"

"No," Dad said. "And he never will."

Oh, yes, he would. The darkness demanded it.

I widened my eyes in mock innocence. "But you didn't do anything wrong. That's what you said. You'd do it again. So why not tell him?"

"No, and that's the end of it." The smell of bacon came right before Dad's frustration slammed into my shield.

"No, it isn't. You tell him, or I will," I said.

A juice glass on the table started to shake.

"Kai, let it go." Mom sounded scared, and I liked it.

"I just don't understand. If you didn't do anything wrong, why not tell Caleb?" I asked.

"No!" Dad shouted.

The glass shattered. Dad's telekinesis—the power he so perfectly controlled—had escaped his grasp.

"Dylan Giles," Mom said his name like a safe word.

Dad stared at the shards of glass that hung in midair. He didn't let them fly out and hurt anyone. "It's okay, Dylan," she murmured. To me, she said, "Leave us."

The shards dropped to the table.

I laughed. I couldn't remember feeling so happy. And that terrified me.

CHAPTER 12

Oliver

I avoided the employee breakroom at Super One Foods. Mickey and I worked overlapping shifts, and I didn't want to end up alone with her. The last thing I needed was for Kai to have one more reason to doubt me.

So, instead, I went out to my car and blasted the heat while I checked voicemail. There was one from Kai's mom. She mentioned her husband's telepathy and a glass in the kitchen. She paused like something worse was coming. "Kai seems to be acting out." Mrs. Guhn didn't provide any details, but there was fear in her voice.

I called home. Kai's mom answered on the third ring.

"Mrs. Guhn, what's going on?" I asked.

She sounded breathless. "I'm just baking some cookies."

"No, I mean today, with Kai. I got your voicemail."

There was silence on the other end. I wasn't sure she was still there. "Mrs. Guhn?"

"Sometimes she acts out," she said each word carefully.

"Are we talking yelling and breaking stuff or something to do with her powers?"

"The latter."

Mrs. Guhn dropped her voice lower, like she didn't want anyone to overhear her. "Kai's always been complicated, Oliver. More complicated than you know."

"And you think she might hurt someone?"

"I don't know what she might do." Her voice fell away like this conversation was too much for her. "Look, it's been a bad afternoon here. I'm sorry I left you the voicemail. I just wanted you to know. It's probably nothing."

I wasn't sure if she was trying to comfort me or herself. If it was me, it wasn't working. "You aren't going to tell me what happened?"

"You really should talk to Kai. I just thought you should know." Something binged in the background. "I have to go. I need to take the cookies out of the oven."

"Wait, Mrs. Guhn—"

She ended the call.

CHAPTER 13

Kai

I retreated to my room after the blowup with my parents. Ten minutes later, the front door slammed. I slipped off the bed and went to my window. Dad and Naomi got in his car and drove off. Looked like Naomi was getting her trip into town after all.

I heard the muffled sounds of cabinets slamming and baking sheets clanging. Mom was still in the kitchen. That was her favorite place to be when she was upset. As if baking something sweet would mask all that was sour between us.

I was still trying to process what my parents revealed. They had sacrificed me for Caleb. The darkness inside me whispered, *They never put you first*. And the darkness understood why. Because my parents never thought I was worth saving. Deep down, there were times when I shared that same awful thought. Everyone would be better off without me.

I felt like my soul was on fire with the pain of being unwanted. It's better not to be loved at all than to be loved only a little.

Tears trickled down my cheeks. Sobs escaped from my mouth. I threw myself on the bed and buried my face in the pillow and let it all out. Just a day ago, I'd been hoping to make my family whole again. Now I knew that wasn't going to happen.

The darkness whispered, *You don't need them. You never did.*

There, in the darkness, I sensed it. A strength that I needed. I started to reach out for it, but stopped. I didn't trust it.

I didn't trust anything. Or anyone.

My hand flew over the page, filling it with images from inside my head. And another and another until there were dozens of landscape drawings scattered across the bed.

"What happened?" Caleb asked from my doorway. If he'd knocked, I hadn't noticed.

I didn't stop drawing. I couldn't. It was all that held me together right now, preserving the thin layer of calm around me. I kept drawing as I told him haltingly about what my parents had said in the kitchen.

When I finished, Caleb was quiet.

I glanced at him.

The look on his face. It was the way he looked when he caught kids picking on me at school. It was the *I won't let this happen to you* face. "Are you fucking kidding me?"

I shook my head.

"You matter as much as I do. Even more to me."

"You've always been the stronger one in their eyes."

"If I have been, it's only because I've always had you."

I bit my lip. "But what if they were right?"

"You would never hurt me," he said without hesitation.

"But in high school, I did horrible things after Kadin died."

"I know."

"But you don't know what I felt. How much I enjoyed it."

"You were a teenager. You'd lost your only friend. So you lost control. It's just that your powers made you a little more dangerous than the average adolescent. And then you went to Grandma Guhn, and she taught you how to protect yourself and everyone else."

"But I think it might be happening again," I whispered as I grabbed Caleb's hand. "Something made me goad Dad until he snapped. Something in me—something that was me, but not me."

This was serious. Neither one of us had ever seen Dad lose control of his telekinesis.

CHAPTER 14

Oliver

Although my Jeep Cherokee handled the icy roads well, I kept it in a lower gear to be safe. One thought rolled around in my head as I drove home that night. I needed to find a way to break through to Kai for a minute, long enough to remind her just how much I loved her. I had no idea how I was going to help her, but I had to convince her to let me try.

I thought I knew everything about Kai. But something had happened, something terrible, something she hadn't trusted me to accept or understand.

That hurt. And I couldn't help feeling a little bit resentful at being cast as the bad guy — the one who had nearly destroyed us by keeping secrets.

I cranked up the drum and bass until it filled the car. I tried to figure out how to start a conversation with Kai. There were so many ways it could go sideways, but I was good at planning. I ran through different scenarios in my head. Every time I came across something that would send Kai running out of the room, I stopped and rebooted the scenario.

Tonight, I would make some progress with my wife. We would have a conversation we'd both been avoiding and I would figure out why her mother was so scared.

I would show her that I was there for her, no matter what she'd done in the past, no matter what she might do now. I'd remind her that I always showed up for her, even if that meant rescuing her from a madman. I needed for her to see me as the hero everyone in town said I was. I'd make her understand that everything I did, I did for us.

CHAPTER 15

Kai

E ven on the worst days, the world can surprise you. A few hours after my conversation with Caleb, I was sitting on the sofa with Lukas nestled beside me. I stroked his mop of dark brown hair. His green eyes peered up at me. He'd seen far too much for a four-year-old, but he was handling it.

He smiled and I felt myself smile back. We'd had a unique bond before the cave, but now it was even stronger. No one else understood what had happened to us.

I was glad Lukas had convinced his uncle Alex to bring him over. Alex sat in the chair near me. His navy sweater deepened the blue of his eyes and set off his pale blond hair. I pushed my own hair back self-consciously, making sure it covered the bare spot in back.

"You look great," Alex said.

When he spoke, I couldn't help staring at his lips. The bottom one was much fuller than the top one. I knew those lips in ways I shouldn't. The memory washed over me. We were back at Copper Falls. And those lips were on mine.

I blinked and looked away. "I bet you say that to all the girls who have just gotten out of the hospital."

"Believe it or not, I don't." His voice was warm and comforting. "How are things?"

Awful. Difficult. Impossible. "Okay."

"Why don't I believe you?" He gave me a sympathetic half-smile with a slight tilt of his head. It was charming.

I shrugged. "Just having a bad day." An incredibly, life changing, family-destroying bad day.

He didn't push for more. He noticed my sketchpad laying on the coffee table and scooped it up.

"These are really good," he said as he flipped through it.

"Thanks."

He frowned.

"What's wrong?" I asked.

"These woods. They're part of the Hoffmanns' property."

I had no idea any of the places I drew were real. They were just images that took hold in my mind and begged to be put to paper. I figured I made them up. But if they really existed, then this drawing thing just got a lot weirder.

I lied, "I must have been there."

His mouth opened. It took a moment for the words to come. "It's nowhere near where you were." He didn't need to add *when Nathan kidnapped you.*

"Must be a coincidence." I tried to sound calm. I knew that my drawing was connected to Nathan. The images probably were, too.

"Maybe." Alex didn't sound convinced.

I didn't know what else to say, so I asked Lukas, "What's going on?"

"He wanted to talk to you in person." Alex patted Lukas's leg, encouraging him to talk.

Lukas didn't say anything.

"What's my favorite little boy want to talk about?" I snuggled closer to Lukas, hoping my nearness would help him feel safe.

Lukas whispered, "The bad man in the beard."

Nathan. His father. We hadn't really talked about him since the cave. "Sure."

Lukas hesitated. "Have you seen him?"

"I went to the hospital. There's a guard to keep him in his room," I said.

"Is he still stuck in his head?" Lukas asked.

That's how his mother Mickey must have explained the coma to him. "Yes."

Lukas hesitated. He looked at Alex, but thought at me, *Did you go there? Into his head?*

I did.

Was he mean?

He was very sick in the cave. Lukas's ability to see illness as colors made him able to find health problems before any doctor did. *Remember you said his head was purple? The doctors fixed it. He's not like that anymore.*

What if he gets like that again?

Is that what you are worried about?

Lukas whispered, "I don't want him to hurt us."

I hugged him. "No one will let that happen. The police, your mom, Uncle Alex—all of them are protecting you. You're safe."

"He got me last time," Lukas said.

I never understood what happened. Lukas was too scared and confused in the cave to tell me. "How did he do that?"

Lukas started shaking. "He came in my room. He scared me more than any monster. He said he'd hurt Gammie and Mommy if I made a noise. I was real quiet. He pulled me out the bathroom window."

Nathan was an empath who could twist people's emotions. He must have enhanced Lukas's fear to keep him petrified.

I kissed the top of Lukas's head. "It's over now. You're safe."

"Buddy, if something like that happens again, you make a noise.

You fight anyone that tries to take you," Alex said.

"But he'd have killed Gammie," Lukas said.

He was right. I'd been in Nathan's head. Lukas saved his grandmother's life with his silence.

"Maybe Uncle Alex can help you learn a few ways to protect yourself? Do they have any self-defense classes for kids around here?"

"I'll look into it," Alex said.

"It's okay to be scared," I told Lukas. "I still have bad nightmares."

Lukas nodded. "It's always so dark in mine. I make Mommy keep a nightlight on."

"You're braver than me. I keep all the lights on in my room at night."

Lukas fidgeted with the buttons on his sweater. His voice was so soft, I almost missed the question. "Why was my dad such a bad man?"

"What he did was very bad." I didn't know why I felt the need to differentiate his actions from his person. It was such a small distinction. Something a child couldn't possibly grasp.

"I don't like him," Lukas said.

"You shouldn't. Not after what he did."

"But he's my dad," he whispered.

For a moment my gaze crashed into Alex's. I opened the window in my shield. I ignored the shadows converging around me. I let the sympathy he felt wash over me. I shouldn't be taking anything from Alex after that kiss. But, when I let Alex in, the shadows receded.

"Sometimes parents aren't good parents. It's their fault. You didn't do anything wrong." And sometimes they sacrifice one child for another.

"Mommy's a good mommy."

Despite my feelings about Mickey, I had to admit it. "You've got a great mom."

Lukas seemed calmer. Like our conversation was helping him let go of some of what happened. I wished it could be that easy for me.

Lukas's thoughts filled my mind. *You got hurt a lot worse. Your head is still pink. Does it hurt?*

Just a little.

Pink meant I was injured, but I'd survive. The scariest moments held a simple choice: survive or don't. So far I always survived. What came next, after surviving, that was the messy part. Dealing with what happened. Processing the pain and feeling each and every emotion you'd suppressed to survive. That was where things got complicated. The aftermath was where everything could fall apart.

What my parents had done to me hurt more than any physical wounds. I wasn't sure this pain would ever end.

Lukas's arm stole around my neck and he kissed my cheek. *It'll be okay.*

He was trying to make it better for me. His love filled my mind. It was unconditional. It smelled of roses, like Grandma Guhn used to. It was the kind of love I needed from my parents. The kind they would never give me. Tears flooded my eyes.

Mom came in with some hot chocolate and cookies. She took one look at me and asked, "Lukas would you like to help decorate some gingerbread men?"

Lukas's eyes brightened. "I love gingerbread." He paused and asked me, "Are you going to be okay?"

I blinked back tears. "Absolutely. Make one for me and one for your mom?"

He nodded and followed my mom into the kitchen.

As soon as Lukas was gone, Alex said, "It's okay to not be okay."

Same advice my brother gave me. I smiled. "Have you been talking to Caleb?"

"I will if it makes you smile like that again," Alex said.

Warmth trickled into my core. A feeling of safety and security. I pulled my legs up and tucked them under me, so I could rest my cast in my lap and resist reaching out to him.

"How are you really doing?" he asked.

"I've been better."

He touched my hand. His fingertips were like feathers grazing my skin.

"Talk to me," he said.

I hesitated.

His fingers glided over mine. "I wanted to come by and check on you."

"Thank you." I laced my fingers through his and squeezed. There was something I wanted to know. Something I couldn't ask in front of Lukas. Something I worried about, especially given my own family's reaction to me. "How's your family dealing with Lukas's abilities?"

"Mickey is still trying to wrap her head around it."

"Has she told anyone?"

He nodded. "My parents and siblings."

"How are they dealing?"

"Dad seems to be having some trouble with it. I think he just needs time. Bottom line, we're grateful to have Lukas home. If he had a second head or a supernatural ability, it wouldn't change how much we love him."

"Sometimes people get scared by the woo-woo stuff. If anyone has questions, I'm here."

"I appreciate that. Is someone scared of your woo-woo stuff?"

He was too perceptive. I couldn't talk about my parents, I just couldn't. But I could tell him what scared me. I hadn't told anyone except Caleb about what was going on inside me. "There's a darkness in me."

"We all have darkness in us." In his eyes, I saw it. There were things he didn't want anyone to know about. Lines he'd crossed that he couldn't uncross.

I knew that better than anyone. I'd heard and seen it all over the years. "Not like this. Maybe it's something about having these abilities or something about my mind. I think Nathan did something to me. I don't understand it exactly, but he awakened something in me—

something terrible—and it's getting stronger every day."

Alex wrapped both hands around mine. I felt their warmth and strength. I wished I could absorb it.

"I'm trying so hard to hold it all together."

"Why don't you let it out?" he asked.

"I've seen what it can do. What I can do. I won't be able to stop." I stumbled over my words. "I'm afraid that I will lose control. That I will become someone I don't want to be."

"How long do you think you can hold it all inside?"

"I don't know."

"If you need anything, I'm here."

I nodded.

His eyes filled with certainty. "You'll figure this out."

"What if I can't?" My voice cracked.

He squeezed my hand. "You will. When you're ready."

The way he said it, I almost believed that I would be able to face everything inside me and not succumb to it.

I didn't realize Oliver had come home from work until he cleared his throat. He stood in the doorway, watching us. The accusation in his eyes sliced through his words. "Didn't mean to interrupt a tender moment."

Alex released my hand. I curled into the corner of the couch.

"We were just talking," Alex said.

"She has a house full of people she can talk to. She has a husband she should talk to," Oliver said.

I didn't need one more person telling me what to do today. "I can talk to whomever I want, whenever I want," I said sharply.

"But I can't?" Oliver demanded. "I've been avoiding Mickey for you."

Did he expect me to be grateful? "Thank you for controlling your urge to see your ex-girlfriend."

"At least I'm trying." Oliver stayed in the doorway.

"My family is here. Lukas is in the kitchen. What sort of torrid affair could we be conducting on the couch?"

Oliver gave me his stern face. "This closeness between you two has to end."

The blood pounded against the tips of my fingers. It felt like daggers of anger were going to shoot out of my eyes. Maybe they would. A part of me actually liked that idea.

Alex started to get up. "I should go."

"No." I put my hand out to stop him. "You're not going anywhere. If Oliver has a problem with that, he can leave."

Oliver clenched his jaw. "Are you seriously asking me to leave my own house?"

"You can't pick my friends. You can't tell me what to feel or how to act. I get to make my own decisions. Deal with it."

Oliver's jaw dropped. "Deal with this." He stalked out of the living room and slammed the front door shut behind him.

Alex didn't move.

I didn't know what to say, so I defaulted to an apology. "Sorry you had to see that."

"I didn't mean to stir up trouble."

"We've been in trouble for weeks."

"Should I go?"

I reached for his hand and squeezed it. "Can you stay?"

"As long as you need me." His smile was a promise made.

CHAPTER 16

Oliver

I needed a drink. I wanted to be around folks who appreciated what I had done for Kai, so I headed to Brennan's Green Brier. It was the kind of place where people might want to buy the local hero a round or three.

Nothing had changed since the last time I had been in this bar. Dozens of trophies filled the shelves on the back wall. Approximately 95% of the trophies were softball. My dad had helped win some of them. The other 5% were from darts, horseshoes, and bowling. Family photos sat in frames below it. That wall displayed everything that mattered to the owner, Mike Brennan.

Posters covered the other walls so that the green paint barely peeked through. The pool table was right where it had always been.

As I had expected, the bartender, Mimi, got the first round for me. I sipped my Jack and Coke, trying to forget what I'd just seen.

Alex Fuchs.

In high school, he'd been my wingman. Now he was holding my wife's hand.

I stared at the bottles lining the back of the bar. A strand of tiny holiday lights made them sparkle. How many bottles would it take to forget it all?

I took another swallow and glanced up at the ceiling tiles. People used to pay a dollar to sign them. I was sitting two tiles away from the one with my mom and dad's signature. Sophie and Reinhard Richter, it said. Sophie was all curly and pretty. Reinhard and Richter were written in stark, straight lines. I wondered if they were together in the afterlife. I wondered if Kai and I would ever be together again.

I shook off that thought and made my way over to the jukebox. I flipped through a few albums. The same songs had been there since the place opened. I picked a few favorites and ended with a special one, "Ring of Fire" by Johnny Cash.

I finished off my drink and ordered another one.

Mimi insisted, "It's on the house."

When I tried to pay her, Mike chimed in, "Your money's no good here tonight."

A few of the other patrons cheered. I smiled and raised my glass. It was pathetic, but I needed the ego boost.

Then I saw someone I knew. Dan Fuchs. This town was full of Fuchses, but he was the only one I wanted to see tonight. He was a couple of years younger than me. When we were kids, he'd tag along with Mickey and me. He'd grown into a hulking guy, but he still had the same golden-retriever eyes he'd always had.

He took the barstool next to mine and ordered a beer. "Care to tell me what you're doing here on a Wednesday night? Alone?"

"No, I don't."

He pointed to my glass. "Is that your first?"

"It was my second." I gulped it down and ordered another one.

"I'm going to need your keys."

I fished them out of my pocket and slammed them on the bar. "Are we good?"

94

"Drink away."

I snorted and took another gulp. It wasn't enough to stop me from thinking about Kai. I couldn't help imagining what Alex and she did after I left. Snuggling on my couch. Kai saying his name and pulling him closer.

Dan interrupted my thoughts. "You remember when we were kids and our dads would come here to drink after a softball game?"

"We'd play that game in the lot next door. What was it?"

"Ghost—"

"—in the Graveyard," I finished. The ghost would go hide and everyone else would stay on home base, cover their eyes, and count.

Dan laughed. "We'd count off by o'clocks, all the way up to midnight."

Then we'd try to find the ghost. If he tagged you, he turned you into the ghost. If you found him, you'd yell, "Ghost in the Graveyard," and try to make it back to home base before him. We spent hours playing that game.

Whenever I was stuck being the ghost for too long, Alex would let me find him. He had been the older brother I'd always wanted, the guy who looked out for me. Now he was looking out for my wife.

My fingers tightened around the glass the way they wanted to tighten around his throat. I took another gulp of Jack and Coke.

"Life was easier back then," Dan said.

"To who we used to be." I raised my glass again.

Dan clunked his Budweiser can against my glass. "You remember that song our dads would sing?"

Alex and I used to sing it when we snuck out to Grandpa Fuchs's barn with a six-pack. We'd spend hours drinking and talking and being stupid. God, that bastard was entangled in every good memory I had of Butternut. And now, he had come between Kai and me just as I was trying to bring us back together. It twisted something in my gut.

I finished my drink and ordered another. "It was set to the tune of 'Alouette.'"

"Oh, how I love her saggy tits," Dan sang.

"Her double chin." Our voices merged together.

We kept going, getting progressively drunker and raunchier with each chorus. A few of the regulars joined in. The liquor and the memories fueled our singing.

By the time we finished the song, I'd forgotten why I was there in the first place. I was starting to feel good again. Then Mickey strolled in wearing black jeans and a green blouse. Her clothes clung to her curves. When I looked at her, I couldn't help remembering how good her body felt pressed against mine.

Dan waved her over. As she made her way to us, her dangly earrings caught the light and sparkled at me.

"What's going on?" she asked.

I gave her a Jack Daniel's-induced smile. Way too happy for the state of my life. "Singing."

"You?" Her eyebrows shot up.

Our eighth grade chorus teacher had asked me to quit—out of respect for the students who could actually sing.

"So what is my gorgeous sister doing at a bar on a weeknight?" Dan asked.

"Alex and Mom are watching Lukas, so I can meet Bryan Brennan for a drink." She toyed with her earring.

"You have a date?" I asked.

"Are you jealous?" she teased.

"Nah, I got Dan." I threw my arm around his shoulder.

Dan shook his head. "You want to help me look after him for a few minutes?"

"I suppose I owe you." She laughed and sat down beside him.

I sucked down my drink. Might have been my fifth or sixth. Didn't matter anymore. Mimi swung by and I ordered another.

I lifted it to toast Mickey.

Mickey and Dan raised their Buds.

She said, "I haven't seen much of you at work."

"Yeah." My gaze slid away from her. "You know how it is. So much to do with the in-laws setting up camp in my house." Pretty good excuse, Oliver. I wanted to high five myself.

"Sure, the in-laws." She sounded like she didn't quite buy it, but she wasn't going to push in front of Dan. She looked at the jukebox and asked, "Any requests?"

I laughed. "I already picked one of your favorites."

"You still remember my favorites?" Her nose wrinkled up in disbelief.

"Ring of Fire" started playing at that exact moment. Her lips melted into a smile.

Mickey's eyes met mine. In that moment, we were seventeen again. She extended her hand. "One dance."

It was how she got me on the dance floor every time.

I slid off the stool. Tipsier than I realized. Didn't matter. She fit perfectly in my arms, just like she always had. Her hair still smelled of coconut. I loved it now as much as I did when we were a couple. A part of my brain knew I shouldn't be enjoying this, but then I flashed back to Kai and Alex holding hands. Kai got to pick her friends? Well, so did I.

"I love this bar," Mickey said.

"Lots of good memories."

"Remember how I used to beat you at pool all the time?"

"You'd wear those tight jeans to distract me."

"You were easy to distract."

I laughed.

We were halfway through the song when I felt a tap on my shoulder. I didn't know who was interrupting our dance, so I didn't let Mickey go. If it was her date, he could wait until the song was over. I turned my head to tell him so.

Alex stood right behind me. His expression reminded me of an angry Norse god. "What are you doing with my sister?"

I released her and turned to face him. "It's just a dance between friends."

Mickey stepped away from me. "Dan and Oliver were just helping me kill time while I waited for Bryan."

He stared at me. "I suppose you're just killing time until your wife recovers?"

"I was told to leave her in your capable hands," I said.

Alex's eyes narrowed. "So you came to drink and dance with your high school sweetheart?"

My words slurred. "Kai would rather be with you." She'd made that clear enough.

Dan came up to us. He kept his voice low. "Alex, just let him be."

"I'll let him be. As long as he lets my sister be," Alex said.

"I'll do whatever I want with whoever I want." Mickey's eyes flashed.

Several patrons turned to look at us. I didn't care.

Alex stepped closer and said in a low voice, "You've got a wife who needs you."

He didn't know what it was like. Living with someone who wouldn't let you help her. He'd never been shut out by Kai. I growled, "Why don't you get your own wife and stop sniffing around mine?"

Alex shook his head. "She asked me to stay."

Those five little words shifted everything inside me. Kai had reached out to him. Kai wanted his help. Kai wanted *him*. Jack Daniel's and anger were a dangerous combination, and Alex's words were an accelerant. My fist flew at Alex's nose.

He dodged it. "That's it. No more free passes."

Mickey gasped, "Oliver!"

Her voice stopped me from taking another swing. I was half-turned toward her when Alex's fist slammed into my cheek. I stumbled back from the blow and tasted blood in my mouth. I lunged toward him, but Dan held me back.

Mike's voice boomed across his bar. "Not in my bar, boys. Take it outside. Now." He might look like a kindly old grandpa, but there was steel in his tone.

I headed toward the door, but Mickey grabbed my arm. "Oliver, whatever's going on with Kai, this won't help it. You need to sober up and go home to your wife."

Dan nodded. "Take my couch and sleep it off."

Alex shook his head. "You've got it all. And you're going to ruin it."

I lunged toward him again, but Mickey got between us. Her eyes locked on mine. "Go home, Oliver."

"It was just a dance," I sputtered.

She gave me a sad smile. "It's never just a dance with us."

CHAPTER 17

Kai

After Alex left, I went to bed early to avoid the rest of my family. I seemed to be fighting with all of them, except for Caleb. I lay in bed, awake and furious at Oliver. I was so busy trying to figure out what was happening to me, I didn't have time to figure out what was happening between Oliver and me, let alone start an affair with Alex. I seethed at my husband's ridiculous jealousy.

Though, I had to admit something. At least to myself. I was actively avoiding thinking about Oliver and me, because once I did take time to really think about us, everything would change. It had to. And I wasn't ready for that.

He wasn't the Oliver I fell in love with. That Oliver loved his action plans. Whenever he did an audit, he made his auditees come up with an action plan and he held them to it. He said it was his way to prove what they'd done was an outlier and would not become a pattern of bad behavior. He saw them as the best way to make sure that the mistake didn't happen again. "A necessary control to mediate risk" is what he called it.

I needed that kind of certainty. I needed him to prove to me that what he'd done to me, to us, over the past weeks was an aberration. That he was still the same man I had married. But he hadn't even tried. Not really. He gave me excuses and explanations, but no action plan. I couldn't be with him if this was the person he wanted to be.

So I hid behind all the other stuff that was happening. Granted, there was a lot of other stuff happening. But I should have been able to turn to Oliver for help, and I couldn't.

The sadness I'd felt dissipated with those thoughts. Now my shield pulsated with anger. Repressed anger. Renewed anger. Rage-filled anger. The shadows danced around the perimeter of my shield. They knew how close I was to giving in, how much I wanted to give in.

I threw back the covers and paced the room. Then I looked at the clock. It was almost one in the morning, and Oliver still wasn't home. What was he doing?

I called his cell. It rang a few times and went to voicemail. Damn. Damn. Triple Damn.

An icy sliver of fear cut through my rage. Had something happened to him? If he had gotten into an accident, someone would have called me. Unless he'd driven off the road and no one had seen it. I couldn't help picturing him trapped in his Cherokee in a field somewhere.

I called the local hospital to make sure he hadn't been admitted. I tried his cell again. I picked up a book, but my eyes kept going to the clock on the nightstand. I watched time tick away.

I thought about waking my parents, or Caleb, but I didn't want to talk to my parents and I didn't want to bother Caleb over what was likely nothing.

I laid in bed certain I would never drift off until I woke to my own scream. With all the lights on in the room, it only took a few moments to see where I was.

Caleb was sitting on my bed beside me.

He squeezed my hand. "It's okay, Kai. I'm here." Once he'd managed to calm me, he asked, "Where's Oliver?"

"He didn't come home."

A thousand responses flitted across my brother's face before he settled on "Is there anything I can do?"

"Can you stay here with me?" My voice came out shaky.

"Of course."

My brother and I stayed up for hours. Sometimes we talked; sometimes we just sat there in silence. Waiting for Oliver to return. Every thirty minutes, I opened the window in my shield and reached out in search of Oliver's mind. If he were within a half-mile of home, I'd hear his thoughts. But each time, I didn't.

Caleb shielded his thoughts and the rest of my family was asleep. Their minds were beyond my reach.

And Oliver wasn't coming home.

I picked up my pencils and sketchpad and started drawing. The stark lines were tightly woven together. Caves. Darkness all around me.

Caleb didn't say anything. He just stayed there with me.

When I stopped, the bed was littered with images of caves.

The cave. That was where everything had changed. What I'd learned there, it changed the way I saw Oliver. He hadn't spoken up for his friend Christian. I understood why teenage Oliver couldn't stand up to his father. I did. But after his dad had died, when Oliver was an adult, he should have come home and faced the truth. He should have said something, done something.

The Oliver I loved would have.

And Mickey. I rubbed my temple. It wasn't just a couple kisses. It was how he'd reached out to her for comfort when things were going badly for us. The first time he'd hidden it from me for years. The second time, I walked in on their kiss. If I hadn't, I'm not sure he'd have ever told me. It made me question every moment of our relationship.

I hated Oliver for his secrets. His lies. His betrayals.

But it wasn't that simple, because I also loved Oliver for all the times he fought for me when I couldn't. I loved the man I thought he was, the man I wanted to believe he could be again.

And all these conflicting emotions were complicated by the fact that something had happened to me, something that tied me to Nathan and made me feel feelings that seemed like they weren't my own.

Oliver had changed, but I had changed, too. I wasn't sure I would ever be the woman I had been. I wasn't even sure I wanted to be that woman anymore.

I let myself think about leaving him. It scared me because for the first time I could imagine a future without him.

At 6:00 a.m., I felt Oliver's thoughts brush against mine. I wasn't ready to know what he was thinking, so I made sure my shield was impenetrable.

Caleb went back to his room so I could talk to Oliver.

A few minutes later, I heard the front door open. The stairs creaked under his weight.

He slid the bedroom door open carefully, as if he was trying not to wake me.

He jumped when I asked, "Where have you been all night?"

His eyes were bleary and bloodshot. His clothes were wrinkled, like he'd slept in them. "Out." He made his way to the closet.

I followed him. "I deserve more than that."

"Maybe." He grabbed a change of clothes and headed for the shower.

His breath was sickly sweet. The mints couldn't completely mask the sour smell. "Were you drinking?"

"Yes." He walked into the bathroom and started removing his clothes.

"What are you doing?"

"I'm taking a shower."

"Right now? Come on. Talk to me, Oliver."

"Sucks when the person you love shuts you out, doesn't it?"

"Are you punishing me?"

He sighed, relenting a little. "I had to blow off some steam. That's it. Then I crashed at Dan's."

I noticed that his cheek was covered in a dark purple bruise. Without realizing what I was doing, I reached out to touch it. He pulled away. "What happened to your face?"

"I was drunk. I must have hit it on something."

"Oliver..."

"I'm tired, I stink. I need a shower." He was down to his boxers.

"I was worried."

"Really?"

"Really. Next time text or call."

"I didn't think you'd notice I was gone."

"Of course, I noticed." I stared into his maple syrup brown eyes.

He stared back at me. "Wanna join me in the shower?" It was a playful question he'd asked hundreds of time, but underneath it there was a hint of uncertainty. And hurt.

"You know, there's nothing going on between Alex and me."

His expression locked up. "There's nothing going on between you and me, either."

"I just need time." I knew that was a lie, even as I said it. I think he knew it, too. I turned to leave the bathroom.

He grabbed me. "Don't walk out on me."

"Let me go."

"I won't do that. Ever. I saved you, damn it. I saved your life. I was there when you needed me most. I was there when you were in danger."

"I wouldn't have been in danger if it hadn't been for your secrets."

His jaw muscles pulsated. "I don't think I'm the only one with secrets. What happened today, Kai?"

105

"Nothing." He had seen everything there was to see when he found me holding hands with Alex.

"Your mom called me. She's worried about you losing control. What secrets are you keeping from me?"

I wasn't expecting that. Emotions cluttered my throat. Not mine, though. His. Oliver's frustration tasted like fried cheese on my tongue. His anger was cinnamon invading my nose. It was nauseating.

"I can't talk about it." I choked out the words and struggled to shield myself.

"So you get to have secrets but I don't?"

"My secrets won't kill you."

"How can you be so sure of that?"

What had Mom told him? "Let go of me," I hissed.

He released my arm and rubbed his hand over his face. He slumped down to sit on the toilet lid.

The scents and smells faded.

His voice came out world-weary. "I don't know what to do anymore, Kai. I know I'm losing you."

"I'm still here."

"Then why does it feel like you're not?"

The darkness swirled inside me, wanting to tell him everything. About what I did to my classmates in high school. What I felt about him. The darkness would say anything to make him leave me. The darkness made it easy for me to imagine—to want—a future without Oliver. But I still wasn't sure what I wanted. I bit my lip until I tasted blood. "I can't do this."

I stumbled backward. I needed space. Room to breathe. He got up and followed me into the bedroom. "Why will you let Alex in and not me?"

The words were out of my mouth before I knew it. "Because I trust him." Shadows swirled around my shield.

"And you don't trust me." It wasn't a question, but a realization. Oliver stormed out of the room.

I hid in Caleb's room the rest of the morning. Now, I stood by the window staring out at the backyard. Fields of white snow stretched all the way to the line of silvery woods in the distance.

"You can't stay cooped up in here forever," he said.

"Just a little while longer."

"What happened?"

I wasn't up for recapping the ugliness that was Oliver and I. "I don't know what to do anymore."

"Good."

"Good?"

"You've been in this crazy stasis since the hospital. It's time you admit it and do something."

I swallowed. "I don't want to make any decisions yet."

"Because you're afraid of the darkness, or because you're afraid of change?"

I didn't need to answer, but I did anyway. "Both."

"Tell me your worst fear. Just say it out loud."

"That I can't save Oliver and me. Maybe because I don't want to anymore."

Saying it out loud brought tears to my eyes. If I let them fall, it felt like I was admitting that my fear was true. So I blinked and swallowed until they no longer threatened to fall.

"What do you need right now?"

"To get away from here."

Caleb smiled. "Why didn't you say so earlier? That's easy."

Twenty minutes later, it was a little awkward when all of us piled into two cars.

I still wasn't talking to my parents, and I had nothing to say to Oliver. Caleb managed to get the three of them into my parents' car.

Naomi and I rode with Caleb. She slid into the backseat and put her earbuds in without saying a word to either of us. I assumed she was still mad at me.

I appreciated the silence. Caleb let me have some time to think. I tried not to imagine what my parents were telling Oliver about me or what he was telling them.

We headed into town to see the holiday display at the Butternut's Area Historical Museum. When we walked inside, the Butternut High School brass quartet was playing "Silent Night." The whole museum was decked out for the holidays. Historical holiday items crammed the shelves. A century's worth of Santa ornaments, snowman toys, sleigh bells, holiday plates, and angels were everywhere the eye could see. There was an entire display case devoted to nativity sets.

It was enough to distract me from everything going on with my family, at least for a little while.

Mom asked Oliver, "Is this what it was like when you were younger?"

"This was a store when I was a kid."

"Really?" Mom asked.

"What did it sell?" Dad wanted to know.

"A little bit of everything," an older woman with curly white hair interjected.

"Mrs. K?" Oliver asked.

"Oliver Richter, how long has it been?"

"Too long." He smiled and hugged her.

Oliver introduced my family to Mrs. K. She'd taught math and science to him in eighth grade. When the introductions got to me, she asked, "You're the tough cookie who saved Lukas?"

I nodded.

"You do Butternut proud."

"I just did what had to be done," I said.

"That's what we do here." She winked at me.

Mom glanced around. "It's so hard to picture this as a store."

"I'm sure Oliver remembers the penny candy and the ice cream, but the owner, Matilda Bortz, sold everything from newspapers to mittens to over-the-counter medications."

"That's enterprising," Caleb said.

"If these walls could talk." Mrs. K leaned in to share a story. "One day, a woman came in asking for some worm medication. Matilda had several medications for de-worming, depending on the animal's size." Mrs. K warmed to her tale. "When Matilda asked her for the dog's weight, the woman said, 'Dog? Hell, I need it for myself!'"

My entire family burst out laughing. To anyone who might have seen us, we were a normal, loving family. But anger and sadness swirled around me in shades of red and blue. Whiffs of bacon filled my nose and chili peppers danced over my tongue. So much frustration and anger.

"What happened to her?" Mom asked.

Mrs. K sighed. "She passed on a while ago. Someone bought the place and lived here for a spell. Then the house went back to the bank. Eventually, the historical society snapped it up."

"You've really made it a treasure trove of mementos," Oliver said. "Is that Mrs. Dietz's nativity set?"

"It is."

Before she could tell us more, someone called out to Mrs. K and she excused herself.

I wandered off with Caleb. As we made our way through the museum, several people stopped to ask how I was, to thank me for saving Lukas, to tell me how strong I was, to wish me well, and to offer their help. I didn't realize how many people recognized me and cared. Everyone acted like the worst was over. I appreciated the sentiment, but it didn't feel true.

I made my way upstairs. Hand-crafted wedding gowns from

another age were displayed on dress forms. One gown was seafoam green with intricate lace details. Another was buttercup yellow with puffy chiffon sleeves that gathered at the elbow. In the corner was a white confection with a long train and lace veil. I could feel the hope sewn into each garment.

I'd worn a tank top and jeans when I'd married Oliver, but I still understood what these dresses meant to the women who had worn them.

Caleb put his arm around me, and squeezed my shoulder. "Brings back memories, huh?"

"We made so many promises to each other that day." I leaned against my big brother.

"Do you still want to keep them?" he asked softly.

"I'm not sure if we can, anymore."

CHAPTER 18

Oliver

Not only did Kai refuse to ride in the same car as me, she continued to avoid me while we toured the museum. As I led her parents around, I did my best to get them to tell me more about Kai's dark secret; they did their best to distract me from that topic. I even tried to pump Naomi for information, but she didn't have any idea what I was talking about.

Kai kept her distance from her parents and me. Naomi did her best to ignore her big sister. Caleb was the only one of us who appeared to be in Kai's good graces. Big surprise. Kai slipped her hand through her brother's arm and leaned against him as we walked around Butternut's tiny downtown. The entire area stretched across two parallel streets. It was really just a short series of one or two story buildings. Some occupied, some not. The town was trying to hold on to what it had been when the mills were at full capacity and the jobs were plentiful.

A wide strip of land lay between the two streets. Right now, that grassy stretch was buried under piles of snow. You could barely see the railroad tracks that ran straight through it. Beside those tracks sat the Butternut Feed Store, a long red and white building with a tin roof and a silo beside it.

What had once been a place for farmers to stock up on supplies had evolved into the perfect pit stop for outdoorsmen and locals. The Feed Store sold a little of everything from hunting boots to Cheetos. Through all its incarnations, it remained the gossip hub for the town.

Grain and feed were still stored in the entrance area that retained its barn-like features. We passed through on our way to the store, which was shaped like a horseshoe with the main part of the store and the cash register in the middle and two sections extending behind it for fishing and hunting.

The owners, Bill and Kathy, were happy to see my wife up and about. Kathy gave the Guhn family a tour of the store, sharing stories about the animals mounted on the wall.

Mrs. Guhn stared at a doe that had been expertly preserved by a taxidermist. "It just seems like a waste to turn these animals into trophies."

"I'd rather they eat the animal than make it into this," Mr. Guhn said.

I murmured to Kathy, "They're from Southern California."

She nodded in sympathy.

Bill came out from behind the counter and explained, "Most hunters use the animals for food, especially the deer. Everything inside is stripped out and used."

"So, really, it's kind of like recycling. Not wasteful at all," I said.

"People here went green a long time ago—out of necessity." He gave my in-laws a sideways glance.

Mrs. Guhn said, "We've been raising chickens since Kai went to college."

"They replaced us with poultry," Caleb said to Kai and she laughed.

"We needed something to worry about after you two left the house," Mr. Guhn said.

"Not like you had another kid or anything," Naomi muttered.

I whispered to her, "Just not one who caused as much trouble."

She gave me a slight smile and walked off to check out the T-shirts. Everyone meandered around the store. Caleb stuck to Kai's side. I watched them move through the aisles in sync, laughing and talking. Kai and I used to be like that when we lived in the city. We'd wander down Broadway, popping in and out of the stores as we made our way to Chinatown for dinner.

After Naomi picked out a T-shirt, I led her back to the register to pay for it. The rest of the family came with us. I was behind a rack filled with boots when I heard a hushed voice from the other side.

Mrs. Wiesner. Somehow, her attempt to be quiet made her voice carry further. "Last night, Oliver got in a fight at the Irishman's bar. A fight over Mickey."

I froze. Naomi bumped into me.

Mrs. Kohler, who loved gossip almost as much as Mrs. Wiesner, didn't even try to speak quietly. "That boy is ruining the Richter name. Thank goodness, Henrich isn't here to see how his grandson turned out."

I closed my eyes and cursed my stupidity. I should have realized the story of what had happened at Brennan's Green Brier would be all over town today. I should have told Kai myself when I had the chance.

"His poor wife is still recovering from saving Mickey's son, and Oliver is out stirring up more trouble for her." Mrs. Wiesner tsked.

"I see why his wife wasn't the friendliest girl in town," Mrs. Kohler said. "Dealing with a husband like him can ruin a woman's temperament."

I glanced at Kai's family. Caleb smirked at me like I'd lived up to his lowest expectations. Kai's parents both wore expressions of concern. Naomi peered around me, annoyed that I blocked her way to the register.

Dreading what I was going to see, I looked at Kai. For a moment, it seemed that she had retreated inside herself. Then something flared in her eyes, a fire I'd never seen before. I took a step away from her without even realizing what I was doing.

Kai walked around the display to face Mrs. Wiesner and Mrs. Kohler. We followed her. Naomi just wanted to make her purchase, but the rest of us needed to see what happened next. When she saw Kai, Mrs. Wiesner had the grace to blush. Mrs. Kohler, however, pulled herself up to her full height. At almost 300 pounds, she was a mighty woman. She looked down at my petite wife and Kai stared back at her without flinching.

"Mrs. Wiesner, Mrs. Kohler." Kai nodded to each of them. "Lovely to see you again."

Mrs. Wiesner asked, "How are you feeling, dear?"

"On the mend," Kai said.

"That's wonderful to hear." Mrs. Kohler added, "Oliver."

"Hello," I said.

"Well," Mrs. Wiesner's voice came out unnaturally high, "we'll let you get back to your shopping."

The elderly ladies stepped aside to let Naomi through, but they didn't give up their prime location for gossiping. They just switched to the church's pancake breakfast while we were in earshot. And what one lady was wearing, or rather, not wearing enough of. They had more than enough judgment to go around.

Kai turned and left the store.

I followed her out to the entryway. The exposed wood made the entire place feel unfinished. Cold seeped through the uninsulated walls.

She stood with her back to me.

I wasn't sure how to begin. "Kai—"

"You lied to me this morning." Her voice was low, almost a growl.

"I told you that I'd been drinking and I was at Brennan's Green Brier. With Dan."

"And you ended up in a brawl over Mickey." Her shoulders tightened, inching toward her neck. "That's how you got the bruise on your face."

"Let me explain—"

She swiveled to face me and held up her hand to stop me. "You had a chance to explain. Instead, you lied."

"It's not how it sounded."

"It never is with Mickey, is it?" Her laugh came out harsh, and it sputtered to a quick death. "You always have an excuse, Oliver."

"I just needed to blow off some steam. I went for a drink. I was hanging out with Dan when Mickey showed up. Then Alex came in." I paused for a moment. "After he left you, I guess."

"So, this is my fault somehow?" Her voice rose with her disbelief.

"It's *our* fault. Things have been bad. I've done my best, but—"

"I won't listen to one more excuse."

"What?"

"Stop. Just stop." Her voice sounded gutted.

I didn't know what to do. I reached for her.

"DON'T TOUCH ME!"

Something pushed me back. An invisible force. A wave of emotions slammed into me. So much anger and hurt and betrayal. I stumbled back.

"Kai—"

"Leave me alone." She stalked away from me.

I tried to follow her, but I couldn't. Something was keeping me pinned in place.

CHAPTER 19

Kai

Inside me, the fury rumbled. All the anger and hurt that I had locked away ignited. It took every bit of strength I had to keep my shield intact. I didn't know what would happen if I let all this rage out.

I kept walking, putting as much distance as I could between Oliver and me. Just past the post office, there was a section of downtown with empty buildings. I saw the boarded up windows. The sign for a butcher shop that looked like it closed down decades ago. No one was down there. There was nothing worth going there for.

I could feel Oliver's desperation to reach me, but I couldn't look at him. If I did, I knew that everything would spill out. Rivers of rage. Hurricanes of hurt.

Oliver had lied to me. Again. After everything we'd been through, he kept lying to me.

This was the real Oliver.

While I had been worrying about him, wondering where he was, he'd been at a bar. With Mickey. He hadn't come home to me because he'd been with her. And he'd gotten into a fistfight with Alex. A fight over Mickey.

Tears blurred my vision. I swallowed, and bitterness burned my throat.

Oliver, my parents—the people who were supposed to love me the most had betrayed me. Again and again.

I couldn't take it anymore.

Suddenly, everything disappeared. The street, the snow, all of downtown Butternut. Gone. All I saw was red. A thick, impenetrable fog of red.

I couldn't see where I was going. I had to stop.

I heard footsteps running behind me. If it was Oliver, I didn't know what I'd do. Sweat burst across my back.

"Kai, wait up!" Caleb yelled.

The red fog faded to a translucent haze.

Caleb wrapped me in his arms, and I clung to him.

I couldn't stop shaking. "I should have known he was with her. He's always finding his way back to her."

Caleb guided me down an alley between two abandoned buildings. A place no one could see us.

"Get the whole truth before you do anything," he said.

I couldn't believe Caleb was defending Oliver. Was my brother going to betray me, too?

"How?" My voice cracked. "How am I supposed to find out the truth when he keeps lying to me? He could have told me what had happened last night, but he didn't. He even made up a story about how he got that bruise on his face. Oliver is a liar. He's always going to lie to me. That's who he is."

"Kai, you have every right to your anger."

I took a shuddering breath. The last thing I needed was therapist-talk from the only person I trusted. Part of me knew that he was trying to help, but my anger overwhelmed me.

Suddenly, there he was, standing inside my shield. The floor was melting beneath us, sucking us both into the abyss. I screamed.

He grabbed my arms and held me. "What do you feel?"

"I hate him. I hate Mickey. I hate this situation. I hate everything that has happened since Oliver brought me to Wisconsin and I hate everything that keeps happening."

I sobbed in his arms. He held me and let me cry.

To anyone walking by, it would just look like my brother was holding me. They wouldn't hear me breaking down. They wouldn't have any idea of what was happening inside me.

When the storm of emotions quieted, we remained inside my shield.

Caleb said, "The fight probably had more to do with you than with Mickey."

I wiped my nose. "I haven't done anything."

"No, you haven't." He added, "You haven't let Oliver in."

"Look at what he does to me!"

"This is what happens when you build walls around your feelings. No one can hold all this inside. Not even you."

I stared at the floor of my shield. It was solidifying again, temporarily cooling down after the eruption of anger.

"I have to. You see how dangerous it is. This kind of rage could ignite half the town. If I let that get out..." My voice trailed off.

"I get it."

For once, Caleb the millionaire and golden boy didn't have a solution.

CHAPTER 20

Oliver

A s soon as I could move, I realized I was shaking from the shock of what Kai had just done to me. I dropped down onto a stack of chicken feed.

Then Caleb appeared in front of me, asking, "Where's Kai?"

It was hard to form the words, but somehow I managed. "She left."

He shook his head and headed after her. Either he hadn't notice how off I was or he didn't care.

It felt like forever before my limbs felt completely mine again. I glanced at my watch. Mere minutes had passed.

I still couldn't believe Kai did that to me. To use her powers to hold me in place. It was awful. I shuddered. What she'd done didn't feel like an accidental flare of her abilities. She knew she was turning her powers outward on me. And she still did it.

I swallowed. Was this what her mother was hinting at?

I didn't know how to handle a Kai who did things like this. I chewed on the inside of my mouth. I feared what might happen if I followed Kai and caught up to her, especially in her agitated state.

Caleb would find her. He was the only one who could talk her down now. All I did was inflame her.

The shaking stopped, but I didn't get up. I wasn't ready to face anyone just yet. I was still sitting there five minutes later when her parents and Naomi came out of the store.

Mrs. Guhn looked around. "Where's Kai?" Her voice rose with concern.

"Caleb and she took a walk," I said.

Her father gave me a dubious look.

Naomi looked from me to Mrs. Guhn to Mr. Guhn. She must have sensed the tension because she took a giant step back. She jerked her thumb in the direction of the store. "Soooo, I'm going back in the Feed Store."

Mrs. Guhn nodded and said, "That's right, dear."

Naomi rolled her eyes and shook her head. She mouthed "Good luck" to me.

My lips twitched, but I couldn't manage a smile. Not now.

Mr. Guhn cleared his throat. "Marriage can be tough at times."

Oh God, no. Please, not the *difficulties of marriage* speech.

"No matter how tough it gets, you're still married to my little girl." He clamped his hand on my shoulder.

My mouth was so dry. It felt like all the moisture had been sucked out. I tried swallowing, but it didn't help. "I know, sir."

"Then act like it. Stop drinking with your ex-girlfriend."

"It's not what you think."

Mrs. Guhn chimed in. "It doesn't matter what we think. All that matters is what Kai thinks. I saw her face in there. She thinks it's true."

"But it isn't." I fumbled over my words. "I'm not doing anything with Mickey. I'm trying to be there for Kai."

"Oliver." The sharpness of her tone cut through all my explanations. "Kai's emotions are her worst enemy. You know she feels everything ten times more than you do. Do you want to make her spiral again?"

"No." I rubbed my palm on my thigh. "I never want that to happen."

"Then start acting like it." Mr. Guhn squeezed my shoulder. Harder than he needed to.

"This gossip isn't good for Kai or you," Mrs. Guhn said.

"I know." I stared at the dirt encrusted floorboards. "I messed up." So had Kai. But I was afraid to tell them that. Because they might do something to make it worse for both of us.

Mr. Guhn said, "You need to fix it."

I nodded.

He and Mrs. Guhn went back in the store to get Naomi.

I stayed there on that feedbag. I didn't know what to do next. I had no idea what words could possibly make any of this okay. Not only what happened last night with Mickey and Alex, but what Kai just did to me. There was nothing that made any of it okay.

CHAPTER 21

Kai

I went to bed as soon as we got home.

I slipped into sleep faster than I had in weeks and deeper than I had since the hospital. I didn't go into a nightmare this time. Somehow, I found my way to the pond in Grandma Guhn's backyard. My entryway to the In Between.

I wanted so much to talk to Grandma Guhn. I knew that she could help me. The fact that she was dead didn't mean that it was impossible to communicate with her, just harder.

I sat down on the giant rock and wrapped my arms around my knees. I had another new problem. My darkness didn't want me to talk to Grandma Guhn. It wanted to take control and do its worst. I clung to the piece of me that didn't want that to happen, but that piece was getting smaller and smaller.

Sitting in the shade of an ancient oak, I watched its leaves make shadows on the rocks and the water. I leaned back, dipped my toes into the pond, and flick-flacked the water. It wasn't cold here, even with the shade, because the water wasn't that deep. I could see all the way to the sandy bottom.

I waited to see if Caleb would join me.

I'd promised Grandma Guhn I'd try to bring him to the In Between with me. And Caleb was eager to see her, too. I just had to figure out how to do it.

Then I felt his presence. I turned to see him walking across the yard to me. He climbed up on the rock and sat beside me.

"You did it," he said.

"It's just the first step."

"A big first step," he reminded me. "Savor it."

I couldn't. There was so much more we had to do to get to Grandma Guhn. I explained that the entrance to the In Between was at the bottom of the pond, and that finding it might be difficult. I told him to look for a glimmer of light amid the sand and rocks.

Then we slid into the water.

Even in my dream, my left wrist was in a cast. I let the weight of it drag me down. I scanned the pond's floor, but I didn't find what I was looking for. Lungs bursting, I surfaced.

We swam in opposite directions to cover as much space as we could. Diving down, coming back up, shouting that nothing had been found, and trying again. And again. And again.

I got desperate. I clawed at the silt, trying to dig my way to the In Between. It didn't work.

Finally, we gave up.

Exhausted and drenched, we stretched out on the big rock beside the pond.

"I can't cross over. We can't get to Grandma Guhn," I murmured.

"Maybe it's different this time," Caleb said. "Maybe you're not strong enough to get both of us through. Not now, anyway. You just need to get stronger."

"Maybe," I replied.

What I couldn't say, not even to Caleb, was that maybe the darkness was winning. Maybe it had already won.

CHAPTER 22

Oliver

After Kai went to bed, I retreated to my study. I couldn't spend another minute with the Guhns. Their judgment started at the Butternut Feed Store, continued on the car ride home, and wasn't stopping anytime soon.

They didn't see what Kai did to me, pinning me in place at the Feed Store. Now, I finally had an idea of what her mother feared. A Kai who lashed out was a Kai who was dangerous to everyone around her.

I wasn't sure what to do next. What would she do if she woke up and found me in bed with her? I didn't know and I was a little afraid. So I stayed in my study, killing zombies on my Wii for a few hours. I considered spending the night on the couch there. But I had to talk to Kai about what happened. And that wasn't going to happen if we weren't in the same room.

I waited until all the Guhns had gone to bed. Then I snuck into my room with Kai and grabbed a pillow and some blankets and made a makeshift bed on the floor. I wasn't expecting to get much sleep.

I don't know when I drifted off, but I woke up when she did.

She got out of bed without even acknowledging my presence on the floor.

"You didn't have nightmares," I said.

She didn't say anything as she put on her bunny slippers and walked toward the door of our bedroom.

I got up. "We can't go on like this."

"I know."

She was almost gone.

I was desperate to keep her here. I blurted out, "That bar fight wasn't about Mickey."

"Wasn't it?" Her spine was so straight. It was like every muscle was working to hold her upright.

"Kai, when I saw you with Alex..." I pinched the bridge of my nose. How could I explain what that had done to me? "It hurt me. I was jealous. I've been trying so hard to be there for you, and you haven't let me—"

She turned to face me. Her blue eyes flashed, dark and dangerous. "This is what you were trying to tell me yesterday. That everything— EVERYTHING—is my fault."

"I'm not blaming you."

Her laugh bounced uneasily off the walls.

"I'm just trying to explain."

"Of course you are. But I'm tired of your explanations, Oliver. If Brennan's Green Brier had been an isolated incident it would be different." She shrugged. "But it was one of a *series* of incidents, Oliver. A *pattern* of behavior. What's your action plan, Oliver?"

At that moment, I was afraid of my wife and of what she might do. But I had to try.

"Let's start with honesty," I said.

Kai cocked her head, listening.

"I was jealous when I saw you and Alex together. I went to Brennan's Green Brier for a few drinks. Mickey showed up. I danced with her. Then Alex came in."

My words stuck in my throat. I was trying to be honest, but I couldn't tell Kai what Alex had said to me. I skipped over it. "So, yeah, I shouldn't have been dancing with Mickey. But Alex shouldn't have been holding your hand."

Kai rubbed her temple. She seemed to be in pain. "I don't want this."

"Me, neither. What can I do to fix this?"

Something in her expression changed. It was like I finally asked the right question.

"Tell me the truth. Show me that Mickey is in the past." Her voice cracked. "Make me believe that I'm the one you want to be with!"

"Can you do the same with Alex?"

There was a pause that I didn't like, but she finally said, "Yes."

I kept going. "I need you to be honest with me, too. Tell me what's going on with you and your parents."

Kai stumbled over her words like she couldn't quite make her way through them. "They picked Caleb over me. They kept him away from me when I was in the institution because they wanted to protect him."

I reached for her hand. She didn't pull away, but she didn't hold on to mine either.

"What about your mom's concerns about your powers? About you using them on others?" Like she did to me yesterday. I bit back those words.

"Back in high school, I did some awful things. I took the thoughts that I heard and I concentrated them. I balled them up and I fired them into people's minds. I used my power as a weapon." She whispered, "Some felt pain. Some got sick. A few needed therapy."

"Was it like what happened yesterday?"

She pulled her hand away from me. "I just pushed you away. That was all."

"Should I be grateful?" I asked.

"I'm not telling you how to feel. But I can hurt people if I lose control. I didn't hurt you."

"I couldn't move, Kai. It was scary."

She heaved a sigh. "You want me to apologize, but I'm not sorry. I had to get away from you for both our sakes."

"Why didn't you tell me any this?" Instead, she'd kept this hidden from me for years.

"It was something I promised I'd never do again. I buried it. As long as I never talked about it, it stayed in the past. It was like some other me did it."

"That's how I felt about Christian's death."

The Christmases I remember with my mother were happy.

After she died, there were several years of fake happy, everybody trying to put on a brave face. Grandma and Aunt Ines prepared Austrian feasts, and my family would hide gifts for me to find on Christmas Eve. The gift hunt was exciting and the food was delicious, but none of it distracted me from what was missing—my mother.

When I first came back to Butternut, I had visions of how Kai and I would celebrate Christmas in Butternut with Aunt Ines. But now Kai's family was here, and their traditions dominated.

Aunt Ines, however, still managed to sneak in a few of our family favorites including kürbiscremesuppe, a Styrian pumpkin soup, and gebackener karpfen, a delicious fried carp.

Mrs. Guhn cooked a four-course vegetarian meal that only her husband and she could possibly enjoy. And no one was talking.

By the third course, I was longing for escape, but then Kai brought out a steaming pot of tteokguk, Korean rice-cake soup with beef brisket. It was something her grandmother had prepared each year for her Korean husband. It was a reminder of how families and traditions blended together. For a moment, I thought we might actually salvage this holiday after all.

CHAPTER 23

Kai

On Christmas day, Lukas called and invited us to join his family for dessert. He whispered, "I really need to see you, Aunt Kai."

I had no desire to spend time with the Fuchses. Oliver had promised to stay away from Mickey, and I wasn't going to contact Alex. But I could not say no to Lukas.

So a few hours later, I was there at the Fuchses with my family in tow. Mrs. Fuchs welcomed me into her home with a big hug. I breathed in her baby-powder scented perfume. Then she released me and bustled off to the kitchen. Aunt Ines went with her to help. My mom offered, but Mrs. Fuchs was firm that the Guhns were guests in her home today.

Each of the Fuchses made their way over to me. Mr. Fuchs, the stern family patriarch, thanked me for saving his grandson. Alex's older brother, Pete, dropped a kiss on my cheek as he took my coat. Kevin, Alex's youngest brother, shook my hand. Thomas, the bookish Fuchs, helped his very pregnant wife Irena waddle over. She squeezed my hand and said, "Thank you for saving Lukas."

"He saved me too," I said.

Dan gave me a bear hug. "Next round of repairs is on me."

He'd helped make our house into a home. "Thank you." Though I didn't think he could fix what was broken in our home.

Then I saw Alex.

He waited until I was alone. "You look lovely," he murmured.

I ran my hand over my azure blue dress, smoothing my skirt. I didn't know what to say, so I blurted out, "So do you."

He chuckled. "That's the first time anyone's said that to me."

Did I just tell a grown man he looked lovely? Heat flooded my face.

Oliver stepped between us and extended his hand. "Merry Christmas."

The tension between Alex and Oliver tasted of blackberry pie. So tartly sweet that I wanted another bite.

"Merry Christmas." Alex gripped Oliver's hand and gave it a shake.

"Aunt Kai," Lukas ran over and grabbed my skirt. "Come play." He tugged me away.

Mickey smiled politely, but red and purple smoke swirled around my shield. Jealousy. Frustration. Red Hots burned my tongue. Anger. Her anger.

I should fortify my shield, but I didn't. I wanted to know what Mickey was feeling. I let her thoughts seep in. *Why was it so important to Lukas to have her here today? It's a family holiday.*

I loved Lukas. We both had special abilities, and we'd been kidnapped together. Those were things that bonded us. Mickey might be his mother, but she could never understand Lukas like I could.

At the same time, I was a little bit worried about my feelings for Lukas. When Alex brought him to see me, I noticed that my attachment to him seemed almost parental. I couldn't help wondering if those feelings weren't mine, but Nathan's.

I tried to shake off those concerns for the moment.

Lukas guided me past the couch and the recliner toward the

132

fireplace. Its mantle was cluttered with family photos. The Fuchses were everything I had wanted the Guhns to be: close-knit, supportive, and loving.

Lukas stopped at his small wooden table. He sat in a little chair and I kneeled across from him. While he colored, I sketched. I tried to listen to his thoughts, but I couldn't catch them. His were always harder to tune in, but I think he was guarding them today.

Finally, I asked, "What did you want to talk to me about?"

He looked around to make sure no one could hear us. "I have to see my dad."

"Why?"

"To talk to him."

"Did you ask your mom to take you to see him?"

Lukas shook his head. "I want you to go with me. Can you ask her?"

I hesitated. I didn't want to talk to Mickey, but Lukas's eyes pleaded with me.

I swallowed my doubts and said, "Sure."

"Did you make that picture for Mommy?" Mickey asked as she leaned over Lukas and me.

"For Aunt Kai," Lukas said.

"That's so sweet." Mickey's smile stayed in place, but her thoughts darkened to cranberry red. Someone needed to teach this woman how to shield. My grip on the pencil tightened, but I tried to stay calm.

Mickey reached over and picked up one of my drawings. "Why did you draw this?" Her voice held a hint of fear embedded in anger.

"Why?"

"That's where Nathan proposed to me." The picture shook in Mickey's hand. "This is exactly how it looked on that day nine years ago." She dropped my drawing back on the table like it burned her hand.

She confirmed what I had suspected. My drawings were actually Nathan's—his skill, his memories. This realization sent a burst of heat through my body, but I'd have to process it later.

Right now, I had to help Lukas. "Lukas wants me to take him to see Nathan."

"Absolutely not," she said.

Lukas looked up at her. "Mommy, I have to see him."

"It's a bad idea," she said.

"I'll go with him. Nothing will happen," I promised.

That seemed to infuriate her. "This is really none of your business. He's my son."

"I think it might help him get over what happened to us if we face Nathan together," I said.

"No," Mickey said. The jaundiced yellow of fear swirled around her. She was petrified of Nathan. And more than a little bit freaked out by me.

Alex must have overheard because he came over to us. "Mickey, I can take them."

Her face softened. So did her thoughts. They turned a gentle sky blue. She liked the idea of Alex and I spending time together. I didn't have to guess why.

Oliver made a point of stepping between Alex and me. "What's going on over here?"

I hated the gleam in Mickey's eyes as she told him. "Lukas wants to see Nathan, and he wants Kai to go with him. Alex has volunteered to take them."

"I don't want Kai anywhere near Nathan," Oliver said.

What Oliver wanted didn't trump what Lukas needed. "I've already been to see him."

Oliver sputtered, "When? How?"

"When Caleb and I went to Wausau." I focused all my attention on my drawing.

"Why didn't you tell me?"

"There was nothing to tell." Nothing that made any sense, anyway.

Mickey didn't say a word. A triumphant feeling seeped out of her. She stepped back to let the tension between Oliver and me build. She was so confident that we would destroy our marriage. What she didn't understand was how many people I could take down with us.

"It's important to Lukas," Alex said.

Mickey stroked Lukas's head. "Baby, do you really want to do this?"

He nodded. "Please, Mommy."

"All right. Uncle Alex will take you and Aunt Kai to see him."

Mickey's thoughts were almost gleeful. *Another wedge between Oliver and Kai. And I didn't have to do anything this time.*

"I guess the three of you have it all worked out." Oliver stomped away.

My emotions were shifting like tides during a storm. One second I was merely annoyed—the fact that she was waiting for Oliver and me to break up was hardly a surprise. But, the next moment, I wanted to lash out at her with everything I had. Inside my shield, the floor became stickier than melted caramel. It would be so easy to let it liquefy and send all those feelings at her.

She deserves it, the darkness reminded me.

If I let go now, I wasn't sure that Mickey would be the only one to suffer. I struggled to keep the darkness contained.

The pencil in my hand snapped.

"Are you okay?" Lukas asked.

I nodded. As I looked into his eyes, I knew I couldn't hurt his mother. *Not yet*, the darkness whispered.

I was staring at the massive platter of Christmas cookies on Mrs. Fuchs's sideboard when Caleb joined me. He looked distracted. Worried, even.

"Everything okay?" I asked.

"Just a business call." He gave me a quick smile that didn't reach his eyes.

"On Christmas? What's going on?"

"Nothing I can't handle after the holidays."

He tried to maintain his usual confidence, but his mind didn't feel so certain to me. I would have asked more, but Oliver's laugh distracted me. It wasn't a polite chuckle. It was a deep-bellied guffaw. I hadn't heard him laugh like that in a long time, so I turned around to see who was making him do it. It was Mickey, of course.

Oliver asked, "So, no shredded pancakes today?"

Mickey leaned into him. "Next time."

Of course she assumed that there would be a next time. A next time for her and Oliver. I stared, wanting her to notice that I saw what was happening. She stared right back, placing a hand on my husband's arm. She was baiting me. Daring me to say something. Wanting me to react in front of everyone.

The darkness in me whispered, *You can stop her.*

I pushed the darkness back. I thought about Lukas. I remembered all the people I had hurt in high school.

But part of me really wondered if I could get Mickey to back off without doing her any permanent harm, without hurting anybody else.

You can, the darkness said. *Trust yourself.*

I moved a little closer to Mickey and Oliver, close enough to catch snippets of their conversation.

"So hard to understand...kids can be cruel...what other abilities he might develop."

Oliver was responding with stuff like "You're a great mom" and "You and Lukas have so much support. We're all here for you."

Mickey was relying on Oliver to help her. And he was letting her. *Trust yourself,* the darkness said.

Inside my shield, the floor burned my feet. I looked down. It was like hot putty. Malleable. So many dark emotions were close to the surface. I could scoop them right up. I reached down and gathered a cluster of deep-purple guilt.

I'd been inside Mickey's mind. I knew the thoughts that haunted her. I infused this ball of guilt with all of them, personalizing it to her pain. *You drove your husband insane. You're the reason your son almost died. Everything you touch, you destroy. You'll destroy Oliver. Just like you destroyed Nathan.* I wrapped layer upon layer of guilt and remorse into a tight ball. Then I fired it straight at Mickey.

She gasped and stumbled.

Oliver caught her. "Are you okay?"

Her eyes were riveted on me. I felt a smile sneak across my face.

"I just lost my balance for a second. Too much Riesling, maybe. I'm fine." Sweat shone on her forehead. The blood rushed out of her cheeks.

Maybe this would make her realize that she was dealing with a new Kai.

"I'll just eat something and sit down for a minute." Mickey grabbed a couple of cookies and headed for the living room. She glanced back at Oliver for a moment, as if she thought he'd actually go with her.

He just watched her leave. Then his gaze slid back to me. His face changed. Concern became suspicion, which shifted to something I never expected to see there. Fear, definitely fear, as he realized that whatever I'd just done, I was capable of infinitely worse.

CHAPTER 24

Oliver

I was almost afraid to step into our bedroom, not just because of what she'd done, but who she'd become, and what it meant for us.

The Kai sitting on our bed was not the Kai I'd fallen in love with. She definitely wasn't the Kai I'd married. She wasn't even the Kai I'd tried to understand and connect with over the past few weeks. Her body thrummed with energy. She didn't just anticipate a fight, she welcomed it.

I could barely contain the anger inside me. I paced the room. "Secrets and lies are what are tearing us apart, right?"

"Your secrets and lies." She looked so serene.

"You didn't tell me that you'd gone to see Nathan!"

"You never asked." She used that tone that most people reserved for talking to little kids.

"Lies by omission still count."

"Do they?" She made it sound like she would have to recalibrate my score because of that.

I might be on shaky ground, but I wanted to understand. I needed to. So I pushed forward. "Why didn't you tell me about seeing him?"

"It had nothing to do with you."

"Nothing to do with me? You're my wife. And Nathan kidnapped you. He almost killed you!" Nathan had also exposed my darkest secrets, but this didn't seem like the time to bring that up. "How can you say that your visiting him had nothing to do with me?"

She shrugged. "What do you want me to say? It wasn't about you."

"What was it about?"

"It was about me."

I was so frustrated that I almost missed the slight tremble in her voice and the way her gaze lingered on the floor. There was something else. About Nathan.

I clamped down on my emotions and focused on hers for a moment. I dropped down onto the edge of the bed and asked, "What happened when you saw Nathan?"

She studied her hands. "I'm not who I used to be, Oliver. You want that woman, but I can't summon her back here. She died in the cave. No matter what I do, she's gone. And the me that's here? You don't know her."

"What happened in the cave changed all of us."

The saddest laugh I'd ever heard escaped her lips. "You don't understand."

"Then explain it to me."

"I can't. I'm still trying to figure it out for myself. That's why I went to see Nathan."

I tried to process the information Kai was giving me, but it wasn't much to work with. "So, when you attacked Mickey—"

Her eyes slitted. "What did the little bitch tell you?"

The violence in her voice startled me. "I saw it myself. Mickey didn't bring it up. I did. But she's afraid you might hurt Lukas."

"Bullshit. She knows I won't hurt Lukas. She's worried about what I might do to her."

"Kai, what you did—you can't do that."

Her eyes went cold. "I can do whatever I want."

I tried to be reasonable. "I know that you're going through a lot. I know that you're not yourself. I know that you didn't really mean to hurt Mickey—"

Kai leapt up from our bed. "It's always about Mickey," she hissed. "Do you know what she was thinking all day? NO! But I do. When we fall apart, she'll be there for you. She's waiting for it."

Her jealousy came out of nowhere. After weeks of pushing me away, now she suddenly acted like I belonged to her. I shook my head. "That doesn't make it okay to hurt her!"

Her voice burned my ears. "You still don't get it, do you? I could have put her in a coma. Or worse. I just wanted to let her know that she couldn't keep pushing me. That I wouldn't stand by and let her steal what was mine."

She was delusional if she thought she could cross that line with her powers and it would be okay as long as someone didn't die or end up in a coma. "Listen to yourself. My Kai would never hurt another person like that."

"Your Kai is dead!" She screamed at me. Her eyes were lit with a maniacal fire. For a split second, she reminded me of Nathan.

I didn't know what to say or do. I glanced out the window. Anywhere but in those eyes. Silence lingered between us.

Finally, I said, "Maybe you're right. Because you're a total stranger to me."

She didn't contradict me.

"We can't figure this out ourselves. We need help." I rolled my lips. My next suggestion was a desperate gambit. "Couples counseling. An hour a week. Will you think about it?"

She snorted. "You can't seriously think that would help. You just want to prove that I'm crazy so that you don't have to feel guilty about leaving me."

Her words were like a slap in the face. "Is that what you really believe? That I'm waiting to leave you? I didn't have to stay by your hospital bed. I didn't have to stick around while you ignored me, while you chose Caleb, Alex—anyone but me. I could have left if I'd wanted to, long before now."

"No, you couldn't." Her voice was low. "I saved Lukas, and you saved me. You like being a hero. Would you still be a hero if you left your poor wife while she was still recovering from the trauma of being kidnapped and almost killed?"

I was about to get up when she grabbed my arm and asked, "Think about it. Why are you still here with me?"

I didn't have a single answer. And that told me way too much.

I went to the closet and grabbed my suitcase. I threw in some clothes. I grabbed what I needed from the bathroom.

"You're leaving me." It was a statement, not a question. Kai almost sounded relieved.

"I can't stay with you if you're hurting other people."

She got up and went to the closet. She emerged with two pairs of my shoes.

"What are you doing?"

"Helping you." She actually smiled.

CHAPTER 25

Kai

"I guess I should have seen this coming," I murmured.

I lay in my bed, staring up at the ceiling and absently stroking the feathers on Herbie's back. The turkey cluck-purred at me in agreement and shuffled closer. Caleb lay next to me. He bent his head closer until it touched mine. The way we used to when we were kids and needed the reassurance of each other.

"I should have known that Mickey would tell Oliver."

"Why did you do it?" Genuine curiosity wound through his words. And maybe a little worry.

"The darkness..." How could I explain it? "I felt like I could use it, like I could control it." I'd felt almost the same while I was helping Oliver pack. I'd had the sense that I was taking charge of my fate.

"You really could have hurt her. You could have hurt everyone there."

"I know." My throat dried up. The initial euphoria had passed. "But I didn't. Don't you see? I have control that I didn't have before."

"Are you going to do this again?"

He had been inside my shield. He understood what I was holding back.

"I might." I added, "But I can control it now."

Caleb was silent for a long time.

"You don't want me to?"

"I'm worried about what you might do to other people. But I'm also worried about what doing that will do to you."

I rolled over and stared into his eyes. "It's not like last time."

Caleb didn't disagree. "I trust you."

I rolled onto my back again.

Eventually, I fell asleep.

I didn't dream.

When I walked downstairs to the smell of bacon, I knew what was coming next.

My parents wanted to talk. I made my way to the kitchen. The table was covered in plates of bacon, French toast, eggs, cinnamon rolls, hash browns, and fruit.

It was going to be a serious talk. Probably an intervention.

I slid into a chair and heaped my plate with French toast and bacon. I reached for the maple syrup, planning to enjoy this meal while I could.

Mom sat down next to me. "Kai, you can't lose Oliver."

"It was his choice to leave." I bit into a piece of bacon. It was real bacon, not tofu. Not even turkey.

"You've been keeping him at a distance for weeks. Even a saint would start to lose hope," Dad said.

I choked. "A saint?" Why was it so easy for them to always cast me as the bad guy? "So he gets into bar fights over Mickey and he's still up for sainthood?"

"No one is perfect, Kai. We gave him a talking to about that," Dad said.

Mom rushed to add, "He did save you—"

"You're talking about when he saved me from Nathan?"

Both my parents looked confused.

Mom answered. "Yes, of course…"

"Do you know why Nathan kidnapped me?"

Neither of them responded.

"Do you know why Nathan almost killed me?"

They shared one of those looks where they said so much without saying a word.

"Because I'm Oliver's wife. Because of secrets Oliver kept from me. Because—" I stopped. I didn't owe my parents any explanation.

"Because what?" Mom pushed.

I wasn't going to tell them about Christian's death, so I went with the truth that had been splashed across all the papers. "Nathan thought that Oliver was Lukas's father."

"That's ridiculous," Dad said.

"Is it?" Bitterness curdled my words. "Oliver hooked up with Mickey while I was institutionalized. While *you* had me institutionalized."

"No." Mom gripped her coffee cup.

"It was a horrible time for him. Men do stupid things when they are dealing with loss," Dad muttered into his coffee.

I couldn't believe what I was hearing. From my own father. But then again, they'd never really loved me. Not as much as they loved Caleb.

"We shouldn't fly out tomorrow," Mom said to Dad. "We can't leave her here like this."

I closed my eyes and took a deep breath. I tried to remind myself that they wanted to help, even if they didn't know how.

"This time, you should let me handle things." Caleb's voice boomed from the doorway.

"You don't understand. Your sister…" Dad struggled to find the right words.

"Is dangerous?" I finished his sentence for him.

"You can be," my father acknowledged.

"You still don't get it." Caleb's voice was like acid. "You're still trying to protect me from Kai."

Neither of my parents could look at Caleb. They couldn't look at me, either.

"What you don't understand—what you won't understand—is that we need each other more than we need you," Caleb said.

Mom's lips thinned to silvery lines. "You can't make us leave."

"Are you sure?" Something in the way Caleb stood reminded me of a mercenary.

Mom looked to Dad, as if she expected him to do something.

He didn't say anything for a bit. Just sat there staring at the table. It was a long while before Dad asked, "If we leave now, will you give us another chance?"

Caleb was silent.

"Son?" Dad asked.

"Maybe we'll be there for Easter in San Diego," Caleb said.

While my parents and Naomi drove to the airport, Alex was driving Lukas and me to the hospital to see Nathan.

The two-hour ride went faster than I expected. Soon, we stood in the hallway near Nathan's room.

Alex knelt down in front of Lukas. "Are you sure you want to do this, buddy?"

Lukas clutched my hand and nodded.

I'd already explained to the police officer on guard that Lukas was family. I was his chaperone.

Alex gave Lukas one last squeeze. "I'll be right out here if you need me." His gaze shifted to me. "If either of you need me."

I tried to look more confident than I felt. Then I opened the door, and Lukas and I stepped inside.

The room was silent except for the steady beeps indicating that Nathan was still alive. His skin was paler than last time as if a little more of his life had slipped away.

"Where's his beard?" Lukas whispered.

"They shaved it off."

"He doesn't look as scary."

"There's no reason to be afraid of him now. He's in a deep, deep sleep. Your mom explained that to you, right?"

Lukas nodded. "Can I talk to him?"

"I'm not sure how much he can hear and understand."

Lukas looked up at me with those big green eyes. "No. I mean inside his head?"

This was what Lukas had come here for, but I was suddenly afraid for him. "Are you sure? We have to get close to him to do it. We have to touch him."

Lukas's face scrunched up in concentration. Then he nodded. "I'm safe with you."

I hoped that he was right.

I held tight to Lukas's hand and touched Nathan's arm. I opened my shield.

Suddenly, I was sitting on a wooden bench. Lukas was next to me. A white and red gingham tablecloth covered the picnic table in front of us.

Nathan sat across the table from Lukas and me. With his baby-blue polo shirt and sad eyes, he looked like a weekend dad.

The biggest sundae I've ever seen sat between us. A dozen scoops of vanilla and chocolate ice cream were piled high on a huge silver bowl and covered in bananas, nuts, sprinkles, whipped cream, and maraschino cherries. Three long silver spoons waited beside the sundae.

Lukas was the first to speak. "Can we eat it?"

A smile flitted across Nathan's face. "Of course."

"Is it okay, Aunt Kai?"

I looked into Nathan's eyes. Sane. Calm. I picked up a spoon, took a heaping scoop of ice cream, and ate it. "Of course."

Lukas picked up a spoon, but before he took a bite, he asked, "Why did you hurt us?"

Nathan rubbed his hand over his forehead. "I was sick. I'm sorry for what I did to you and to Kai."

Lukas seemed satisfied with this answer. At least enough to take a bite of ice cream.

Nathan picked up the third spoon, and we all concentrated on the sundae.

Lukas stuck the spoon into the ice cream and moved it around. "What's going to happen to you?"

Nathan shrugged. "I don't know."

Lukas fidgeted. He didn't like that answer.

"Whatever happens, you will never hurt Lukas again," I said.

"Never." Nathan's voice was thick with emotion. "That I can tell you for sure."

Lukas returned his attention to the sundae. It was a few more bites before he asked, "Will I see you, when you get better?"

"Only if you want to." Nathan's voice held a note of hope.

I noticed clouds on the horizon. "There's a storm coming."

Nathan glanced up at the sky and frowned. "It's time for you to go."

"Why?" I asked.

"You don't want to be here when the storm hits."

The wind kicked up, whipping my hair around my face.

"Get Lukas out of here," Nathan yelled.

I scooped Lukas up in my arms and prepared to run. Everything around us faded away. A moment later, Lukas and I were back in the hospital room.

CHAPTER 26

Oliver

"I hate soft mattresses," I said.

After all the nights of barely sleeping because of Kai's nightmares, I'd thought that getting a solid night's sleep would be a perk of staying in Aunt Ines's guest room. I was wrong.

The chairs in the breakroom at Super One Foods didn't help either. All plastic with no lumbar support. I stretched my arms over my head and a couple vertebrae cracked into place.

"I can't believe Kai's still at your house and you're with Aunt Ines," Mickey said.

"It was my choice to leave."

"I hope it wasn't because of me."

"What Kai did to you on Christmas—lashing out like that. She could have really hurt you."

"It," Mickey dropped her voice, "reminded me a little of Nathan."

I had the same awful feeling.

Mickey changed the subject. "I bet Aunt Ines loves having you around."

"She loves packing my lunch." Today's was a wiener schnitzel sandwich and a slice of gugelhupf, a Bundt cake that included almonds and cherry brandy and a drizzle of white icing.

Mickey tapped the back of her front teeth with her fingernail. She used to do that in high school when she had something to say.

"What's on your mind?" I asked.

"I don't know how to do this." She looked down at her sandwich.

"Do what?"

Her voice was barely a whisper. "Raise a special kid. I don't want to do the wrong thing with Lukas."

"You're a terrific mom. He loves you. Just keep loving him." Even as I said those words, I thought about Kai's parents. They loved her, but they kept hurting her.

"But what if it's not enough? What if he turns out like Nathan?"

Kai was so much better equipped to answer these questions than I was. "Kai's been a mess lately, and I can understand if you don't want to talk to her, but Aunt Ines can pass along any questions you have. Kai would do anything to help Lukas."

She looked off to the side like she was considering my offer. Then she gave me a serene smile. "Alex has been so supportive. I bet Kai would talk to him."

I looked at Mickey to see if she was actually trying to torture me. She just sipped her soda.

I tried to steer her away from Alex. "You know Aunt Ines was also friends with Nathan's aunt Sabine. She knew about Sabine's powers. She's a great person to talk to about the woo-woo stuff."

"I will then." She touched my arm. "Thanks for all your support. I couldn't get through this without you."

CHAPTER 27

Kai

I could think of one person who could help me understand the connection between Nathan and me. Unfortunately, that person was dead.

Caleb had continued to join me during my dream visits to Grandma Guhn's pond. Together, we'd searched and searched, but we hadn't found a way through to the In Between. Tonight, Caleb decided not to join me. He wanted to see if I could make it through on my own. So did I.

As soon as I fell asleep, I stood on the rock at the edge of the pond. The water sparkled at me, inviting me to try one more time. I jumped in and swam deeper and deeper. I scanned the bottom of the pond for the telltale sparkle that marked the entry to the In Between. I was about to go back to the surface for a breath, when something caught my eye, a faint glint. I swam closer and dug through the rocks. My lungs began to burn. I needed air.

But I couldn't stop now. This might be my only chance. Frantically, I yanked at the rocks. Suddenly, a ray of light burst through the silt.

White light. The water grew warmer and warmer. The light encircled me, heating me to the bone. It was almost painful. My lungs screamed for air. I had to breathe, but I couldn't. I was engulfed in brightness and lost consciousness.

I don't know how long I was out for, but I woke up floating on my back in a giant lake. The shore looked to be miles away. The sky above was an afternoon blue. Was this the In Between? I looked around for a sign of Grandma Guhn.

I saw a boat floating in the distance. I waved at it. As it came toward me, I realized it was a gondola.

I heard the concern in her voice before I saw Grandma Guhn's face. "Sweet Pea, what are you doing back here?"

She leaned over and her auburn braid trailed in the water. She reached for me and I grasped her hand. She tugged me out of the water like I was weightless. The moment I got into the boat, my clothes were dry.

"Caleb and I have been trying to get here for weeks, but we couldn't find our way," I said.

She squeezed my hand. "So you came alone?"

"We needed to figure out if I could still get through." I feared the problem was me—that I was too broken to ever see Grandma Guhn again. Relief swept over me. A feeling of rightness settled in my belly.

"The way will not be open to him until he is ready."

"But he can get here?"

"He'll need your help, of course. But he won't find the entrance if there is any fear in his heart."

"Why?"

"The way through is not easy. Fear makes it impossible to find."

"What's he afraid of?" I asked.

She gave me that patient smile that I missed so much. "Sweet Pea, you're the mind reader, not me."

I had been so caught up in my own need to see Grandma Guhn that I never sensed Caleb's fear.

"Caleb will find his way when he is ready to see us." She tilted her head. "Everyone does things in their own time. Be patient."

I nodded.

"I'm not just talking about Caleb. You've been having trouble with your emotions again. It's not like that time with Kadin. I know you think it is, but this is different."

"What is it?"

"I'm not sure. I need to take a closer look at your aura." She closed her eyes and gently ran her hands over the air that was a few inches from my body. She blanched. "What did you do?"

"Nothing. Why?"

"Your energy. Your soul. It's off." She frowned.

I confessed, "I think I came back wrong. Nothing's been right after the cave. I haven't been me."

"Your aura isn't just yours anymore. You pulled someone into you." Her lips bunched with concern. She touched my third eye. Her eyelids fluttered and she breathed, "Nathan."

"He's still in a coma."

She opened her eyes. I saw the worry in them. "When he almost died, you were together. You pulled a piece of his soul into you."

"How?" I'd never done anything like that before. If I'd known I could, I would have taken a piece of Grandma Guhn's, so she wouldn't have died. I wouldn't have been able to stop myself.

"Your powers. The way they interacted must have created a strange connection."

"I figured something of me stayed behind. That a part of me died. But there have been signs that I took something from him." I shivered, despite the warmth of the day. "Or had some of him forced on me."

"He's rippling through you."

"Can you fix this?" I whispered.

"I'm not sure I can untangle your souls without damaging both of you. This is something you and Nathan did. I think you might be the only ones who can undo it."

"Is that why I don't hate him?" I had been trying to understand my lack of anger toward him.

She nodded.

I hesitated. "So my fights with Mom and Dad? Me pushing Oliver away? My lashing out at Mickey? Was all that caused by Nathan?"

"It's impossible to know how much is him and what is truly you. But I don't think he could force you to do anything you truly didn't want to do."

I bit my lip. "So the darkness in me..."

"Is his, yes, but it's also yours."

"But he said it was all mine."

"He may not be able to recognize it as his own anymore."

There was so much more I needed to understand. "He says he's in the Neitherlands. Is that where people in comas go?"

She nodded. "Yes, it's a pocket between the living world and the In Between."

"So that's where I went in my coma? I don't remember it."

"Most people don't."

"How long can he stay there?"

"It depends on the strength of his mind. He has to maintain that space. The longer he's there, the more energy it takes to keep it going."

That must have been what he meant about drawing the place—it was how he maintained the Neitherlands. Her words made me flash back to the storms there and Nathan's terror.

"But he can come back from there? I mean, he can return to the world."

Her lips thinned. "It depends on how strong he is."

"What if he doesn't? What if he dies?" My voice rose. "What happens to me?"

"I'm not sure, Sweet Pea. It might mean that you'll always have a piece of him inside you."

I woke up with one thought in my head: Go see Nathan. Caleb and I set out as soon as we could. On the way to the hospital in Wausau, I explained what I had learned from Grandma Guhn.

When I finished, he said, "It kind of makes sense."

"Really? You think me having a piece of someone else's soul inside mine makes sense?"

"It's a relief, actually. Because now I know that you alone aren't choosing to do everything you do."

"And that makes you feel better?" I asked incredulously.

"It does when you start lashing out at people and playing mental warfare."

"I guess," I muttered.

I let the conversation peter out as I tried to figure out how to tell him what Grandma Guhn said about his fears keeping him out of the In Between. I wasn't sure this was the best time or place for that conversation.

Luckily, Caleb made the choice for me. "What else did Grandma Guhn say?"

I told him everything.

His eyes tightened and his fingers gripped the steering wheel until his knuckles turned white.

It made me nervous, so I babbled, "I mean it's freaky that I can go to the In Between. I've never brought anyone there. It's completely normal to be afraid of it."

Caleb shook his head. "That's not it."

"What is it then?"

He shrugged.

"Are you scared to see Grandma and Grandpa Guhn?"

Images flitted through his mind. I didn't have my shield completely up, so I saw it all. Grandma Guhn lying in the hospital bed, her body ravaged by cancer. She wasn't just pale, she was sunken and shadowed.

"She's not like that anymore, I promise."

He nodded. It wasn't just Grandma Guhn, though. Another memory rose up. Far worse to behold. Caleb was only twelve when we were in a terrible car accident. He had been trapped for hours with Grandpa Guhn and me.

He thought we were both gone, empty bodies that would never come back to life. Grandpa's sightless eyes stared straight ahead. Caleb reached for his arm. It was lifeless. No pulse. Nothing. Gone.

Caleb couldn't reach me in the back seat. My eyes were closed. And that was the hope he clung to: They might open again.

"I'm sorry that's your last memory of him."

"I couldn't do anything to help him. He was gone." His voice broke. "I couldn't reach you in the back seat. I thought you were dead, too."

His pain swirled in my mouth, tasting of crème brûlée. Agonizingly sweet and tender once you got past the thin, protective layer.

I touched his arm. "I'm still here. And I'm not going anywhere."

"If I'd lost both of you in that moment..."

One car accident changed everything. Our grandfather died. We never knew if it was losing him or being that close to our own deaths that activated our powers. Either way, after the accident, we would never be the same again.

My heart thumped in my ears as I approached Nathan's room. The cop frowned at me. I was pushing the limits of his tolerance. I made my way toward him, trying to look apologetic.

He glanced around. "I can't keep bending the rules, even for you."

"This is the last time." I hoped I wasn't lying.

He stood aside to let me pass.

As soon as I pressed my hand to Nathan's arm, I was inside his mind. We sat on a blanket in a grassy meadow. He wore a pale blue-and-white-striped seersucker suit and a straw hat. I was in a gauzy pale green dress that swished and swirled around my feet. It was just like the picnic we shared in his mind when he had me trapped in the cave.

"Why are we back here?" I asked.

"This is where it all began. You felt everything I felt. You wanted to help me."

In that moment, I had wanted to die to punish Oliver. It was the only way to help Nathan and I wanted desperately to help Nathan.

"My grandmother says I have some of you inside my mind. That's why I smell and taste emotions. That's why I can draw now—and why I draw scenes from your memories. That's why I have all this darkness inside me. Some of it is my own, but not all of it."

He stared at the horizon. "It makes sense. I have some calm in me. I can think more clearly now. Maybe that's because of you."

"So, how do you think we 'untwine' ourselves?"

"I don't know. I don't know how I or we did it, so I don't know how to undo it." He scratched the corner of his face where his ear and cheekbone met. "I remember how you wanted to save me and I wanted to save you. Maybe that's why we got tangled up in each other."

"Why didn't you tell me before?"

"I didn't know. I'm just trying to work it all out."

I could barely handle my own darkness, how would I manage his? "What controls your darkness?"

"Revenge. That's the only think that forces it back."

I closed my eyes. Moments flitted through my mind. Pushing my father until he lost control of his telekinesis. Attacking Mickey at Christmas. Fighting with Oliver. Those were acts of revenge. Now I understood why every aggressive outburst felt justified. Why upsetting others helped me feel more in control.

The horror of who I'd become hit me. "I'm a ticking time bomb. I've been lashing out. I've been fighting with everyone. I've been destroying relationships."

He closed his eyes. "And you only have a little of what was inside me."

But I had my own darkness, too. "How do you live with this inside you?"

"You've seen what I did."

I'd have to find another way.

CHAPTER 28

Oliver

I was in Aunt Ines's kitchen, sitting at her 1950s-style chrome and vinyl table. The metal chairs had iridescent yellow sparkly cushions. Her fridge was turquoise. The entire kitchen was done in shades of yellow and turquoise. The white curtains had bright yellow daffodils printed on them. Pure Aunt Ines.

She scooped gefüllte paprika onto my plate. "How's work?"

"Fine. Thanks." I loved her stuffed peppers. "This is a treat."

"They're easy to make. I could teach Kai."

I'd been gone for four days. Kai hadn't called or texted once. "No point in that," I mumbled.

Aunt Ines's lips turned down and her chin tightened like an angry turtle. She had no idea how to make this better for me, so she tried to distract me by launching into a story about her book club. Then she went on about the fundraiser she was working on with Mrs. K for the Butternut Area Historical Museum. I didn't have much to contribute, but I enjoyed listening to her talk. The good food and her company were almost enough to take my mind off the wreck of my marriage.

After we finished dessert, I confessed, "I don't think Kai and I are going to make it."

"If I had the whole story, I could help." Before I could say anything, she wagged her finger at me. "And don't go trying to sell me what you told everyone else. There's more that you haven't told me. I feel it in my bones, Oliver Herwig Richter."

I winced at the use of my middle name.

The truth came in a jumble of facts and memories. I was excavating emotions I'd kept under control for so long that I'd let myself forget how much it all hurt.

Every time I told the story of what Schneider had done to Christian, I felt as powerless as I did back then. I was twelve all over again and it was the night Christian disappeared. Then I was sixteen, finding out how Dad had helped Schneider cover up the crime. I felt the pain, the shock, and the betrayal as deeply as I had the first time.

After I left for college, I never came back. As long as I stayed away, I could pretend I wasn't a part of their lie. I didn't let myself think about it. I boxed it up and shoved it into the closet of my memories.

She pressed her palms to the sides of her face as if she had to hold it all together. "Oh, Oliver." Her eyes filled with tears. "He didn't."

I was afraid she'd defend my father or demand proof I didn't have. I needed Aunt Ines on my side. She was my only living relative.

"He did. It's the truth."

She looked dazed. "I can't believe my brother would do that."

"I think he saw himself in Schneider." At least, that's how I tried to rationalize it. I never understood how my Dad could do it. Break the law he swore to uphold. Tarnish a kid's memory to save a guy like Schneider.

"Reinhard and Sophie loved Schneider and Heidi. Schneider was there when Reinhard lost your mother. Heidi came and took you to play with her daughter. They were like family to us."

Heidi had been my mother's best friend. I hadn't thought of her in so long. Her daughter, April, was only five when she died in that house fire. I barely remembered her. That had to be why my father felt like he had to protect Schneider. The man had been through so much, and my dad would do anything for family.

"This is what destroyed your relationship with your father? It's why you never came to visit?"

I nodded.

She patted my hand. "I'm so sorry you had to keep this secret for him."

"I did it for you and Grandpa, too. I never wanted to harm your memory of Dad." My throat tightened, making it hard to get the words out.

Her eyes teared up. "You always cared too much about others." She hugged me. "I understand now why you had to leave. Why you couldn't come back."

A warm feeling loosened the muscles in my chest. I wasn't going to lose Aunt Ines, too. I let the moment linger.

She settled back into her chair. "Is that everything?"

I hesitated.

"Best to get it all out now, Oliver."

I told her that I had made out with Mickey while Kai was institutionalized. I told her how Nathan threatened Kai because of me. Everything that happened to Kai in that cave had been my fault.

"So the rumors about you and Mickey are true?"

"Sort of."

I explained about the bar fight and what Kai did on Christmas Day. When I was done, I had a dull ache in the base of my skull. I rubbed the back of my neck, but it didn't help. "Mickey and I are friends. I haven't done more than kiss her since we came back here."

Aunt Ines shook her head. "Please tell me that's not what you said to Kai."

"No."

"Do you want Kai back?"

I wanted the Kai I knew and loved back, not the twisted, cruel version of her that Kai had become. "Not if she's like this."

"But maybe you can help her."

"She won't even let me try!"

"Of course she won't, not as long as you're seeing Mickey. You've got to cut that out."

"I work with her."

"Then it's time you get a new job."

I laughed. "Where?" Butternut was a small town. Everyone had to eke out a living here. That's why so many people ended up moving away.

"I'll put the word out around town." She sounded confident.

"No manual labor."

"I think it's time you get back to what you're good at." She winked at me.

CHAPTER 29

Kai

When I didn't think about everything that was going on and just stayed in the moment, it was almost peaceful at the farmhouse. Herbie napped beside me on the couch. Caleb built up the fire until it blazed in front of us. Then he sat next to me with his feet resting on the coffee table. I'd given him those pink and blue argyle socks a couple years ago for his birthday.

"I don't like people. They don't have many redeeming qualities," he murmured.

"I take it your meeting didn't go well."

He frowned. "I missed it."

"You never miss meetings." Caleb had been scheduling his life since elementary school. The only difference was that now he used an iPhone instead of a Trapper Keeper.

"Something went haywire with my calendar." He sipped his hot chocolate. "It's the second investor call I missed. Someone moved it and, somehow, I wasn't notified."

"That's unusual."

"I should have gotten an email. It should have been automatic." He rubbed his hand over his eyes. "I'm not sure what's going on, but I'll get to the bottom of it."

My brother always sounded confident, but worry lines lingered around his eyes.

"I wish I could eavesdrop on their thoughts for you."

"Who?"

"The people you work with."

"You'd have to go to London or New York."

I sat up. "Then take me to New York."

He smiled and patted my knee. "Thanks, but I've got it handled. I'll stop in the New York office and ruffle the right feathers on my way back home."

I bit my lip. "When do you leave?"

"When things are sorted out here."

"So, never?"

He laughed. "I know you have a plan."

"How?"

"Since we saw Nathan last, you've had that *What do I do next?* look in your eyes and now you have that *I've got to do something* face."

He was right. I was done running from myself. I put my hot chocolate on the coffee table. "I don't want to become like Nathan. I don't want to lose control like that."

"So, what are you going to do?"

"I want to face the darkness and the shadows. But that means letting out everything that I've walled away inside myself."

"Kai..."

"The emotions inside me aren't just my own worst feelings. Some of them are Nathan's. I don't know what will happen," I admitted. "And I won't risk hurting you. If I'm going to do this, I need you to leave and take Herbie with you. I have to know that you're outside my telepathic range."

"What if something goes wrong? What if you can't handle it?"

"Then the only person who gets hurt is me. I couldn't live with myself if I took you down with me."

"You wouldn't."

The words scraped against my throat. "I might."

"I hate this plan," Caleb said.

"I know, but it's the only thing I can do."

The next morning, I bundled up and walked out to the backyard because I didn't want to damage the house. Under extreme stress, like at the Butternut Feed Store, my emotions had physical manifestations. My nose burned from the cold air. I pulled my hood up around my head and tied it shut to keep the wind out. I folded down the fur trim to protect my face.

I laid a tarp and then a sleeping bag on the snowy ground. I sat on it with my legs bent under me. There was only one way I could find out what was inside me. I had to go inside myself and face everything. I had to drop all barriers and let the shadows in and the darkness out. I was scared, but it felt like the first step to learning how to control my emotions again.

I took a deep breath in for a count of four, held it for a count of seven, and released it for a count of eight. I did it over and over again until I felt calm and centered. Then I visualized my shield. The walls were bulletproof glass. One by one, I made them disappear. I stood exposed on a pulsating red floor. My inner shield was all I had left to dismantle. It was the one I'd erected to protect me from what happened in the cave, and the aftermath.

Deep in meditation, I visualized my mental landscape—barren, cracked earth with mountains edging the horizon. In the distance, I saw the shadows. Masses of them. They moved so stealthily. I almost didn't realize they were approaching me until they were everywhere, all around me, swooping in. I ducked, but they weren't trying to get to me. They slid along the floor of my shield, as if they were desperate to find a way in. They wanted to get at what I had been trying so hard to keep contained.

They wanted all that darkness? They could have it. The floor liquefied. The shadows dove in and disappeared. I followed them, swept into a churning sea of emotions. Tidal waves of feelings pulled me under.

What I felt in the cave with Nathan came for me. Desperation— Nathan's and mine. They blended together. Violent attempts to save ourselves. We hurt and we lashed out. We were righteous and insane.

Then my mind surfaced in a memory. I was reliving the moment when Oliver shot Nathan. I was so tangled up in Nathan's mind that it was as if Oliver had shot me. The bullet burrowed into my shoulder. Pain radiated across my chest. Throbbing, burning, aching. All at once. Sharp, then dull. Pain, so much pain. I'd never felt anything like it. Then the cold stole over me, creeping up from my extremities and snuffing out all the warmth in its wake. I knew that this was the chill of death.

My body fought it. My teeth chattered and my muscles trembled. But my mind welcomed an end to all this suffering. It wanted a release from all this pain.

The man who should have protected me had killed me. My husband. His last betrayal. But it felt right somehow, that the man who had saved me so many times would be the man to take my life.

Nathan grabbed my hand. We were dying together, all twisted up in each other's minds. Then, as he slid into death, he pushed me away. Nathan saved me.

All the things I'd buried inside me, I was facing them now. The worst of what had happened in the cave, and everything that had come after. My disappointment in Oliver. My anger at my parents. My jealousy over Mickey. My desire for Alex. My strange connection with Nathan.

Before I could make sense of any of it, I sank further into my past. The worst moments had to be relived. I felt my grandparents' deaths all over again.

I heard a howl, like a wounded animal begging to be put down. It was coming from me.

The sun was high overhead when I emerged from the darkness. Early afternoon. Hours had passed. I tried to stand, but my legs were asleep. The pins and needles helped bring me back to the present and the outside world.

I understood what had happened to me. At least, I thought I did. Nathan and I had become intertwined because neither one of us was strong enough to survive alone. How we did it remained a mystery, but I knew why we did it: survival.

Now, the shadows no longer hovered around the periphery of my shield. They weren't gone; they were part of me, part of the darkness that I still carried. I didn't know what that meant for me. But the floor of my shield was solid wood again. It didn't pulsate or feel sticky. It felt stable. *I* felt stable—for now, anyways. I didn't know what came next, but I felt a little more confident that, whatever it might be, I could handle it.

I called Caleb. He picked up on the first ring.

"Are you okay?" He said it so fast the words blurred together.

"I think so."

"Can I come back?"

"Yeah." My voice was raspy, like I hadn't spoken in days. I sketched out what had happened while he drove back to me.

"I think this will take some time to work through," he said.

My laugh fled into the trees. "You think."

"I know, I know." He was laughing, too, now.

"Can you keep talking to me until you get here?" I didn't want to be alone.

"Absolutely."

Grains of gold and silver glittered in the black and tan sand. The sky was a bright blue with gauzy clouds. The ocean roared in my ears. I was dreaming of Torrey Pines Beach. This was one of my favorite places in the world, but it wasn't where I needed to be. I needed to be in the In Between. I tried to visualize Grandma Guhn's yard. I concentrated on summoning the pond.

And there it was.

I slid into the water and dove to the bottom. I found the passageway without any trouble at all.

This time, I didn't emerge in the lake, but on its shore. Grandma Guhn stood next to me.

"What's going on?" she asked.

"Nathan doesn't know how to undo what we did, and neither do I. I don't know what I'm doing, but I feel like I need to do something." I rocked on my heels, unable to stand still. "I tried embracing my emotions and a swarm of shadows invaded my mind. I don't know if I made things better or worse."

Grandma Guhn hugged me. "Sweet Pea, I wish I could do more for you." She took my hand and led me along the shore.

Movement helped me get my thoughts together. "What are those shadows? What will they do to me?"

"When someone dies, the shadows come for your pain."

"Who died?"

She looked straight into my eyes. "You did."

"No, Nathan pushed me out of his mind in time."

"I'm not talking about that. You've said it yourself. Pieces of you died. Everything you found out in the cave, it destroyed parts of you. They are gone."

I gripped her arms. My voice sounded hysterical even to me. "But I'm still alive."

"Not the way you used to be." The sadness in her voice made my heart hurt. "I've been thinking about it since your last visit. Meditating on it. I think your experience in the cave left a hole in your soul. A space Nathan could occupy."

It made a terrible sort of sense. The kind I didn't want to be true.

I fell into her arms. She held me and stroked my hair, like I was a little girl again. I wanted to stay that way forever. But I didn't know how much time we had before I woke up. I had more questions to ask.

"This darkness, do you think being in Butternut makes Nathan's presence stronger in me?"

"It's his hometown. There are so many triggers for him there." She paused, considering. "I suppose it's possible that being there makes it more likely for his darkness to emerge."

"So I could hurt Mickey?"

"You might. But only if some part of you wanted to. Remember he can't take control of you."

Hurting Mickey would hurt Lukas, and I didn't want to do that. I just didn't trust myself not to. "If I went away..."

"Then the part of him that's in you might be weaker."

The next morning, I woke up to the scent of chocolate chip pancakes and caramel sauce. As I neared the kitchen, I heard the slurp of whipped cream being sprayed from a can. Caleb and I had invented this breakfast back when he was ten and I was eight. I slid into my seat at the kitchen table and devoured what was on my plate. It tasted like happy memories.

When I was on my second stack and had half a cup of coffee in me, I told him about my dream. He listened without interrupting. I loved that about my brother.

I explained about the shadows and the darkness. Then I licked the last of the caramel sauce from my fork. "So you see why I can't stay here anymore."

"The house or Butternut?" Caleb asked.

"Both."

"What about Oliver?"

"I can't tell him about Nathan."

"Why?"

"What if he thinks I'm losing it? What if he tries to get me committed for my own good like Mom did? I can't risk being locked away. I won't let anyone take control of me again. Ever."

"Are you going to San Diego?"

"I can't turn to Mom and Dad."

"Do you want to go stay at Grandma Guhn's house?"

Caleb had inherited it when she died. "I want to go to New York with you."

"Do you think that's a good idea?"

"It's better than being here."

He didn't look convinced.

I leaned forward. "I need to go back there. I need to remember who I used to be before everything happened here. New York is my turf." I added, "I need to face everything I left behind there. And besides, I want to help you with whatever is going on at work."

"Are you sure?"

He didn't say *don't come*. And that's how I knew he needed me. "Positive."

"When are you going to talk to Oliver about it?"

"Tonight."

"When do you want to fly out?"

"Tomorrow."

CHAPTER 30

Oliver

Not even the lime green and grape juice purple of Aunt Ines's living room could brighten my mood. I sunk into her overstuffed paisley sofa and rested my feet on the purple ottoman shaped like a pig.

Every tabletop and shelf was cluttered with mementos. Family photos, spoon rings, souvenir thimbles, and cows. Lots of cows. Glass cows, porcelain cows, ceramic cows, plastic cows. Cows were her latest weakness.

I turned on the TV.

Aunt Ines fluttered in wearing a flamingo-print dress with a bright green sweater. "Have you seen my book?"

"Which one?"

She lifted the pillows off the couch to check behind them. "The cooking school mystery with the pies on the cover."

I looked around the room. "I don't think it's in here."

"I need it for my book club tonight."

"Oh." I had hoped we'd have an Oliver and Aunt Ines night. I'd grown to rely on her company to distract me from the fact that Kai still hadn't called.

My aunt's shoes clacked on the hardwood floor as she made a loop around the room. "Found it!" She pulled it from between the cushions of the lime green chair in the corner, slid it in her purse, and went to the front closet to get her coat.

Before she put her coat on, she popped back into the living room. "I meant to tell you, Mr. Kohler wants you to stop by the Bank of Butternut tomorrow to talk about a job. Something to do with anti-money laundering. That's what you used to do, right?"

"It was part of my audit work. How did you score that?" Mrs. Kohler made it clear I'd never get a job inside her husband's bank when I'd first arrived back in town.

"You're a local hero. And I happen to have the ear of several ladies in town who are close to Mrs. Kohler."

I chuckled. "You used her position in town against her?"

"A few friends reminded her that she shouldn't pass up the opportunity to reward a hero. That's all."

"Thanks." I stood up and hugged her. "I really appreciate your help."

She patted my cheek. "Of course. Now you have no reason at all to see Mickey."

I knew I was supposed to stay away from Mickey, but I had to tell her that I wasn't working at Super One Foods anymore. I owed her that. When I called, she said she'd love to stop by. I hadn't actually invited her over, but she was off the phone before I could tell her not to come.

Then she was on the front porch. With Lukas. There was no way I could say what I needed to say with him around, but I couldn't just send them away, either. So I invited them in for tea.

We headed back to the kitchen.

Mickey looked around. "Ines definitely put her stamp on the place."

"You mean the daffodil print curtains?" I asked.

"I meant that." She pointed to the ceiling. "How did she get yellow and turquoise glitter embedded in the white paint?"

I had the same question when I noticed it. I couldn't help smiling. "She's Aunt Ines."

Mickey laughed. She had a beautiful laugh that made you want to join in.

"I'm hungry," Lukas announced.

"You wouldn't be if you'd finished your dinner," Mickey chided.

"I wasn't hungry then." He gave me the *I'm just a little kid* face.

I fixed him a small plate of leftover wiener schnitzel and potato salad. Between mouthfuls, Lukas asked, "Where's Aunt Kai?"

Mickey flipped her dark hair over her shoulder. "She's at her house."

"Why isn't Uncle Oliver there?" Lukas asked.

"She wanted some time with her brother." Lukas didn't need to know the truth.

"Mommy and Uncle Alex like to hang out, too."

"Family is important." Not just blood ties, but the people you love and trust by choice, like the Fuchses. God, how was I going to do this? How was I going to push Mickey out of my life?

Mickey seemed to sense my need for a serious conversation. "Maybe Lukas can have dessert in the living room?" After I nodded, she asked him, "Would you like to watch some cartoons, sweetie?"

"Okay," he said.

I put three chocolate chip cookies on a plate and poured him half a cup of milk. Then we headed to Aunt Ines's living room. He sat on the floor, using the coffee table as a table. She flipped to a show he liked.

When we got back to the kitchen, Mickey touched my arm. "If you need to talk about Kai, I'm here for you."

Her offer just made this harder. "Thanks. But after what happened with you and Kai at Christmas, I wouldn't put you in that position."

"I don't mind."

"But I do." I tried to tell myself that, given Kai's current state, it was better for Mickey if we didn't see each other.

Mickey stepped back. "Well, I know you'll do your best to work things out."

But I wasn't ready to say goodbye to Mickey. Not yet. I stalled and asked, "How are things going with Lukas?"

"Ines told my dad about how Nathan's aunt Sabine had powers. Dad grew up with her. He saw what a good person she was. That helped him. I'm going to try to talk to the Hoffmanns, for Lukas's sake. Hopefully, they can shed more light on the powers in their family. I have to smooth things over for my son. If they can help, they need to be in his life."

She'd always kept her former in-laws at a distance. It wouldn't be easy to have them back in her life, but she would do it for Lukas. "That's why you're such an awesome mom."

Mickey's smile made my stomach flutter. "And someday you are going to make an awesome dad."

I wasn't sure I'd ever get to have kids. Not anymore. "I hope so."

"I know so."

My tongue felt like sandpaper rubbing against the roof of my mouth. I sipped my tea. It was a temporary relief. How was I going to tell her we couldn't be friends anymore?

She must have seen it in my face. "What is it, Oliver?"

I had to just say it. "If my marriage is going to have a chance, we have to stop seeing each other."

"But we're friends."

"It doesn't matter what we are to each other because everyone else thinks it's more. Kai thinks it's more."

"What are you going to do? Ignore me at work?"

"It looks like I have a new job. I need to put some space between us. I've got to show Kai that you aren't a threat."

"I can't believe you're cutting me out of your life." Hurt flared in Mickey's gray-green eyes.

I hated myself for putting it there. "I don't want to. You're like family. But it's the only way I can make a go of my marriage."

"You still think you have a chance?"

"Mickey..."

"I get it, Oliver. She's your wife. You have to do this for her." Her voice quivered. "But if it was your choice?"

I shouldn't say it, but her voice begged for the truth. "We'd always be friends."

CHAPTER 31

Kai

I could have asked Oliver to come over, but I couldn't say what I had to say and then leave him alone at the farmhouse. That just seemed cruel.

"Are you sure you want to do this?" Caleb asked.

We were halfway to Aunt Ines's house.

"I have to. Oliver was right. I'm not the Kai he knew. But I'm not sure I even want to be her again." The shards of Nathan embedded in my psyche guaranteed that I would survive anything. I might decimate others, but I'd survive. That was what Nathan did. Oddly, what scared me in the beginning was becoming a source of comfort as I tried to unravel what was him and what was me.

"But leaving Oliver and coming to New York is a major step. It's not like when he moved across town for a few days."

I leaned my head against the passenger window. The cold glass soothed me. "Oliver and I don't work. I don't know how to fix us. What I do know is that we don't have a chance unless I can figure out who I am now, and I can't do that here. The best thing I can do for everyone is leave."

175

"Are you running away?"

I stared out the passenger window. The night was cloaked in darkness. I could barely make out the silhouettes of the trees and houses that we passed. "I'm not running away. I'm running toward my own future."

Caleb didn't say anything else. He let me have some time to gather my thoughts before I talked to Oliver. When we pulled up to Aunt Ines's, Mickey's car was parked in the driveway.

Anger surged through me, but I didn't give in to it. Not this time. I probed it. Most of it was mine, but I could tell that some of it was Nathan's.

Right now, I wanted to hurt Mickey. I wanted to make her pay for all the times she hurt me. I wanted her to suffer the way I'd been suffering. This desire scared me, and yet, it felt so good to be this way. Powerful. Strong. Decisive.

Caleb reached over. "Don't let her get to you. You don't know why she's here."

"I don't need to know why she's here. It's enough that she's here at all."

"Maybe we should come back later?"

I wasn't letting Mickey run me off. "I'm going inside."

"I'll come with you."

"No. I need to do this on my own."

Caleb looked uncertain, but he didn't insist. "I'll be out here waiting. Just remember why you're leaving. You don't want to do anything you'd regret right before you go."

My eyes locked on my brother's. "The problem is, I don't think I'd regret it. Not anymore."

I got out of the car and walked toward the front porch. On my way, I opened a window in my shield. Oliver's thoughts slipped though. They tasted of cherry wine—lonely and bittersweet. He was trying to push Mickey away, and he hated having to do it. He was doing it for us. I should appreciate it, but the fact that it was tearing him up so much just made me angrier.

Mickey's emotions smelled of apple pie. *I can't believe he's choosing his crazy wife over me. But his marriage has already fallen apart, and, when he finally realizes that, I'll be there waiting for him.*

Rage churned within me. I wanted to unleash it on her. I was so close to letting go.

Then I heard Lukas's thoughts. *I want another cookie, but I don't think I should bother Mommy and Uncle Oliver.*

I took a breath in for a count of four, held it for a count of seven, and exhaled to a count of eight. I did it again. And again. I felt a flicker of calm, but the rage still whirled inside me.

If I needed proof of why I had to leave Butternut, this was it.

I focused all my thoughts on Lukas. I let my love for him build a bulwark against the anger. I could do this.

As I reached for the doorbell, the front door swung open. Mickey stepped out with Lukas in tow.

She froze at the sight of me.

Lukas's face lit up. "Aunt Kai!"

"Hey, Lukas." I bent down to hug him. When I stood up, my gaze locked on hers. "Mickey." I couldn't help imbuing both syllables with dislike.

"Just stopping by for a quick visit?" she asked.

"I'm here to talk to Oliver. My husband."

"He's in the kitchen. Just go straight back. It's on the left."

"I've been here before." My neck tightened. I felt a muscle start to spasm.

"But it's been a while, hasn't it?" She gave me a defiant look.

It took every ounce of control I had not to lash out at her. "You'd better get going."

She reached for Lukas's hand. "I do need to get this little guy home."

I shut the front door and pressed my back against it. I was shaking. Blueberry muffins of hatred burst over my tongue. I closed my eyes and took another 4-7-8 breath.

"Everything okay?" Oliver asked.

I opened my eyes. "I hate that woman." Sweat trickled down my back. Why was it so hot in here? I yanked off my coat and scarf.

Oliver looked shocked. I couldn't tell if he was surprised to hear me admit it, or alarmed by the vehemence in my voice.

Before he said a word, I blurted out, "I really, really hate her. Like, eternal blood feud hate her."

"I get it."

"Do you? Then why do you keep seeing her?" I demanded.

"The Fuchses are part of my family."

"And what am I?"

"My wife." Oliver gave me a crooked smile. "I told her we can't be friends anymore."

"I'm so sorry that it's come to that." I couldn't keep the sarcasm out of my voice.

"I've known her my entire life. It wasn't an easy decision."

"I know," I said through gritted teeth. "I heard your thoughts."

"Then you know that I'd do anything to get back what we had."

I threw my stuff down on the bench in the hallway and followed him back to the kitchen. He turned on the kettle and pulled out mugs for us. He offered me a cookie.

"I'm not hungry." My stomach was a knot of tension.

While we waited for the water to boil, he asked, "How did you get here?"

"Caleb brought me over."

"Is he waiting outside?" When I nodded, he said, "Tell him he can leave. I'll drive you home later."

"No, that's okay."

He opened his mouth like he was about to insist, but the words died on his lips. Now that I was here, I didn't know how to say what I'd come here to say.

Oliver filled the silence. "I've got a new job, I think."

"What?"

"Aunt Ines hooked me up with an interview at the Bank of Butternut."

"What will you do there?"

"They've had some compliance issues."

"Is it permanent?"

"I don't know. I have the interview tomorrow."

"Good luck."

"Thanks. Does that help with the Mickey situation?"

"I suppose it does. Thank you."

The kettle whistled and Oliver made our tea.

He put my cup in front of me. "So what did you want to talk about?"

"You were right about us. About me. I'm not the woman you married. But you're not the man I married, either."

He gave me his disappointed face. Partly hurt, partly resigned. "I'm sorry we ended up here."

"Sorry doesn't fix what's broken."

"We can't undo what happened."

"I know." I looked into my tea. Anywhere but into his eyes. "I can't stay here any longer."

"Are you going back to San Diego?"

I shook my head.

"To Grandma Guhn's house?"

"I'm going to go with Caleb to New York."

"Shitfuckingdammit." Oliver leapt up. His chair tipped over and slammed against the floor, but he didn't seem to care. "Absolutely not. You know what the city does to you."

"I know what it did to me. You said it yourself. I'm not the same person I used to be."

"So, you're leaving me?" he asked.

"You already left me."

"I moved across town, not across time zones."

"I need to figure some things out. I can't do it here."

"What things? How are we supposed to fix our marriage if we don't work together?"

"It's not always about us, Oliver. This is about me."

"Did Caleb suggest this?"

"Caleb doesn't want me to go back to New York any more than you do."

Oliver glared at me for a long moment. "I feel like there's something you aren't telling me. I thought we decided no more secrets."

I wasn't ready to tell him about Nathan. "I have to go."

He changed tactics. "When we came to Butternut, you said you'd give it six months."

"We didn't come to Butternut, Oliver. You *took* me from New York and dragged me out here to Butternut. Against my will. And it's been five months. Close enough."

"I didn't pull you back from the edge to let you go rushing back to it. I can't sit by and watch it happen again. I won't." He splayed his hands on the table and leaned over me. "That city does things to you. And you can't see it when it's happening. You don't know what you might do there."

"You'll just have to trust me to take care of myself."

"And if I can't?" he asked.

"Then that's your problem, not mine. I'm going to New York."

He righted his chair and sat back down. "For how long?"

"I don't know."

"What if you start to lose it again?"

He didn't understand how close I was to losing it here. "Caleb will be there."

"I'm still your husband. Does that mean anything to you? Anything at all?"

"It does. But I can't stay here. I've got to figure out who I am before I can figure out if we can work again."

"If you leave, this is you giving up on us. It's a separation."

An ultimatum. I guess I should have expected that, but I didn't. "Don't threaten me."

"It's not a threat, it's the reality of what's happening to us."

"According to you."

"It's your decision."

It felt like he was trying to control me. The darkness in me revolted. I wasn't letting anyone I loved manipulate me anymore. Not my parents, and not Oliver.

I'd moved my wedding ring to my right hand because of the cast on my left. I tugged off the thin gold band and slammed it on the table. "Fine. It's a separation."

I stormed out of the house.

CHAPTER 32

Oliver

Kai was gone. No matter how many times I told myself it was
true, it still felt unreal, like at any moment I'd wake up from
this nightmare and find myself lying in bed beside her.

But the truth was indisputable.

After my interview, I'd gone back to Aunt Ines's house to pack up
my things. With Kai gone, I might as well go home.

I sat at Aunt Ines's kitchen table while she stacked a week's worth
of meals inside two shopping bags. Wiener schnitzel, jägerschnitzel,
gulaschsuppe, semmelknödel, and käsespätzle. All of my favorites.

I wasn't looking forward to eating alone.

"You didn't have to do all this." I loosened my tie and undid the
top button of my dress shirt.

"I didn't have to. I wanted to."

"I don't know what I'd do without you. You're all I have left."

"Kai loves you. I know she does. It's just that so much has come
between you two."

I slouched in the chair. "You don't understand. You've never lost a spouse."

Aunt Ines stopped packing up the Tupperware. "You're not the first person to lose someone you love."

"I know, I know. You've lost your parents. My dad. But this is different. Marriage is different."

"A ring doesn't define a relationship." Her voice was sharp—almost angry. "Do you remember Sabine?"

Of course I did. Nathan's aunt. "She was your best friend."

"She was my everything, Oliver." Her voice didn't waver.

Her everything? Oh. I worried that Aunt Ines never had someone, but I should have seen it. My aunt had found love in her lifetime. A love that spanned decades. Just not a love that she could proclaim at that time. "I'm glad you had someone special."

"I did." Her eyes misted over.

Sabine had passed away several years ago. "How did you go on without her?"

She sat down beside me at the table. "I focused on what I still had. I had Grandpa. I had you. And I had the memory of everything Sabine and I shared."

"I'm sorry you lost her."

Her eyes got a dreamy look. "Sometimes I forget she's not here. Something happens and I pick up the phone to tell her. I lived my entire life loving Sabine. It's not something that death can stop."

I reached over and squeezed her hand. "You were lucky to have each other."

Her eyes focused on me again. She tried to shake off her sadness. "Tell me about your interview at the bank."

I gave her a half-smile. "I got the job."

She clasped her hands together. "Oliver, this is wonderful news. Congratulations."

"Thanks."

"When do you start?"

"Tomorrow."

"Do you like the new boss?"

"Mr. Kohler's a saint to put up with his wife."

"Have you met his assistant?"

"Ms. Brown? She's very protective of him."

"Isn't she though?" she asked with a knowing look.

"You mean…?"

"Let's just say there's a reason Mr. Kohler has been able to tolerate Mrs. Kohler all these years."

"How long have they been together?"

Aunt Ines's face compressed in concentration. "Going on forty years, I think."

"I wouldn't want to spend forty years with three people in a marriage," I said.

"Oh, don't be so sure that it's just three."

"Mrs. Kohler?" Impossible.

"I know it's hard to imagine now, but she was a looker in her day."

And that's when a terrible realization trickled over me. The nine years I'd had with Kai might be all I ever got. I yanked off my tie and draped it over the chair. "What will I do here without Kai? So much of my life has been about taking care of her."

"Maybe it's time you start taking care of yourself."

Two things had defined my life since I'd come back to Butternut—Kai and my father's secret. Kai was gone, but my father's secret remained. "I think it's time I try to do something about Schneider."

"He's not someone you want to tussle with."

The worst had already happened. Kai had left me. "What can he do to me now?"

Her mouth puckered. "What about the Fuchses? What about me? Schneider wouldn't have a problem using us to get at you. Look what he did when Kai was missing—making you sign that false statement before he'd help look for her."

"But he wouldn't actually hurt anybody, would he?"

Aunt Ines looked wary. "Your daddy used to say Schneider was like a sleeping black bear. Leave him be, and all is well. Poke him, and you don't know what might happen."

"I owe it to Christian. It will all come out at Nathan's trial anyway."

"Then there's no reason to make yourself a target."

"The Hoffmanns need to know. And what if Nathan never wakes up?" I knew I wasn't making a lot of sense, but I needed to get out from under my father's secret.

Aunt Ines rested her chin on the back of her hand. She stared at me as if she saw something I didn't. "Do you think if you can make things right for Christian, you can make things right with Kai?"

"It'll mean something." It had to. Maybe when Kai saw what I was doing for Christian, she'd realize that the Oliver she loved was still here. And maybe the Kai I loved would find her way back to me.

CHAPTER 33

Kai

When I opened the window, cold air seeped in, horns blasted from the streets below, a siren screamed past. New York. A wave of panic crested against my shield. The person in the ambulance was hurt badly. A gunshot wound. If I let it, his pain would become mine. Part of me wanted to do it. Just to test if I could handle it. That was my darkness. It always wanted to push the limits of everything.

I took a deep breath and reinforced my shield. No doors. No windows. Locked up tight. The way I had to be in the city.

It was oddly familiar and almost comforting to slip back into my old lifestyle. I knew with absolute certainty the Kai I had to be to survive here.

I turned back to my suitcase. It was nearly empty. I was almost settled into my room. Despite the modern sleekness of most of Caleb's place, he'd furnished this room with my tastes in mind. All the furniture had character and charm. The sleigh bed was hand-carved. Oil lamps that had been converted into electric lamps sat on the dresser, nightstand,

and desk. The walls and draperies and bedding were all shades of cream and pale blue.

"How are you settling in?" Caleb asked from the doorway.

"Great." I'd spent the afternoon exploring and getting used to being on the west side in Tribeca, while Caleb headed into the office to catch up on things.

"You like your room?"

"I love it." All this decorating took time and planning. "How long have you had this place?"

"I closed the deal last October."

"Why didn't you tell me?"

"I wanted to surprise you."

That was my brother. Always thinking of me. I threw my arms around him.

Caleb's cell buzzed. He pulled back and checked it. His lips twitched.

"Work?" I asked.

He shook his head.

"Are you seeing someone?" I teased. He was always involved with someone in some way. Never too seriously, though. My brother was married to his career.

"I've seen her a few times."

My brother had dated men and women since college. Tall, short, White, Black, Asian, Latino. He always said that it was the soul, not the body, that intrigued him.

"Her?" I asked.

"For now, yes."

"What about Mateo?" They'd been dating for a while when he lived in London.

"His job keeps him in London." He said it like that explained everything.

"Are you still together?"

"Not when we're on separate continents." He typed away on his phone. "He's free to see anyone he wants."

"And when you're in London?"

"That's when things get interesting." He grinned.

"Please tell me everyone knows about everyone else."

"When you're honest, people will surprise you." Caleb sat on my bed. He patted the place beside him. "Enough about me. How was your first day back in the city?"

I sat beside him. "I'm fine."

"Of course you are." He nudged me with his shoulder. "But how was it being here?"

"New York still feels like home. I lived here for so many years."

"With Oliver."

The city was one giant emotional imprint of us. "When I turned the corner to your apartment, I was certain I'd run into the old Oliver and me, fresh from college. Or maybe I'd see us celebrating our second anniversary at Nobu."

I had lived so much of my life in one place that I felt like the me of each moment was still here, splintering off to live another version of my life or continue along the path I was on until everything changed. Unfortunately, all these memories and emotions were potential triggers for my own darkness.

"How's your shield?" Caleb peered at me, trying to read my mental state from my expression. "Any headaches, thoughts you can't block out, moodiness?"

"My shield is much stronger than when I left."

"Nathan's influence?"

I nodded. It was the best thing about having my soul entangled with someone like Nathan. It made me more resilient.

"If it gets to be too much being here, you'll let me know?" he asked.

"Of course."

"You can go back to Butternut any time."

"No. I really can't. Not until I know I can control it all—including the piece of me that used to be Nathan." I glanced out my window at the busy streets below. "How was work today?"

His voice sounded less confident than usual. "My boss wants me to stay in New York a while. They've got me doing meetings with Compliance and Audit this week."

"Is that normal?" I asked.

"It means there's concern about what I'm doing. A big enough concern to pull me away from client business."

"It sounds like you're in trouble."

"They're watching my activities more than usual. Things are off." He sounded distracted.

"Let me know if you want me to eavesdrop on anyone's thoughts."

He frowned. "I don't want you straining yourself."

"I won't."

"It's not necessary. Not yet."

"I'm strong enough."

He rubbed the back of his neck. Worry lurked in his expression. "I can feel things shifting. Power balances. Allegiances. It's all subtly moving. Things are off. It's driving me nuts because I can't get into my managing director's head."

"Why not?"

"He's an insomniac."

Caleb couldn't dreamwalk into someone's consciousness unless they had a close relationship and they were both dreaming at the same time. Insomniacs were a definite problem.

"I don't know the new auditors well enough to get into their minds. My compliance contact resigned over the holidays to go backpacking in Africa and find himself. More likely he'll find malaria."

"Isn't there anyone else in Compliance that you know well?" I asked.

"No one involved with what's happening to me."

"I don't really understand what you do." I probably should if I was going to help him.

"I invest clients' money in private deals."

"Why didn't you say that over Christmas?" I asked.

"I try to keep it complicated to impress people."

"Or to shut Dad down."

"That, too."

We talked about the little things that had been going wrong. Things that made my incredibly competent brother look incompetent: missed meetings with important people, deadlines exceeded, reports gone awry. It sounded like someone was sabotaging him. Now, he was under more scrutiny and subject to more oversight. Responsibilities were shifting away from him and back to his boss. He didn't like it. He never liked having his decisions questioned.

I curled up on Caleb's cream-colored, wrap-around couch in the middle of his huge sand-toned living room. The colors reminded me of the beaches back home in San Diego. I wondered if that was why he picked them. Caleb was sentimental at his core. He just didn't let most people near his core.

I settled back into the cushions. The open concept design of Caleb's place meant that I could watch him making popcorn in the kitchen. We were on the thirty-eighth floor, so a couple hours ago when I stared straight ahead, I had the most amazing view of the sun setting on the Hudson River through a wall of windows. The kind of view Oliver and I could never afford.

Caleb dropped the bowl of popcorn between us and started searching for a cheesy slasher flick to watch. They were our favorites growing up. We were twenty minutes into a movie about zombie beavers when the doorbell rang.

He got up to answer it. From the couch, I turned my head to see our guest. A tall, platinum blonde woman stood there. Her medium blue eyes had the kind of makeup every woman strives for: accenting, but not noticeable. She was dressed in New York black. Everything fitted and dark, but I bet her heels had Louboutin red soles.

She almost smiled when she looked at Caleb. "Darling, you didn't answer my call." Her voice carried a faint Russian accent.

"I told you I had company." He gestured at me.

I waved from the couch.

Her eyes narrowed on me. "I just need to grab something from the bedroom."

He let her in. "Of course."

Instead of heading to his bedroom, she prowled around the couch. I felt her eyes move slowly over me like she was cataloguing every detail of my appearance. "Smart decision staying in. Doesn't she have anything presentable?"

He came over and said, "She's my sister, Natalia. She'll be staying with me a few weeks, so be nice."

"Nice was never part of our arrangement." She fondled his collar.

Caleb gave her a patient smile. "An addendum."

She patted his chest. "I may have a few of my own."

"I look forward to negotiations."

She swiveled back toward me and my brother introduced us. She gave me her hand like she expected me to kiss her knuckles. I didn't.

Then she breezed past my brother and went into his bedroom. On her way back, she handed him the bracelet she'd retrieved. "Be a dear and help me?"

He fastened it around her wrist. "All set."

She leaned in and kissed him. Not a quick goodbye kiss, but a *let's get things started* kiss. Right in front of me.

When she pulled away, her voice was all husky. "I'll see you soon."

After the door shut behind her, I couldn't help blurting out, "I don't like her."

"Most people don't."

"But you do?"

"She's an acquired taste."

"That's one way of putting it."

"She's a Manhattanite."

"I was a Manhattanite. I wasn't like that."

"She's one of the top futures traders at my investment bank. She makes more in a year than most people make in a lifetime. Everyone is an ally or an antagonist to her."

"Which one are you?"

"I'm never quite sure. That's what I like about her." He touched his lips.

I rolled my eyes. Caleb always liked a challenge.

CHAPTER 34

Oliver

I should have been headed a few doors down to Jumbo's for lunch, but my feet took me elsewhere. I needed to clear my head. Walking used to help me do that when I lived in the city. Unfortunately, it was the kind of day that iced over your breath and froze your fingertips. Ten minutes. That was all I could take out there in the Northwoods' cold.

I tugged up the collar of my wool overcoat to ward off some of the chill. I planned to make a loop around the center of town. It had been two days since Kai had left Butternut. I hadn't spoken to her. I didn't know what the protocol was for a separation.

I might not be able to fix my marriage, but I could fix some things here in Butternut. I just had to figure out how to bring Schneider to justice. Well, the best/least dangerous way to do it.

I was so lost in my thoughts that I didn't see Mickey until I nearly collided with her in front of Brennan's Green Brier.

"You really need to watch where you're going." Her voice was tartly sweet.

"You're all the foot traffic I've encountered," I said.

She put her hand to her ear. "Wait. Is that Oliver Richter's voice that I hear? Speaking to me here? In public?"

I might not know the protocols for separation, but I did know that staying away from Mickey was no longer a priority.

"Stop." I bumped my arm into hers. "I'm sorry about that. You know I am." I tugged her across the street, toward the stretch of green that was covered in snow.

She pulled out of my grasp. "So now that Kai's gone, you can talk to me? I can't take the whiplash of being your friend."

"I had to show her that you and I are in the past."

"Who says I want to be in your future?" she demanded.

"Fair enough." I blew out a cloud of white. "Look I need to tell you something."

She must have heard the seriousness in my voice, because there was no witty retort. "What?"

"I want to prove what Schneider did to Christian."

"We decided not to do that. It's too risky. He could come after us or our families." She tilted her chin defiantly.

"I know. But I can't live with this lie anymore."

"So, now that Kai is safely in another state, you're willing to take a chance?" Her voice shook. "What if he comes after me? Or Lukas? I can't go through that again."

"I'll do it by myself. You won't be involved. He won't go near your family."

She gripped my coat sleeve. "What if he hurts you?"

"I'll be careful."

She stared at me like she was trying to figure me out. "I can't let you do this all by yourself. It's too dangerous."

"It's safer for you that way."

"But you'll be safer with a partner." She stepped closer. "You need someone who can watch your back. Like when we were in the cave."

"Aunt Ines will help me."

She looked doubtful. "I can get into places she can't."

I didn't want Mickey involved. But I saw that familiar spark in her eyes. If I didn't let her help, she might go rogue. "All right."

"All right?" She looked up at me through her thick black lashes.

"You can help with research. Nothing dangerous."

I didn't quite trust her when she murmured, "Nothing dangerous."

CHAPTER 35

Kai

For two years, City Hall Park was where I used to mark the beginning and the ending of each workday. The 6 train dropped me there and picked me up. My office at the Children's Administrative Services building was a five-minute walk away. Some days, it felt like five hours to get from the office to the subway.

I sat on a bench in the center of the park. The fountain in front of me was shut off for the winter. The city had filled it with evergreen boughs, but the fountain would have to wait for spring to fulfill its real purpose again.

In Butternut, I'd felt like that fountain—waiting to fulfill my purpose again. Now that I was back in the city, I felt like I was ready to rediscover my purpose.

It felt good.

I felt right.

I was in charge again. I would fix the relationships Oliver broke when he made me leave the city. I had to start with my boss and end with my friends. I needed to apologize and try to explain why I'd left so abruptly.

While I sat there, thousands of thoughts clinked against my shield, but they weren't breaking through. They weren't even making any dents. I was much stronger now. I sent a silent thank you to Nathan. It was beyond bizarre to be grateful to him after everything he did to me, but I was. And I wasn't going to fight it.

What I was going to do was celebrate each and every good day here in the city. They used to be pretty rare.

I didn't have long to wait for my old boss Angela to join me. I looked up and saw a dark-skinned woman in a red coat with black trim. Her hair was longer, but I recognized Angela and waved. She waved back at me.

When she got to the bench, she gave me a hug and sat next to me. "It's good to see you again."

"I'm sorry for how I left." I never would have disappeared on her like that. Oliver had offered my resignation without my consent or knowledge. He'd said it was the only way to save my life. I didn't agree, but it was one of his unilateral decisions.

"This job does things to us. I know you would have stayed if you could."

"I never wanted to abandon the kids." I hated thinking of the little ones suffering because I wasn't there to help them. Or of my coworkers, already stretched so thin with their own caseloads, having to shoulder my work, too.

Her voice was firm, but understanding. "You were at your breaking point. You were probably beyond it for a while. We all saw it. You have to take care of yourself before you can help others."

"Still, I should have given notice."

"We worried that something serious had happened. But your husband emailed me a few times to let me know that you were doing better, that you were coming back to yourself."

She glanced at my left hand. The cast peeked out of my coat. "Are you doing better?"

"I'm getting there." I sketched out the details of the kidnapping and rescue. I ended with "Luckily, no one was hurt badly besides the kidnapper."

Angela's eyes locked on mine. For a split second, I swore she glimpsed the darkness inside me. "I think a lot of people got hurt. And some of them are still struggling with it."

I studied the slate beneath my feet.

"Do you remember what I told you when you started?"

"Surviving is all these kids know how to do."

"What you've been through, it makes you a survivor, too."

She was right. What she didn't know was what I might do to survive. The silence lingered between us. I wished I had some coffee to sip. Something to do with my hands. Finally, I asked, "You want to sign my cast?" It was covered in signatures from Butternut.

"I'd love to."

After she finished signing it, she checked her watch. "I wish we could talk more..."

"...but you've got to get back to work," I finished for her.

She leaned closer. "It's okay that you left. It's okay that you couldn't stay."

My eyes burned. "I wish I had done more."

"We all wish that we could every single day." Angela patted my shoulder. "You did your best for as long as you could. That's more than enough."

As I watched her walk away, I realized her words might not just apply to my job, but to my marriage.

CHAPTER 36

Oliver

"**I** don't like it." Aunt Ines shoved her chair back. It screeched across the linoleum floor in her kitchen. She stomped over to the kitchen sink and rinsed her dessert plate.

Although she hadn't been thrilled when I told her about my plan to try to find evidence that linked Schneider to Christian's death, she'd come around and even offered to help. Then I mentioned Mickey's involvement. That was what caused this reaction.

"If I told her no, she'd just go off on her own. You know how hot-headed and stubborn she can be." I forked a piece of Bundt cake.

"That's my point. We need to be careful. She isn't." Aunt Ines shoved her plate into the dishwasher and wiped the counter down the way she wanted to wipe Mickey out of my life. "The only reason she wants to help is to stay close to you."

"She was good friends with Christian, too. Lukas was kidnapped as leverage to get the truth about Christian out of me. Trust me, it's personal for her."

"Oh, it's personal for her," Aunt Ines muttered. "She wants you back."

"What? No. She understands that I'm only separated from Kai."

Aunt Ines snorted. "She's using this situation to spend more time with you and rekindle things."

"Why do you hate her so much?"

"I don't." Aunt Ines sighed. "But I've seen all the hurt she's caused. She's brought nothing but trouble into your life."

"Come on Aunt Ines, that's not fair."

"I know she's the first girl you...you know."

"Aunt Ines!"

"Well, she is. And she broke your heart."

"So did Kai."

"Kai's your wife. She gets to break your heart."

I laugh-groaned at her logic. "It's too late. I can't stop Mickey from helping."

"Then have her talk to me about it. Not you."

I couldn't imagine that going over well with Mickey. "That's ridiculous. Trust me, nothing will happen."

"You've already kissed her too many times for someone who loves someone else."

I winced.

"Do me a favor, then. Make sure your contact with her is by phone. No late nights together at the farmhouse."

"Seriously?"

"I know how girls like her think."

"She's a single mom."

"In need of a husband and a daddy for her son."

She didn't know Mickey like I did. "That's not how it is between us."

"I have eyes, Oliver. I've seen how things are between you."

I felt the heat creep over my face. I didn't know what to say, so I finished off my slice of Bundt cake.

CHAPTER 37

Kai

Dinner with friends shouldn't have been so hard. There were only three of them because my telepathic depressions made it difficult to maintain friendships. I had met Enrique and Marc back when I first moved to the city and worked at the New York Times. We bonded at a company retreat. I'd probably still be wandering around the Bronx looking for the zoo if it weren't for them. Ariana, the blonde pixie, had been my college roommate freshman year. She kept in touch after school, and I'd helped her get her first job in the city three years ago.

When I lived in Manhattan, all of us used to brunch together once a month. Or rather, we were supposed to. But those last few months I was in the city, I couldn't seem to get it together enough to attend.

From their closed mouthed expressions and crossed arms, I knew I had a lot of work to do with them. They had every right to be mad at me for disappearing from their lives. I'd barely texted them before Oliver dragged me away to Butternut. After I got there, I just stopped. I mean, there was so much going on between Oliver and me, and I didn't want to try to explain any of it.

Even now, I danced around the truth, trying to keep things light. They weren't having it.

So I took a deep breath and told them everything—or close enough to everything. I skipped over the extremes Oliver had taken to get me out of New York. I told them how I was kidnapped by Nathan. My near-death experience and recovery. I finished with Oliver and I being separated.

"No!" Enrique sounded both scandalized and excited.

Marc reached across the table to take my hand. "I'm sorry."

Arianna gave me her sad face. "Do you think it's totally over?"

"I don't know."

"Oh, sweetie," Enrique flagged down the waiter down. "We're going to need another pitcher of margaritas."

I nodded, but stuck to virgin margaritas because telepaths and liquor don't mix.

My friends spent the rest of the meal alternating between telling me I'd be fine without Oliver and assuring me we could still save our marriage.

By the end of the night, we were hugging and laughing. I had my friends back. They made me pinky-swear that I would stay in touch. This time I knew I would.

When I got back to Caleb's, he wasn't home. Probably out with Natalia again.

After a day of apologizing and explaining, I was drained. I got into bed and fell asleep immediately. I spent what felt like an eternity waiting for Caleb to join me in my dream. Then, he was there with me on the rock beside Grandma Guhn's pond.

"Are you ready?" I asked.

Tonight I was going to try once more to take him to the In Between. He assured me that he was ready, that he wasn't afraid anymore.

Together, we jumped into the water and swam for the bottom.

This time, we found the passageway without any trouble at all. Bright white light encircled us.

And then we were standing in a forest. Giant sequoias surrounded us, creating a canopy of shade. It was somewhere I'd never been before.

Our clothes were dry. The air was summer warm and slightly humid.

Caleb grabbed my hand and squeezed it. "So, this is the In Between?"

I nodded. We'd done it.

"It's beautiful here. Why didn't you tell me it was like this?"

"I've never been to these woods before."

I glimpsed a person moving toward us through the trees. As she got closer, I recognized Grandma Guhn. Her long auburn hair was tied back in a braid. When she saw Caleb her smile widened.

Caleb dropped my hand and enveloped her in a hug. "You're okay." He swung her around a few times.

"Of course, I am. It's the two of you I worry about." Her dark blue eyes met mine as she said, "The living can get in far more trouble than the dead."

He put her down and kissed her cheek. "I've missed you."

She patted his cheek. "I'm always watching over you kids." She looked back through the trees to someone in the distance. "He's waited a long time to see you."

"Grandpa Guhn?" Caleb whispered.

She nodded. "He wants to talk to you."

Caleb started forward. Then he stopped. "Kai?"

It was rare for Grandpa Guhn to be in the In Between. I wanted to go too, but I knew Caleb needed to see him alone.

Before I could say anything, Grandma said, "You need your time with Grandpa. Kai and I will be along in a bit."

Caleb hesitated.

"Go," I shooed him away.

I didn't mind waiting. Without looking back, Caleb headed deeper into the woods.

We'd really done it. *I'd* done it. A warm feeling pooled in my stomach and spread out to my limbs. I felt strong, stronger than I had in a long time.

"You're feeling better."

"I am. Thank you for helping me get here."

Grandma Guhn looked me over with solemn eyes. "You left Oliver."

"I had to."

"Sometimes you grow back into your life. And sometimes your life no longer fits you."

"I think it might be the latter."

She reached out and plucked invisible things from the air an inch from my cheek. "Your aura has shifted. Nathan's still there, but he's not as prominent as he was."

"Being in New York helps."

"It's your city. It will call to you more than to him. Which means that it won't trigger his darkness. But it might trigger yours."

"I know. I'm just hoping that I'll be able to deal with it."

Grandma and I talked for a while about my parents and the holidays. She didn't offer me any advice, just listened. Confiding in her always helped.

I heard Grandpa Guhn's voice through the trees. "Lillian?" He said her name with a faint Korean accent. "Bring *Sown-yah* over here."

He always called me "Granddaughter" in Korean.

"We're on our way, Jae," she said.

Caleb and I were back with the two people who loved us best. After all the drama with my parents, it felt good to feel like a family again. Part of me wished we could stay here with them. But our visits here were only meant to be temporary. Our lives weren't over yet.

Whatever had happened between Grandpa and Caleb, it had

erased the shadows from my brother's eyes. He looked peaceful—not a typical look for him.

Grandpa Guhn turned to me. "Sown-yah."

I walked into his open arms and let him wrap me in unconditional love.

The next morning the smell of coffee summoned me from bed. It was 7:30 a.m. when I stumbled down the hallway to the kitchen. The wall of windows looking out over the Hudson River let way too much light in. I squinted, not quite ready for that kind of brightness.

The countertops were white marble with veins of gray. The gas stove had six burners and two ovens and looked like something a professional chef would use. The rest of the appliances were equally imposing. Six steel stools wrapped around the island of marble in the center of the room.

Caleb looked up from his phone as I padded into the kitchen. "Love your hair."

I checked my reflection in the toaster and had to laugh. "Bedhead pompadour. I hear it's all the thing in Brooklyn."

"Don't go hipster on me," he grumbled.

I got a cup of coffee and slid onto the stool beside him. "I can't make any promises."

"Thanks for last night."

"You did the hard part. How'd you overcome your fear?" I asked.

"I realized that being with all of you was the most important thing. And anything that stopped that from happening had to go."

"What were you afraid of?"

Caleb stared into his coffee cup like the answer swam inside it. For a second, he reminded me of Dad. "Being left behind."

"I won't do that."

"If you die, you will."

"Then I won't die."

"That's an impossible promise to make."

"I do impossible things everyday."

He gave me a quick smile. "Seeing Grandpa again meant everything to me." His voice thickened with love.

"That's why I pushed you to keep trying."

For a moment, every emotion was there in my brother's eyes. He finally forgave himself for not being able to save Grandpa.

"It wasn't your fault," I said.

"It always felt like I could have done something." He toyed with his spoon.

"Grandpa didn't blame you."

"He said it was his time, not ours."

"Do you ever," I lowered my voice, "wish we'd died with him?"

"Do you?"

"Sometimes. When my powers were really hard to control or kids were being cruel."

"But not lately?"

"Not lately."

My brother got quiet. It started to feel awkward, so I got up to help make breakfast. I was in charge of the toast and the bacon. Caleb scrambled the eggs. We'd fallen into a nice rhythm, timing everything just right for the perfect hot breakfast. Nothing worse than cold eggs or barely warm toast.

He waited until we were eating to ask, "Have you talked to Mom about Oliver?"

"I got a ten-minute lecture on the dangers of being here and leaving Oliver there. It started with how I'll lose my mind and ended with how I'll lose my man."

"She raises some good points," he said into his coffee.

"She doesn't understand me. She never has. Not like you do."

"Nice spin."

I winked at him. "Maybe I could go into PR?" It was the first time I thought about a different career. Taking another path. Being someone new. It was enticing and terrifying.

"How's your morning looking?" he asked.

"Very open," I said.

"Can you swing by my office at ten and eavesdrop on a few people's thoughts?"

"Absolutely." I couldn't help sounding surprised that he'd changed his mind.

"Are you sure you're up for it?"

"Of course." I was eager to help him. And at that moment, I was feeling up for anything. "What am I looking for?"

"There's a meeting with Audit, Compliance, IT and my boss today. It's the best way to get a glimpse of what's really going on without breaking any laws."

"Are you planning on breaking any laws?" I asked.

"Would it matter?"

"Only if someone catches you."

Caleb gave me his wicked grin. "I've never been one to get caught."

The things he got away with in high school still amazed me. "Let's try it the lawful way first."

"You do realize it's pretty amoral to snoop on people's thoughts."

"I said we were going to avoid the illegal. I didn't say anything about the amoral."

I mentally anchored myself in my brother's office by studying everything in the room. It was so Caleb—all sleek and elegant. I sat behind his mahogany desk. Its vast surface contained only one nonessential item: an old photo of Caleb, Grandma Guhn, and me. Two sumptuous leather armchairs faced me across the desk, and a matching sofa stretched along one pristine white wall with three huge windows that looked out over Midtown.

I turned my attention back to the photo. Caleb and I were thirteen and fifteen. I looked like a mini-version of Grandma—same blue eyes, red hair, pale coloring. Caleb was mostly Dad. He had the surfer confidence and ease that I lacked. He was already tall, but still skinny. He wouldn't get muscular until college.

As far back as I could remember, Caleb had been taking care of me. It was nice to be able to return the favor. I knew how much his career meant to him. It wasn't just about the money. It was about the independence it afforded him. He could do what he wanted, whenever he wanted.

I needed to help him and I was pretty certain I could, but my knee still bounced up and down under the desk. It had been months since I'd been around this many minds and opened up my shield. I wasn't sure what would happen.

I was stronger now, though. I'd gotten Caleb to the In Between. I'd left Oliver. I could do this.

I took a deep breath, closed my eyes, and envisioned my shield. It was sealed up tight. I carved a window and opened it a crack. So many voices and emotions. Truckloads of thoughts. An express train of emotions. All coming toward me like Time Square and Grand Central colliding at rush hour.

Breathe. Just breathe. Focus.

I listened for Caleb, trying to find his thoughts in the chaos. Everyone's thoughts are distinct. Minds are like fingerprints to me.

Kai, can you hear me?

There he was. *Yes.*

I bent the walls of my shield outward, creating a tunnel from my mind to his. I used his thoughts as a beacon, letting them guide me to him. Then things got tricky.

I needed to be able to listen to the thoughts of everyone in the conference room while keeping everybody else out—everybody in the building, everybody within a half-mile radius. It would be a challenge, and I wasn't entirely sure about my plan.

As I stretched my shield around the minds in the room, I could feel all the thoughts and emotions rushing at me. I struggled against the onslaught. I wasn't going to be able to keep a handful of minds inside while keeping hundreds of thousands of others out for long. My head ached. Sweat beaded on my lip.

I knew what I had to do. I reached for the darkness. I felt it rise up. I used it to reinforce my shield.

The cacophony receded. I'd done it.

Now there were just a few voices. I spent a couple moments absorbing the chatter, without trying to make any sense of it. Not that I could make much sense of it. There was a lot of technical jargon that I didn't understand. Unknown acronyms—AML, KYC—that meant nothing to me, but quite a lot to the people in that room. Emotions flowed around the room. I tasted the tangy sweetness of anxiety and the cinnamon of anger filled my nose. Underneath it all was an orange candy of fear dissolving on my tongue.

I'll cover his ass only until my ass is on the line.

A strong thought from a determined mind. It had to be Caleb's boss. I focused on that mind.

He'll explain everything. Compliance is just looking for a scapegoat for their mistakes. There better not be a paper trail back to PE. How fucking long are they going to keep us waiting? Audit is five minutes late to a meeting they called. They must have something on us. Enough to waste my time and Caleb's. Shit. Scroll through the Blackberry. Look annoyed. Get ready to put them in their place.

Caleb's thoughts distracted me. *The new compliance guy looks like he doesn't know why he's here. We're still waiting on Audit and IT. What's taking them so long?*

I replied, *It's something to do with AML and KYC. What are those?*

He didn't respond, so I tried to slip back into his boss's head.

I couldn't. Caleb's boss was gone. Everyone was gone. Utter silence.

I risked a tiny window in my shield. Nothing. It was like the entire population of Manhattan had disappeared.

The quiet was terrifying. My palms grew damp.

It was one thing to actively block out other minds. I still felt their presence, and I knew that I could reach out if I chose.

This was the obliteration of it all. My heart raced. Sweat burst across my scalp. It trickled down my forehead. I wiped it away. Panicked, I tried one more time to connect with Caleb. I had to be able to find my brother.

But I couldn't. I was completely alone.

By the time Caleb returned to his office, my telepathic powers were just starting to come back online. I knew that he'd be stressed about the meeting, so I decided to wait to tell him what had happened to me.

Instead, I told him what I'd heard during the brief time I was inside his boss's head, and I did my best to relay the random chatter I'd heard.

"KYC and AML," he repeated.

"What do they mean?"

He rubbed his forehead. "Know Your Customer and Anti-Money Laundering. Both are Compliance's job when we take on new investors. Compliance has to screen them."

"What does that have to do with you?"

"Not much. I gather the investor information, but Compliance makes the decision whether or not to approve new investors from an AML/KYC standpoint."

"Huh."

"Did you get anything from IT or Audit?"

"No, I didn't."

He raised a questioning eyebrow.

I shifted nervously in my seat. "I sort of lost my telepathy for a while."

"You had trouble hearing people's thoughts?" he asked.

"I didn't hear anything for a while. Total radio silence."

He leaned back in his chair. "Has this ever happened before?"

"Kind of." I told him about when Jenny had died and our minds were connected. I collapsed on the sidewalk, but by the time I got home, my telepathy had rushed back and overwhelmed me. "It never lasted this long or came back this gradually."

He looked worried.

"My first thought was that it might be the head injury, but I've had so many scans and tests, and why would the problem only show up now?"

He nodded for me to continue.

"Then I started thinking about Nathan, and how our powers interacted. Maybe it's something like that. Maybe there was somebody in the room with the power to shut me down?"

"You mean someone who sensed that you were there?"

"I don't know. It could have been somebody who didn't even know what he was doing to me."

Caleb pulled his lips to the side of his face. His evaluating-things face. "We need to figure this out. First, we'll have a doctor check you out and rule out any new health issues." He picked up the phone and made a couple calls. In ten minutes, I had an appointment with a specialist for the next morning.

"Then what?" I asked.

"Let's table that discussion until after we get the test results."

Before I could reply, Natalia stuck her head in the door. "Caleb, do you have a minute?"

Her eyes narrowed as she looked at me. I opened the window in my shield, curious to see how much I could hear now. Natalia thoughts were like flaming snowflakes. I couldn't miss a single one. *Is that sweater from a mall? Where does she get her jeans? And those sneakers...*

Out loud, she said, "Oh, I didn't realize you were busy." She didn't bother to sound like she cared.

Caleb waved her in. "I'm never too busy for you."

She smiled and it reached her eyes. For a second, I glimpsed what Caleb saw in her.

I stood up. "I should get going."

"I'll see you at home," he said.

"He might be a little late tonight," Natalia said.

I lay back in bed and cradled the phone to my ear.

"How are you doing?" Alex asked.

His voice sounded deeper on the phone. I liked it. "I've had better days."

"You sound pretty good."

"I'm definitely feeling stronger. How's Lukas?" I asked.

"The nightmares eased up after you took him to see Nathan. Thanks for calling him yesterday. He was so happy to hear from you. What's going on in the big city?"

I hadn't meant for it to happen, but, before I knew what I was doing, I told him about what had happened to my telepathic abilities. And then I just kept talking. Everything I'd kept from Oliver, I shared with Alex. My darkness, Nathan's presence in me, Caleb's troubles at work. All of it came tumbling out.

"You know," his voice dropped so low it gave me shivers, "there's a prospective client who wants to meet me. I wouldn't usually travel all the way to New York just for the chance of a new job, but..."

"You're coming to New York?"

"Only if you promise to show me the sights."

"Of course!"

I knew I shouldn't be so excited to see Alex. But I was.

CHAPTER 38

Oliver

I slid onto a stool at the counter at Jumbo's, the only place to grab lunch downtown. Facing a wall of wood paneling, I listened to the conversations flowing around me. Grandmothers bragging about their grandkids. Wives commiserating about their husbands' shortcomings. Old men reminiscing about their glory days. Background noise that distracted me from all the quiet in my life. I bit into the fried fish sandwich. It was good, but not good enough to stop me from dwelling on what was wrong.

When I talked to Aunt Ines I sounded like I was ready to take on Schneider, but I did worry about the fallout. I needed a solid plan, but I didn't have one. Not for Schneider and Christian. Not for Mickey and Aunt Ines. Not even for Kai and me.

I couldn't believe my wife and I had reached this point. We couldn't have kept going the way we had been, but this separation felt final. I hadn't been able to reach her for a long time, and now I worried that I never would again.

I dropped my sandwich and fumbled for my phone. I dialed her number.

She answered on the third ring. "Oliver?"

"Hey."

"Hey." She said tentatively, like if she spoke too loudly everything between us would explode.

"What's going on?"

"Nothing."

It was a nothing that encompassed everything. "Talk to me."

"About what?"

I leaned my head in my hand. She was still pushing me away. "How are you?"

"Okay."

"How's Caleb?"

She tripped over her words. "He's fi-okay."

"Is he fine or is he okay?"

"Uh, it's just something at work. No big deal."

"If he's having trouble at work, maybe I can help." I wasn't eager to help Caleb, but I'd do it to reconnect with Kai.

"I appreciate the offer." Her voice warmed a bit.

"Tell me what's going on."

"Something to do with AML and KYC."

"That's not part of his job. That's Compliance."

"We're still trying to put the pieces together. They're keeping him in New York for a while longer. He has some meetings with Audit and Compliance."

"The meetings could be part of an annual review, but if he's based in London, I don't understand why they'd be doing that in New York."

"He splits his time between the two offices now," Kai said.

"But this is a review of last year's work when he was based in London."

"He was in New York a couple months too. Should I be worried?" she whispered.

"Concerned," I said.

Kai got quiet.

I didn't know what else to say, so I went with the truth. "This separation is hard."

"I don't know how to act," she confessed.

"I wish there was a procedures manual."

"I'm not sure it would make it any easier."

"Probably not. Just clearer. Is it okay to call to check in on you?"

Before she could reply, Mickey's voice came from behind me. "Hey, Oliver."

I turned so she could see my phone and waved her away.

Mickey whispered, "Sorry."

I mouthed, "It's Kai."

She made a pained face and went over to a table.

"You're with Mickey?" Kai's voice chilled me.

"I'm at Jumbo's, finishing lunch. She just came in."

"Oh."

"It's a small town, Kai."

"Maybe just text me next time." She hung up on me.

I stared at my cell. Shitfuckingdammit.

I stalked over to where Mickey was sitting and slammed my palm on the table.

A few people looked over. "Sorry," I said to them.

I got a few nods of acknowledgment.

I sat down across from Mickey.

"Is something wrong?" Mickey widened her eyes.

"Didn't you see that I was on the phone?"

She shrugged. "I didn't mean to intrude."

"But you did." I pinched the bridge of my nose. "You do. You intrude."

She tilted her head to the side. "Do I?"

I dropped my hand from my face. "Yes."

"Maybe you should ask yourself why."

I took a deep breath and tried to stay calm. She had a way of getting under my skin.

"Not everything happens the way you want it to."

"You think I don't know that?" I was raising my voice again. I took a deep breath. "It's just that your timing really sucks."

"Oh, I don't know, Oliver. You might be glad that we bumped into each other." A look of self-satisfaction passed over her face.

"What do you mean?"

"So I'm allowed to talk now?"

"Go for it."

She glanced around to see if anyone was in earshot. Then she leaned across the table. I did the same thing until our noses were inches apart.

She whispered, "I've poured over all the old newspaper articles about Christian's accident, but there was nothing we can use in there."

I didn't think we'd find a smoking gun in the paper. Dad and Schneider were too clever for that.

"So I started talking to people in town," she said.

I knew she'd go rogue. "You should have talked to me first."

"Relax. Everyone believes my cover story that I want to do something to celebrate Christian's life."

"And?"

"People have been helpful, but they don't remember much about that night or the days afterward. Or all they remember is what they read in the paper."

"Schneider's going to find out that you've been stirring things up."

She lifted her chin defiantly. "It's a good cover story."

"It won't be good enough for Schneider."

"Well, what have you done?" she demanded.

"A lot more thinking than you."

"How's that working out?"

"Not so great," I muttered.

She gave me an *I told you so* smile, but she didn't say the words. "I need you to do something for me. You were with Christian that night. Can you write down everything you can remember about what he was wearing and what he had with him?"

"Why?"

"I'm thinking maybe we can find a discrepancy in the police file. Something that shouldn't have been at the scene. Or something that should have been there but wasn't."

"That won't be enough to pin anything on Schneider."

"Do you have a better idea for our next move?"

"No," I admitted.

"How much did that hurt to admit?" she asked.

"Too much."

CHAPTER 39

Kai

When Caleb and I were kids, we'd talk about how different things would be when we grew up. We would be in control of our lives. Of course, it hadn't turned out quite the way we'd envisioned. Caleb's career was careening out of his grasp. And I was walking around with a piece of somebody else's soul.

It wasn't just that I had no idea how to separate Nathan from me. I wasn't even sure I wanted to get rid of him anymore. I was stronger now than I used to be, and some of that strength came from Nathan. Still, it was hard not being able to separate my emotions from his.

I kept going back to my last conversation with Oliver. Part of me knew that what he'd said made perfect sense. Butternut was a small town; he was going to bump into Mickey. But another part of me was furious. I couldn't stop myself from imagining Oliver and Mickey together. The darkness in me stirred. I felt its power. I wanted to lash out—at Oliver, at Mickey, at both, at either. When the darkness was in charge, I knew that Oliver and I were over. But, even when I wasn't burning with rage, I didn't care much if we were. And the feeling was so surprising that I had to wonder if it was coming from Nathan, too.

I flicked on the TV to distract myself. I watched a black-and-white movie about a cat terrorizing the people who murdered its owner. By the time it ended, it was midnight. Evidently, Natalia had been serious when she warned me that Caleb might be coming home late.

When he did get back, he took one look at me and started making hot chocolate.

A short time later, he came into the living room, sat down beside me, and handed me a mug of it.

I took a sip. It wasn't Jacques Torres. "Marie Belle?"

He smirked. "Vosges."

I liked it. "So, how was Natalia?" I asked.

"Delightfully exhausting." He leaned back into the couch and gave me a mischievous smile.

"Okay, then." I didn't press for details.

"Thanks again for your help at the office today."

"I just wish I'd been able to help more."

"We'll know tomorrow whether or not everything's okay," Caleb said.

"The doctor's not going to be able to tell me anything about my telepathy."

"He'll be able to see if your brain is working the way a normal brain is supposed to. Humor me. I need to know that you're okay."

"I'm sure I'm fine." I leaned closer. "The more I think about it, the more I think it was somebody else. Somebody whose powers interfere with mine."

"How many people like us do you think are out there?" Caleb sipped his hot chocolate.

"I have no idea. It's not like there's a registry."

He snorted. "Well, there's me and you and Dad and Grandma Guhn. There's Nathan and Lukas and Sabine. And that's just two families."

"For all we know, one in ten people could have secret abilities."

"Then why don't you sense them more often?"

I gave the question some thought. "Maybe because I only sense them when my shield is down." And I usually kept it up in the city.

"But you didn't sense this mystery person at the office today."

"But this mystery person shut down my power to sense anything!"

"Right. So, let's go with your hypothesis. There's someone in my office with the ability to shut down your telepathy. How do we find him?" Caleb put his mug on the glass coffee table.

"Good question. It's not like I can read his mind. But maybe I can read his face."

"What do you mean?"

"I take him by surprise. I see how your coworkers react to me."

"There are thousands of people in that building."

I shrugged. "Obviously, we start with the people in the conference room."

"Obviously." He gave me a dubious look.

"Can you get me a visitor's pass?"

"I can if you tell me what you plan to do with it."

"I'll make my way through your office building and run into each of the people from that meeting."

He sighed. "All right. I don't love this plan, but I don't have a better one." He looked me up and down twice and grimaced.

"What?"

"You can't go back to my office in that sweater and those jeans. Or those sneakers." He pulled out his wallet and handed me his black Amex card. "Try to keep it under $20k."

"I'll try." I rolled my eyes.

His expression didn't change.

"Wait, you're serious?"

"The card doesn't have a limit, but I don't like to carry a balance. I pay it off each month."

I only needed an outfit or two. "Twenty thousand dollars?"

"Fine. Thirty, but that's it. You'll hit Bergdorf's and Barneys first. I'll set you up with a personal shopper at both. Then swing by Wempe. I'll pick a watch for you, but you'll need to have it fitted to your wrist."

"Seriously?"

"A watch is a status symbol in my world. It opens doors. That reminds me. You're going to need a handbag. Preferably Hermès. Pick one you like." Caleb must have thought better of it. "Actually, I'll order something for you and have it delivered here."

Apparently, I couldn't be trusted to pick out my own purse.

He rubbed his chin. "You need to blend in. Ask yourself, What would Natalia wear?"

I groaned. "Fine, as long as I don't have to ask myself, What would Natalia do?"

"She's not all bad."

"I didn't say that she was."

He shook his head. "It's written all over your face." He reached over and gently tugged a lock of hair into our line of sight. "We're going to need to do something about this hair, too."

I jerked away from his hand. This was getting insulting. "I'll call my old stylist."

Caleb looked like he was going to insist on someone else, but he stopped himself. "Text him. Tonight."

I'd left my phone in my room, so I went to get it.

I texted my stylist as I walked back to the living room.

We finished our hot chocolate. Caleb wasn't sleepy yet and neither was I, so we found another cheesy old horror flick and settled in.

During a lull in the action, Caleb asked, "What's going on with Oliver?"

"What do you mean?"

"You keep looking at your phone. I'm assuming that he should be trying to get in touch with you, but he isn't. So, what happened?"

I told him about how I hung up on Oliver.

"Oh." Only Caleb could color one syllable with so many questions.

"He promised to stay away from Mickey. Then he's out having lunch with her. God only knows what else he's doing with her now that we're separated. Not that my being with him ever stopped them before."

"I'm sorry."

"Oliver and I used to be so good together." I punched the cushion.

"Were you?" He quirked an eyebrow.

"We had our problems. But we were better than we are now."

"But even back then, he was keeping secrets from you. He was lying to you."

"I know."

"And you hate secrets and lies."

"I know." I sighed. "Still sometimes I think if I could go back to that life and believe in him like I did then, I would."

"Did you give him a chance to explain about Mickey?"

"He gave me a line about accidentally running into her," I said flatly.

"How do you know it wasn't true? It's not impossible that two people looking for lunch would end up in the same restaurant, given how tiny Butternut is."

He was right, of course. And I knew that—or at least part of me did. But trusting Oliver had hurt me so deeply. It was just easier to think the worst of him.

CHAPTER 40

Oliver

I went home that night and dug through one of the worst memories. I sat at the desk in Grandpa's study, trying to remember everything I could about the night Christian died. I'd spent so many years burying that memory. It was hard to dig up the details. They came to me in fragments.

We were playing Super Mario Brothers on my PlayStation. Christian had his feet on the coffee table beside the bowl of Pop Secret. I could see his beat-up black Converse high-tops. There was a hole forming in the right toe where a bit of blue sock peeped through.

My mind skipped ahead to when he was leaving. His black-and-grey plaid flannel shirt was tied around his waist. He grabbed his book bag—L.L. Bean, hunter green—and ran out the door. I chased after him. When I tried to get him to stop, he pushed me away. His green T-shirt glowed in the porch light. He wore the hemp and bead necklace Mickey had made for him.

I tried to remember if he was wearing anything else. Did he have a jacket? A ball cap? I couldn't see anything. All I could see was the look on his face right before he turned to leave. Like I'd betrayed him. I hadn't known that he was in love with Mickey, too. He never told me. But I should have known.

He leapt on his bike and rode off. It was a moonless night, and he disappeared from view quickly. I never saw him again. I never got to explain or apologize. I never got to fix what I'd broken. I swallowed, but I couldn't dislodge the wad of guilt in my throat.

I struggled to see if there was anything else I could remember, anything that might help Mickey and me. Nothing.

I emailed what I had to Mickey. Then I went to bed.

I didn't want to be back here. The place my father had loved above all others—the chief of police's office. It was a non-descript room with a grey filing cabinet, a cheap metal desk, and a couple of chairs. Nothing had changed since it was my dad's office. The only difference was that John Schneider sat behind that desk now. My father's best friend, and the man who had killed my best friend.

John's thin, dirt colored hair stretched across his scalp. His girth filled the chair.

Mickey sat beside me. We'd both been summoned here by Schneider.

I tried not to show fear; I infused my voice with annoyance. "Why are we here?"

"It's a real shame about what Nathan did," he said.

Mickey gripped the arms of her chair.

"Yes, it is," I said. "We're hoping he comes out of his coma soon, so that the trial can start."

"I'm sure we can all agree on that." Schneider spread his broad hands out before him on the desk. "It's my job to protect the innocent."

Mickey didn't say a word. She didn't have to. Her lips tightened, one eyebrow rose, and her eyes squinted. Her face betrayed her inner thoughts—blatant disbelief.

"You have something to say, Mickey?" Schneider asked.

I reached over and touched her hand to steady her.

"You didn't protect Lukas," Mickey said.

I released the breath I was holding. Whatever she was feeling now, it wasn't about Christian, or, at least, not entirely. She was angry mama bear now.

"My officers and I, we did our best." He leaned back in his chair, but his eyes were alert. "The investigation is ongoing. We're still doing everything we can to make sure Nathan pays for what he did to your son." Schneider turned to me. "And your wife. It might help me to know why you and Mickey were searching the Hoffmanns' property for Lukas."

Lukas and Kai had gone missing days apart, and from different locations. Kai had last been seen walking in the woods near the Hoffmanns' house. It made sense to start looking for her in that area. But we'd have to come up with an explanation for why the Fuchses were there, searching for Lukas.

"And don't try telling me 'because of a dream' again. I didn't buy that the first time."

The thing is, that was the truth. Caleb had managed to find Kai through dreamwalking, and that's how we'd learned where Kai and Lukas were.

I shrugged. "Crazy as it sounds, it was a dream."

Schneider sighed. "I guess we all have our secrets to keep." He sucked on his teeth for a moment, seemingly lost in thought. "It's a shame about the Hoffmanns. Guess instability runs in that family. Christian was reckless. Nathan's insane. Let's hope Lukas takes after your side of the family."

I glanced at Mickey. She was about to lose it.

"Well, Chief," I said, trying to bring this meeting to a close. "If that's all you wanted to know—"

229

"I've heard some things around town." Schneider wasn't going to let us go just yet. "You're trying to raise bike-safety awareness? Because of Christian?"

Mickey nodded.

"Well, that's nice, Mickey. Maybe the department should be involved."

Mickey's gaze darted to me. Her fingers tapped nervously against the armrest. The bike-safety awareness thing was just her cover story.

"But there's something I need to understand first." Schneider leaned forward now, fixing her with his stare. "Why did you request a copy of the police report on Christian's death?"

A cold sweat broke out on my forehead and upper lip. I knew Mickey was planning to sneak a look at the files, but I had no idea she had requested a copy of the police report. Of course Schneider was going to find out. This was why I wanted to take things slow.

Mickey fumbled over her words. "Christian was my friend. His death was such a shock. I never understood why he was riding his bike so late at night. I just want to understand what happened."

"After all these years, Michaela, do you really think you can lie to me?" He didn't break eye contact until she shrank back in her chair and looked down. Then his gaze slid to me. "I expect better from you, too, Oliver."

I was out of options. All I could do was tell the truth.

"Nathan had a gun to my wife's head. He wanted to know what had really happened to his brother. I told him."

Schneider nodded, like I'd confirmed what he'd already suspected. "Well, I don't know what you told Nathan, exactly, but I do know that any new inquiry into Christian's death isn't going to look too good for your father. He was the chief back then. I was just a junior officer, following orders."

"You can't blame Oliver's father for what you did," Mickey blurted out.

"Oh, Michaela, you have no idea what I am capable of." Schneider folded his fingers together and rested them on his desk. "Kids, I've got some advice for you: Let the past go and look to the future. We've got a psychotic kidnapper in a coma, and what happens when he wakes up is something I can help you with."

"How?" I asked.

Schneider gave me his Cheshire cat grin. "I've got some sway with the judge and the prosecutor. I can get them to plea bargain Nathan into a mental institution. No trial. No dirty laundry. No need for little Lukas to testify or for fragile Kai to relive the trauma. We can make this whole situation go away."

"If we leave the past alone?" I asked.

"Seems fair. Let the past go and have a better future." He spread his hands wide, as if he was showing us everything that he was offering us.

"What about you?" Mickey asked.

For a split second, Schneider's mask of indifference slipped. "I lost my wife and daughter in a fire. Do you know what the charred flesh of a loved one smells like? I do, and I can't forget it. Every day I live without them is my punishment."

"You need to step down," Mickey said.

Schneider shook his head. "Can't. Pension requirements."

"What about the Hoffmanns?" I asked.

"We can't bring back Christian. But we can spare them a trial for Nathan. A trial where their grandson would be a key witness."

"They should know what really happened to their son." There was plenty of angry mama bear in Mickey, enough to spare for another child, another family.

"I'll let you two decide. Is a dead boy more important than your living son?" Schneider turned to me. "Is Christian more important than Kai?"

"Are you threatening them?" I asked. Not that I knew what I would do if he was.

"Merely pointing out that there are worse things ahead for all of us if you two don't let the dead lie."

CHAPTER 41

Kai

After enduring hours of poking and prodding, I was back in the specialist's office. He flipped through the scans and the test results and assured me that everything looked normal. My skull was healing and there were no signs of swelling in my brain. Just what I'd expected. I texted Caleb to let him know.

Then, I set out for Bergdorf Goodman. The personal shopper eyed my cast for a moment, considering how to work around it. Luckily, she was up to the challenge. She brought me dozens of things to try on.

I stared at myself in the mirror. I wore a black St. Laurent pencil skirt and a short-sleeve silk chiffon Chanel blouse. My shoes were black Louboutins with two-inch heels. I was surprised to see how easily I slipped into Caleb's world. Well, almost. My hair hung shapeless and heavy around my shoulders, but I was going to fix that. I got a kick out of imagining what my stylist would think of the new me.

After a few more stops, I had added a gorgeous dove-gray Dior coat with bell sleeves and two more skirts. A couple more blouses, and a cashmere sweater cape that I was sure Natalia would deign to wear. And, even though I knew that there was a delivery from Hermès waiting for me at home, I let my brother treat me to a Céline bag that I just loved. I figured he owed me for subjecting me to this extreme makeover.

After I got my diamond-studded Rolex fitted at Wempe, I headed downtown to my old hairdresser at 2B Salon in the Financial District. I asked him to give me my standard layered bob with bangs, but he took one look at my shopping bags and assured me that I needed something different. I emerged with a cut that was similar to my old style, but sleeker, edgier.

There's something about chopping off my locks, it's like a reverse-Samson effect. It made me feel even stronger.

When I got back to the apartment, I felt a mix of exhilaration and exhaustion. It had been a long day, and shutting out the city took a toll. Though I had to admit that shopping without worrying about money was fun. I was looking forward to taking my new look to Caleb's office tomorrow.

Tomorrow was Oliver's birthday. I'd never missed a single one of his birthdays since we'd met. And this year, I had totally forgotten.

I heard the door open and close. Caleb was home.

When he saw my haircut, he said, "You look great!"

"Just wait until you see the new clothes."

"You're ready for the office tomorrow?"

I nodded. "I left your Amex on the kitchen counter."

"Did you melt it?" He grinned at me.

"Let's just say Natalia would be jealous."

He chuckled, and then he got serious. He handed me a few sheets of paper. "These are all the people from the meeting."

I scanned the pages, memorizing their faces, names, and jobs. They included his boss, the compliance guy, two audit people, and the IT person. "Hello, David, Harry, Montgomery, Igleka, and Stellan." I asked, "And my visitor pass?"

"Waiting for you at the front desk. Are you sure you're up for this?"

I bit my lip. I had one concern. "Do you think anyone will remember me from a few days ago?"

Caleb's face contorted. He struggled to find a nice way to put it.

I bit back a laugh. "I know, I know. But now I've got a new hairstyle, new clothes, and this." I lifted my right wrist to show him the watch.

"I knew it would look great on you."

I held up the black Céline bag I'd selected for myself. "Can I keep it? And return the Hermès bag?"

"Nice choice." He swatted the air. "Keep them both. So, what's your game plan?"

"Guys love to rescue a damsel in distress."

"What about Igleka? She won't fall for that."

"Oh, that's easy. 'Where's the bathroom?'"

"Clearly, you've thought this out."

I had.

Caleb got quiet. He had to be thinking about the day ahead, worrying about his job and about me.

I was thinking about the next day, too. "It's Oliver's birthday tomorrow."

"Are you going to call him?"

"I should."

He took my hand and squeezed it. "It doesn't make you a car when you stand in a garage."

I knew what he was trying to convey: Just because Oliver and I stayed in our marriage didn't make it a real marriage anymore.

CHAPTER 42

Oliver

I had gone to Aunt Ines because I knew that she could help me, but I stayed because of the Sacher torte. The moist chocolate cake was covered in chocolate icing. The first mouthful was heaven. Tartly sweet apricot jam lined the icing and the middle of the cake. The shock of the sugar icing. The textures and flavors intoxicated the tongue.

"I wanted to be the first one to wish you a happy birthday. Even if it's not officially until tomorrow," Aunt Ines said.

"Thank you. This means a lot to me."

"I thought we could have dinner together tomorrow."

"Would you mind if I passed? I'm not really in the mood to celebrate." Especially since it was my first birthday without Kai.

"I'm not talking about a party. Just a quiet dinner here with me?" She tried not to look hurt.

I relented. "All right."

A smile lit up her face. "I'll make all your favorites."

"Thanks."

It was nice to make someone happy for once. I enjoyed my cake as I watched her putter around the kitchen.

When I told her about the meeting that Mickey and I had had with Schneider, her good mood vanished.

"You should stop this foolishness before someone gets hurt," she said.

I couldn't. "Do you think there might be any evidence that still exists?" It had been sixteen years since Christian died.

"How would I know?" Her cheeks flushed and her voice rose. "Your father didn't tell me anything. Not even after you left." She made her tea in silence. By the time she returned to the table, her frustration was replaced with wariness. "This is all new to me."

She stirred her tea slowly, lost in thought. Finally, she tapped her spoon against her dainty rose-painted teacup. "Is this what you really want?"

"Yes."

"Even if it means that Schneider might try to hurt you. And Mickey. And Lukas. And Kai."

"He thinks we're considering his offer. That buys us a little time."

"You're not answering my question."

"I'll do what I have to do to protect everyone." I wished I felt as sure as I sounded.

She sipped her tea. "Would you accept your father's help?"

What a weird question. "He's dead."

Her eyes locked on mine. "If he could help you, would you accept his help?"

Would I take his help? Despite everything that happened, he was the only person who might be able to get me out of this mess. "If it meant clearing Christian and punishing Schneider? Yes, I'd take his help."

"That's all I needed to know." Aunt Ines slapped her hands on the table, got up, and left the room.

I ate pre-birthday cake while she was gone. By the time I was starting on my third slice, she reappeared with a big cardboard box in her arms. I rushed to take it from her. Someone had written *Linens* on the top, but it didn't weigh much at all and things rattled inside. Definitely not linens.

"When your father brought this to my house and asked me to keep it, he told me that you might need it someday. I figure that someday has come," she said.

I set the box on the table. It was taped shut. I grabbed a knife, sliced it open, pulled the flaps back, and looked inside. The first thing I saw was a picture of Mama, Dad, and me. I couldn't have been more than five years old. Dad and Mama were smiling. Dad looked so happy. I'd forgotten he could smile like that. He never did after she died.

I put the photo on the table. Underneath the photo was a gold pocket watch.

Aunt Ines peered over my shoulder. "That was your grandpa Eder's."

My mother's father. He'd died before I was born. I clicked open the watch. Inside was an inscription in Austrian German. *Immer mache zeit uer wichtig.*

Always make time for what matters.

Next, I found a piece of wood carved into a snowflake. "A Christmas tree ornament?"

"I don't know what it is, but I think it belonged to your mother," Aunt Ines said.

"What are these?" I asked as I pulled out several notebooks. The top one was a very thick volume bound in brown leather. It looked like it could hold a few years of daily entries. The others were slimmer and in purple satin. I flipped open the fat notebook and recognized my father's starkly straight handwriting. The flowing script in the others belonged to my mother. Journals. I never would have guessed that either of my parents had kept a journal, but they both did. Mom's stack of journals proved she was the more prolific writer.

I looked into Aunt Ines's warm brown eyes. "Thank you for sharing this with me. But I don't understand how it's supposed to help me." Mom died four years before Christian did. Dad was too smart to write about his crime in a diary.

Aunt Ines patted my hand. "I have no idea, Oliver. I just know that, after you left, I promised your father that I'd keep all these things safe, and that I'd give them to you if it seemed like you needed his help after he was gone."

After Dad died, I suppressed every feeling I'd ever had toward my father—good and bad. I just wanted to be free of the secret to which Dad had bound me. Now all those feelings came rushing back. They cluttered my chest making it hard to breathe. Feelings I'd killed years ago reincarnated. All these years I believed my father didn't care. It made it easier to stay away and deal with his death. I choked on the words, "He cared," and buried my face in my hands.

Aunt Ines hugged me. "Oh, my sweet boy, I know he didn't always show it, but he did love you. He never stopped loving you."

I sat at Grandpa's desk, with a bottle of Jack Daniel's beside me and my father's journal in front of me. I poured a shot of whiskey and downed it.

Then I opened the journal.

I searched for the day that Christian died. I didn't think my dad would have written anything incriminating, but there was still a tiny chance he might have recorded something then that might help me now.

All he wrote that day was: *I've given Schneider a second chance. I pray he takes it.*

I scanned through the entries after that. He described the search for Christian, and I couldn't help recoiling from his words. All that time, he'd known where Christian was, and he'd known that Christian was dead. On the day Christian was "found," he wrote:

When I saw that boy's body, all I could think of was my own son. Christian was Oliver's friend. He was with Oliver that night. What if it had been Oliver instead?

Telling the Hoffmanns that their boy was dead was one of the hardest things I've ever done.

There was nothing I could do to save him.

I kept skimming until I got to the day that I discovered the secret that my father was keeping for Schneider.

Oliver knows. God help me. I didn't think he was home. But he was here, and he heard everything. My son can barely look at me. Maybe someday he'll understand. I couldn't save Christian, but I could save Schneider. I traded the dead for the living.

There isn't a day that goes by that I don't feel for the Hoffmanns.

I flipped to the final entry, needing to know what my dad's last thoughts were. The entry was dated September 7, seven weeks before my father died.

Time lets you see where your choices led you. I wish I could go back and choose better. When Sophie died, most of me died with her. If I could have taken her place, I would have. Oliver deserved to have a mother. He reminded me so much of her that it hurt to be near him. I didn't realize what my distance did to him. I thought I was teaching him to be strong, but I was teaching him to keep it all inside.

I know why Oliver left. I thought that I could help John. I thought that he'd been through enough, losing his wife and daughter. But I didn't realize that, in trying to help my friend, I'd lose my son. By the time I understood, it was too late. If I spoke out about what John had done, he would have said that Oliver was an accessory after the fact. And nobody was going to say that about my son. I wasn't going to make him suffer for my mistakes.

I didn't know whether to laugh or cry.

I'd suffered from my father's mistakes. Hell, I was still suffering for my father's mistakes. It did, however, help to know that he'd tried to protect me.

It might not be much, but this journal was the beginning of a case against Schneider.

My cell phone rang and startled me. I looked at the number. It was Kai. I couldn't talk to her, not right now. I let the call go to voicemail. I went back to reading. Entries were sporadic at times. Several months could pass without my dad writing a word. Then there were short entries about me, like when I made National Honor Society or won the math award in high school. It mattered enough for him to write it down. There was so much of him that I never knew. That I would never know. All those years I stayed away, I lost them. I lost my father.

Twenty minutes later, the doorbell rang. I put the journal down and went to see who it was. I found Mickey on my doorstep, rubbing her mittened hands together.

"It's freezing out here." She darted inside without waiting for an invitation.

I shut the door behind her. "What are you doing here?"

"I don't know how much time yesterday's meeting with Schneider bought us. We need to get to work now."

I rubbed my jaw. "It's late, can't this wait until tomorrow?"

She looked at her watch. "It's 9 p.m., old man. You can spare an hour or two."

"I guess so."

"What's going on? You're usually not such a pushover."

"Nothing."

She touched my arm and softened her voice. "You promised to keep me in the loop."

"I'm reading my dad's journal."

Her face scrunched up in sympathy. "Oh, Oliver, that must be so hard."

She wrapped her arms around me. I leaned against her and breathed in the scent of her coconut shampoo. It made me feel better.

Finally, she let me go and took off her coat. "Why don't we go through it together?"

"Two people can't read one journal."

"I bet there's other stuff I can work on while you're reading it." She hung her coat in the hall closet and kicked off her snow boots.

She followed me back to the study. I showed her everything my dad left me in the box. She touched each item with care, knowing how much these things meant to me. When she got to my mom's journals, she said, "I could read them for you."

"I'm not sure there's anything helpful in there. She died four years before Christian was killed."

"But your dad thought it would help you, so, who knows?"

"You don't mind?"

She picked up the journals. "I always liked your mom."

These were my mother's private thoughts. I wasn't sure I should be reading them, let alone Mickey. I reached to take them back.

She didn't let them go. "If I find anything that should stay locked in the journal, that's where it will stay."

I let her keep them. "Thanks."

We spent hours pouring over the journals. We didn't find anything else incriminating Schneider, but we learned so much about who my parents were.

"Oliver, you should read this." Mickey passed my mother's journal to me. It was open to one of her last entries.

241

I worry about Reinhard. He doesn't know how to handle loss. He just shuts down. I've always been here to pull him back, but after I die, I'm afraid no one will be able to reach him. This shouldn't be happening. I was supposed to grow old with him, to watch Oliver grow up, to help raise my grandkids. Ines and Heidi promise they'll help out, and I love them for it, but it's not fair. I hate the thought of Oli growing up without a mother's love.

My throat constricted. I never wanted to lose her either. If she had lived, our lives would have been completely different. I couldn't help imagining the possibilities. Christian might be alive. He might have a son of his own now. Even if he had died, Dad wouldn't have covered for Schneider. Dad would have done the right thing because my mother would have made him. Nathan never would have come for Lukas or Kai. Mickey and I might never have broken up. Lukas could have been mine.

For a moment, I wished I could step into that alternate world. The moment passed, and I went back to reading my father's journal.

I dreamt of Sophie again. She was alive and sitting beside me at Oliver's high school graduation. I could smell her perfume. Chocolate. She always smelled of chocolate. I held her hand in mine. It was so warm and full of life. When they called Oliver's name, a smile broke across her face and radiated joy.

I woke up alone in our bed. I could still smell her. My hand was warm where it had held hers, but she was gone.

My father never wanted to be separated from my mother. She was always in his thoughts even a decade after her death. They had the kind of love I thought Kai and I had.

I looked at the clock. Almost midnight. I'd be twenty-nine in a few more minutes.

"Mom wants you and Aunt Ines to come over for dinner tomorrow," Mickey said.

"Why?"

She squinted at me. "We have to celebrate your birthday, silly."

"I thought I'd skip the festivities this year. It's just going to be Aunt Ines and me."

"But Lukas is excited for cake and candles. You can't disappoint a little boy."

"My aunt already planned a dinner for us."

"My mom will call her in the morning. They love to coordinate things."

She wasn't taking no for an answer. "What time should I be there?"

"Six-thirty. And I'll even make kaiserschmarren with homemade plum jam."

"Why didn't you say so?" Mickey's shredded pancakes were my favorite dessert. "I'll be there."

She leaned close to me. So close we shared a breath. I didn't move an inch. She shifted left and brushed a kiss against my cheek. "Happy Birthday, Oliver."

In that moment, it was.

CHAPTER 43

Kai

I glanced around at the other people in the elevator. A woman in business casual. A few men in suits. One had white hair. He wore his tan suit so naturally. It felt like an extension of who he was. He looked familiar. Then I realized he was Montgomery from the Audit Department.

When he got out on the twelfth floor, I followed him. I walked as briskly as I could in my new Louboutins, and then I pretended to stumble.

He grabbed my arm and helped me steady myself. I thanked him and smiled.

He smiled back. "Are you all right?"

He was touching me, and I could still hear the murmur of other people's thoughts just outside my shield. Montgomery wasn't the person I was looking for.

"I'm so sorry. Thank you for your help." I released him and tucked my hair self-consciously behind my ear.

"Are you interviewing here?" he asked.

"I'm meeting a friend for lunch." I unbuttoned my Dior coat. Then I swept my hand over my fitted skirt, trying to distract him from further questions.

His eyes skimmed over my new outfit and returned to my chest. For a second, I thought he might invite himself along to lunch. Then his phone pinged.

He glanced down at it and frowned. "I'm late for a meeting. Have a good lunch." He rushed down the corridor.

Montgomery was the third person on my list that I'd ruled out. I'd already managed to run into David, Caleb's boss, and Harry, the compliance guy. I had two more people to find.

I went in search of the other auditor, Igleka. When I found her, she was in the break room, making coffee. I approached her sheepishly and asked her for directions to the ladies' room. Before I walked away, I complimented her on her glass bead bracelet. I touched her wrist as I marveled over it. She seemed pleased by the compliment, but that was it. I didn't get the sense that I was anything more to her than a nice stranger who had to pee.

Nothing changed with my telepathy either. Emotions still surrounded my shield like familiar riders smushed next to me on a crowded subway car.

I made my way back to the elevator banks. IT was down on the fifth floor. I got off the elevator, but there was no one to sneak in behind. I stood at the glass door for several minutes. Looked like I needed to change tactics. I tugged the visitor sticker off my lapel and pretended I couldn't find my keycard. I looked as helpless and frustrated as possible. Finally, an IT guy took pity on me. He let me in as he was heading out.

I switched to my New York walk, moving confidently and quickly, so that no one questioned my being there. I searched the maze of cubicles for Stellan's. I found it, but he wasn't there. Damn it. I was trying to figure out what to do next when everything went silent outside my shield. It was abrupt and awful. The absolute obliteration of my telepathy. I hadn't been this alone in decades. Everything around me was muted. I couldn't perceive the world the way I usually did. It made me feel off.

The mystery person was close.

I rounded the corner and stumbled.

A tall guy with wavy, medium brown hair caught me. He had the kind of eyes that refused to commit to green or brown. He tried to hide them behind the thick black frames of his glasses, but I saw his eyes. And they saw me.

He was Stellan Petersson, the IT guy.

He steadied me. When he touched me, I felt far away from everything. It reminded me of bath time as a kid. Submerged in water with a layer between me and the rest of the world. Except it wasn't affecting my ears. It was drowning out my telepathy. I shook my head and tried to focus.

"Are you okay?" he asked.

"First day in the new heels," I mumbled and pulled away from him. "Thanks for the save."

"Anytime." He gave me a slow smile. "You look lost."

I was. This was new territory for me. But I played along. "I'm trying to find my brother."

"What's his name?"

"Caleb Guhn."

Nothing in Stellan's expression changed. I don't know what I expected to happen, but I was disappointed by his non-reaction.

"You're on the wrong floor. The big wigs are up on thirty-five," he said.

"We had a bad cell connection. I swore he said five."

He pulled out his business card and scribbled something on the back before he handed it to me. "It's a big building. If you get lost again, feel free to call for help."

I took his card. Was he flirting with me? Being helpful? Giving me a clue? Without my telepathy, I couldn't tell what his motives were.

I looked down at his card. "Thank you, Stellan."

"You're welcome, I didn't catch your name."

"Kai Guhn."

Fifteen minutes later, I dropped into the leather chair across from Caleb in his office. "Found him."

"Really? Was it Montgomery? I had a feeling it was Montgomery."

I shook my head. "Stellan."

"Stellan Petersson?" He made it sound like it was the most absurd thing I'd ever said.

"Yes."

"Are you sure?"

"Being close to him shut down my telepathy. Completely."

"But, Stellan Petersson is such a…dork. Are you sure you got the right Stellan?"

"How many Stellan's work in IT?" Dork wasn't a word I'd use to describe the man I'd just met. "He's got that dangerous, quiet thing going on. The smart, mysterious hacker."

Caleb snorted. "Stellan isn't geek chic. He's just geek."

My brother and I had very different taste in guys, but I didn't understand his opinion of Stellan at all. "Well, whatever you think of him, he's the one who shut down my telepathy."

Caleb tapped the tips of his fingers together. "We're not even sure that it has anything to do with me, though. Maybe it's just a coincidence."

"Maybe. But I can't get inside his head to find out." I looked down at the card Stellan had given me. "He works with you?" I asked.

"He's the IT guy for Private Equity and for Futures."

I didn't know much about computers. I tried to remember my interactions with IT at Children's Protective Services. Well, beyond their patent advice to reboot the computer. "IT is in charge of who has access to what, right?"

"Yeah. So?"

I stared at Caleb. I didn't understand why my very smart brother was suddenly so dense. "Think about what you just said. Stellan has access to a lot of information, and he controls who has access to that information."

"I'm not sure what you're getting at, Kai."

I knew what Stellan could do to me. Now I wondered if he was doing something to my brother. "I think he's impacting your perception of him. You're way too dismissive of him."

Caleb rolled his lips outward like he was considering it, but only for a moment. "It concerns me that his powers interact with yours, but I don't see why he'd want to cause any trouble for me."

I sighed. "That's my point. If he's playing with your perceptions, you wouldn't."

Caleb frowned. "Valid. I'll think it over." He leaned forward. "I need another favor. David is coming by in a few minutes." He got up and opened the door to the coat closet. "Would you be so kind?"

"You want me to get in there?"

"I need you to sneak into my boss's head to get more intel on what's going on. It's this or under my desk."

I peered inside the closet. "It's not exactly a walk-in."

"You're tiny. You'll be fine."

"How long will I be in here?"

"It won't be more than fifteen minutes, I promise."

I nodded.

He shut the door.

My brother's coat and spare suit hung in the closet. When I pushed them to the side to give me more room, a whiff of sandalwood hit me. Standing there, I realized how much my feet ached. I eased off the heels and stretched my toes.

I heard the door to Caleb's office open and shut.

"Guhn, we need to talk," David said.

"What's going on?" Caleb asked.

I opened a tiny window in my shield. Thoughts swept in. I searched for David's.

Fear. Minty fear assaulted my nose. He was afraid Caleb had crossed a line in acquiring new investors. *KYC.* There it was again. *Know Your Customer.*

There better not be a money trail. I'm only five years away from retirement. I don't need this shit. Even if Caleb made everyone's bonuses better last year. Audit won't let this go. Fuck.

I tried to listen to his conversation with Caleb as I followed his thoughts. He sounded calm, but I sensed how much effort that was taking. "Audit got lucky with Compliance, but they'll keep digging. You know how they get when they think they found something."

"I do," Caleb said.

David struggled with how much to say and what to say. Finally, he settled on, "Well, keep your nose clean. We want new investors, but we don't want any trouble."

After his boss left, I slipped out of the closet and sat down. I told Caleb what I heard in his boss's head.

Caleb pulled his lips to the side of his face. It was his thinking expression. "Unfortunately, that doesn't tell us a whole lot that we didn't already know. Except that David is scared, and that scares me."

Caleb was lost in thought for a few minutes before he spoke again. "It started off with little things that made me look careless—like the missed meetings. Now, though, it's impacting the investor approval process, which is a regulatory landmine."

"But you told me that's not part of your job."

"It's not, really. But I gather and document the background information on potential investors before the firm allows them to invest their money with us. It's how we make sure we aren't taking illicit funds—money from terrorists, drug dealers, people like that."

"So, you take down the information, but who reviews it?" I asked.

"Compliance ultimately approves all new investors. I provide them with the basic investor information. They run all the checks on them."

"So you should be okay?"

"I should be." His voice was tinged with uncertainty. "But how do I prove a negative? That I didn't do something wrong?"

"We need to know more."

He gave me a tight smile. "I might have an in with Audit. Igleka hides it pretty well, but I think she likes me. If I can build on that, I can get into her dreams." He turned his full attention on me. "Are you sure you can do this? I hate asking you to manipulate your shield with so many minds around you."

"I can handle it. I'm a lot stronger than I was." What I didn't tell him was that I was drawing this new strength from my darkness.

He rolled a pen across his desk. "You know, you never asked if I did anything wrong."

"I don't care. You're my brother."

CHAPTER 44

Oliver

I hadn't wanted a big celebration, but that's what I got. Mrs. Fuchs served my favorite meal—wiener schnitzel and spätzle. True to her word, Mickey had made a special plate of kaiserschmarren with homemade plum jam for me. Aunt Ines made me another Sacher torte to share with the Fuchs family. It glowed with a single giant "29" candle. Mickey had insisted.

As everyone told me to "Make a wish," I closed my eyes and thought about what I wanted. I only got one birthday wish, so I had to make it count. My thoughts turned to Kai. I couldn't forget that she'd hung up on me the last time I called. I didn't think that a birthday wish could fix what was broken between us.

So, I wished that Schneider would finally have to face the consequences for what he'd done.

I blew out the candle.

While Mrs. Fuchs cut the cake, I asked, "Are Alex and Pete coming?" Neither was at dinner. I figured they were working late, but Pete wasn't one to miss a Sacher torte.

Mrs. Fuchs looked at Mr. Fuchs. They had one of those secret looks that passed critical information between them. Then she said, "Pete had a move down in Milwaukee."

"Alex is with him?" Despite the tensions between us, I figured he'd show up to a family dinner, even one in honor of me.

For a moment, no one said anything.

"Alex is in New York," Mickey said.

"New York?" My imagination conjured up images of Kai and Alex walking hand in hand down Hudson Street. Her taking him to all our favorite spots in Central Park. All the things Kai and I once did together, she'd do with him.

Mrs. Fuchs's words came out flustered and rushed. "It's for a job."

The cake suddenly tasted like chalk in my mouth. I took a gulp of coffee to wash it down. "I figured the guys had to be out of town to miss Sacher torte."

"You figured right." Mickey studied my face, waiting for a response.

I tried to act nonchalant, but it took everything I had to keep my voice level. "How long will they be gone?"

"Just a few days for Pete," Mickey answered. "Alex wasn't sure."

Alex was in New York with no immediate plans to come home. That irked me.

"Kai called me last night," Lukas said.

"That's great, buddy," I said.

Then I remembered that she'd called me, too, and I hadn't answered. But she hadn't left a message. I thought about calling her back tonight, but that would just mean lying about how I was spending my birthday. And it would mean knowing that, while I was talking to her, she might be with Alex.

When I came out of the bathroom, Mickey grabbed my wrist and tugged me toward her bedroom.

"What are you doing?" I asked.

"Shh."

Something in her eyes made me obey.

Her room was the same dark purple that it had been when she was a teenager. The movie and band posters had been replaced with photos of family and the places she longed to visit. Her old twin bed was now an adult-sized full.

After she shut the door, she picked up a small box on her dresser and thrust it at me. "Here."

"What's this?"

She tapped her fingers against her thighs like she was nervous about my response. "A birthday present."

I lifted the lid. Inside was a braided leather bracelet. I'd made it when we were in middle school and given it to her when we started dating. I ran my finger over its worn texture. "You saved it all these years?"

"It's a souvenir of one of the best times of my life."

I swallowed. "Mine, too."

"When things felt hopeless, I would hold this and know that there was hope. I thought you could use it now."

"Thank you." I hugged her.

She wrapped her arms around me and held me close. "You'll get through this."

I closed my eyes and sank into the warmth she offered. It was a moment of calm in the uncertainty of my existence. Mickey was always there, guiding me back to myself.

A few moments later, she stepped back. She picked up my mom's journal. "I wanted to show you this." She flipped to an entry.

Oliver amazes me every day. His smile. His love. He is everything I dreamed of when Reinhard and I talked about having a baby. Reinhard is so gentle with him. So careful. He says it's because Oli is a piece of me, but Reinhard doesn't realize how much of his strength Oli has. I see the same stubbornness in Oli's eyes when he demands his bottle at 3:41 a.m.

"They really loved me." I sank onto her bed.

Mickey sat beside me. "Of course they did."

Before I had Kai, I'd had my parents. Parents who loved me. A family. But both my parents were dead now. So were my grandparents. And my wife had left me. "They're all gone. My family is gone."

Mickey rested her hand on my back. "That's not true. You have Aunt Ines. You have us Fuchses. We're still here and we love you."

"Even you?" I asked.

Her eyes were the softest, lushest green. "Especially me."

CHAPTER 45

Kai

The next morning, I returned to Caleb's office building. I wanted to know if I could sneak into Stellan's mind if I caught him unawares.

I sat on a bench outside the building and slid open the window in my shield. A firestorm of thoughts came hurtling at me. Too many for me to handle on my own. But I didn't have to as long as I reached out to my darkness. There was so much strength there, and I just needed a little of it.

When I reached for it, I felt something in me shift. Like the darkness was reaching for me as I reached for it. I should have recoiled from it, but I didn't. I let its power course through me. I had to be strong enough to handle whatever might happen.

I could hear so many minds. I took a deep breath and focused. The chatter separated into distinct voices. Rich baritones, gentle whispers, cries of pain. I heard everyone in a half-mile radius. Their voices reverberated through me.

I searched for Stellan, but, since I'd never heard his thoughts before,

I didn't know exactly what to listen for.

I tried going inside the building, loitering around the lobby. Same problem. I went upstairs to another company's office and tried from their waiting room. Nothing worked. I couldn't find Stellan. Maybe he wasn't here today.

Finally, I went to his floor. I still couldn't find him.

And then, all it once, the voices were gone. It was so sudden that I felt certain that Stellan knew what he was doing. He'd sensed me before I found him.

I was halfway to the Bluebell Café when my telepathy finally came back online. The din of thoughts started with intermittent gasps. They morphed into continuous whispers. Then, finally, a steady stream of chatter. I let it wash over me for a minute before I closed my shield again.

I'd spend so much of my life seeing my telepathy as a curse; I never realized how much I relied upon it or how much it defined me. Until now. Every time Stellan took my power away, a part of me feared it would never return. I couldn't imagine a lifetime of that kind of silence. It was suffocating and terrifying.

When my cab got stuck in traffic, I watched the people moving about on the street. My thoughts slipped to Oliver. The last time we'd spoken, I'd hung up on him. The next day, I called and didn't leave a message. What was I supposed to say? *Happy Birthday, too bad our marriage is falling apart.* I hadn't really expected him to call back, but it stung that he hadn't. I'd been pushing him away for so long. I shouldn't be surprised that he'd finally taken the hint.

I felt the darkness stir inside me. It whispered in my mind, *Oliver is gone. You need to let him go.*

I was trying.

I pushed open the glass door at the Bluebell Café and the sounds of the city faded away. Country music played in the background. Mismatching, hand-stenciled tables and chairs stretched across the aged wooden floor. A rustic hutch filled with dishes nestled against the wall. This place sucked the city right out of you. It reminded me of Butternut, and that was why I'd pick it for Alex.

I scanned the tables, looking for him. He stood and waved at me from the back of the restaurant. His eyes were so blue. A blue I could drown in. I couldn't help rushing toward him.

"That's New York fast." He laughed and enveloped me in a hug. I held on tight. "A Butternut welcome."

He helped me out of my coat. "All too rare in this city."

"So, tell me about this client you're after."

"I can't say too much until the deal's done. She's got five houses that need to be packed up. Everything is going out to her relatives in Wisconsin."

"How exciting."

Before I could say more, the waitress came over. She stared at Alex the entire time she was taking our drink order. It started to get annoying. I mean I got it. He was a good-looking guy, but there are plenty of good-looking guys in New York, and this one was with me.

I was looking forward to a chance to talk, but the waitress was back with our drinks mere minutes after we'd ordered them.

She put his hot chocolate in front of him and practically purred, "I put extra whipped cream on it for you."

She'd also carved a heart into the cherry she put on top.

"Thank you. It looks amazing." He took a sip. Whipped cream dotted the tip of his nose.

She giggled.

"What?" he asked.

"Let me help you." Her eyes shone with anticipation. She couldn't wait to touch him.

"I got it." I reached over and used my finger to wipe the cream away. Then I licked it off my finger.

"Thanks." Alex didn't take his eyes off me.

The waitress finally got the hint and left, so Alex and I could catch up on what had been happening in Butternut with his family, Aunt Ines, and, of course, Herbie.

Finally, he added, "Oliver's doing okay."

I didn't want to talk about Oliver with Alex, but I couldn't help saying, "He's been spending time with Mickey."

Alex leaned forward. "I think they are trying to fix what happened with Christian."

"Oliver can do whatever he wants, we're separated." I meant it.

"Does he know we're having lunch?"

"Did you tell Mickey?" I asked.

"Yes. Why?"

"Then Oliver knows we're having lunch." Mickey would make sure to pass that information along.

Alex sipped his hot chocolate for a few moments. "Do you miss him?"

"Sometimes." Though it was getting less and less frequent. "But we don't work anymore."

He tilted his head. "But you might again. There's a chance?" I wasn't sure if he was rooting for Oliver and me to get back together or hoping that we wouldn't.

"We aren't the same people who made those vows, so how can we be expected to keep them?" We were living separate lives, two people who used to love each other.

After lunch, Alex and I wandered around Gramercy Park. On any given street in the city, you can discover something—an amazing building, a hidden cemetery, a forgotten mural. The city was filled with unexpected beauty if you took your time and looked around.

We stumbled upon a gothic church, found a bench inside the church grounds, and sat down.

"Tell me more about what's going on with your brother," he said.

There were people milling about. "I can't really talk about it here."

"Can you tell me telepathically?" he whispered.

"I can try."

I envisioned a window in my shield. I made the glass clear so I could see Alex. He stood outside. No shield. Nothing. Totally open to me.

It made it so much easier to share thoughts with him. I envisioned my shield as a tunnel connecting his mind and mine. It blocked out all the other minds around us. We were able to communicate silently as the city swirled around us.

I told him what had been happening at Caleb's job. How he had been made to look careless and less competent. How it was escalating to illegal activities that involved compliance and money laundering.

With Caleb, I always tried to be optimistic; with Alex, I could let the worry show. Warmth spread through me. Hope. Alex made me feel like I could fix this for Caleb.

We could have lingered on that bench all day, but the cold seeped through our down coats and weaseled its way under our clothes. We needed to move around. Besides, I'd promised to show him the tourist attractions.

The Empire State Building was first on my list. A weekday early afternoon usually meant shorter lines and quicker access. We made our way into the building, showed our IDs, and got in line. We passed the time by making up ridiculous backstories about other people in line.

An hour later, we crowded into the elevator and headed to the main deck on the eighty-sixth floor. I was pushed so close to Alex that I could

261

feel the warmth of his body. He smelled like sunshine and summer. I tried not to think about the other people. I blocked out their thoughts and their feelings by focusing on Alex.

I heard his thoughts. *This is a perfect day. But Oliver. Damn it, she's still his wife. I can't get in the way.*

I probably shouldn't have eavesdropped on his thoughts, but I couldn't help thinking back at him, *You're never in the way.*

He looked startled, but whispered, "I try not to be."

His gaze held mine. For a moment everyone else disappeared. I swear my heart sped up to match his. My throat went dry. Was this really what I felt? Or was it the darkness, intent on the annihilation of my marriage? I didn't know. I wasn't even sure I cared.

When the doors opened, we were at the main viewing area. We stepped outside onto the wrap-around balcony. The view to the east stretched past the East River into Brooklyn and Queens. To the south was the Statue of Liberty. She looked so tiny from up here. Everything was less intense. More manageable.

We meandered around so he could get pictures from each angle.

Alex asked, "How has it been? Being back in the city?"

"Amazing. I forgot how much I loved living here." Because it used to be much harder. Nathan had changed that for me. Fleetingly, I wondered if he was behind my growing attraction to Alex. A final push to end Oliver and me. That was what Nathan had wanted. But it felt like what I wanted, too.

"It must be hard to be here without Oliver," he said.

The darkness inside me stirred, pushing the truth to my lips. "I don't belong with Oliver."

It wasn't enough just saying it, though. I had to do something. I could reach out and touch Alex. I wanted to, and I didn't try to fight it.

I caressed his cheek. "Some things can't be denied."

I saw my darkness reflected in his eyes, a desire that burned my soul and threatened to devour both of us. I stood on tiptoes and brushed my lips across his. His arms wrapped around my waist. I clasped my hands around his neck. I wasn't letting go. All the tourists faded away. Every worry fled my mind. There was just Alex. His lips, his hands, his breath.

The kiss was desperate, passionate. He wanted it as much as I did. His desire tasted like a candied apple. But then he pulled back.

I can't take advantage. She's vulnerable right now. His lips abandoned mine.

Through a haze of desire, I watched them move. He was saying something, but I could barely hear him over my heart thundering in my ears. All I wanted was for him to kiss me like that again.

I shook my head and tried to focus on his voice.

"You've got so much on your mind right now, with your brother and with Oliver. It's not the time to start something," he said.

"But we already started something. That moment at Copper Falls. That was the beginning of something."

His thoughts went back to our first kiss. We'd stood gazing out over the frozen waterfall. It looked like a root beer float. The water was amber colored, but the waterfall was coated in white ice. Desire swirled around my shield. I knew he wanted me. I'd closed the distance between us and kissed him. He knew it was wrong, but in that moment he wanted me more than he wanted to be right.

His memory faded. His voice came out hoarse. "Sparks. You can't control sparks."

"It's never been just sparks between us." I pulled him in for another kiss. Not sparks—fireworks. A Fourth of July extravaganza. This time he didn't let go.

CHAPTER 46

Oliver

I didn't know why I'd brought my mom's ornament to work. Maybe just because it had been so long since I'd had anything of hers, and I didn't want to let go. After she died, Dad had packed away all of her things. Every reminder of her disappeared from our house like she'd never been there.

I hung the ornament inside my cubicle in my line of sight, thinking the more I saw it, the more memories it would shake loose. They were all I had left of her.

I heard Mr. Kohler's footsteps coming down the hall before I saw him. I didn't need to look at my watch to know it was 1:45 p.m. This was the time he swung by my cubicle every day. He wore a three-piece suit and wire-rimmed glasses. He had a full head of white hair. Despite being in his seventies, he looked like a fifty-year-old. I wondered if his secretary had something to do with that.

He stood there while I gave him a five-minute update on my progress. When I finished, he pointed to my mom's ornament and asked, "Where did you get that?"

"I found it in a box of my mom's stuff," I said.

"Mr. Fuchs made one for me, too."

"Mickey's dad?" I asked.

He shook his head. "Georg, her grandfather."

He had passed away several years ago. "He used to carve ornaments?"

Mr. Kohler look confused. "Ornaments?" Then he chuckled. "That's a key, Oliver."

"To what?"

"It depends what Mr. Fuchs built for your mom. Could be a box, a safe, a piece of furniture, a wall. He was ingenious at making hiding spots."

I must have looked stunned, because Mr. Kohler added, "The families that settled here from Austria and Germany wanted to protect what was important to them. It's why many of the old houses have secret rooms."

That made sense. Probably why Grandpa Richter had a safe in his office. "So, what does your key unlock?"

Mr. Kohler smiled. "That's between old Georg and me."

After work, I headed over to the Fuchses, hoping Mr. Fuchs could tell me more about his father's work.

Mr. Fuchs was in the living room when I arrived. He was a tall man with dark hair like Mickey's, except age had streaked it with gray. His blue eyes studied the snowflake carving as he turned it over in his hands. "This is definitely one of my dad's."

He found a magnifying glass and showed me the signature carved into the design work on the back of it: Georg Viktor Fuchs.

"He made them for special customers. He loved the challenge of making it look like nothing important. Hiding in plain sight, so to speak."

"What is it a key to?"

Mr. Fuchs shrugged. "That's a secret that died with my father and your mother."

Mickey wandered into the room. "What secret?"

I handed her the ornament and explained how it was a key to something.

She turned it over in her hands. "This is so cool. Pop Pop really made it?"

Mr. Fuchs nodded. "Where do you think the boys get their woodworking talents?"

I flashed back to the day Alex walked Kai and me through the Fuchs Storage Center. Kai's fingers had glided over the hand-carved mirror made by Alex's grandfather. Kai had flirted with Alex that day to get back at me. She was probably flirting with him right now. That thought hurt, but not as much as it once had.

Mickey pulled me out of my memories by asking, "It was your mom's?" She flicked her nail against the back of her front teeth.

Something was on her mind. "Yes. Why?"

She got up and waved me to follow her. As soon as we were in the hallway, she murmured, "I think I read something about a key."

I trailed her back to her room. "In my mom's journal?"

She nodded and shut the door. "She mentioned a key. I didn't realize she meant that." She pointed at the ornately carved wood.

It never would have occurred to me, either. Thank goodness for Kohler's daily pop-ins.

She picked up one of my mom's journals and pointed to a passage.

I still keep everything important in my secret hiding spot. When he's older, I will share it with Oliver.

After she put it down, she picked up another slim volume and flipped closer to the end of it.

It won't be me who shows Oliver the secret hiding spot. I trust Reinhard to do it. I want Oliver to have that piece of my family's history.

"Dad never told me about it," I said.

Mickey picked up a third volume and flipped to an early entry.

When Mommy and Daddy died, I inherited everything, including Daddy's desk. I still have the key that unlocks my secret spot. Daddy had it made by Mr. Fuchs so I'd have a place to play while he worked. One day I will share it with my child. And we will have hours together at the desk just like Daddy and I did.

"All we have to do is find the desk," Mickey said.

"I don't know where it is." I explained how my father had gotten rid of all my mother's things. Whatever she might have left in that compartment for me was gone. Another bit of my mother disappeared from my life.

Mickey touched my arm. "Maybe your aunt Ines will know something?"

"Maybe." But I wasn't holding out much hope for that. "Why did Dad wait so long to give me the box? Why didn't he reach out while he was still alive?"

Mickey's eyes were kaleidoscopes of understanding. "He made mistakes. He wasn't the father you needed, but he's the only father you had."

"He could have given me my mother's journals. He could have saved that desk for me. How could he keep her from me?"

"Maybe it was too painful for him?"

"He lost his wife, but I lost my mother. Then I lost all the reminders of her." I couldn't remember what the desk looked like. I couldn't remember her favorite dress. I lost all those things. Because it was too painful for my father, I had to lose every memento that would have kept the memory of my mother alive.

CHAPTER 47

Kai

I was sick of letting things happen to me. The darkness wanted me to make things happen, so I invited Alex back to Caleb's place.

When he sat down on the couch, I sat beside him and rested my hand on his thigh.

"We shouldn't." He grabbed my hand, but he didn't remove it.

"I'm separated," I whispered in his ear. Then I kissed his neck.

I could feel his desire for me. It stirred in the depths of his soul. A little darkness of his own. He was tired of taking the high road. He wanted to take me instead. It was delicious.

I slid into Alex's lap. I laced my fingers through his hair and sucked on his earlobe.

"No regrets?" he asked.

"Never with you." I stared into his eyes.

My hands glided over the muscles of his shoulders and down to his chest. My cast made it a little difficult, but I started unbuttoning his shirt. "We deserve a little happiness, don't we?"

Something in his eyes evaporated. I think it was the last of his restraint. His hands slid around my waist. He pulled me closer and kissed me. The blood soared through my veins. It felt so good. I didn't want it to stop. I wanted to give in to every impulse I had with Alex.

I struggled out of my sweater, desperate to get closer to him. His skin felt so warm against mine. There was just Alex and me.

Then Caleb opened the apartment door. "Well, this is quite a homecoming." His voice poured over us like ice water.

I leapt away from Alex. "What are you doing home so early?"

"It's 7:30 p.m.," Caleb said dryly.

"Is it?" I'd lost track of time. I snatched my sweater off the floor and put it back on. Thank goodness my jeans were still on.

Alex fumbled with the buttons on his shirt. "I should head out."

Caleb's eyes danced with amusement. "Don't leave on my account. I haven't seen my sister this excited in months."

A slight blush crept over Alex's cheeks.

"Caleb, don't tease him."

My brother ignored me. "If you're going to get close to my sister, especially on my couch, I think we should get to know each other better."

I shot Caleb a withering glance. He ignored it.

Alex sat down. "That's fair."

Caleb poured drinks and I rustled up some snacks from the kitchen. We made a few rounds of small talk until an awkward silence fell over us.

"She's almost over Oliver, you know," Caleb said.

I choked on my wine. "Caleb!"

"It's true," he confided to Alex. "I've been watching her fall out of love with him for weeks. Thanks for helping her face it."

Alex cleared his throat. "I didn't mean to," he glanced at me, "I mean, I meant to kiss you." He tried again, "I just..."

Caleb grinned, clearly enjoying Alex's embarrassment.

"How was work?" I asked through gritted teeth.

"You told him about what's been going on?"

I nodded.

"Of course you did, because you trust him," Caleb said.

Alex stuffed a few chips in his mouth to avoid having to respond.

"I dreamwalked into Igleka's head last night."

"What did you find?" Please let it be something helpful.

Caleb rubbed his fingers over his lips. "There's information missing from the KYC files of several of my big investors, but I know it was there when I sent the files. If Compliance received them without that information, they should have rejected them and punted the files back to me so that I could complete them. But instead they approved them as investors."

"So that's Compliance's mistake, right?" I asked.

"It is if the necessary paperwork was missing when they approved the investors."

"So you think someone removed it after the approval was done? Why?"

"To make it look like Compliance was rubber stamping my new investors."

"Why would anyone do that?"

"Because that would cast suspicion on me."

"So, who has access to those files?" Alex asked.

"Electronically? Anyone in Private Equity, our admins, IT, Audit, and Compliance," Caleb said.

"What about the paper documents?" I asked.

"Compliance keeps the paper files in their department," Caleb said.

"But someone could sneak in and alter them?" Alex asked.

My brother nodded.

"Stellan could poke around in the electronic files without arousing suspicion," I said.

"True, but there are plenty of other people who had access to those files," Caleb said.

A look of confusion passed over Alex's face. "But, after everything Kai told me, I mean, Stellan was in that meeting, and he's been preventing Kai from using her telepathy. So it makes sense that he's involved."

I appreciated Alex's help, but I wasn't going to try to argue with my brother about Stellan again. "Fine, Caleb. Let's explore the theory that it could have been anybody. Do any of your coworkers have a grudge against you?"

"Not that I'm aware of," he admitted.

Caleb had been popular in high school. But he was also the kind of guy people secretly hated. Luckily, my brother had a knack for amassing some powerful allies over the years. He enlisted them to help search for me when I'd been kidnapped. He was someone who always had people. People I never met who could do things that were best left unsaid. "Can you get someone to look into your coworkers' pasts? See if anyone might have a secret grudge against you?"

"I already made a few calls," Caleb said. "And yes, I'm having Stellan checked out. But so far there's no motive for him, just opportunity."

At least he was considering Stellan. That was progress. "Did you get any more details about the files from Igleka's head?"

"There's one file for the Valasquez family. She thinks I didn't do proper KYC because I wanted to allow them to invest funds from questionable sources. With their money, I was able to make shitloads more for my group." Caleb rubbed the center of his forehead, like his third eye ached. "It gets worse."

"How could this get worse?" I asked.

"Igleka has someone investigating wire transfers into my accounts. She's looking for kickbacks. She thinks I might have paid off the compliance associate, Thaddeus, to approve my investors," Caleb said. "That's why the paperwork missing from the other files is so concerning. One investor approved without proper paperwork is an oversight. Several become a pattern of rule breaking."

"But you didn't, so there won't be anything to find," Alex said.

"There shouldn't be," Caleb said.

"What about Thaddeus? Can't he testify that he didn't get any kickbacks from you?" I asked.

"He's backpacking in Africa. Completely off the grid. No way to get a hold of him," Caleb said.

"That's really convenient," I said.

Caleb shifted and looked at his hands.

He used to do that when he was hiding something from Dad. "What aren't you telling us?"

"I dabbled in the gray. Just once. The Valasquez file is the only file that I sent Compliance with the KYC paperwork incomplete."

"Why would you do that?" I asked.

"Sometimes things slip through," Caleb sighed. "It wasn't right, but one slip wouldn't have been a big deal. That investor made our bonuses last year. But Audit is digging deep now, looking for a pattern of behavior."

I took a deep breath. "If it was just one mistake, we can fix it."

"I haven't been responsible for most of my recent fuckups. Clearly, someone is setting me up. We're talking about someone capable of getting into the investor files and altering them to make Compliance, and by extension me, look bad. This person would have no trouble setting up a dummy account in my name."

This seemed like an awful lot of work to destroy my brother. Why would anyone do this?

I leaned back into the couch. My shoulder brushed against Alex's. I didn't move away. Neither did he. "Setting up a dummy account is something an IT guy could probably do? Somebody who knows his way around computers and finance? Somebody like Stellan?"

"Or just about anybody else in IT."

"Caleb! How many other IT guys are preventing me from helping you by blocking my telepathy?"

"But you said it yourself. He might not even know what he's doing. It might have nothing to do with me."

"It's possible," Alex conceded, but he didn't sound convinced.

"Everything we know so far points to Stellan." I needed for Caleb to believe me. "I'm going to talk to him."

"How?" Caleb asked.

"He gave me his card when we met. His cell's on the back. I'll just give him a call."

"And do what?" Alex asked.

"Meet him for a drink," I said.

"I don't like it. If you're right, he's dangerous," Caleb said.

Finally, he was coming around. "I'll pick a crowded bar in your neighborhood."

Caleb wanted to be there, just in case. But I was afraid Stellan would see him and leave. We compromised. Alex would stay out of sight in the back of the bar and I would keep him on the phone through the entire meeting so he could eavesdrop and swoop in if needed.

CHAPTER 48

Oliver

Aunt Ines's kitchen had become my oasis of calm. I didn't want to go home. I hated walking into an empty house, so I delayed the inevitable by stopping over Aunt Ines's for dessert, for conversation, and for companionship.

She'd put out milk and chocolate chip cookies for me and poured herself a cup of tea. "How are things with Herbie?"

"We've reached a détente."

She chuckled. "And Kai?"

I looked down at my plate.

"What happened?"

"Alex is with her in New York."

"You're busy with Mickey," Aunt Ines said.

"I'm trying to bring Schneider to justice." Mickey and I weren't hanging out and exploring the city together like Kai and Alex. "Kai missed my birthday. No gift. No card. No call. Not even a text."

On our wedding day, she promised she'd never miss a birthday or a holiday. That I'd never be alone again. She'd broken that vow.

Aunt Ines absorbed that information without comment. Then she changed the subject. "Did you read the journals?"

"Dad's."

I told her about the entries where Dad hinted at Schneider's guilt. "But I need real evidence from the crime, something to take to the authorities and help them prove that Schneider killed Christian and covered it up."

"Schneider must have disposed of everything by now." Aunt Ines tapped her nails on her teacup.

"I know. Maybe there's something he missed, though." I tried to keep hope alive, but I wasn't sure what to do next. "What if he gets away with it?"

"He can't escape his conscience."

I snorted. "I don't think he has one."

"I wouldn't be so certain. He stopped the heavy drinking after what happened to Christian. I never put the two together until now."

"The Hoffmanns—"

"Deserve better. I agree. But Schneider can make your life here impossible. He could target Lukas or Mickey to get to you. And for what?"

I wrestled with the fear of what Schneider could do to us. The more I thought about it, the more I questioned if I should keep doing this. Maybe it was time to let it go, even if it meant I would remain a part of the cover-up. Forever.

Maybe I couldn't fix what my dad broke.

It wasn't the only thing bothering me, though. I'd lost another link to my mom when my dad got rid of her family's desk. "Grandpa Eder's desk had a secret compartment. The key was in that box you gave me, but I have no idea where the desk itself is. Dad got rid of all of Mom's stuff when she died."

"That's not true. He couldn't keep her things in his house, but he kept them safe. The desk is right there in your study." She broke a piece of cookie and popped it into her mouth.

"What?"

"Grandpa Richter's desk used to belong to your mother, and, before that, your grandpa Eder."

"I have the desk." I couldn't believe it. The desk I'd sat at for the past six months, it was my mom's desk. Grandpa Eder's desk. The desk that was meant to be mine.

"My father always wanted you to have something of your mom's kin. He knew how much Mr. Eder and your mom loved that desk. It was the only piece of furniture he ever dusted."

"He did that for me?"

"Oliver, don't you know how much he loved you?" Her smile broke my heart.

All those years I'd stayed away—they caught up with me. "I missed out on so much with Grandpa."

Aunt Ines didn't say anything. She just gripped my hand.

My eyes burned. The table blurred. The pain of what I'd lost was magnified. Bone chilling grief overwhelmed me. Hot tears trickled down my cheeks.

Aunt Ines wrapped her arms around me. "Oh my sweet boy. It's all right. Let it out."

I cried for everything and everyone I'd lost. My grandfather, my mother, even my father. I cried for all the people that I would never see again.

I'd called Mickey as soon as I left Aunt Ines's house. Now, she and I were in my study, standing in front of the desk. It wasn't just a piece of furniture; it was a tangible connection to Grandpa Eder and Mama.

Mickey broke the silence. "Let's start with the outside."

"Sounds good." I gave her a tentative smile. "Thanks for coming over." I don't know how I would have gotten through the past few days without her.

We explored every surface, looking for a hidden hollow spot. My fingers tested the wood for a sliding panel or a section that popped out, somewhere we could try the key. Mickey tapped on the wood, listening for a hollow sound.

While we were working, I thought about Grandpa Eder. He'd died before I was born, but more than one person had told me that I took after him. I couldn't help wondering if my life would have been different if I'd known him.

"Do I always run away?" I asked.

Mickey's tapping came to a slow stop. "Not always."

"What's the exception?"

"Back in high school. When I broke up with you. You tried to fight for me. After I pushed you away, you shut down. It's how you survived the pain."

It still hurt to remember that time. I'd tried to fight for Kai, too. Before I pulled back and tried to survive the pain of losing her. "You make me sound so cold."

"We all have our methods of dealing. Yours might not be the best way, but it lets you continue and sometimes that's all we can do—continue."

I thought about what she said as I moved onto the drawers and looked for false bottoms. Mickey went under the desk. I wasn't sure I wanted to be that way anymore. Maybe I...

"Oliver, I found something," Mickey said.

I crouched down beside her, my body pressed against hers. She shined her flashlight on a smooth panel of wood.

"What am I looking at?" I asked.

She slid her fingers over a faint seam. Then she pressed on it. A square piece of wood popped out. Underneath was the impression of a wooden snowflake.

I slid out from under the desk, grabbed the key, and handed it to her.

"Ready?" she asked.

"Do it."

She put the wooden snowflake into the space in the desk. Nothing happened.

"Can you turn it?"

Mickey pressed harder. The key sunk deeper into the wood until we heard a click. Then she used the openings carved in the snowflake to turn it.

The panel popped open to reveal a hidden compartment.

CHAPTER 49

Kai

New York bars are all the same at night. Too many people crammed into a tiny space with too many emotions brought to the surface by alcohol. It was bad enough when I sensed these heightened feelings without smelling and tasting them, too. The sweet coconut scent of the desperate. Honey everywhere, heavy on my tongue. It was the taste of irresponsibility. Sometimes the scents and smells came from the same person. It made my head spin.

I hated these places. Avoided them in college. Ran from them when we lived in the city. All the tastes and scents would make me instantly disoriented on a Saturday night.

Wednesday night wasn't that bad. It was the beginning of the descent to the weekend. There was still hope. A whiff of possibility. Like peanut butter, it clung to the girls.

The guys, they were different. If they didn't find someone here, they kept a cache of booty calls on their phones. Worst case scenario, they hired someone for a night. It didn't make much difference where they stuck it in. Just that they got to stick it in somewhere.

Emotions pressed against my shield. Sucking and licking at it. Trying to weaken it. I couldn't let them slip through and get to me. I closed my eyes and took a 4-7-8 breath. Then I took another to center myself before I touched my darkness. I'd been doing that a lot lately. I could feel it seeping into me. There was so much strength in it. But it also contained every bad impulse, every self-destructive desire, and every cruel instinct. All the pieces of me that I fought to control, I had to release them to reinforce my shield. And each time I did it, it was an exhilarating rush that I craved more and more.

Fuchsia and indigo fog encircled my shield. The fuchsia was lust; the indigo was loneliness. So much loneliness here.

It called to my darkness. I wanted to exploit it. Things shifted inside me. I felt wicked. Powerful. Willing to do anything to get what I needed. I draped my coat over the stool and sat down at the bar. I leaned forward, showing enough cleavage to get the bartender's attention.

"What would you like?" His gaze slid from my breasts to my face and back again.

Hard liquor, much like pain pills, interfered with my shield. It's one of those things you did once and never again. Like drinking until you blacked out. Once and never again. Though, tonight, I had to fight the urge to order tequila shots.

"A Chardonnay," I said.

He gave me a generous pour.

I sipped my wine. I didn't look for Alex. I didn't need to. I could feel his mind brush against mine. *Everything okay?*

I'm great.

Be care—

His thoughts cut off in mid-sentence. Silence. Infuriating silence. The fuchsia and indigo outside my shield vanished. White light shone in, obliterating everyone else's thoughts and feelings.

My telepathy was gone.

I didn't tell anyone why it scared me so much. It reminded me of the quiet before I lost control. The quiet of not being here. The quiet of death.

It also meant that Stellan was here. I scanned the crowd until I saw him. He made his way toward me, weaving around people, in no particular hurry. He knew I'd wait for him.

He slid onto the stool beside me and ordered a Manhattan.

I didn't have to shield around him. It was the worst silver lining ever.

I tried making small talk for a few minutes, but something in his eyes told me that he knew what I wanted to ask him, so I did. "How long have you been able to do this?"

"Do what?" He gave me a look of mock surprise.

"Shut down my special abilities."

A smile spread slowly across his face, as if he was more pleased than he expected to be. "Is that what I do to you?"

"Isn't that what you do to everyone?"

"Something like that." He sipped his drink. "So what special abilities do I shut down?"

"Tell me about yours and I'll tell you about mine." I batted my eyelashes.

He chuckled. "You remind me of your brother."

"Gorgeous?"

"Practical."

"How long have you been able to do it?" I asked again.

"A while. What about you?"

"The same." I could be as vague as he was.

"And your brother?" He adjusted his glasses.

"He's pretty normal," I lied.

"Are you sure about that?"

He knew more than I realized. I wasn't sure what to do next. But the darkness did. I let it take control. I leaned closer to give him a good view of my breasts. "What makes you think otherwise?"

He smirked and sipped his drink.

281

I slid a finger around the rim of my glass and used my bedroom voice. "You don't like my brother, do you?"

He shrugged. "Like, not like. It's irrelevant."

I didn't know what he meant and I couldn't pry into his mind. I needed to knock him off his game. I slid my hand up his thigh.

His voice warmed. "Ms. Guhn, are you flirting with me?"

"Would you like me to flirt with you?" I stroked his inner thigh.

"It might make me more inclined to answer your questions." Amusement glinted in his eyes.

I tucked my hair behind my ear and smiled coyly. "If you hated Caleb, you could find a way to hurt him without anyone ever finding out?"

He widened his eyes. "Could I? How?"

I leaned closer and whispered in his ear. "You'd think of something."

"You'd be surprised by all the things I can think of."

I was close enough to share a breath. "It takes a lot to surprise me."

"Really? Let me see if I can do it."

When he closed the distance between us, I swore he was going to kiss me. Instead, he whispered in my ear, "Someday, you'll ask me the right question and I'll answer it." His voice was low, but I heard every word. "The who and the how can't save your brother. Only the why."

"Can *you* save my brother?"

"I just did." He tossed back the rest of his drink and left the bar.

I puzzled over Stellan's cryptic words, but none of them made sense to me. My gaze wandered around the bar and I glimpsed Natalia sipping a martini. She was flanked by two gorgeous dark-haired, dark-eyed men. They looked rich, powerful, and ready for anything.

She raised her glass to me. I lifted my Chardonnay. She disentangled herself from her companions and sashayed toward me.

I started noticing the murmuring of other minds. Stellan must have left the area. Quickly too. I erected my shield and plastered a smile on my face for Natalia.

"Nicely done," she said.

"Excuse me?"

"You can play the sweet wife all you like, but I saw you with that guy. And he wasn't your husband."

"How do you know?" I asked.

"Wives never flirt with their husbands like that," she said. "If they did, they might not stray." Natalia checked out my outfit. "Nice shoes. Great coat. The city is clearly rubbing off on you."

She made it sound like I was turning into her or something. "How do you do it?"

"Do what?"

"Share Caleb."

She tossed her platinum locks behind her shoulder. "Haven't you realized we are all lending and sharing? No one truly belongs to anyone else in this world."

"That's not true."

She sipped her drink. "It's all contracts, and we're always on the lookout for a better deal—whether we admit it to ourselves or not."

"How can you live without love?"

"I don't." Natalia laughed. "I just don't lie to myself. I accept that love is ephemeral. I grab it when it comes and I let it go when it leaves." She turned and made her way back to her table. After she rejoined them, one of the men nuzzled her ear.

I wasn't sure if I felt sorry for her or jealous.

I picked up my phone and told Alex, "I'll meet you outside."

"Sure." He hung up.

I grabbed my coat and headed for the door.

CHAPTER 50

Oliver

I shined my flashlight into the six-inch deep compartment in my grandfather's desk. Inside was a stack of letters tied together with a ribbon. I pulled it out. The ink was faded and the envelopes were yellowed. The graying ribbon had spots of bright blue that hinted at its former beauty.

Each envelope was labeled in careful handwriting for a different situation. *Going to college, fighting with your father, losing your grandfather, after your dad dies, when you get married, when your marriage has problems, birth of your first child, when you feel like giving up, if you get divorced, if your wife dies.*

Mickey peered over my shoulder. "They're all from your mom?"

I traced my finger over the curvy handwriting. "She left them for me."

"Why didn't your dad give them to you?"

I shrugged. "Maybe he didn't even know they were in there. This was my mother's desk."

I started to open an envelope, but Mickey said, "Wait. There's something else in there."

She squeezed around me and reached inside. A single letter in Dad's handwriting had fallen behind the pile of my mother's letters. The envelope and writing weren't as aged as the others. I scooted out from under the desk, so I could read it.

> Dear Oliver,
>
> I'm sorry this is all coming so late to you. That's my fault. I couldn't read your mother's last letter to me. She begged me to do it as soon as she passed on, but it was too painful. It took me years to look at it and that's when I found out that she'd written all these letters for you. Trust me, I had no idea what I kept from you.
>
> It was only in her final letter to me that she asked me to pass them on to you and to give you the key and the desk. I should have read her letter like she asked. Then I would have given you her journals and these letters earlier. By the time I knew about them, it was too late. You'd already left for college.
>
> I planned to reach out to you. If I didn't, something happened to me before I could. If you're reading this, it means you've come home and you got the box of things I left with your aunt Ines. I was afraid John might snoop around, so I had to keep this letter hidden in the desk. I had to make sure it was somewhere beyond his reach until you could find it.
>
> There are some things I need you to know. I'm sorry to burden you with more secrets, but you're the only one I can tell.
>
> John thinks we disposed of everything after Christian's death. He destroyed Christian's clothing. I was supposed to get rid of Christian's bike, but I didn't. I guess a part of me always knew John couldn't be trusted. The bike is safe inside a hidden room at Grandpa Richter's farmhouse. Aunt Ines knows where this room is, and she can let you in. There are paint marks on the bike that I suspect are from John's car, a tan 1990 Buick Regal. This is the only physical evidence left connecting John to Christian's death.

Son, I'm sorry I made you keep my secret. I was wrong. I thought I could save John. I never guessed that it would mean losing you.

Love,

Dad

CHAPTER 51

Kai

As I stepped outside the warm bar, a burst of cold air burned my cheeks and stung my legs. Stockings were no defense against the January frigidness. I buttoned up my coat and searched for my gloves.

"Are we done here?" Alex sounded impatient.

I did a double take. "Is everything okay?"

"Did you get what you needed?" he asked curtly.

"Stellan's definitely involved. I just don't know why he's doing this."

Alex nodded once and set out for Caleb's apartment. I had to scamper to keep up.

"Slow down. I can't move that fast in these shoes."

He let me catch up. "You seemed to move very fast at the bar."

"What?" It took me a second. "Oh, the flirting. With Stellan." I laughed. Alex didn't. "Are you jealous? I couldn't use my telepathy, so I had to fall back on my *other assets*."

"Well, it was quite a performance."

"Are you serious?"

"And I heard what that woman had to say to you. I'm not looking for a better deal, Kai, and I don't share."

"Neither do I. If I did, I might not have minded about my husband and your sister."

Alex flinched a bit at that. "But you were willing to flirt with Stellan."

"To save my brother, I'd sleep with Stellan."

Alex looked genuinely shocked.

"Wouldn't you do the same thing for Mickey?"

"Stellan's not my type." Alex's lips twitched. The ghost of a smile appeared there.

"You know what I mean."

"I'd do anything for my family."

"So you get it. There's something else I need for you to understand." I grabbed his arm and pulled him to a stop. I didn't care how much the other people on the sidewalk glared. I looked up into Alex's blue eyes and said, "When I came out of that cave, I brought darkness with me. I'm willing—and able—to do things that I couldn't do before, and the things I do aren't always nice. If you can't handle that, you should walk away now."

He stepped closer and leaned down until his nose almost touched mine. "I like a little darkness in my woman."

I whispered, "I've got more than a little."

"Good."

A delicious tension coiled inside me. Maybe it was the wine. Maybe it was New York. Maybe it was all the lust and desire from the bar. Maybe it was Natalia's words. Most likely, it was all of that plus the darkness dancing in Alex's eyes. His darkness called to mine.

I closed the distance between us, pushing him up against the nearest building. My lips found his. My hands slid under his coat, needing to get closer. The entire world narrowed to us.

I lost track of time until the world began to intrude again. Wolf whistles and shouts of encouragement.

Alex pulled away, murmuring, "I'd better get you back to Caleb's."

CHAPTER 52

Oliver

I woke up with my head buried in Kai's pillow. It still had the faint scent of her pear shampoo. I missed that smell. In that moment, I missed her. But I'd been missing her less and less often like I was getting used to her absence.

I rolled over and stared at the clock—5:01 a.m. It was too early to call Aunt Ines. I tried to get back to sleep, but I couldn't, which was surprising, because I'd been up so late the night before.

After we read my dad's letter, Mickey and I had turned the house upside down trying to find the secret room he mentioned. We knocked on walls for hours. At 2:00 a.m., exhaustion crept over us. She crashed in a guest room. I went to my own room. I figured I'd sleep until my alarm clock rang. But I didn't. Too much nervous energy inside me.

My need to expose Schneider was no longer just about making amends to Christian or letting his family know the truth about his death. Or even proving to Kai that I could do the right thing. Now, I was doing this for my father, too.

I lay there in the dark and thought about what Schneider could do to me and Mickey and the people we loved. He could turn the police force against us. He could bring false charges against us. Or worse, use his position to hide what he'd done—just like he had when he killed Christian. I had no idea how Mickey and I could continue digging while protecting ourselves and our families.

And then it came to me. It was so simple. We'd let him think he'd won, that we'd taken his advice and chosen the living over the dead.

If we were careful—and convincing—it would buy us time to build a case against him.

I watched each minute pass on my clock, waiting until I knew that Aunt Ines would be awake. At 6:00 a.m., I dialed her number.

She answered on the third ring, "What's happened?"

"Too much to explain over the phone. Can you come over?"

She must have heard the urgency in my voice. "I'll be there in thirty minutes."

I hung up the phone. Mickey stood in the doorway, rubbing the sleep from her eyes.

"Coffee?" I asked.

"Coffee."

We headed to the kitchen to brew a pot.

It was good to have Mickey there, drinking coffee in my kitchen; it had been good to have her there when I was reading those letters from my parents. She understood me.

We heard the front door bang open. "Oliver?"

"In the kitchen, Aunt Ines."

When she joined us, her cheeks were flushed. Herbie trailed behind her. He ducked his head for a pet.

"What's going on?" she asked as she absently stroked his feathers. Her gaze settled on Mickey and she frowned.

I ignored my aunt's disapproval. "We found something." I led her back to my study and showed her everything we'd found inside my mother's desk. "Dad left me a letter." I handed it to her and she read it.

"Oh, Oliver, I'm so sorry about your mother's letters." She shook her head.

I couldn't think about that right now. "Can you help us find the secret room?"

"Of course. It's in my old room."

Mickey and I followed Aunt Ines upstairs to the room that had been hers growing up. When we got there, Aunt Ines opened the closet. I'd given it a quick once-over the night before, but I hadn't found anything.

The closet was only two feet deep. Its walls were made of cedar paneling. I could tell from the way the wood smelled. There was a shelf along the back. I looked again, but I still didn't see any suggestion of a doorway.

"What's the deal with a secret room anyway?" Mickey asked.

"A lot of old houses around here have them. Yours probably does. Ask your father," Aunt Ines replied. To me she added, "Grandpa didn't trust banks. He used to keep money and family heirlooms in there."

"What about the safe in his office?"

Aunt Ines chuckled. "He used to call it his bait. He left enough money in there to appease a robber and keep him from searching further and discovering the real treasures up here."

"So, how do we get in?" I asked.

"Grandpa made sure there was no door frame or visible seam," Aunt Ines said.

I ducked my head to avoid the shelf and took two steps inside the closet. I ran my hands over a few sections of paneling. "He did a great job."

Aunt Ines smiled proudly. Then she showed me how to remove the shelf from the back wall. I laid it on the bed. She stood facing the right wall and placed her hands on the cedar panels. Her left hand was about a foot off the floor and her right hand was about two-thirds of the way up the wall. She pressed both palms against the paneling until something popped. The back wall swung inward on a small, dark room.

Mickey handed me a flashlight and I stepped into the space. It couldn't be larger than six feet by six feet. Everything was covered in sheets. When I pulled one off, dust sailed through the air, choking me. I sputtered and coughed. It must have been years since anyone had been in here. Beneath the sheets were pieces of furniture in perfect condition. Was that Mama's old dresser and nightstand? I wanted to take a closer look, but I had to find the bike. I slide between them and headed toward a lumpy shape in the back.

As I pulled the sheet off, I heard something crinkling underneath it. I let the sheet drop to the floor. There it was: Christian's bike, wrapped in plastic. The handlebars were twisted and the front wheel was bent at a forty-five-degree angle.

Very carefully, I maneuvered it out into the larger room. Through the plastic, I could see that scratches marred the dark blue paint. Tiny tan paint flecks were embedded in them. Schneider's car. Had to be.

"Your dad did a good job preserving the evidence," Mickey said.

"Too bad he hid it in the first place." I couldn't help thinking of all the stress this cover-up must have caused my dad. It had to have taken a toll on his health. If he hadn't chosen to protect Schneider, maybe he wouldn't have had that heart attack. Maybe he'd still be here. Maybe I wouldn't have left Butternut. I might never have met Kai on that library rooftop. So many "what ifs" and "if onlys."

I'd made the wrong decision, too, when I'd decided to run away instead of confronting my father. I was still paying for what he'd done, but reading that letter helped me understand him in a way that I never had before.

"Oliver, are you okay?" Aunt Ines's forehead crinkled up with concern.

"Just trying to process everything."

Mickey touched my sleeve. "What should we do with the bike?"

"We need to get it to a crime lab. But not anywhere around here."

"Ashland County?" Mickey asked.

"I think we should take it to the state police," Aunt Ines said.

"Even at that level, someone might owe Schneider a favor. Cops protect cops." That was what my dad had done.

While Mickey and Aunt Ines debated county vs. the state police, I considered our next steps. I wanted to confirm that there was evidence on the bike before we surrendered it to the authorities, so that meant an independent lab.

"I need to make a call." I put the bike back in the secret room and went downstairs. I dialed Brett, an old friend in the prosecutor's office in New York. I'd helped him out with a money laundering case. He said he owed me one. Today, I'd find out if he'd meant it.

He sounded surprised to hear from me, but after I explained the situation with the bike from a closed case, he gave me the name and address of a reputable lab in Chicago. He warned that it would run a couple grand. I didn't care. This might be the evidence I needed.

When I hung up, I explained to Mickey and Aunt Ines that I needed to take the bike to a lab in Chicago.

"Will Mr. Kohler give you time off?" Aunt Ines asked. "You just started working there."

"I'm ahead of schedule. I'll tell him it's a personal emergency. I just need a couple days."

"What about Schneider?" Aunt Ines asked.

"I'll tell him that Mickey and I are going to take his advice and drop our investigation."

"I'll come with you," Mickey said.

Aunt Ines shook her head.

"Once I get the bike to the lab, I'm going to New York. I need to see Kai." I hadn't known it was true until I said it out loud.

Aunt Ines gave me a nod of approval. "Good."

There was something percolating in Mickey's eyes. Not defiance, no, certainty. "I want to be there when you talk to Schneider. And I'm going with you to the lab. I'll bring your car back here and you can fly on to New York."

"Oliver can do this alone," Aunt Ines insisted.

I could, but I didn't want to. "Can you be ready in an hour?"

"Yes," Mickey said.

CHAPTER 53

Kai

I dreamed of Alex. Of all the things I wanted to do with him. The dream me indulged every dark desire she had. I woke up at 6:30 a.m. to rumpled sheets and the smell of coffee brewing in the kitchen. I padded down the hall.

When Caleb saw me, he fanned his face. "Those were some hot dreams last night."

My cheeks burned. "You didn't."

He held up his hand. "As soon as I saw what was happening, I left your dreams."

I climbed onto a stool at the island and rested my elbows on the cool marble counter. My skin still felt warm from dream Alex's caresses.

Caleb handed me a cup of coffee. With a smirk.

I didn't like admitting it to myself, but Natalia might be right about love. Maybe the kind of love Oliver and I had only existed for a certain amount of time. Maybe we had a built-in expiration date that neither of us saw coming. We were foolish to think that it could be forever.

Bleak thoughts like this came so easily to me now. They felt like they were my own, but were they really? If they came from the darkness in me, some of that was Nathan. I had no way of telling whose pessimism I was indulging. In any case, the distinction seemed more and more meaningless with each passing day. The darkness was bleeding into me. It felt like every time I reached for it, it became a bigger part of me. It gave me a freedom I didn't know I'd been longing for.

Ever since my telepathy had manifested, I'd been learning to control it. I spent so much energy trying to protect myself and everyone around me. The darkness made it so much easier to defend myself, and it made me a little less concerned about what my powers might do to anybody else. I thought about what Natalia had said. If life was all about balancing costs versus benefits, I felt like I had been paying too high a price.

Caleb waved his hand in front of my eyes. "Earth to Kai."

He startled me back to the moment. "I'm here."

"Have you told Mom and Dad?"

"About what?" I had no idea what my brother had been saying.

"Have you told them that you're divorcing Oliver?"

Divorce. I hadn't said the word out loud. I hadn't even thought it yet. "For now, let's focus on your problem, not mine."

"Are you using me to avoid dealing with the end of your marriage?"

All I could say was "Oliver and I should talk. In person."

I got up to get myself another cup of coffee. Caleb finished getting ready for work.

Before he headed out the door, he said, "I've got two private investigators looking into Stellan." He said it like it was an afterthought.

"So you finally believe me?"

"I don't see what you see, but I trust you."

"We'll fix this," I promised.

I puttered around the apartment, mulling over Stellan's last words to me: *Someday, you'll ask me the right question, and I'll answer.*

I still wasn't sure what he meant, so I called him. When he answered, I asked, "What did you mean last night?"

He didn't say a word. Just hung up on me. Not the right question.

I called him back. "Why are you doing this?"

He hung up again.

The third time I called, it went to voicemail.

For the first time, I had to admit to myself that Caleb might be in real trouble. Despite all his resources and our abilities, we might not be able to figure out what was going on and make everything right.

What if Caleb went to jail? Images of my brother locked away assaulted my mind. My heart sped up. Sweat burst from every pore. My skin felt so clammy. I wanted to peel it away.

The din outside my shield grew louder; the voices grew more distinct. Thoughts and emotions thundered against my shield. I watched in horror as a tiny crack appeared in my shield.

I could reach for the darkness. It would save me. But, all of a sudden, I felt reluctant.

I didn't want to let any more of the darkness into me. I had to try something else. I remembered how drawing had helped me back in Butternut.

I found paper and a pencil in Caleb's home office. My hand flew over the page. Sketching, shading, shaping. The lines took form. A lake. Trees. A summer day. I felt the warmth of the sun on my skin. I heard the birds chirping in the trees. I breathed in the fresh scents of spring.

The din of voices receded. It was still there, but not as loud. I continued to draw until images littered the table. Scenes of Butternut, I assumed. Places I'd never been.

Finally, I could hear myself think again.

I took a deep, shuddering breath. I'd done it. I'd kept the city at bay without calling on the darkness. It was reassuring to know that I could still do that.

Something told me that if I reached for the darkness again, I wouldn't be able to step away from it.

CHAPTER 54

Oliver

Schneider stared at us from across his desk. The desk that had been my father's. "You two look exhausted."

I sighed. "We were up all night talking about this."

Mickey nervously crossed and uncrossed her legs. She shot me a few glances that were laced with a blend of annoyance and resignation.

The chief's gaze settled on her. "And what did you decide?"

I looked down at my hands and mumbled, "We don't have anything to prove what really happened. It's just my word against yours."

"So you kept looking, did you?" He didn't sound surprised.

"We had to." Mickey flicked her nails.

"Sixteen years is a long time." He leaned back in his chair.

"It's not okay—what you did, what my dad did, what I did. It will never be okay. But we can't undo any of it." I made sure to mix the right amount of frustration and defeat into my tone.

Schneider looked pleased, almost paternal. I hated him for that. "Oliver, life must go on. I'm glad that you're thinking about the future, making the best decision for Lukas and Kai."

"That's the only reason I'm doing this."

Mickey sat forward. "I won't let my son be hurt anymore. No trial. No testifying. And Nathan goes away where he can never hurt Lukas again."

I slouched in my chair. "And I'll leave this alone if you can do the same for Kai. She deserves that."

"I'm glad you two finally see the big picture." A Cheshire cat grin sliced across his face.

"The living for the dead," Mickey agreed.

When we were an hour away from Butternut, Mickey asked, "Do you think he really bought it?"

I kept my eyes on the road while we talked. "I think so. But it's hard to tell with Schneider."

"If he didn't..."

"Let's just trust that he did." I tried to sound confident, but I couldn't help checking my rearview mirror every five minutes for the state police.

"If you go a little faster, we might get there before midnight," Mickey said.

I glanced over at her. Her feet were in turquoise and purple unicorn knee socks. The kind that looked like gloves for her feet. I knew because they rested on my Cherokee's beige dashboard.

"I'm staying at five over the speed limit. We've got evidence from a murder in the car. Do you want to get pulled over?" I asked.

"Not really." She ripped open a bag of Sour Patch Kids and handed me a green one. It was my favorite when we were kids. It was her least favorite.

I popped it in my mouth. "Thanks."

"Just being a good co-pilot." She opened a water bottle and handed it to me.

"What did you tell your parents about the road trip?" They were watching Lukas while she was away.

"I said you needed a ride to the airport."

"And they didn't mind?"

"It's just one night."

"You spent last night at my house. Your parents have to suspect something's up."

"I told them you needed a shoulder to cry on. That we fell asleep on the couch talking about Kai."

She fished out two red Sour Patch Kids and tossed them in her mouth. "Remember when we used to see how many we could eat without making a face?"

"Ten was your best." Christian always grimaced at four. Mickey and I would keep going. Sometimes we'd swap our favorites and force each other to eat them. "We were so competitive back then."

"I wonder how many I can do now," she said.

Mickey was trying to distract me, and I loved her for it. "Five bucks says I can do more."

"Still the same Oliver."

With her, I felt like I was.

She handed me two red ones. "Let's see how many you can take."

I popped them in my mouth.

"Nice." She handed me two more.

The sour factor doubled. I fought to keep a straight face.

She handed me four more.

"You're grimacing. Pay up!" She laughed.

"Next pit stop, snacks are on me."

Half an hour later, I got off the highway at a gas station with a convenience store. She browsed the aisles, picking up Slim Jims, Doritos, Dr. Pepper, and a banana.

When we got back into the car, I asked, "Why the banana?"

"It makes up for all the junk food," she said as if it were a given.

We snacked in silence, until I asked, "Are you sure you don't mind driving back to Butternut alone?"

"It's too late to change my mind." She flicked on the radio and hunted for a song. "We're almost past the hard part. Once we get the bike to the lab, we're okay."

I wanted her to be right, but I knew that she wasn't. We still had a lot of work ahead of us. "Why did you do this? You're risking so much."

"For Christian, and for you."

"But what about Lukas? Don't you worry Schneider might try to hurt him?"

"Every day. But I also worry about what Lukas will think of me when he's older. If he learned that I stood by and did nothing, he would never look at me the same. Christian wasn't just our friend. He was Lukas's uncle. His death is what drove Nathan to do all those awful things. I'm standing up for my family, and for my friends. I don't know if Schneider will go to jail or just lose his job as chief of police. But I have to do something."

I nodded. There was something else I needed to talk about. "I know that Kai is not one of your favorite people."

"It's not just what she did to me. I don't like the way she's treated you."

"I wish you could have met her when I first knew her. Or when we had just gotten married. She was a different person then. I just don't get her now."

"Who could?"

"Caleb." He was the one person who always got Kai.

"They're like the Wonder Twins."

I chuckled. "I really appreciate your help. I'm not sure I could have done any of this without you."

"I owed you," she said.

"No, you didn't. After everything that happened in the cave, I owe you."

"We've always had each other's backs."

Mickey was always there for me when the bad stuff happened.

"Don't look so serious, Slim Jim."

I laughed. She nicknamed me Slim Jim when we took a road trip to Niagara Falls with Alex during our junior year.

This road trip with Mickey was a far cry from my last road trip with Kai. When I brought Kai from New York to Butternut, she kept trying to get away from me. She made it impossible to relax. She couldn't see that I'd done it to save her.

It had been so hard. The past few years were the most difficult of our marriage. I always thought it was worth it. We were building something solid. We were moving toward the future we dreamed of. Now, I wasn't so sure.

Life was hard without her, but a different kind of hard. A "hard" that had hope that easier was around the corner.

When I'd mapped out our trip, I hadn't factored in a six-car collision. We arrived at the lab three hours after it had closed. We tried knocking, just in case there was somebody still working, but we got no response.

We sat in the parked Cherokee and tried to figure out our next move. I'd been running on adrenaline the last few hours. I was about to crash. I didn't have a backup plan and I couldn't formulate one. I leaned my head back against the headrest and stared up at the roof, waiting for a solution to appear.

"I can drop you at the airport so you can get on the next flight to New York. Tomorrow, I'll bring the evidence to the lab," she said.

"I can't let you do that alone." I needed to see this through.

Mickey used her phone to search for a hotel, navigating while I drove. We self-parked. We didn't want anyone nosing around in the trunk and finding the bike.

We were both about to drop when we got to the front desk.

"I have one king room available," the front desk clerk informed us when I asked for two rooms.

"We need two rooms," I said.

"I'm afraid I don't have two rooms available. I have one."

I looked at Mickey. She looked at me.

"Do you mind sharing?" I asked.

"What about Kai?"

"I'll deal with that tomorrow."

We got our key cards and headed to our room. As soon as we were inside, Mickey grabbed all the extra pillows from the closet and built a wall down the middle of the bed. I doubted that would matter to Kai, but I appreciated the effort.

"Thanks." I flicked on the TV.

Mickey sat on her side of the bed. "Do you think Christian knows what we're doing?" Her voice sounded so small.

I reached over the pillow wall and squeezed her hand. "I hope so."

"After everything that happened in the cave, I haven't been able to get him out of my thoughts."

"I know." I'd spent years blocking it out, pretending the loss of him didn't hurt. "I wish I could go back to that night when we were twelve..."

She laced her fingers through mine and held on. "It wasn't your fault. Schneider shouldn't have been on the road when he was drinking. He shouldn't have covered up hitting Christian."

Her hand was so warm. I clung to it. "My silence helped him."

"Your father forced you to go along with their cover-up. You were a kid. You couldn't have changed anything."

"I didn't try. I did what my father told me to do, and then I ran away."

"Most people would have done the same thing." She reached over and swept the hair out of my eyes.

It felt good. "Alex wouldn't have." That's what made it so hard. "He'd have told the truth."

"If it meant destroying our father, he wouldn't have."

"Your dad was worth saving."

"Your dad is your dad. None of us gets to choose." Her phone rang. She let go of my hand. "It's Lukas."

She chatted with him while I flipped through the TV channels. I stopped at the Discovery Channel and settled into an episode of Bear Grylls trying to survive in the jungle. For twenty minutes, I lost myself in the show.

"I'll see you soon, baby," she said as she ended the call. She offered, "I can go to the lobby, if you want to call Kai."

"I'll see her tomorrow."

"Oliver..."

"There's no point. I'll have to tell her where I am and who I'm with. Then she'll just get mad and hang up. Triage can't be done long distance."

I woke up hours before Mickey. During the night, our hands had reached across the pillow wall and found each other. I didn't want to let go, so I stayed still and watched her sleep.

Her dark hair fell across her face. Her breath was slow and calm. She was in a deep slumber. I released her hand and gently pushed her hair back so I could see her face. She was as beautiful as she had been at seventeen. Back then, there were so many nights we snuck away together, not just for sex, but to be in each others' arms.

Looking at her, I missed that.

Mickey's voice came out sleepy-slurry. "Oliver? What are you doing?"

I hadn't realized that I was stroking her hair. "Um, just pushing your hair off your face. I didn't want you to have trouble breathing."

She snorted. "I've never heard of anyone suffocating on their own hair."

"Probably because of good Samaritans like me."

She laughed.

Then we got up, grabbed some food, checked out, and headed to the lab.

Even if we paid for a rush on the testing, it would be a few weeks before we knew anything.

Mickey's eyes met mine. "We can wait."

I got the feeling she wasn't just talking about the test results. I had a lot to discuss with Kai.

She drove me to the airport and hugged me before I got out of the car.

"Thank you for everything."

She gave me a bittersweet smile. "I've always had your back."

I watched her drive away before I headed into the terminal.

The plane had reached cruising altitude before I pulled out my mother's letter, the one marked, "When your marriage is in trouble."

> *Dear Oliver,*
>
> *I wish I could be there to listen, but I can't. So all I can do is tell you what I've learned from my own experience.*
>
> *Marriage is a promise that isn't always easy to keep. To love someone through everything is the greatest challenge in life. Living means changing and there will be changes that shake your faith in your relationship.*
>
> *I loved your daddy with everything I had, but we had our ups and downs like all couples do. It always came down to two simple questions: Can I live without this person? Do I want to?*

If your answer to both is no, then you keep fighting. If it's yes to both, then it's time to let go. If your answer is yes and no, that's when it takes some figuring out.

Marriage is like Grandma Richter's garden. You must tend to it. You must be willing to get your hands dirty and dig deep to keep the roots healthy and flourishing.

Love with all your heart, my darling boy.

All my love,

Mama

I knew what my answer to the first question was. I could live without Kai. Our time apart had taught me that.

So, the real question was, did I want to?

I spent the rest of the flight grappling with that question.

I pulled Kai's wedding ring out of my pocket and stared at it. I remembered our wedding day in Death Valley. The wind had whipped her hair around her face like wildfire. I slid the ring on her finger and promised to always be there for her. So much had happened since that day. A part of me wanted to slide it on her finger again. A part of me was afraid of what would happen if I did. How much more would I have to take before we'd be okay again?

I didn't know.

I put the ring back into my pocket as we prepared to land.

CHAPTER 55

Kai

We were all waiting for the call.

Caleb sat on the couch with his phone resting on the glass coffee table in front of him. Alex put his arm around me, trying to offer comfort. I took what I could from him, but it wasn't enough. I stared out the window. Tiny bits of light sparkled in the windows of buildings across the river, but the darkness encroached on everything.

Alex squeezed my shoulder. He talked about Lukas to distract me. He opened his mind to me and let me see his memories. Lukas as a tiny bundle snuggling in Alex's arms. Lukas's big green eyes. The sweet baby smell that enveloped him. I lingered in Alex's memory and breathed it in.

For a moment, I felt like I could handle this.

Then Caleb's phone rang. My body tensed, preparing for the worst. I hated not knowing what was happening. I could push into Caleb's mind and hear his thoughts, but he'd asked me not to. I wasn't sure if he was protecting me or needed a little time to process what he found out.

All I heard was Caleb's side of the conversation. "I understand" was followed by "How much time?"

I shifted closer to Alex, trying to escape my own anxiety. It didn't work. The din of thoughts clinked against my shield. My neck muscles clenched up and tugged at the back of my head, triggering a dull pulsing in my right temple.

It felt like my entire body was vibrating on a higher frequency. I couldn't sit still a moment longer. I got up and paced around the room to dispel some of this energy.

Alex followed me. He whispered, "He's going to be okay."

"You don't know that."

"You'll find a way through this."

"What if we can't?" My voice quivered.

Caleb lips compressed and his eyebrows pulled together. He ended the call with "Just do what you can." He didn't need to say another word. His face told me this wasn't good.

"How bad?" I asked.

"My friend looked into my financials," Caleb said. It was his polite way of saying the hacker got back to me.

"And?"

"He found a couple accounts in my name that I never set up. They're showing large wire transfers to Thaddeus Williams."

The smoking gun. As soon as Audit discovered this, Caleb would be in serious trouble. He would be fired, for sure, and completely unemployable. And that was the best-case scenario.

I scrambled to find a way out for him. "Is there any way you can make it go away?" If Caleb had friends who could find this information for him, maybe he had friends who could make it go away. I was no longer interested in what was legal or what was ethical. I just wanted to save my brother.

Caleb rubbed his lips. "If we had more time, yes. If we try now, my friend thinks that something even worse will pop up. He said whoever set this up is good. Really good. This involved months of intricate planning that he can't trace to its source."

"How long before Audit uncovers it?" My voice came out breathy.

Caleb tapped his phone against his thigh. "A week if I'm lucky."

"And then what happens?" Alex asked.

"They turn me over to the authorities," Caleb said.

I closed my eyes. One week. We had less than one week. Then they would take my brother away.

I couldn't let this happen to him. And I didn't know how to stop it. I opened my eyes.

"Are you going to be okay?" Caleb's gaze never left my face.

I forced a smile and lied, "I'm not the one in trouble."

"I've got to make some calls. We'll talk more. This isn't over." Caleb walked out of the room. He didn't say don't worry.

Muscles I didn't know the names of tightened in my back. Tremors rocked my body. My teeth chattered.

Pain. Excruciating pain. Stabbing through my brain. Short circuiting everything. So much loss. I'd lost Grandpa Guhn. Then Grandma Guhn. My marriage was over. I'd never have the family I needed. I couldn't lose Caleb, too. I wouldn't.

Red Hots scalded my tongue. Rage. My rage. It was greater than anyone else's. It was fueled by fear. Sweet buttercream fear. Nausea overwhelmed me. The room pulsated around me.

The din outside my shield was deafening. A migraine hit. Alex came toward me. His lips moved, but I couldn't hear him. My shield cracked. Everyone's pain came streaming at me.

A woman fifteen floors below sobbed inside my mind. She lost her three-year-old daughter to leukemia. Oceans of grief. A man on the street below lost his girlfriend of eight years to a younger man. An aching loss. So much loss. Everywhere. All around me. I couldn't. I couldn't. The crack widened into an abyss. Thousands of voices screamed in my head. They begged for help that wouldn't come.

I clutched my head. My brain cramped and spasmed.

Something at the core of me shattered. Everything inside me started to break apart. If I let it happen, it would destroy me. As everything pixilated into purple snow, I did the only thing I could. I reached for my darkness and pulled it close.

CHAPTER 56

Oliver

It was dark when I climbed into the taxi at JFK and headed for Manhattan. I tried to think about what I wanted to say to Kai, but my thoughts kept returning to Mickey. I couldn't help smiling when I thought of our road trip. The pillow wall that she'd built was a hilarious attempt to protect my virtue. I texted her that I'd landed okay in NYC. She replied that she was back in Butternut and wished me luck with Kai.

The cab ride was quicker than I expected. I was almost in Manhattan. I felt the energy building as I closed in on the city. The minute I crossed the bridge, it rose up to greet me. Kai used to say that the city had its own heartbeat. People were its blood and they flowed through the streets and into the subways, cluttering up restaurants and stores along the way. They were everywhere. Coming back, I could see what she meant.

We were almost at Caleb's when it occurred to me that I should shield my thoughts before I got to Kai. I hadn't had to do that since she left me in Butternut.

I took a deep breath and closed my eyes. Marble. Black marble.

Solid walls of marble all around me. A floor of marble below me and a ceiling of marble above me. Impenetrable. A tomb of marble to bury every thought and emotion inside.

I was a few blocks away from Caleb's place when I felt something. A gentle pulse against my shield. It was a weird sensation. The closer we got to Caleb's building, the stronger it became.

Stepping out of the cab was like walking into a war zone. A couple was fighting on the sidewalk. She flailed her arms; he stamped his foot. A child wailed in a stroller, and his mother sat on the pavement, sobbing right along with him.

A delivery guy bumped into me. "Watch where you're going, jackass."

"What?"

He turned around. "Did I stutter, you stupid piece of shit?"

One look at his face and I knew that he was about to take a swing at me. I made a break for Caleb's building. Surprisingly, there wasn't a doorman out front to greet me and open the door. Didn't matter, I yanked the door open and rushed inside.

At first glance, the lobby was an improvement. There was the soothing sound of water cascading down a wall of gray granite. White marble lined the walls and pale wooden flooring led the way to the front desk. It was all very serene—except for the young woman screaming at the front desk attendant, "You have to let me in!"

He didn't seem to care. "You locked yourself out. You find a way in."

"But you have to let me in! You have my spare keys back there."

"I'm so tired of you entitled little brats. Hey, Ahmed. Did she give you a tip at Christmas? I mean, a good tip." The guy at the front desk directed his question to an older man slumped in a plush chair. Judging from his uniform, he must be the missing doorman. He just shook his head.

"That's what I figured. She didn't give me shit, either." The front desk attendant returned his attention to the woman in front of him.

"If you can't be bothered to give us a decent tip at Christmas, I can't be bothered to find your keys."

I'd never heard a front desk attendant treat a tenant with such disdain. I had a terrible feeling that all this craziness had something to do with Kai.

I ran to the elevator. No one tried to stop me. I pressed the "38" and then repeatedly jabbed the "door close" button.

As the elevator rose, the thumping on my shield grew, like I was closing in on the source of all this. I got a sick feeling in my stomach as I made my way down the hall to Caleb's apartment. It couldn't be Kai. She wouldn't.

I found his apartment and thumped on the door.

Alex opened it. He was more surprised to see me than I was to see him.

"You shouldn't be here."

I detected a note of fear in his voice. "Should you?" I asked.

He barred my way. His eyes darted into the living room. "It's not safe here," he whispered.

A second later, anger slammed into my shield. A tiny crack formed. That had never happened before. "Is this Kai?" I whispered.

He nodded. "I don't really understand what's happening. I don't know how to describe it."

"Let me in, Alex. I can help."

He hesitated. "She's not herself."

I stared him down until he stepped aside. I went a few feet into the living room and saw her. Kai was standing by the wall of windows in the living room, looking out. Caleb was standing a few feet away.

He edged toward her.

"Don't come any closer." Her voice was like molten lava. It burned my skin.

I wasn't sure if she meant me or Caleb.

I retreated toward the front door, pulling Alex with me. "What happened?" I asked.

He spoke softly. "Caleb's in trouble. She was so scared. I thought she was going to pass out. Then," he bit his lip, "she got so calm. Suddenly, Caleb started crying. I mean, like a little kid." Alex paused like he didn't want to tell me what came next but he had to. "I was balling, and I didn't even know what I was upset about. It felt like I was crying about everything that I've ever cried about. And then it was over. Caleb and I were both fine. That's when the neighbors started yelling and throwing things."

Alex rubbed the back of his neck. He'd thought he'd known what Kai was like, but he was only just beginning to learn.

I almost felt sorry for him.

"Caleb says that she's turning her emotions outward," he said.

I felt it. The emotions rolling off her slammed into my shield. The vibrations made my teeth ache.

"Kai," Caleb said her name like a command. He had edged closer and was still trying to reach her.

She turned to him and smiled. It was the scariest smile I've ever seen. The smile of someone doing something awful and enjoying it.

"Kai?" he whispered.

"I have to do this," she said brightly.

"Do what?"

"Make them face it."

I had no idea what she meant, but I knew that, whatever it was, I didn't like it.

"You don't," Caleb said.

I admired the firmness in his voice.

"I do." She made it sound like a necessity.

I heard someone wailing a floor below us. Glass shattered. Something flew out a window. I prayed that it wasn't a person. There was so much yelling.

"Kai, you can stop this," Caleb said.

"I don't want to," she said.

There was no hint of doubt in her voice. I shuddered.

"You're hurting people, Kai." Caleb said it slowly, like he was speaking to a child.

"They were already hurting. I'm just helping them understand that the hurt will never end."

I looked at Caleb's face, and I saw something I'd never seen there before. Terror. And that terrified me. I'd always resented Kai's relationship with her brother, especially the way that his wealth meant that he could help her in ways that I couldn't. But, now, I realized how much we—Kai and I—had depended on him.

"Kai, I need you." Caleb didn't even try to hide the fear in his voice. "Remember the Kai who played with me in the tidal pools. The sister who would risk her sanity to save me."

"She's too weak," she hissed. "She can't help you. She can't handle it."

"I'll always need my sister."

She wavered. If there was anyone she would come back for, it was her brother. Then she saw me.

"My husband." She turned and opened her arms to me, but her words was full of loathing.

That was when Caleb noticed me. "Alex, get him out of here. Now!"

Alex was shoving me back out the door when Kai shattered my shield. She reached inside my mind and found the worst pain. She forced me to relive it. The smells, the voices, the people. I was back at Mama's funeral. Except, I couldn't see anything but Mama lying dead in her coffin.

The loss overwhelmed me.

In the distance, I heard Caleb say, "Kai, don't."

"He has to pay." Her voice didn't even sound like her own.

I felt such agony. I thought I might pass out. That would have been a blessing. But I didn't.

Kai took me back to the worst moments of my life. She made me relive each and every one of them. Somehow she combined them all so that I felt every emotion at once. Suddenly, I was staring at Christian's closed coffin, knowing I would never see him again. Then she took me to the moment I realized that my father had covered up the death of my best friend. She summoned up every time Mickey rejected me during senior year. She made me watch Mickey with Nathan at the games, at the dances, at the parades. She let me wallow in my loneliness.

She wasn't done. She added in all those times I thought that I'd lost her—the razor blades in the bathroom, the pill bottle in the living room.

Please stop, I begged.

But she still wasn't done. Now I was in Aunt Ines's kitchen when Kai slammed her wedding ring on the table. Finally, I stood in the cemetery by my grandparents' and my parents' graves.

I'd lost everyone. Everyone.

And then I lost consciousness.

CHAPTER 57

Kai

I was barely awake when Caleb appeared in my doorway. "Can we talk?"

Memories from the night before rushed at me. They were hazy, but they were enough. I groaned.

Caleb took that as a "yes." He came into the room and climbed into bed next to me.

I threw my arm over my eyes. "Please tell me Oliver wasn't here."

"I can't."

When I had unleashed the darkness, it had gone after anyone in its path. I'd used most of my strength to keep it away from Alex and Caleb. I hadn't expected Oliver.

I couldn't remember what I had done to him, but I knew that it was horrible. I also knew that Oliver was just the beginning. My mouth felt drier than the Mojave Desert. "How many people did I hurt?"

He hedged. "Well, it's hard to say. There were no fatalities—that I know of—in this building."

I waited for a sign that he was kidding.

He wasn't kidding.

"I don't know what you might have done to Oliver if Alex hadn't gotten him out of here."

I felt bad for the strangers who had suffered from my breakdown. As for Oliver…

"He came here to see you. He still wants to see you."

"Probably not a good idea." Saying that was easier than saying that I didn't want to talk to my husband, that I'd rather hurt him than talk to him.

"I tried to explain that to him, but he doesn't care. Do you think you can control yourself around him?"

I sat up and considered Caleb's question. Whatever had happened the day before, I had survived it, and I was stronger for it. "Yes."

"How are you feeling? Really feeling." He studied my face like he could read the truth there.

"Calm."

"Maybe you needed to lose control. Next time, though, let's do it somewhere else. Somewhere slightly less populated." Caleb wrapped me in a hug.

After he let me go, I followed him out to the kitchen. He fired up a burner and started making breakfast. I had wanted to be here to help him, but yet again he was helping me.

"What are you going to do?" I settled onto a stool at the island.

"Make scrambled eggs. White toast. Sound good?"

"No, I mean about what's happening to you. The fake accounts with the bribes."

"There's nothing I can do about them."

Caleb tended to his eggs.

I had to do something to help him. "Stellan could have set up the fake accounts."

"He'd just need some of my personal information and a valid form of ID."

"Where do you keep that stuff?"

"In my desk in the living room."

"Someone could have snuck in and taken them for Stellan."

"There's a list of people who can get into my apartment undetected. It starts with my cleaning lady, my super, my doormen."

"And Natalia."

He frowned. "She has no reason to do it."

"Neither does Stellan." And we were sure it was him.

He scooped the scrambled eggs onto our plates and sat down beside me. "How would you feel if we could only see each other in our dreams?"

I hated the question. "You're going to run."

"I don't think I have a choice. I need to disappear until I can figure out what's going on and prove that I've done nothing wrong."

I sipped my coffee. "Then I disappear with you."

"What about Oliver? And Alex?"

"You mean more to me than either of them. If you go, I go with you."

I saw Oliver before he saw me. He was hunched over on the bench, staring at his hands. His posture cried out in exhaustion. His face was drained. I knew that I was to blame for that. I wondered if he hated me. I knew that it would be easier for me if he did.

When he looked up and saw me, he gave me his crooked New York smile—happy that I was on my feet and worried about what I'd do next.

He rose from the bench where he'd been waiting. We set out through the Ramble, a wooded area in Central Park that twisted and turned until you forgot you were still in the city. Oliver and I came here when we needed to have a deep conversation.

"Are you okay?" I asked.

"Last night was the worst night of my life. It was all my worsts at once."

"I wish you hadn't been there."

"What happened to you last night?"

"Things are bad for Caleb. He might be arrested soon." I studied the ground. "It hurt so much. I couldn't handle it. I had to let the darkness take over."

"Or what?"

"Or I'd lose myself."

"But you did lose yourself. To the darkness."

"No, I didn't." I pressed my palm to my chest. "I'm still here. I just can't keep turning it inward."

"All those innocent people, Kai." He'd never sounded more disappointed in me.

"I didn't hurt them. I just helped them understand their pain better."

He looked shocked, like he expected remorse from me. "You hurt me. And I think you enjoyed doing it."

He had me there. No point in lying. "I did."

"Do you think it was Nathan?"

I couldn't even remember what I'd told Oliver and what I hadn't. It had been so long since I was used to confiding in him. "What do you mean?" I asked.

"After Alex took me back to his room last night, I was trapped inside my nightmares for hours. When I finally woke up, I couldn't believe you could be that cruel. Alex defended you. He told me about how Nathan's darkness merged with yours."

Damn Alex for his honesty.

"Why didn't you tell me?" he sounded distraught.

"I'm still trying to understand it," I said quietly. I didn't bother to tell him that I hadn't trusted him with the truth. We were well past that now.

He stared straight ahead. "You have a choice. You don't have to be like this."

"Like what?"

He glanced over at me. He started to speak, and then thought better of it. We kept walking in silence. I watched a squirrel race up a tree and heard a bird calling for its mate.

Then he stopped walking. I stopped, too, and turned to face him.

"I miss who we were. I miss what we were," he said.

"So do I."

There were so many memories of us here in New York. Right now, it felt like we were wandering through the graveyard of our love and neither of us was courageous enough to admit it.

We stood there facing each other for an eternity. Until a dog walker forced us to start moving again.

There were things I needed to say to him. Things that would help him move on. "The girl who married you is gone, Oliver. So, if you came looking for that girl, you're not going to find her in me."

"What if I'm still not willing to let you go?"

"Think about last night, I freaked out because I was worried about Caleb. I managed to protect him and Alex. But I lashed out at you."

"What if I can forgive you?"

"I made out with Alex."

"And I kissed Mickey. So what?"

I kicked at a stray rock. It skittered off the path. "I'm not talking about the past. I mean, I made out with Alex a couple night's ago."

"So that's it? You're throwing us away for him?" The shock and hurt in his voice reverberated through me. "I always thought I was the weak one. I beat myself up about Mickey. About one moment of doubt. But what you're doing—it's cowardly. You're afraid I'll hurt you again, so you run away from everything we have."

"I'm not afraid. Not anymore." I made him look at me. "I don't love you enough for you to hurt me. Not that way."

For two heartbeats, he stared into my eyes, trying to read my soul. "I can't believe it."

I wanted to say that I was sorry, but I couldn't, so I said nothing.

His face spasmed in pain. He took an involuntary step back.

"Oliver..." Some old impulse reached toward him.

"No, don't." He put his hand up to ward me off.

"I—"

"No." He turned and ran from me.

I watched him go. Inside me, the darkness purred.

CHAPTER 58

Oliver

I strode through the park, dodging runners, cyclists, and babies on parade. I had to get as far from her as I could. Her words echoed in my head.

She didn't love me anymore. Not that way.

I finally had the answer to my mother's second question. I didn't want to live with Kai anymore. But the anger inside me refused to dissipate. So I hailed a taxi and headed back to the hotel where Alex was staying. I returned to the room he'd taken me to after Kai attacked me.

I pounded on the door.

He opened it. "What's going on? Is Kai okay?"

"You can't have her." I pushed past him. Even if we're over, you can't be with her. You can't."

Alex didn't say anything. He wasn't bothering to fight me for her. He knew that he'd already won.

"I thought you were a good guy." I shoved my hair off my forehead. "And now, you've ruined my marriage."

He rubbed his chin. "I've made mistakes, but this isn't all on me, Oliver. You lied, you cheated, you put her life in jeopardy. You ruined your marriage all by yourself."

The blood sped through my veins and pounded against my fingertips. I rushed at him and slammed him into the wall. He punched me. I hit him again. His fist slammed into my belly. All the air left me. I doubled over, gasping for breath.

"I can't believe that you'd do this to me. YOU WERE THE CLOSEST THING I HAD TO A BROTHER!" I shouted.

"Oh come on. You left town and you never looked back. You went on with your life and I went on with mine. Did you expect me to be waiting for your return?"

"I thought we could pick up where we left off. I thought you'd still have my back."

"I tried to be your friend again. And I also tried to be a friend to Kai."

"Friends don't french friends." I laughed. It was a joyless laugh.

"No they don't." He sighed. "I'm not going to pretend it's okay. It just is what it is."

"You have no idea what life with Kai is like."

"I'm willing to find out."

"Last night didn't scare you off?"

"She protected me. She attacked you. You figure it out."

"So you're willing to overlook what she did to your sister on Christmas Day?"

"What are you talking about?" Confusion rippled across his face.

I couldn't wait to tell him. "She used her powers to attack Mickey. She got inside Mickey's head and hurt her. It's why I moved out."

"Mickey never said a word to me." He sounded dazed.

"Ask her."

"I will."

"And then ask yourself how you could be with someone who did that to your sister."

The shock on Alex's face was the last thing I saw before I slammed the door behind me.

CHAPTER 59

Kai

The tidal pools beneath the Ocean Beach Pier were one of my favorite childhood places. During low tide, Caleb and I would go exploring for hours. While we napped, we met there in a dream. The wind tossed my hair around my face. A few strands stuck to my cheek. I pushed them behind my ear, but the wind yanked them free again.

Our bare feet curved around lava-colored, cratered rocks. We tried not to slip on the green algae. We made it to a nearby pool and peered in, searching for the creatures inside.

I gently poked a sea anemone, watching it curl inward to protect itself.

Caleb sat down next to me. "You always loved them the best."

"The way they change shape and survive. It's really cool." I glanced at him. "I know what you're doing."

"What?" He gave me his most innocent face.

"Trying to remind me how real these dreams feel. It's almost as good as being together in real life. But it's not good enough for me.

Don't you get it? You're the only family I have left."

"I get it." Caleb trailed his fingers through the water.

"What's going on?"

His lips compressed and his eyebrows gathered together. He wasn't happy. "Stellan remains our best lead in terms of ability and opportunity. But even after my friend hacked into Stellan's phone records, we can't find anyone he's in touch with that would want to destroy me. I still can't figure out his motive in all this."

I reached for his hand. "We will. We just need time to discover it." Time we would secure by going on the run.

"When we leave, you can't say goodbye to anyone."

"I know. I've already sent Oliver away. I'll do the same with Alex. I just want one more day with him."

Caleb studied me. "Will that really be enough?"

"It'll have to be."

CHAPTER 60

Oliver

I stalked around Midtown, trying to exhaust my anger in a blur of tourists and crosswalks. Along the way, I bumped shoulders and nearly tripped over hesitant idiots. Blaring horns and loud conversations echoed in my ears. By the time I got back to my hotel, all I wanted was a meal and a nap.

When I opened the door to my room, I found Schneider occupying the lone armchair. He was in jeans, a navy polo shirt, and a khaki sports jacket. His gut hung over his belt. He looked like any other tourist, unless you noticed the gun bulge under his coat.

I glanced around the room to see if anyone else was with him. The bathroom door was open. The shower curtain was gathered to one side. No one was in there.

"It's just me, Oliver," he said with a chuckle.

"How did you get in here?"

"I told the front desk that I was your uncle and I left my keycard in the room. They made me a new one." He held it up for me to see.

"They didn't ask for identification?"

He gave me a slow smile. "I showed them my badge."

Of course he did. "What are you doing here?"

"I came to check on you. How's that brother-in-law of yours doing?" he asked.

Not a question that I was expecting. "Caleb's fine."

"That's not what I hear."

A small town chief of police shouldn't know anything about a Wall Street investment guy. "What are you talking about?"

"Let's cut the bullshit. I know that Caleb's in trouble. I also know how much your wife cares about her brother, and I know how much you love your wife."

Schneider had no idea how I was feeling about my wife at the moment, and I didn't like where he was going with this.

"Did you really think you could fool me?" he asked.

My pulse quickened. I echoed his words. "Fool you?"

"You and Mickey put on a good show, but it wasn't good enough." Before that could sink in, he added, "I know about your trip to Chicago."

My stomach tightened. I felt like I might vomit and pass out at the same time. I dropped onto the bed because I wasn't sure I could keep standing. "How?"

"I put a tracker on your car when you got back to Butternut. I figured it was best to know what you were up to."

"Is Mickey okay?"

"You don't need to worry about her. Not yet, anyway. It's Caleb you should be worried about. As I understand it, he could be facing jail time. Something about the USA PATRIOT Act, if I remember correctly." Schneider tsked and shook his head.

If Caleb was going to be charged with violating the USA PATRIOT Act, he really was in serious trouble. But how the hell did Schneider know anything about this? Caleb didn't even know it yet.

He shouldn't. Unless.... The realization rocked me. "You're the one. You're setting Caleb up."

He nodded, looking pleased with himself.

"But why?"

"I didn't want any trouble from you when you came home, and without your daddy to keep you in line, I needed leverage over you. I knew that you'd do just about anything to protect your wife. Just like Reinhard would for Sophie."

I was still baffled. "You couldn't have done this on your own."

"Outsourcing is the new American dream. The right leverage over a key person can do wonders."

"Who?" I asked. "How?"

He laughed. "Let's just say, you live long enough and you see enough good people do bad things. And those people will do anything to avoid those bad things coming to light. Even do more bad things."

"Do bad people ever do good things?" I asked.

"You're still alive aren't you?"

That was the proof that he'd done something good. Not killing me.

When I looked into his eyes, I finally realized something. It wasn't two people who died in that tragic house fire all those years ago, but three—his wife, his daughter, and his soul. The Uncle John I loved as a child was dead and he was never coming back. For a second, I wondered if Dad had the same realization. It was awful to look at someone and see they were no longer there. Just a husk of the human being you once knew.

"What do you want?" I struggled to keep my voice even.

"The same thing I've always wanted from you. I want you to leave the past alone. At the moment, that means you and me flying to Chicago and getting that bike back from the lab." He sucked on his teeth and muttered to himself. "Should have known better than to trust your father with that piece of evidence."

"And if I say no?" I asked.

"Caleb goes to jail, and your wife learns that you could have kept him out of prison if you'd wanted to."

"If I give the bike to you, you'll help Caleb?" I needed to be certain what his terms were.

"I'll make sure that there's no longer any case against Caleb."

I didn't know what to say. Caleb's future hung in the balance. Not just his reputation, but his actual freedom. If I gave Schneider the bike, I'd lose to my last chance to prove that he killed Christian. I'd let a killer remain free.

He eased himself out of the armchair. "I think I'll go see some sights, as long as I'm here." Schneider sauntered to the door. "I'll give you a couple hours to think it over. When I call, I suggest you answer quickly."

The door clicked shut behind him, leaving me in a situation with no good choices.

But a choice still had to be made.

CHAPTER 61

Kai

I hadn't expected to see Oliver again. I thought we'd said everything we needed to say in the Ramble. But there he was, standing in Caleb's doorway, wearing that stern German face. The one that always made me nervous.

"Schneider's here," he said.

"In the city? Why?" I stepped aside to let Oliver in.

"To see me" was all he said. Before I could formulate a follow up question, he asked, "Is Caleb here?"

"He's in his room."

"Can you get him?"

"Why?"

"Just get him." Frustration singed his words.

I cracked open the window in my shield. Hundreds of thoughts poured in. They didn't overwhelm me. Now that I'd embraced my darkness, I was able to slow them down and hunt for Oliver's thoughts amid the chaos. I didn't hear them. Then I saw his crypt of black marble, where he kept his thoughts sealed up. No door. No way out. No way in.

I went and got Caleb.

Oliver explained what Schneider was doing to Caleb.

"There's no way Schneider could have set me up like that. He had to have help," Caleb said.

"Of course he did. I just don't know who," Oliver said.

"Stellan," I breathed. "That's why we couldn't figure out a motive, Caleb. The motive wasn't Stellan's; it was Schneider's."

"Who's Stellan?" Oliver asked.

"The IT guy for my group at the investment bank," Caleb explained.

"If we can figure out what Schneider has on Stellan we might be able to turn things around," I said. "But we need some time."

"We need to stall Schneider," Caleb said.

"Can you go along with his plan, at least for now?" I asked Oliver.

Oliver's face tightened. "I don't know. How much time would you need?"

"A day or two?" Caleb looked at me for confirmation.

I gave him a quick nod. I hoped I could get through to Stellan in that time.

"I'll do what I can," Oliver said.

"What if we need more time?" I asked.

"I can't give Schneider the evidence. I won't. It's the only proof I have of what he did."

"Damn it, Oliver. Christian's dead. Caleb's alive, and he needs your help."

Oliver looked down. "I want to help. I'm sorry Schneider pulled Caleb into this. I'll do anything I can to help, short of giving Schneider the bike."

I was so focused on saving Caleb that it took a moment for my emotions to catch up to everything Oliver had told me. I tasted cinnamon on my tongue right before the anger engulfed me. "I can't believe this all comes back to you. First your secrets put me in danger, now my brother." The darkness rose up in me. "Why don't I just have a little talk with Schneider?"

"What would that accomplish?" Oliver asked.

"Maybe after I've made him relive the worst moments of his life, he'll find it in his heart to help Caleb."

My brother frowned. "I don't like this idea, Kai. We can't risk you losing control again."

"So what do we do?" I demanded.

"He started setting Caleb up before I even moved home. Schneider is always a few steps ahead of me. God only knows what other plans he has in place for us," Oliver said.

"I don't suppose you happened to record that conversation?" Caleb asked him.

"What?" Oliver asked.

"When Schneider laid out all his dirty deeds, did you think to record it on your phone?" Caleb tilted his head. "Probably not, from the look on your face."

"It wasn't like I was expecting to see him in my hotel room!"

Caleb sighed. "Do you think you can get him to talk about it again on tape?"

"I don't see him rehashing the details. The guy's spent decades evading paying for his crimes," Oliver said.

"Aren't you even willing to try?" My voice squirreled up the wall. He should be doing everything he could to help Caleb.

"I can try," Oliver said quietly.

Caleb squinted at him. "That isn't encouraging."

"You want me to try to entrap a murderous blackmailer, who seems to always anticipate my next move. Yeah, I'm not feeling too confident about that."

"But it isn't your next move. I suggested it. He might not see it coming." Caleb walked to the window. He peered out at the river. It was so dark and impenetrable at this time of night. He thought at me, *If this goes sideways with Stellan or Schneider, we're going to have to run sooner than we thought.*

Let me try to get through to Stellan first.

Oliver was still talking. "Once I take Schneider down, I'll find a way to help Caleb. I promise."

"Maybe you really are sorry, and maybe you actually intend to keep that promise. But right now, you're choosing to sacrifice my brother," I said.

Pain flared in Oliver's eyes. "I hope you can understand one day."

"I won't," I growled. "Now get out."

"Oliver's in an impossible situation," Caleb said.

I couldn't believe my brother was siding with Oliver. "No, he's not. It's entirely possible for him to save you." My bare feet slapped against the hardwood floor as I paced around the living room.

"It's more complicated than that. He's not doing this for himself. I think he wants to show you that he can do the right thing."

"How is letting you go to prison for something you didn't do the right thing?"

"It's not, but neither is letting a man get away with murder."

"Yet he didn't have a problem doing that for 12 years. And why are you defending him? He's throwing you to the wolves!"

"We both know I'm not going to jail."

"But he doesn't. He has no idea that we're planning to run."

I marched to the window and stared out at the Hudson River. The darkness outside no longer frightened me because I knew what hid in its depths. I welcomed it. "What if they catch you?" Caleb could still go to jail.

"You're a telepath. I'm a dreamwalker. We can stay ahead of them." He sounded so certain. "I've already got new passports for us."

"How will we live?"

He smiled. "I have an offshore account that no one knows about it. We can live off it for a few years."

"You think we can do this?"

"I know we can," he said.

"If I'd never met Oliver, none of this would be happening," I whispered. Inside me a storm was building. The darkness flooded me.

"This is not your fault." Caleb got up and hugged me.

"It's Oliver's," I said into his shoulder. We might be fugitives for the rest of our lives. I couldn't let that happen. "This isn't the life Grandma and Grandpa Guhn wanted for you, for us." I pulled away from my brother. "I need to call Stellan now."

My phone and his card were in my room, so I headed down the hallway.

He answered on the third ring. "Kai, what a pleasant surprise."

"How can I help you?" I held my breath, praying that I'd finally found the right question.

"Meet me at the Rusted Nail in Williamsburg." He gave me the address. It wasn't more than a 20-minute cab ride.

"I'm on my way."

I threw my coat on and headed to the door.

Caleb leapt up and followed me. "Where are you going?"

"I have to meet Stellan."

"Not alone." He reached for his coat.

"I can't bring you along."

I yanked the door open and found Alex on the other side, just about to knock. He looked startled. "Kai, can we talk?"

"Sure, but I'm on my way out," I said.

"You can't go alone." Caleb was on my heels.

"I won't. Alex is here. I'll bring him. I'll call you after I talk to Stellan." I slammed the apartment door.

I grabbed Alex's arm and dragged him toward the elevator.

"Where am I going?" he asked.

"To watch over me while I talk to Stellan."

"Why?"

"Because Oliver thinks Schneider is behind everything that Stellan is doing to Caleb. If I can figure out why, I might be able to save Caleb."

"When did all this happen?" Alex asked.

"Ten minutes ago."

"Things are really getting crazy," he murmured.

"It's okay. You don't have to come with me. I just needed to get out of the apartment without Caleb tagging along."

"Caleb would kill me if I let you go alone."

"I'll be fine."

"I'm coming," he said.

When we reached the entrance to Caleb's building, the doorman stepped into the street to hail a taxi for us.

"What was it you needed to talk about?" I asked Alex.

Something flickered in his eyes. Regret? Concern? Anger? It was gone so quickly that I couldn't be sure.

"It's okay, we can talk about it tomorrow."

"Is something wrong? Is Lukas all right?"

"He's fine. This can wait." He sounded so certain.

The cab pulled up. "I think we'd best arrive in separate cabs." I told him the address and sent him ahead to Williamsburg. I took the next cab.

I called Alex on my cell. He was quieter than usual. "Are you okay?"

"Yes. It can wait."

"We've got twenty minutes to kill before we get to Williamsburg."

"Tell me your plan then."

CHAPTER 62

Oliver

After I left Caleb's apartment, I headed uptown. Walking helped me think. Bitter cold nights like this sharpened my mind. The streets down here were quieter at this time of night. No one bumped or jostled me as I made my way through Soho.

I would never forget the look in Kai's eyes when she told me to get out of Caleb's apartment. I knew that she'd changed, but I kept making excuses, refusing to see who she had become. But I couldn't deny it any longer. Something had fundamentally shifted inside my wife. She no longer abided by any of the rules she'd established for herself. She didn't care if she hurt others. She only seemed to care about herself and Caleb. And Alex, maybe.

Even if I could record Schneider saying something that exonerated Caleb, she still wouldn't forgive me. At this point, I didn't really care if she did. But Caleb, no matter how much I disliked him, I still had to find a way to help him without letting Schneider get away with murder.

My footsteps echoed off the sidewalk. My breath came out in clouds of white. I just kept walking. There was nothing else I could do, but move forward.

The street noises faded into the background as I turned everything over and over in my head. Five blocks later, my cell rang.

When I answered Schneider said, "Meet me in the lobby of your hotel in thirty minutes. I'll want your answer."

CHAPTER 63

Kai

My telepathy cut off four blocks from the Rusted Nail.
I watched Alex get out of his cab and walk toward the
bar. I stayed inside mine. When Alex got to the entrance, I
slid my phone into my coat pocket so he could hear what was happening.
I paid the cabbie, hopped out, and followed Alex toward the dive bar.
It was overflowing with hipsters and a smattering of people who came
for the beer and the music. Stellan intercepted me at the door.

"I didn't realize it would be so crowded tonight," he said.

"It's fine."

He shook his head. "Let's find somewhere a little quieter." He took
me by the arm and led me back toward the street.

Alarm bells sounded in my head. "Why don't we talk right here?"

"The sidewalk isn't the right place to have this kind of conversation."
He stepped into the street and hailed a taxi.

"I'm not getting in a taxi with you."

"Suit yourself." A cab stopped beside Stellan and he climbed inside.
He left the door open.

Damn it. If I let Stellan leave, I'd never find out what his connection to Schneider was, but changing the location of our meeting was risky. I looked back at the bar entrance. Alex shook his head at me. He didn't want me getting in that taxi. I didn't want me getting in that taxi. But I still got in the taxi and shut the door.

"I'm going to need your cell phone," Stellan said.

"Why?"

"Because I don't want anyone overhearing what we say."

I clicked end and handed it to him. The passenger door swung open and Alex slid in next to me. "Got room for one more?"

Stellan didn't seem surprised. "I'll need your phone too."

Alex handed it over.

Stellan leaned forward and gave the cabbie an address.

Alex found my hand and squeezed it. I held on tight.

The taxi stopped in an unfamiliar part of Brooklyn. When I got out, I peered up at an old industrial building that looked like it had been converted into lofts.

"Is this where you live?" I asked.

"It's a friend's place," Stellan said.

I gripped Alex's hand. We were at a random person's place in a neighborhood I didn't know. Suddenly, I was concerned about Stellan's intentions. If Alex weren't with me, I'm not sure I would have been able to do this.

We rode the elevator to the fourth floor in a nervous silence. Stellan directed us down the hall to apartment 4F. The place was barely furnished. A couch, two chairs, and a coffee table were the only furniture in the living room.

Stellan shut the door and flipped every lock back in place. I had no idea if this was sinister, or if this was concern about an up-and-coming neighborhood. Without my telepathy, I couldn't read Stellan at all.

I rubbed my arms. "How can I help you?"

"Why don't I brew some tea?" Stellan said.

"We don't need anything but answers." I wanted to get out of here as quickly as possible.

"Let me take your coats. Your purse too."

I shrugged out of mine and handed my purse over. He wasn't going to let us keep anything. If we were going to be here a while, I should get a look around the apartment and see if there was another way out or a weapon I could stash in my pocket. "Where's your bathroom?"

"Down the hall on the left," Stellan said.

I stopped at the bedroom. When I looked back, they weren't watching me, so I slipped inside. The windows opened, but there was a four-story drop to the ground. The bed was just a headboard and mattress. The desk had nothing on it. The top drawer contained a pen and paper. I grabbed the pen and slid it up my right sleeve. It wasn't much, but it was something. If it came down to it, a pen to the eye could disable someone.

I continued down the hall to the bathroom. I searched the cabinets, but they were empty like no one lived here. I flushed the toilet and headed back to Alex. Safety in numbers.

When I got back to the living room, they weren't there. "Alex? Stellan?"

"In the kitchen," Stellan called.

He was microwaving water for tea. It took a second for me to find Alex. He was on the floor, slumped against the cabinets.

My heart leapt into my throat. I dropped down beside Alex. "What happened?"

"I wanted to have a private conversation with you, but he insisted on joining us," Stellan said.

"Why didn't you make me leave him at the bar?" I cradled Alex's face in my hands. He didn't respond to my touch. Fear frosted my veins. What if? No. He had to be okay. *Think, Kai, think.* My fingers went to his neck. His pulse was strong, but without my telepathy, I couldn't reach inside his mind to make sure he was okay.

"Where did you hit him?" I asked.

"I didn't need to." He took two mugs out of the microwave and added tea bags.

I searched Alex's scalp for a sign of injury, but there was no blood. My fingers danced through his hair, trying to find any bumps. Nothing.

"Did you use your abilities on him?" I asked.

He stared down at me as if he was debating how much to reveal. "I made him lose consciousness."

He dampened my telepathy. It seemed like he skewed Caleb's perception of him. Now he'd knocked Alex out. "What exactly are your powers?" I hated how my voice trembled.

"I can play with perception. Alex here thinks he got hit on the head. He'll remain unconscious until I release him." He must have seen the fear in my eyes because he explained, "You needed a reason to not be difficult. If anything happens to me, he won't wake up. Not for a long time."

Alex wasn't physically hurt. I wanted to feel relieved, but I couldn't because he was at Stellan's mercy. My chest tightened. It felt impossible to breathe. I stole tiny swallows of air. Panic was taking over. It couldn't help Alex, so I fought it. But I could feel myself losing until the darkness pulled me back from the edge.

"Is that how you made Caleb think you were harmless?" I asked.

"It was easy. With the glasses and the IT background, he already dismissed me as a spineless nerd."

"Why do your powers work differently with me?"

He shrugged. "I'm not sure. I haven't known many people like us. Your powers and mine seem to counteract each other."

I swallowed. "Are we really going to talk or did you just say that to lure us here?"

"We'll talk once we're all settled in the living room. Grab the mugs." He hauled Alex into the living room and dropped him into an armchair. Alex's head lolled back.

I thought about flinging the hot tea at Stellan, but I worried that hurting Stellan would hurt Alex.

Stellan seemed to guess what I was thinking. "Please, put the tea down. I have no desire to hurt you."

I stared into his eyes. Today they looked more green than brown. They were compelling and clear. Sane. Logical. I wanted to believe him, but I couldn't because of what he'd done to Alex. "Then let us go."

"I can't."

As I stood there staring at him, my mind raced with possibilities. Hundreds of thoughts passed through in a moment. I had a green belt in karate, but my cast hampered me. Still, I could fight. I could scream. I could try to get away. But I couldn't carry Alex and I wouldn't leave him behind. And I still needed information that only Stellan could give me to help Caleb.

I put the tea mugs on the coffee table and sat down on the couch. "What do you need from me?"

Stellan was calm and deliberate. I couldn't hear his thoughts, but I didn't feel like he was crazy. I might be able to negotiate my way out of this.

"Under other circumstances, I like to think we'd have been friends." He sat beside Alex.

A chill raced down my spine. "But now?"

"I don't have a choice. I have to use you as leverage."

"Because of John Schneider?"

Recognition lit his eyes. "He needs something from your husband."

"Evidence that he killed a boy. Did Schneider tell you that?"

Stellan's expression remained the same. "He didn't."

"Does that change anything for you?"

"I wish it did."

"What does he have on you?"

Stellan got a faraway look on his face, like he was reliving a moment he wished had never happened. "We were just having fun. High school kids blowing off steam. Pushing our limits. Everyone tried it. Ketamine and Red Bull. I didn't give it to Emma. I'd never give her a line of anything. She was too tiny to handle that much. A bump. If she'd have just done a bump, she'd have been fine. They dared her to do a line. I should have taken it away from her, but I thought that she knew her limits. But at seventeen, everything feels limitless."

"What happened to her?"

"She did two lines. She seemed okay. I thought she was okay." His eyes implored me to believe him. For some reason I did. "Until she stopped breathing. I tried to do CPR. I told them to call for help. But everyone scattered. They left her there."

"What did you do?"

"I stayed." Bitterness crusted his words.

"Where were you?" I asked.

"Butternut Lake," he whispered. "My family has a vacation house there. My great aunt was born up there."

And suddenly it all made sense. "Schneider found you."

He nodded. "She died on my parent's property. I was eighteen. Her family could have sued. I could have gotten arrested. It would have destroyed my family."

"Schneider helped you cover it up," I murmured.

"He moved her body to another area of the lake. I don't know what he did, but everyone thought she had an undiagnosed heart condition and suffered a heart attack. No one ever found out about the drugs."

Stellan continued, "At first, I thought he was a decent guy. He saved her family from the shame of a drug overdose death. He was giving me a second chance. Then, I figured he'd call in a favor from my family for what he did for me. We're well off and my father's connected in Chicago."

"But he didn't?"

Stellan shook his head. "I finished college and got a degree in computer science. I landed a job on Wall Street. I relaxed, thinking that the past was the past." His fingers absently tapped against his thigh. "I was wrong."

"What happened?"

"A year and a half ago, Schneider got in touch with me. He reminded me about the favor he'd done for me at the lake. He said he was calling it in. He told me I had to find a way to set up Caleb. When I asked what he wanted me to do, do you know what he said? 'Get creative.'"

"So you took a job at my brother's firm?"

"It wasn't that simple. None of this was. I had to get the IT guy for your brother's group to quit and the HR rep to push my resume to the top of the list."

"If you could do all that, why didn't you just use your powers on Schneider?"

"I've tried. I went back to Butternut because I have to be near people to impact their perception. I was in the same room with him and my abilities had no effect on him. I can't alter his perception."

"Has that happened before?"

"No." He took a sip of tea.

"Sometimes people's abilities interact with mine. Yours counteract mine. Maybe there are other people who are immune to us."

"Can you read Schneider's mind?"

"I've never tried. Does he know what you can do?"

"Of course not. It's not exactly something I want people to know, and I sure as hell didn't want Schneider to. Who knows what he would ask me to do if he knew?"

"Are there others like you in your family?"

Stellan looked at his hands. "My sister."

The more we talked, the more I understood Stellan. And I needed to understand him to fix this mess. "When did you find out about your powers?"

"After Emma died. When I lied, people believed me. Little by little, I found I could shift someone's perception. I used it to help with minor things. Fix a bad test score in college, ace a job interview, nothing diabolical." He adjusted his glasses. "I thought I was going to get out from under what happened in Butternut. I have a good life here."

"So, after you do this for Schneider, what happens?"

"He said we'd be even."

Stellan believed that giving in this one time would get him out from under Schneider. "You really think you'll be free? After this, Schneider will have even more to hold over your head. He might not know all the details of what you're doing to my brother, but he knows enough."

Doubt crossed his face. "Schneider promised."

"Well, if a blackmailer promised..." I waited for that to sink in before I dipped my voice. "You don't have to do this. How can Schneider hurt you without exposing his own crimes?"

For a second, I thought I had him. Hope flickered in his eyes; then it disappeared. "My life is over if this comes out."

"What are you going to do with us?"

CHAPTER 64

Oliver

Before I went into the hotel, I hit the record button on my phone. If I could get Schneider to incriminate himself, it might help Caleb. I had to try.

The lobby was filled with tourists on the move. People on their way somewhere important or coming back from something fantastic. I pushed through them and found Schneider sitting on a couch off to the side with a glass of bourbon. His eyes locked on me and a slow smile spread across his face.

I made my way over to him. "I don't want to do this. But I don't have a choice." I sighed. "You win."

He didn't say anything, but the smile faded. He took a sip from his drink. "Maybe you're telling the truth. Maybe you're stalling. You might want to call your wife before you play games with me."

My throat went dry. I swallowed. It didn't help. I wished I had a drink in my hand. "I'm not playing games." I prayed that my face mirrored the conviction that I'd forced into my voice.

He lifted his gaze to meet mine. "Things can change in an instant.

You really should give her a call."

My hand shook as I called Kai. It went straight to voicemail. I told her to call me back immediately.

Schneider murmured, "I wonder why she didn't pick up."

"What have you done to her?"

"Nothing." He leaned back in the chair. "Not yet."

"If you hurt her..."

He waved my concern away. "She'll be fine. As long as you're a good boy and stick to the plan. We'll fly to Chicago and you'll hand the bike over to me tomorrow morning."

"I want to talk to my wife."

"Our flight leaves at 6:00 a.m. I'll meet you here in the lobby at 3:45."

"All this, because I know you killed Christian? Setting up my brother-in-law? Kidnapping my wife?"

Schneider replied, "3:45, Oliver. Don't be late."

My hands were still shaking when I got outside the hotel. I fumbled to shut the recording off. It wasn't much, but at least I'd gotten something from Schneider. He hadn't directly acknowledged anything, but he hadn't denied anything, either. It might help convict him. But it wasn't going to help me find Kai.

Damn. Damn. Triple damn.

I called Caleb. "Kai's not there, is she?"

"She went out," Caleb said.

"She's not answering her phone."

"She's not answering for you."

He didn't understand. "My call went straight to voicemail. You try her."

He must have heard the urgency in my voice. "What's going on?"

"Just call her. Now."

Caleb came back on the phone. "It went straight to voicemail. She's supposed to be with Stellan."

"How could you let her do that alone?"

"I didn't. Alex went with her."

Relief brushed against me. But Schneider seemed so confident. I rubbed my forehead. "I just met with Schneider. I think he might have her."

Caleb sounded angry. "I shouldn't have let her go. She was trying to get Stellan to turn on Schneider. For me."

"Where was she going?"

"A bar in Williamsburg. The Rusted Nail."

"I'll check there."

"I'm going to stay here, for now. In case she comes back. Let me know what you find," Caleb said right before I hung up.

I hailed a cab and headed to Williamsburg. I called Alex, but it went straight to voicemail, too. Maybe that meant he was still with Kai. For most of the cab ride, I let myself hope that they were just in a crowded bar with bad cell reception.

I was five blocks away when traffic snarled to a stop. I leapt out of the taxi and raced to the bar. I pushed through the line of patrons getting their IDs checked by the muscular bouncer. I flashed a picture of Kai. The bouncer ignored me.

I slid him a twenty. "Have you seen this woman tonight?"

He glanced at the picture. "She was here."

"Is she inside?"

He didn't say anything. Just went back to checking IDs. I gave him another twenty.

"She never went in. She got out of a cab and then got right back into another one with a guy. Another guy rushed out of the bar and joined them. Then they left."

"Was one of the guys a tall blond?"

"Yeah."

Alex was still with her. Or at least he had been. "When?"

"Had to be an hour or two ago."

I tried texting Alex and Kai. No replies. I turned onto a quiet side street. I called Alex again. It went straight to voicemail. I tried Kai's phone one last time. No answer.

Suddenly, my cell rang. It was a blocked caller.

I answered immediately. "Hello? Who is this?"

"It's Kai," she said. There was a slight echo. She was on speakerphone.

"Are you okay?"

There was a pause. "Sure."

She wasn't okay. "Are you with Alex?"

"Yeah."

"Can I talk to him," I asked.

"No. He's..."

Something muffled the phone.

"...not available," she said.

"Where are you?"

"Hanging out with Stellan," she said.

"Tell me where you are, I'll meet you."

"I can't."

Shitfuckingdammit. "When are you leaving?"

"He says that depends on what you do next."

"I'm going to fix this," I promised.

The call was disconnected.

CHAPTER 65

Kai

Alex lay there in the armchair. Two hours went by without him stirring.

"Please, let him wake up," I begged.

"He's fine. Check his pulse again if you don't believe me," Stellan said.

When I touched Alex's wrist, there was a steady beat of blood beneath the surface. I pried his eyelids open to see his pupils. They were equally dilated and shrank down in the light of the room. Normal reactions. Good signs. Whatever Stellan was doing to him, Alex appeared to be physically fine, just unconscious. But the longer someone was out, the worse it was. Everyone knew that. I almost died that way in the cave. If Grandma Guhn hadn't healed me, I would be dead.

Alex didn't have someone waiting in the In Between to save him. If he died...

My heart seized up. It felt like someone was crushing it beneath his fingers. The pain overwhelmed me. "What if he dies?"

"He won't." Stellan's voice came out confident.

"You've done this before?"

He didn't bother answering.

I massaged my temples and tried to figure out what to do next. Even if Oliver did what Schneider wanted, there was no guarantee we'd be released. What would stop Schneider and Stellan from disposing of Alex and me? I finally got Oliver's reasoning for not giving into Schneider. It was impossible to trust him. Ever.

I couldn't just sit here and hope Schneider kept his word. I might not have my psychic abilities, but there were two survivors in my psyche—Nathan and me. We had to fight back. We had to do whatever it took to get Alex and me out of this mess.

I sunk into my darkness.

Stellan was acting on Schneider's orders. I needed to offer him something Schneider couldn't. "The only way to get out from under a blackmailer is to take him down."

"Or to give him what he wants," he said.

"You spent so much time making Caleb look guilty. The evidence is overwhelming. Do you have any proof of his innocence?"

"Why?"

"Because I am very motivated to help you if you do."

His gaze didn't waver, like he was sizing me up.

I stared right back at him. "I'd do anything to save my brother."

"I wasn't letting Schneider pin this on me. I kept copies of everything. I recorded a few of our conversations. I can testify to how I doctored the electronic and paper files for the investors."

"I'm a telepath. Caleb's a dreamwalker. We could add our skills to yours. Can you pull yours in so I can use mine?"

He gave me a brief smile. "Yes."

"Good, because I'll need to be able to get into the prosecutor's head and the judge's head."

"And do what?"

"I can figure out what they want and make sure we give it to them."

"And if you can't?"

I swallowed. "I can do things to people's feelings. I can get inside someone's head and manipulate their emotions. Even rewire their thoughts, if I need to." My darkness was completely capable of that. "Caleb can influence their dreams, sway them toward you."

"And you'd do that for me?" Doubt weighed down each word.

"I'd do that for Caleb." I licked my lips. "You didn't just mess with the files, you set up those accounts for the kickbacks, didn't you?"

He nodded. "I got Natalia to smuggle out his passport and the documents that I needed to set up the accounts. She thinks she gave me some tickets to a show that she didn't want. She had no idea what she really did."

"What about the compliance guy, Thaddeus? Caleb never agreed to pay him kickbacks."

He chuckled. "I met with Thaddeus to cement the deal. I played with his perception so he thought he was meeting with Caleb. He believes they made a deal where he would approve any new investors Caleb sent his way."

"You thought of everything," I whispered.

"I had to." He wrapped his fingers around the fist of his other hand. "It was the only way I could get out from under Schneider."

I leaned forward. "He won't let you go. You're too valuable. You've proven it."

Stellan's brow tightened and his eyes squinted. I wasn't sure if he was processing what I said or simply annoyed at me for saying it.

"If you help me, Schneider will get arrested and go to jail for a long time. He'll be stripped of his power. That's the only way you'll ever be free."

"After what I've done to Caleb, he'll come after me."

"Caleb doesn't want to hurt you. He just wants to save himself. If I make a deal with you, he'll stick to it."

"You want me to trust you two?"

I scrambled to get him on my side. "If Caleb turns on you, you can turn on him. You have mutually assured destruction. If he hits the button, you hit the button."

"I'll go to jail for what I did to Caleb."

"We'll make sure you don't. We can negotiate immunity for you."

"My career will be ruined."

"You probably won't get an IT job at an investment bank again, but Caleb knows people who could use your skills. You can get a job somewhere. A clean slate—for real, this time." I prayed Caleb could do everything I was promising.

Stellan didn't say anything. I hoped he was considering my proposal.

"I want to believe you, but..."

"Let's call Caleb." If this worked, Caleb and I wouldn't have to run away. My brother could keep the life he loved.

Stellan dialed my brother's number and put him on speakerphone.

"Kai, where the hell are you?" Caleb sounded anxious.

"I'm with Stellan," I said.

"Are you okay?" he asked.

"Yes," I said. "We may have a change of plans."

CHAPTER 66

Oliver

A single image haunted me: Kai and Alex in coffins. Their faces were so pale. Their eyelids closed forever. Their souls claimed by death.

My marriage was over. Alex was no longer the friend that he had been. But I couldn't let anything happen to them. I knew better than anybody what Schneider was capable of.

I had no choice. I had to do what Schneider asked. I had to let go of the last chance I had to bring him to justice.

When my cab pulled up in front of my hotel, I got out, but I didn't go inside. I couldn't, not yet. The walls of my room would suffocate me. I needed to be outside, so I headed south. It was the only way I could get ahead of the panic that surrounded me.

My feet took me to 59th Street and Fifth Avenue. Then I walked west along the side that overlooked Central Park. At least my father and Christian were dead and beyond Schneider's reach. One thought ran through my head. My dad had wanted me to do the right thing. And right now, that was saving Kai and Alex.

CHAPTER 67

Kai

After an hour of intense negotiation over speakerphone, Stellan and Caleb reached an understanding. We would work together to bring Schneider down and to protect Stellan. In exchange, Stellan would clear Caleb of all wrongdoing.

When he hung up, Stellan said, "I'm counting on you."

"You have my word. I will get you out of this. Now, please release Alex."

Stellan leaned over Alex and said something in Swedish. Alex's eyelids opened. His blue eyes focused on me. It was like someone had taken all the air out of the room and then as I struggled for my final breath, they pumped it back in.

"Are you okay?" Alex asked.

"Me?" I choked out. "You've been unconscious for hours."

Relief coursed through my veins. He was alive. He was okay. Before he could stand, I rushed into his arms. I crushed his lips in a desperate, life-affirming kiss.

"That's a wonderful way to wake up," Alex murmured.

Stellan cleared his throat. "I hate to break this up, but we have somewhere we need to be."

Stellan was right. We had to go to the courthouse to meet Caleb and the lawyer he'd retained for Stellan.

Alex frowned and touched his head. "We're not going anywhere with him. He hit me."

I shook my head. "He just made you think he hit you."

"My head hurts. He hit me," Alex insisted.

I tried to explain about how Stellan could manipulate perceptions, but Alex refused to hear me. He set me aside and stood up. "I won't let you hurt her."

"Relax. We've come to an agreement. I'm going to save her brother and she's going to save me," Stellan said.

Alex asked me, "You're going to help him?"

"It's the only way."

Alex raised an eyebrow and his lips flattened with doubt.

"I'll explain everything later, but, for now, I need you to trust me," I said. "Can you do that?"

Alex stared into my eyes for what felt like an eternity. There was a struggle going on within him. Finally, he said, "I can," and headed for the door.

"Where are you going?" I asked.

"To help set your plan in motion," Alex said.

Stellan, Alex, and I met Caleb and the lawyer at the courthouse downtown. Together, we went into a private room to meet with the district attorney. True to his word, Stellan pulled back his abilities, so I was able to use my telepathy again.

While Stellan's lawyer talked, I focused on the DA's thoughts. He needed a career-making case. A big fish to take down. Stellan wasn't it, but P.W. Brown & Sons was. If he could make something stick against them, it would be splashed across all the newspapers. A banking scandal wouldn't just make the headlines; it would make his career. Then he could run for Senate. It had been a lifelong dream.

I mind-linked with Caleb and passed all the information along.

Caleb cleared his throat. "Can we take a five-minute break?"

The DA frowned. "Right now?"

"Just a few minutes."

The DA conceded.

Caleb filled the lawyer in on what the DA really wanted.

"What Stellan did to you points to rampant, systematic lack of controls and supervision at P.W. Brown & Sons. Regulatory breaches that don't just mean major fines for the bank, but serious regulatory ramifications. Cease and desists being issued. Possible criminal proceedings," the lawyer said.

"That's the kind of scandal the DA is salivating for," Caleb murmured to me.

Once the DA returned, Stellan's lawyer was able to negotiate the terms of Stellan's immunity. Stellan wouldn't serve a single day in jail. He might have to plead down to a lesser charge or two, but they would be minor and the fines and community service would be reasonable.

Caleb's dreamwalking would come in later. He'd keep focusing the DA on P.W. Brown & Sons and away from Stellan. He'd influence the judge, if needed.

Stellan kept us in the meeting to make sure we saw everything he did for Caleb. He revealed where all the correct documentation had been stored. He brought a flash drive that showed the before and after of the electronic files he'd altered. He walked the DA through how he manipulated the system controls to do everything that he did. He even pointed out what managerial controls and oversight would have prevented him from doing it.

When it came to Thaddeus, Stellan couldn't admit to his perception-altering abilities, so he improvised. "I drugged Thaddeus to make him think he was meeting with Caleb, but it was actually me."

The fact that Schneider had been pulling the strings from Wisconsin meant the crime crossed state lines and that the FBI would need to be involved. I listened to everyone's thoughts to make sure it was safe for Stellan and no one was going to try to double-cross him.

The hardest part was Emma's drug overdose in Wisconsin. None of us knew what evidence Schneider had on Stellan. The DA felt that had to be handled by his counterpart in Wisconsin. Stellan glanced at me.

I knew what I had to do. I had to compel the DA to do what we wanted. I didn't just have to listen to his thoughts; I had to get inside his head and alter them. I didn't know what it might do to him, but it didn't matter. I had to get him to help Stellan.

Playing with the very fabric of the DA's mind, I wove webs of logic and emotion to shift his choice. It should have bothered me how easily I slithered into his thoughts and corrupted them, but it didn't. I had to honor all the terms of the bargain I'd struck with Stellan. It was the only way to save my brother.

CHAPTER 68

Oliver

I sat beside Schneider at the airport gate. He was so certain he'd get away with everything for eternity. I guess when you spend decades trading in favors, you learn that everyone can be manipulated.

I hated that he was right. "Kai and Alex will be released as soon as you get the bike?"

"As soon as I dispose of the bike."

"Why did you entrust it to my dad?"

I had the recorder on my phone on, hoping to get as much as I could out of him. It was all I could do now. I didn't need to do it for Caleb, but I needed to do it for myself.

"We shared in the blame. We shared in the cover-up."

"He didn't kill Christian. You killed Christian."

Schneider sighed. "Aren't we past this?"

"How am I supposed to trust you?"

"I've got no interest in harming anyone."

"What about Caleb? What about all the evidence against him?"

"I'm sure the case has some holes in it." He didn't sound particularly concerned about Caleb's fate.

I swallowed.

We'd be boarding soon. I got up for one last trip to the men's room. I was five steps away from Schneider when I saw several officers coming toward us. Most of them looked to be NYPD, but one flashed an FBI badge. I heard Schneider unholster his gun.

Suddenly, the officers were shouting. "Get down on the ground. Hands where we can see them."

I froze. Someone shoved me to the ground. I didn't fight back even when the carpet bit into my cheek. I couldn't see what was happening, but I heard scuffling and grunting.

Then it was all over.

Schneider had been disarmed and handcuffed. He kept saying, "This is a misunderstanding. I'm not the person you're looking for."

But no one listened to him.

I tried to explain to the nearest officer that Schneider had hostages. The officer asked, "You're Kai Guhn's husband, right?"

I nodded.

"Your wife and her friend Alex are safe. Call your brother-in-law; he can explain everything. We need to take you down to the station to get your statement."

I dialed Caleb's number.

"What the hell is going on? Schneider's being arrested," I said.

He explained what he and Kai had been able to do and gave me a summary of the deal they'd negotiated with the DA. He ended with "Kai's safe. Alex is okay. I'm going to be fine. Tell the NYPD and the FBI everything Schneider did."

"Are you sure?" I asked.

"Yes," he said.

"What are they charging Schneider with?"

"For what he did to me, they have him on blackmail, extortion, conspiracy to commit kidnapping, and conspiracy to forge documents.

They'll probably have more charges after they talk to you about what happened to Christian."

"Can I talk to Kai?" I asked.

"She's giving her statement. She'll call you when she can," he said. There was a ton of noise in the background. "Oliver, I've got to go." He hung up.

CHAPTER 69

Kai

After spending so much time with the authorities, I was glad to be squished between Caleb and Alex in the back seat of a town car. I needed the reassurance that they were both safe.

"I'm so sorry you got hurt," I said to Alex.

"I heard you the first twenty times. And there's nothing to forgive." He gave me a sweet smile. Then he squeezed my hand. "I'm happy it was me and not you. You've taken way too many hits to the head in the past year."

"You weren't..." I stopped myself. No matter how many times I explained it to him, he still swore he'd been knocked out.

Caleb stared out the window. He'd been uncharacteristically quiet.

"Are you okay?" I asked.

"Fine." His face pinched together. Something was still bothering him.

What's wrong?

You took too many chances.

I'd do it again to save you.

"You were great with the district attorney," he said out loud.

"I just figured out what he really wanted and made sure we gave it to him."

"You did more than that."

The darkness in me had altered the DA's thoughts and emotions to suit my purpose. This was who the darkness made me. Someone who would do anything—anything—to save the ones she loved.

When we got to Caleb's apartment, the three of us sat down in the kitchen and caught up on the meals we'd missed.

Caleb glanced at his watch. "I need to shower and change. Then I have someone I need to see."

"Natalia?" I asked.

"I need to celebrate." He winked at me.

"But she helped Stellan."

"He made her do it. And she doesn't even know she did it."

I didn't know how my brother could be so forgiving. He disappeared into his room.

Alex sipped his coffee and stared at the counter. I realized we'd never talked about whatever it was he needed to discuss with me. "Why did you stop over last night?"

"Now's probably not the best time. It can wait."

"After everything we just went through, you can tell me anything."

He had the look of someone who dreaded what he had to say. "Oliver told me about what you did to Mickey on Christmas Day."

"Oh."

"Make me understand what happened."

"It was before I understood what was going on with me and Nathan and the darkness."

"You hurt my sister, Kai." His eyes were deep blue oceans of sadness. "I deserve more of an explanation than that."

"I'm sorry I lost control." I traced the veins in the marble counter, trying to think of something that would make it forgivable to Alex. "When I realized what I was capable of and that it wasn't just my darkness but also Nathan's, I left Butternut. I made sure I couldn't hurt Mickey or Lukas."

"Would you have? If you stayed?" There was an edge to his voice.

I pressed my palms to my knees to keep from fidgeting. "I'd like to think no, but I can't say for sure."

"What about now?" he asked.

"They are completely safe. I can't do anything beyond my half-mile telepathic radius."

"No, I mean when you go back to Butternut." He leaned closer and lowered his voice. "I've seen what you can do. What if you lose control around my sister or Lukas?"

"I love Lukas. The part of me that's Nathan loves him, too."

"But you don't like my sister."

"Can you blame me?"

"I suppose not." He gave me the slightest smile. "But I can't let anyone hurt her, even you."

"So where does that leave us?"

"Can you promise me you won't hurt my sister?"

My breath caught in my throat. The words refused to leave my tongue. I pulled them back and rearranged them. I didn't want to lose Alex, so I told him what I hoped would be the truth. "I think I can control the darkness." My hand was inches away from his on the counter. So close. I wanted to reach over and touch his.

He looked down. "Are you and Oliver really over?"

"Yes." I snuck my hand closer to his until they were touching. He didn't pull away. So I slid my hand over his. His was bigger and warmer than mine. "When Stellan had you like that..."

"I know. I was scared, too." He stood up and pulled me toward him.

I fell into his arms. I rested my head against his chest, listening to the reassuring beat of his heart. I brushed my lips beneath his jaw.

His lips were inches from mine. I stood on tiptoes and closed the distance between them. His desire surged through me. I felt it override his fear and uncertainty about me. Somehow, I managed to keep kissing him as I pulled him toward my bedroom.

"Are you sure?" he asked.

"I've never been surer."

I shut my door. My fingers fumbled with the buttons of his shirt.

He chuckled, "Nervous?"

"A little."

He stilled my shaking hands and undid the buttons himself.

I pulled my sweater off and tossed it aside. Then my shirt. I needed to feel my skin pressed against his. We were here and we were alive. Everything else, we could deal with later.

His mouth was on my neck. His hands were in my hair. His fingers glided down my back, leaving a trail of warmth behind them. His palms rested on my hips. His leg slid between mine.

I wanted this.

I pushed him back on the bed and climbed on top of him. His lips. His mouth. Those strong hands were everywhere. I couldn't get enough of his touch. His heart raced with mine. The anticipation and excitement coursed through us. I let him inside my mind. Every kiss. Every touch. Every thrust. Amplified. Intensified.

I lost all sense of where he ended and I began.

CHAPTER 70

Oliver

I looked for Kai at the police department, but she'd already left. I had to make sure she was all right. I cabbed over to Caleb's. As soon as she opened the door, I hugged her. When I stepped inside the apartment, I realized her hair was a mess. Her shirt was on backwards. Her lips were red and swollen as if they'd been kissed too many times. She smelled like sex.

"Where is he?" I demanded.

"Who?"

"Don't," I hissed at her. "Alex, get out here."

She put her hand on my arm. "This is between you and me."

I jerked away from her and stormed around the living room, shouting "Alex!" to an empty room.

There was one place left—Kai's bedroom. I spun around to head there. Alex met me in the hallway. His clothes were rumpled. His hair was tangled. He had bedhead from fucking my wife.

The blood surged through my veins. My skin felt burning hot. I lunged at him and we crashed into the side table. A glass vase shattered.

My momentum took Alex and me to the floor.

"YOU FUCKED MY WIFE," I screamed at him as we rolled around in the hallway. He tried to gain the advantage, but my rage kept me on top.

"You're separated," he said.

"That doesn't make it okay!" I punched him in the mouth.

"STOP IT!" Kai screamed.

I couldn't. The rage was too much. The pain was impossible to stop. Suddenly, a wave of calm slammed into me. I couldn't fight it. It had to be Kai's doing.

"Kai! Get out of my mind."

"Calm down." Her voice was deep and soothing.

I closed my eyes and imagined black marble all around me. It should have been enough to block her out, but it wasn't. My anger evaporated and a feeling of peace overwhelmed me. I released Alex. "What are you doing to me?"

"I told you to calm down." Her eyes burned with a fire I'd never seen before.

"Get out of my head," I growled.

"Pull yourself together and I will."

She was mind-fucking me. And I couldn't stop her. In that moment, I hated her. Truly and completely. And then that feeling dissipated, too. She wouldn't even let me have my hatred. "If you get out of my head, I'll stop."

"Stop, and I'll get out of your head." She knelt beside Alex. "Are you okay?" She wiped the blood from his lip tenderly.

I wanted to throw up. "I can't watch this."

"Then don't," she said. "Go."

I couldn't. Not yet. So I just stood there.

They whispered to each other.

"What are you talking about?" I demanded

Alex looked at me. "Don't hurt her."

"Hurt her?" I gave a derisive chuckle. "She's the one hurting me."

She helped him up and he went back to her room.

"Can you control yourself?" she asked.

I snorted. "I'm not the one sleeping around or fucking with people's minds."

She tilted her head. "It's because I'm in control that I can do that."

Suddenly, my mind felt like mine again. "I hate you."

"I'm not too fond of you right now." She rubbed her cheek. "It's been a very intense day. I didn't plan for this to happen—with Alex, I mean."

"You just fell onto his dick?"

"I meant like this. Right now."

My fingers tightened into fists. "I was trying to save Caleb. I got a few recordings of Schneider for you. I wasn't going to let Schneider hurt you."

"I know. Caleb told me about what happened at the airport."

"Yeah, thanks for calling me back." I couldn't keep the hurt out of my voice.

"I was going to..." Her voice trailed off.

"After you fucked Alex?"

She walked into the living room. "Do you want a drink?"

"I can't stay." Not with her. Not like we were now. It all felt surreal. But it was all real. Everything was happening so fast. The airport arrest. Her and Alex. "The FBI is confiscating the evidence from the lab in Chicago to run its own tests," I said. "And I gave them my recordings. The police know that Schneider killed Christian. There will probably be more charges after they open up a new investigation."

"That should help put Schneider away for a long time," she said.

"Are you coming back to Butternut?"

"Once things are settled here."

"Where should I send your stuff?" I didn't want it in my house anymore.

She flinched. "I'm not sure yet."

"I'll send it to Alex's. You two can sort it out there."

"What about Herbie?" she asked.

"As soon as you get back, you can pick him up."

She nodded.

I couldn't look at her anymore. I didn't want to see Alex again. "Goodbye, Kai." I headed to the door and didn't look back.

CHAPTER 71

Kai

O n my last night in New York, I made sure all my bags were
packed and ready to go.

Caleb stood in the doorway to my bedroom. "Are you
sure this is what you want?"

I nodded. "Stellan's safe. You're safe."

"You can stay here as long as you want."

The crazy thing was, I could. Because of the darkness, I could live
in Manhattan again. But there were things I needed to take care of first.
"It's time for me to go back to Butternut."

"To Alex?" he asked.

"And Nathan." I had to face him again.

"What are you going to do about his darkness?"

"I don't know." I bit my thumb. I liked what I could do now. I
didn't want to risk losing this control. "But I have to go back and help
Nathan wake up."

"If you need me, I'm only a phone call and a short flight away."

"Thanks."

"So what about you and Alex?"

Alex had stayed a few nights in New York before heading home. I didn't know what we had. I liked not knowing. "We'll see."

"How are you going to explain your relationship to everyone back there?" Caleb asked.

It was a small town. I was still married to Oliver. Tongues would wag. It was inevitable. "I'm going to tell the truth. My marriage fell apart. I changed. Oliver changed. It happens."

"Are you going to stay at Alex's place?" Caleb asked.

"I probably shouldn't. Though I'm looking forward to seeing him."

"I don't think 'seeing him' is all you're looking forward to."

I felt the heat creep over my cheeks. "Caleb!"

"Not to worry, I got this." He tossed a set of keys at me. "I got you a used SUV. It will be at the airport waiting for you. I also rented a small cabin on Butternut Lake for you. Now you have your own place for as long as you want it."

"I can't take all this." It was too generous.

"Think of it as a thank you gift. You risked everything to help me. You saved my job. You kept me out of prison. You risked yourself for me. A used car and a small cabin barely begin to repay you."

I flung my arms around my brother. "I'd do it all again to have you safe."

That night, it didn't take my brother and I long to find the way through to the In Between. When we emerged from the water, we stood on a beach beneath a bright summer sun. Blue-green water stretched to the horizon and white sand warmed my feet, reminding me of a family vacation in Kata Noi, Thailand. In the distance, I saw Grandma Guhn walking toward us.

We didn't wait for her. We ran up to her and enveloped her in a group hug.

After she released us, she stepped back and her full gaze rested on me. "How are you?"

"I'm okay," I said.

She ran her palms over my aura and smiled. "You're ready."

"Ready?"

"You can go back and face Nathan. You can help him now."

"What are you talking about?" Caleb asked.

"Last time I saw her, Kai was still healing. She couldn't do anything to help Nathan."

"But now I can?" I asked.

She nodded. "You've accepted your darkness and his. You've grown stronger. Your abilities took a leap. I think you have the power to pull him back to life or to release him completely to death. You can break your bond now. Or you can keep it."

"Keep it?" Caleb asked.

"Because she likes who she's become," she said as if it were clear to all.

Caleb looked around. "Where's Grandpa Guhn?"

"It's rare for him to come to the In Between." She gave him a sympathetic smile. "Be careful with your young lady. She may act like she doesn't have a heart, but she does, and you can bruise it more easily than you realize."

Caleb looked like he wanted to ask Grandma what she knew about Natalia, but then thought better of it. "Kai's now the heartbreaker in our family."

"Caleb!" I punched him lightly on the shoulder.

"It's true. Alex and Oliver were fighting over her. Broke a nice vase of mine, too."

Grandma Guhn lifted my chin so our eyes met. "You picked the one you want?"

I nodded.

"Tell me all about your Alex." She turned to Caleb. "And your Natalia." She linked arms with me and Caleb. I had a family again.

EPILOGUE

Oliver

I stood alone in front of my mother's white headstone. The cemetery was so quiet. I'd have to get used to quiet like this. The quiet without Kai.

I looked down at the pink roses I'd brought. They were the closest I could find to blue. Snow crunched in the distance. I wasn't alone here, but I didn't look up. Mourners needed their privacy. The crunching stopped next to me.

"Oliver?" It was Mickey. "I brought something for your mom's birthday."

She held out a bouquet of blue roses. She remembered. Not just the blue roses, but my mom's birthday.

"Where did you find them?"

"I made them," she said. "You always brought them here when we were kids. For her birthday and Mother's Day."

"You remembered her birthday?"

"I bring them every year for her. I know you would have if you were here." She shrugged like it was no big deal.

I hardly knew what to say. A warm feeling filled my core and spread outward. The feeling of being cared for. I stared at the blue roses. "How do you make them?"

"Blue dye and patience. I'll show you."

"Thanks." I always thought it would be Kai here beside me. Kai going through all of this with me. But it wasn't. And it never would be again.

Love like Kai's and mine, it didn't just disappear, but I'd never forget what she'd done to me. Screwing with my emotions after she screwed Alex. It was time to open Mama's letter, the one marked, "If you get divorced."

Mickey placed the roses on the grave and squeezed my shoulder.

"I didn't understand what my dad was going through back then," I said. "I mean, when my mom died."

"You were a kid. How could you possibly understand any of it?"

I slid my hand in hers and squeezed. "Thank you for always being here."

"Thank you for setting things right for Christian."

Schneider was in custody in New York for the crimes he committed there. They set his bail at one million dollars. I didn't think anyone would pay that for him. Stellan, Caleb, Kai, and I would all testify against him for his recent crimes against Caleb.

In Wisconsin, the Ashland County Sheriff's Office had reopened the investigation into Christian's death. The police department had Schneider on unpaid leave pending the investigation. From what I understood, my testimony would help them charge him with manslaughter, destruction of evidence, tampering with evidence, bribery, interfering with an investigation, creating false evidence, and preparing false documents.

"I couldn't have done it without you."

Mickey leaned closer. "I'll always have your back, Oliver."

She kissed me.

AUTHOR'S NOTE

As this is a work of fiction, I've taken artistic license with the town of Butternut to suit the story's needs. Some places are represented as they are and others are completely fictionalized. Butternut, Wisconsin, is a real town with an amazing population. When I was originally researching the town back in 2010, the population was at 407. I've been there a couple times to visit and am lucky enough to call many of its residents my friends. In 2014, when I last visited the population was at 375. However, since the story is set between 2012-2013, I use the older population number.

The Butternut Feed Store is described as it was on my visit in 2014 and from the photos I took at the time. It is owned by Bill and Kathy. The Butternut Area Historical Museum exists and does have those holiday decorations on the main floor during the Christmas season and the wedding gowns are part of the permanent collection on display upstairs.

Brennan's Green Brier is owned by the amazing Brennan family and is recreated faithfully on the page. Jumbo's is the best place to grab lunch downtown. Cruise Inn Spring Creek is a great restaurant and bar on the outskirts of town owned by the Bayers.

Super One Foods is the local grocery store in the neighboring town of Park Falls.

The Park Falls Herald was the name of the local paper up until 2013. Then it became the Price County Review. Since this story takes place in 2012-2013, I continue to use the Park Falls Herald as the local paper to be historically accurate.

There are actual homes in Butternut with secret, hidden rooms. It was a really cool fact that Terry Brennan and Maxine Kilger shared with me, and I spun into my fiction.

There is no First Bank of Butternut. That was needed for story purposes. There is also no Butternut Police Station or Butternut police force. In reality, Ashland County provides police coverage for Butternut. The town hall is actually its own separate building, but that didn't work for my story. The fire station is beside Brennan's Green Brier, but it doesn't house the town hall or police station. In the past, it did have a small office for the Butternut police station.

A few of the actual residents of Butternut do make cameo appearances in this book purely for fun and because I adore the people of Butternut. They include: Mrs. K at the Butternut Area Historical Museum, Bill and Kathy at the Butternut Feed Store, Pam Bayer at Cruise Inn Spring Creek, and Mimi and the much loved and dearly missed Mike Brennan at Brennan's Green Brier. When I have used real people in the book, I am using them in a fictional manner.

ACKNOWLEDGMENTS

Many thanks to my parents for their constant support while I devoted years to writing and revising this book. To my mom, for being a great beta reader and encouraging me when my doubts were out of control. To my dad, for listening to my tirades about revisions.

To Kat Bender, for always listening and letting me lose my mind on a regular basis and somehow knowing just what to say to pull me back. I couldn't keep on this journey without your moral support. To Emerson Langley, for knowing when I needed company and being there to help me through all the rough moments—you are the best dog and most loyal companion a girl could ask for!

To Jessica Jernigan, for taking this editing journey with me again. You're the only person I could entrust with Kai and Oliver. Thanks for finding the story and making it the best it could be.

To Abby Brown, for being a fantastic intern and researching things in Butternut when I couldn't get there in the winter. To Maxine Kilger and Terry Brennan, for helping me flesh out so many of the details and loving my story. I couldn't write this series without you two! To Pam Bayer and Mikki Parchim, for being my sounding boards and cheering me on. To Jacqueline McDowell, thanks for all your support online and in person! To everyone in Butternut who opened their town and their lives to me, it's a pleasure to know you and I'm so glad we keep in touch on Facebook. To the Third Story Writers Guild of Park Falls, thank you for welcoming me into your group and your town. To the Cheeseheads, thank you for your constant support, insight, and rallying around me! I couldn't write and promote without all of you.

To Gwen Stephens, Audra Majewski, Brett Helgren, and Mom, your beta reader comments truly helped shape this book. Thank you for the time and care you put into it. To Gretcher Archer, thanks for being there and helping me on my writer journey. I am so incredibly lucky to have met you in the elevator at KN! To my blog buddies—Jacqueline,

Carrie, Sue, Kate, Phil, Pete, Kelly, EllaDee, Dianne, August—and everyone who is with me week in and week out in the blogosphere. Your encouragement means everything to me. Thanks for sticking with me!

To Nick DeSimone, thanks for your tireless work on the internal layout and formatting of the paperback. To Rik Hall, thanks for all your dedication in formatting the e-book. To Creative Paramita, many thanks for creating the perfect cover for my book!

And to you my readers—without you, there would be no one to shares the joys and sorrows of Oliver and Kai's journey. Thanks for asking for the sequel and coming back to read more of their story!

READER DISCUSSION QUESTIONS

1. Consider the title of the book. Since Highway 13 runs through Butternut but doesn't connect to Manhattan, what is the author suggesting about the journey that Kai and Oliver take in this book?

2. Discuss the book cover. How does it convey the central concept for the story? Consider the positioning of Oliver and Kai and the smoke and clouds.

3. What do Kai's nightmares tell you about her true emotional state?

4. Discuss Kai's relationship with her family. What can you gather from her interactions with her mother and father and Naomi? Compare her relationships with them to her relationships with Caleb and Grandma Guhn.

5. One of the running themes in the book is how the past influences the present. For Oliver, the loss of his mother, Christian's death, his rift with his father, and the breakup with Mickey in high school tend to define who he is now. For Kai, her parent's fear of her abilities, her friend's death in high school, losing her grandmother, and her breakdown continue to shape her daily life. Discuss how who we are is always tied to what happened to us in our past.

6. The story has two separate storylines for Oliver and Kai. Discuss how this mirrors their relationship breaking down in the book.

7. Why does Kai give up on Oliver? Why does she never give up on Caleb?

8. Discuss how Kai's and Oliver's characters evolve over the course of the story. Who are they at the beginning, middle, and end of the story?

9. Compare the relationship between Kai and Alex with the one between Oliver and Mickey. Why are Kai and Oliver drawn to these other characters?

10. What does the darkness represent to the story? Do you believe everyone has some darkness in them?

11. Was it wrong for Kai to turn her powers outward instead of inward? Why or why not?

12. Discuss how having her own mother institutionalized impacted the decisions Kai's mom made for Kai.

13. Discuss the symbolism inherent in the shields used by Kai (frosted bulletproof glass), Oliver (black marble crypt), Caleb (titanium fortress), and Kai's mother (armored tank). How do their shields tie into who their characters are?

14. There are a lot of smells and tastes associated with memories and emotions. For example, Oliver's reaction to the smell of coconut (Mickey's shampoo) vs. Kai's reaction (at the bar). Find and discuss a couple other examples of smells and the emotions they evoke.

15. Kai seems to be motivated by a fear of being locked away again. It's her rationale for hiding so many things from Oliver. Where does it come from and why is it so central to her character?

16. Why do you think Oliver and Kai's love altered over time? Is love forever or does it have a built-in expiration date? Or is it that it can be destroyed by lies and betrayals?

Want to have author Kourtney Heintz join your book club discussion for *HIGHWAY THIRTEEN TO MANHATTAN*?
To learn more, visit
www.kourtneyheintz.com/contact

DELETED SCENES

*This was originally part of Oliver and Kai's
walk in Central Park in Chapter 57.*

"Do you remember our first fall in Central Park?" Oliver asked.

"That was seven years ago," I said.

"We collected leaves down by the Dairy."

It was a picturesque Victorian gothic building that once served as a place for children to get fresh milk. Crowds weren't a big concern for me back then. We wandered for hours trying to capture the prettiest leaves. I favored reds and oranges. Oliver loved the bright yellow. We collected dozens of them and brought them back to our small studio apartment. We got out the iron and wax paper and arranged them into collages of our first fall in the city.

"We had a magical life together back then." It felt like I was wandering through the graveyard of our love.

*This was originally part of the scene after Kai came back
to Caleb's after a day of shopping in Chapter 41.*

I cabbed home with all my stuff and put it in my room. I still had an hour before Caleb would be home so I puttered around his apartment.

My mind drifted to Oliver. Tomorrow was his birthday. I did something I shouldn't have. I pulled out my iPad and looked through my old photos. It was a weird mix of happy and hurt to sift through pictures of the life I had led. Grandma Guhn and I laughing at Christmas six years ago. Oliver and her making silly faces for the camera. He'd been a part of every important moment in my life up until now.

It hurt to remember how happy we had been.

I lay back, sinking deeper into the couch cushions. Memories flashed through my mind. After I was released from the institution and on the mend, Caleb went back to London. Grandma Guhn was gone. Oliver stayed with me. The day he proposed, we were out on the sandbars at Torrey Pines Beach.

He stood facing me. I saw the stark truth in his eyes as he said, "I can't do any of this without you."

I grabbed his hand. "I'm getting better. I won't leave you again."

He laced his fingers through mine. "Saying goodbye to you would break me."

I leaned in so that our foreheads touched. "Then let's never be apart again."

"Is that a promise?" His voice was tentative. Hopeful.

"If you take me back to New York, I'll make it permanent." That was my one condition. We had to go back to the life we loved.

"Is this your way of proposing?" he asked.

"Take me home, Oliver. Take me back to our home. And we'll build a life together."

"And if I say no?" Uncertainty lingered in his eyes.

"I love you, but I won't marry you unless we pick up where we left off."

His Adam's apple bobbed in his throat. "New York is no good for you. There are too many people."

I shook my head. "If it gets to be too much, we leave. But it won't. Whatever we do, we do it together."

"Together." He pulled a diamond ring from his pocket and slid it on my finger.

His lips were so warm against mine. Our minds intertwined. Our emotions ran so high. Everything we felt, we felt together. This was love. This was what our marriage would be.

The front door opened and pulled me out of my memory. I was

sitting on the couch in Caleb's apartment again. Caleb stood there looking dashing in his gray suit and camel colored cashmere coat.

Q&A WITH KOURTNEY HEINTZ
BESTSELLING AUTHOR OF
Highway Thirteen to Manhattan

WHAT CAN YOU TELL US ABOUT THE TITLES OF *THE SIX TRAIN TO WISCONSIN* AND *HIGHWAY THIRTEEN TO MANHATTAN*?

For me, love is a journey, never a destination. So my titles are meant to be thematic and hint at the difficult journey my characters will take. In the first book, *The Six Train to Wisconsin*, Oliver and Kai live in the East Village near the 6 subway line. Oliver gets to his job in Midtown by taking the train to 51st Street. Kai travels downtown to City Hall to get to her own place of work.

They both love New York, but it becomes impossible for them to stay there when Kai's telepathic abilities spiral out of control. Oliver takes Kai back to his hometown of Butternut, Wisconsin. Obviously, the 6 train doesn't leave NYC and can't take them to Wisconsin. The title is meant to convey the difficulty of the journey they take and the changes they undergo after leaving New York and settling into Butternut.

In *Highway Thirteen to Manhattan*, Kai and Oliver are dealing with the aftermath of everything that happened at the end of the first book. Highway 13 is a state highway that runs through Butternut, but does not leave the state of Wisconsin. However, in this book, circumstances cause both Oliver and Kai to return to Manhattan. It isn't an easy journey for either of them.

THE PAPERBACK EDITIONS OF BOTH BOOKS IN THE *SIX TRAIN TO WISCONSIN* SERIES INCLUDE YOUR OWN PHOTOGRAPHS. WHY DID YOU DECIDE TO ADD THEM?

Paperbacks are so much more expensive than e-books, so I wanted to provide bonus content for my paperback purchasers. I wanted to add a personal touch as a thanks to readers who invest in the paperback. I've always preferred books with photos or illustrations. It's more common in children's books, but my inner child demanded that adults be given books like that too.

The places in the book hold so much significance to my characters and to me. I've been everywhere that Oliver and Kai have been. Those are some of my favorite places, so I wanted to immerse the reader in these places not just with my words, but also with my photography.

The photos aren't the only bonus content I've added to the paperbacks. I included the original short story version of *The Six Train to Wisconsin* in the first book. In the second book, I share a couple deleted scenes and an author interview. Both paperbacks also have book club discussion guides.

Is Butternut a real place?

It's a very small town in Ashland County located in the Northwoods of Wisconsin. When I was picking the location for my story, I wanted a small town in the Midwest. Somewhere completely different from San Diego or New York. I searched my atlas and I found Butternut. It fit all the requirements of my story and I adored the name. When I went to visit, I fell in love with the town and its people.

Butternut is the kind of place where people care about their neighbors. I've been to visit three times while I worked on these books and am lucky enough to count many of its residents among my friends. Several of them helped spread the word about my books and gave me feedback on the cover designs and title choices as part of my amazing street team, The Cheeseheads.

YOU WRITE INCREDIBLY FLAWED AND AT TIMES SOMEWHAT UNLIKABLE CHARACTERS. DID YOU INTEND FOR THEM TO BE THAT WAY?

I did, actually. When you dig deep into someone's motives and emotions, very few of us are truly selfless or completely selfish. It's easier to live in a black and white world of good and bad, but I've seen awful people do wonderful things and wonderful people do awful things. I think we all live along a broad spectrum of behavior, and some days we can be kind and other days we aren't. Sometimes we react based on a darker emotion. And sometimes we rise above and do something truly heroic. I think that's the beauty of human beings. I wanted to capture that and convey it on the page.

WHAT AUTHORS AND BOOKS INSPIRED YOU WHILE YOU WERE WRITING *HIGHWAY THIRTEEN TO MANHATTAN*?

The Harper Connelly series by Charlaine Harris taught me that it's okay to write flawed characters. Her Sookie Stackhouse series inspired me to write my own version of a telepath. I love the language of Alice Sebold's and Alice Hoffmann's books. I wanted to give this story a little literary bent. I like an element of mystery and suspense in my stories. The darkness and the suspense in the Mara Dyer trilogy by Michelle Hodkin definitely influenced how I handled this installment of the series.

YOUR BOOKS DEFY GENRE. HOW DID THE STORY COME TO BE THAT WAY?

I'm a big fan of mystery and suspense. I've never written a story that didn't contain elements of both. I've always been fascinated by the paranormal. I can't seem to write fiction without something paranormal at its core. But it's not about genre for me. I always set out to tell a good story. I love to get inside my characters' minds and explore their true motives and deepest emotions. That tends to contribute a more literary flavor to my writing in this series.

CAST OF CHARACTERS
Highway Thirteen to Manhattan

KAI GUHN

A 28-year-old telepath who can hear the thoughts and sense the feelings of anyone within a half-mile radius. She can mindlink with those she is close to and share thoughts when they are nearby, too. Psychic powers run in her dad's side of the family. While she is recovering from a near-death experience, her telepathic powers start to change. She senses a darkness growing inside her, a force that amplifies her powers and compels her to use them as a weapon. She doesn't tell her husband what's happening to her. Instead, she confides in her brother, Caleb. And in Alex—a friend who may be more than just a friend.

OLIVER RICHTER

Kai Guhn's husband and college boyfriend, he has remained by her side during her mental breakdown and self-destructive behavior. He hoped that taking her from Manhattan to his hometown of Butternut, Wisconsin, would help her. Instead, his secrets put her life in jeopardy. His lingering closeness with his high-school girlfriend, Michaela, has put an additional strain on his marriage. His need for justice further complicates his marriage as he teams up with Michaela to try to find evidence of Chief Schneider's role in the death of Oliver's best friend.

CALEB GUHN

Kai's older brother is a millionaire Wall Street guy. He sticks by her side during her recovery and helps her face her inner darkness. He has the ability to walk into people's dreams and communicate with them across great distances. He is the person Kai trusts most in the world.

MICHAELA FUCHS

Oliver's high-school sweetheart and close friend. Michaela is always there for Oliver, especially when things go wrong. She knows his secrets and wants to help him in his quest for justice against the chief of police.

ALEX FUCHS

Michaela's older brother and Oliver's former best friend. He is one of the people Kai turns to for comfort instead of Oliver. Alex does his best to be there for Kai as he fights his growing attraction to her.

CHIEF SCHNEIDER

Second in command to Oliver's father, he was like an uncle to Oliver until he killed his best friend. Schneider continues to blackmail Oliver into keeping his deadly secret.

ABOUT THE AUTHOR

Photo by Brett D. Helgren

Kourtney Heintz is the award-winning and bestselling author of The Six Train to Wisconsin (2013), the first book in *The Six Train to Wisconsin* series. She also writes bestselling young adult novels under the pseudonym K.C. Tansley. She is a member of the Mystery Writers of America, Sisters in Crime, Romance Writers of America, and Society of Children's Book Writers and Illustrators.

She has given writing workshops and author talks at libraries, museums, universities, high schools, conventions, wineries, non-profits organizations, and writing conferences. She has been featured in the *Republican American* of Waterbury, Connecticut; on WTNH's *CT Style*; and on the radio show, *Everything Internet*.

She resides in Connecticut with her warrior lapdog, Emerson, and three quirky golden retrievers. Years of working on Wall Street provided the perfect backdrop for her imagination to run amok at night, envisioning a world where out-of-control telepathy and buried secrets collide.

You can find out more about Kourtney and her books at: http:// kourtneyheintz.com

Made in the USA
Middletown, DE
09 January 2017